PRAISE FOR *THE FII*

'Crackling with energy, irony, wit and terror, *The First Friend* is a timely and cautionary reminder of the stifling, murderous logic of strong man politics.'   Tim Winton

'Razor-sharp, wildly imaginative, bold, brilliant and often as dark as the inside of a coffin. Another triumph from a truly extraordinary writer.'   Trent Dalton

'*The First Friend* is not just a cracking read, it's a masterclass in Machiavellian manoeuvres. This is a magnificent piece of gallows humour, bitingly funny and horrifyingly grim at the same time.'   Kate McClymont

'Bleak, intelligent and fearsomely well-researched—I kept telling myself I shouldn't laugh, but couldn't help it.'   Michael Robotham

'Shocking, distressing and, yes, discomfortingly hilarious, *The First Friend* rocks and rolls through the paranoia, and the maniacal and murderous egomania, in the aftermath of the Great Terror. It is nothing less than Amisian in ambition and achievement.'   Paul Daley

'A witty, absorbing and at times disturbing depiction of the banalities of horror. We know what's coming but can't turn away. Malcolm Knox has hit on a great idea and delivered a wonderful book: A gripping black comedy that is both a reflection on the past and a warming for the future.'   Michael Brissenden

PRAISE FOR *BLUEBIRD*

'As a scabrous social satire, and as a narrative that satisfyingly weaves together every dangling thread, *Bluebird* is sublime. Knox's best novel to date.'   *Sydney Morning Herald* and *The Age*

'A story about community, and a satire of the Australian dream . . . *Bluebird* is a novel that becomes more enjoyable the deeper you dive into the layers of narrative . . . readers can immerse themselves further into Knox's gentle but incisive commentary on the Australian dream, and whether it has ever existed at all.'   Zoya Patel, *The Guardian*

'*Bluebird* is consistently excellent, rich with spot-on social observations that are sharp, funny and affecting. As a comment on Scott Morrison's Australia, and an exploration of the casualties and boons of progress, it's very good.'   *Australian Book Review*

'A huge, powerful novel about the corrosiveness of keeping family secrets.'   *Good Reading*

'Ambitious and mature . . . the work of a writer comfortable in his skin and in full command of his material.'   *Weekend Australian*

'Reads like an updated answer to Tim Winton's *Cloudstreet*.'   *Books + Publishing*

'Malcolm Knox has written a novel that is layered, affectionate, amusing, dark . . . Read this book, you will be much the better for it.'   Michael McKernan, *Canberra Times*

'A quintessentially Australian story about mateship, family, betrayal and the corrosive effect of shame.'   *The Age*

'Brilliantly written.' *Weekly Times*

'*Bluebird* is engrossing: a sharp-witted and exact satire about our contemporary world and our contemporary families. Yet the satire is never smug and the characters never lose their complexity or their individuality. Malcolm Knox's writing now has such confidence and clarity that he is exhilarating to read. He's a maestro, and I didn't want *Bluebird* to end.'   Christos Tsiolkas, author of *Damascus* and *The Slap*

'Malcolm Knox is in scathing top form with this brutal takedown of white male nostalgia, real-estate greed, wasted privilege and bronzed-Aussie delusion.

'Gordon's an unlikely hero, trapped in the collapsing halfway house of his marriage, his elderly father's crumbling tyranny, loyalty to his abysmal friends—and the toppling Lodge, the symbol of everything he can't bear to lose. The novel perfectly skewers the hypocrisy, racism, class warfare and misogyny at work in the power-plays of ageing surfside gladiators, clinging to their personal and communal mythologies of an Australia that no longer exists, if it ever did. It's a mark of Knox's supreme skill that he can render his protagonist's failures with such ruthless clarity, yet somehow elicit such genuine sympathy that I found myself desperate for Gordon, urging him on to step up, and save himself.

'Filled with biting observations about our culture and our families so starkly insightful they make you gasp and read them out loud, *Bluebird* showcases Knox's dexterity as a satirist more savagely astute than ever.'   Charlotte Wood, author of *The Weekend*

PRAISE FOR *THE LIFE*

'A vivid and essential piece of work.' *Australian Book Review*

'It confirms what ought to have been more widely recognised, that he [Knox] is one of the most considerable of our novelists in what is at least a silver, if not a golden, age of Australian fiction.' Peter Pierce, *Sydney Morning Herald*

'Malcolm Knox explores the inner life of men with both surgical insight and heartfelt compassion . . . *The Life* digs in deep.' Michael McGirr, *The Age*

'Plot is one thing, mere reviewer's necessity, but voice is another. Here is where the novel seduces and converts . . . it is clear Knox is on to something here. He has written a vivid and essential piece of work.' Adam Rivett, *Australian Bookseller & Publisher*

'*The Life* is just a bloody good read.' Stephen Romei, *The Australian*

'You don't have to be a surfer or be familiar with the story of Peterson to appreciate Knox's superb storytelling and his rhythmic, evocative prose in homage to one of Australia's most intriguing sporting characters.' Greg Stolz, *Sunday Times*

'Knox has never written better than in *The Life*. Page after page is radiant with the energy.' Geordie Williamson, *Weekend Australian*

'The book is worded in the crackling stream of detritus that flows from Keith's broken mind—a sort of *Catcher in the Rye* for Antipodean surfers.' *Inside Sport*

'I envy the confidence and the naturalness of this book—it moves and shrugs, completely itself, like a wave.'   Charlotte Wood, *Bookseller & Publisher*

'If Winton is an aria, Knox is early Rolling Stones.'   *The Guardian*

Malcolm Knox grew up in Sydney. Since 1994 Malcolm has written for the *Sydney Morning Herald* and has won three Walkley Awards and a Human Rights Award. His novels include *Summerland*; *A Private Man,* winner of the Ned Kelly Award; *Jamaica*, which won the Colin Roderick Award and was shortlisted in the 2008 Prime Minister's Literary Awards; *The Life*; *The Wonder Lover*; and *Bluebird*. His many non-fiction titles include *Boom: The Underground History of Australia; From Gold Rush to GFC*, which won the 2013 Ashurst Business Literature Prize; and *Bradman's War*, shortlisted in the 2013 Prime Minister's Literary Awards.

THE FIRST FRIEND

MALCOLM KNOX

ALLEN&UNWIN
SYDNEY·MELBOURNE·AUCKLAND·LONDON

This is a work of fiction. Names, characters, places and incidents are sometimes based on historical events, but are used fictitiously.

First published in 2024

Copyright © Malcolm Knox 2024

All rights reserved. No part of this book may be reproduced or transmitted in any form or by any means, electronic or mechanical, including photocopying, recording or by any information storage and retrieval system, without prior permission in writing from the publisher. The Australian *Copyright Act 1968* (the Act) allows a maximum of one chapter or 10 per cent of this book, whichever is the greater, to be photocopied by any educational institution for its educational purposes provided that the educational institution (or body that administers it) has given a remuneration notice to the Copyright Agency (Australia) under the Act.

Allen & Unwin
Cammeraygal Country
83 Alexander Street
Crows Nest NSW 2065
Australia
Phone: (61 2) 8425 0100
Email: info@allenandunwin.com
Web: www.allenandunwin.com

Allen & Unwin acknowledges the Traditional Owners of the Country on which we live and work. We pay our respects to all Aboriginal and Torres Strait Islander Elders, past and present.

A catalogue record for this book is available from the National Library of Australia

ISBN 978 1 76147 043 1

Set in 13/17.5 pt Granjon by Bookhouse, Sydney
Printed and bound in Australia by the Opus Group

10 9 8 7 6 5 4 3 2 1

The paper in this book is FSC® certified. FSC® promotes environmentally responsible, socially beneficial and economically viable management of the world's forests.

Don't regard it as a document, for it is not a document . . . Regard it as a work of art. And you will agree that you've never read anything like it in all of world literature. What well-defined characters! What a grandiose plot, and how cohesive and integrated everything was. It's just too bad that the characters were living people, otherwise you might be able to stand reading it.

Vladimir Voinovich, *The Ivankiad*

AUTHOR'S NOTE

LAVRENTIY PAVLOVICH BERIA (1899–1953) WAS A MASS MURDERER of the twentieth century. As chief of security in the Soviet Union from 1938–53, the second half of Josef Stalin's rule, Beria was a connoisseur of homicide, whether with the stroke of a pen or his bare hands. One of the keys to Beria's survival—he outlived the dictator's rule—was his success in surrounding himself with loyal henchmen from his home republic of Georgia. Like Stalin, who was also Georgian, Beria exercised power through a personal mafia following codes of fealty and violence common to criminal gangs. Another element of Beria's success was his reputation for intelligence, efficiency, attention to detail and an unquenchable appetite for work. Beria saw himself as more than just a secret policeman. For the seven years before Stalin appointed him as his security chief, Beria was governor of Georgia. Like the man he yearned to succeed, Beria was part mobster, part tireless bureaucrat and part true believer in Communism. An American assessment of the time held that Beria was the only one of Stalin's inner circle who possessed the competence to run a medium-sized US corporation.

UNION OF SOVIET SOCIALIST REPUBLICS, 1938

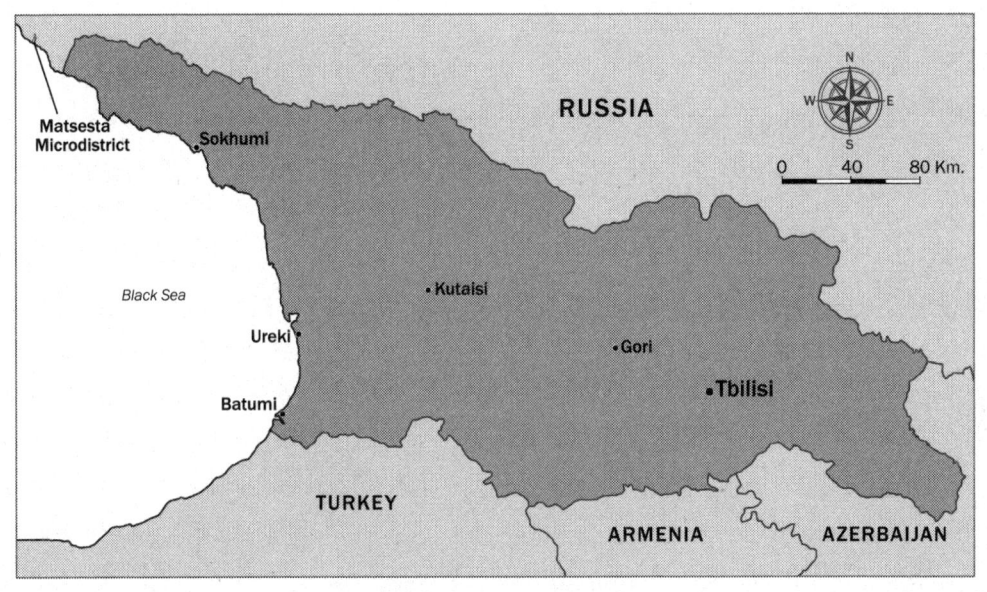

REPUBLIC OF GEORGIA, 1938

BACKGROUND TO EVENTS

1878: Josef Stalin born as Josef Vissarionovich Dzughashvili in Gori, Georgia.

1899: Lavrentiy Pavlovich Beria born in Merkheuli, near Sokhumi, Georgia.

February 1917: Revolution overthrows Tsar Nicholas II. The Provisional Government is installed under Alexander Kerensky with the support of the Menshevik faction of the Russian Social Democratic Labour Party (RSDLP).

October 1917: The Bolshevik faction of the RSDLP overthrows the Provisional Government. Stalin joins Bolshevik leader Vladimir Ilyich Lenin's governing inner circle.

1918: Soviet Russia, Britain, Turkey and Germany tussle for control of Georgia, which declares independence under Menshevik rule. Beria, who is studying architecture in Baku, Azerbaijan, spies for the Bolsheviks and also for the Mensheviks.

1919–21: Led by Leon Trotsky, the Bolshevik 'Red' Army defeats the counter-revolutionary 'Whites' in the Russian Civil War, cementing Soviet rule. Beria begins his career in the Bolshevik secret police, the Cheka.

1921: The Red Army invades Georgia and the Bolsheviks topple the Mensheviks. Georgia becomes an 'autonomous republic' of the Soviet Union.

1924–27: After Lenin's death, Stalin defeats Trotsky in a power struggle and consolidates supreme rule over the Soviet Union. In Georgia, the Cheka helps defeat a nationalist uprising. Beria receives the Order of the Red Banner and is appointed to lead the Georgian wing of the Soviet secret police, now known as the OGPU.

1927–33: Stalin orders mass collectivisation which results in seven to nine million deaths, mainly from forced famine, across the USSR.

1931: Beria becomes Communist Party chief and governor of the Transcaucasian republics of Georgia, Armenia and Azerbaijan.

1933: Adolf Hitler is elected Chancellor of Germany.

1934–36: After years of purging landowners, peasants and class enemies of the regime, Stalin turns on the 'Old Bolsheviks' after his close associate Sergei Kirov is assassinated.

1937: Appointed by Stalin to head the Soviet secret police, now called the NKVD, Nikolai Yezhov leads the Great Terror, in which at least 1.6 million people, many of them members of the Bolshevik Party and the military leadership, are arrested, tortured, forced to 'confess their crimes' in show trials, and deported to slave labour camps or executed.

1938: Stalin visits his birthplace. Beria, as Georgian ruler, is his host.

PERSONS

MURTOV AND FAMILY

Vasil Anastasvili Murtov—Beria's oldest friend, Assistant Communist Party Secretary, personal driver
Babilina—Murtov's de facto wife
Ana—Murtov and Babilina's elder daughter
Melor—Murtov and Babilina's younger daughter
Anastas Karvelashvili Murtov—Murtov's widowed father

BERIA AND STAFF OF THE COMMUNIST PARTY OF THE SOVIET REPUBLIC OF GEORGIA

Lavrentiy Pavlovich 'Lavrushya' Beria—First Secretary of the Georgian CP; governor of the republic
Natia Meskhi—First Assistant Secretary of the CP

Vsevolod Merkulov—head of state security
Evgenii Dumbadze—head of secret police
Sergei Kruglov—head of Party security
Sergo Goglidze—head of internal affairs
Bogdan Kobulov—'The Samovar'
Amayak Kobulov—'The worst man God put on the earth'
Ketevan Nozadze—Beria's personal private secretary
Adam Adamashvili Adamadze—trainee driver

COMMUNIST PARTY OF THE SOVIET UNION SIGNIFICANT PERSONS, 1937-38

Josef Stalin, 'Soso', 'Koba', 'The Vozhd', 'The Steel One'—General Secretary of the CPSU
Vyacheslav Mikhaylovich Molotov, 'The Hammer'—Premier of the Soviet Union
Sergo Konstantinovich Ordzhonikidze—People's Commissar of Heavy Industry
Kliment Yefremovich Voroshilov—People's Commissar of Defence
Lazar Moiseyevich Kaganovich—Deputy Chairman of the Council of People's Commissar
Anastas Ivanovich Mikoyan—People's Commissar of Foreign Trade
Nikita Sergeyevich Khrushchev—General Secretary of the Communist Party of the Ukraine
Andrei Aleksandrovic Zhdanov—First Secretary of the Leningrad Party branch
Nikolai Ivanovich Yezhov—head of state security (NKVD)
Georgy Maksimilianovich Malenkov—deputy to Yezhov
Aleksandr Nikolayevich Poskrebyshev—Stalin's personal secretary
General Nikolai Sidorovich Vlasik—Stalin's personal bodyguard

THE FIRST FRIEND

STALIN'S FAMILY

Ekaterina 'Keke' Geladze—mother
Yakov—elder son
Vasili—younger son
Svetlana—daughter

Prologue
ALTERNATIVE FACTS

AN END

MATSESTA MICRODISTRICT, RUSSIAN SOVIET SOCIALIST REPUBLIC
1 JULY 1938

MURTOV DID NOT SEE THE WOMAN'S FACE WHEN SHE WAS SHOVED through the doorway. His eyes were focused on two palm leaves decorating the whitewashed wall. Through a small window he could see the sky and the sea, the many shades of Georgian blue that had survived the workers' and peasants' paradise.

He was incapable of turning his head towards the woman. His wrists and ankles were chained to the four posts of the bed and his neck was roped to an iron hook below the window. He had nowhere to hide, nor words to explain, his failure. Was he nakedly prepared for pleasure or for torture? Was there any difference? As Beria liked to say, walk westwards to your death or eastwards to your life, and one day you will meet your fate.

Murtov contemplated the blueness of the Black Sea. Despite everything, the Soviet Union could still turn on the colours. Water merged with sky; Murtov thought of infinity. Outside was a day glorious enough to tempt thoughts of an outlawed God. Let the sky in, he thought. Nobody cares what noises come out and nobody can see in; it's all ours from here.

The woman moved into his line of sight. She wore a robe the colour of her skin and her face was concealed by a curtain of black hair.

A hum rose through Murtov's interior, low at first, reminding him of a crowd of Party functionaries gathered for an official address. That gurgle of anticipation. From the top of his stomach it filtered into the base of his chest.

Shame, he thought as he contemplated the woman, that the last person he saw in this life should be the punchline to a joke. A joke, he thought, that his last hours should be spent with his hands cuffed in shame.

✻

A wall away from this room, he had been at lunch.

Beria barked into the telephone the hotel manager kept ferrying to and from the table. Between calls, Beria told stories. Six bald men laughed. The youngest, Adam Adamashvili Adamadze, made sure the others laughed just long enough. Their hands, through four hours of lunch, left their guns only to attend to their food. Murtov had lost the use of his hands and his gun. He had only his eyes. He stared across the table at AAA, who stared back; a competition the workers' paradise permitted.

Suddenly Beria announced that he was shouting his buddy

Murtov a dose of afternoon delight. 'Something to silence the voices in his head!' The six men laughed and went back to their guns.

'My treat,' Beria told Murtov while having him taken to a room where his handcuffs were exchanged for chains and ropes attached to bedposts and wall hooks.

Murtov didn't understand the flow of commerce in the Soviet Union, never had. The boss was comped everything; the boss was comped his life. It was the hotel manager's pleasure to comp a wing of this joint for First Secretary Beria plus his security guy, his Party guy, his operations guy, his other security guy, an additional security guy and that guy's brother, and Murtov, who until yesterday was Beria's everything-else guy. Beria called these men his 'friends'. They relied on him for their livelihoods and their lives. Friendship was a transaction, all barter, all taken care of, and when you thought about it, as Murtov was thinking about it now, it was impossible to say where the means came from and how it happened. Money was a river that flowed through Beria, who converted its energy for those downstream, in the form of gift and favour and don't you worry about that.

No mystery about what was coming: the last high, the shot to end all shots.

Here she is, Murtov thought. He felt as light as a cloud, but then his muscles and his bones, his tendons and his internal organs tightened with a pulse of fury so convulsive that his ears stood out from the sides of his head.

She was not who they said she was. Had they said she was anybody? When she allowed him her face, Murtov discovered who they had been laughing at.

He wished, as he convulsed, to break his chains like Hercules.

Murtov thought he'd got Beria. He thought he'd got him good. But no, it was the boss who got Murtov, and was now, as they said in the workers' paradise when they dared speak of such matters, sending him to the other world. The first friend would have the last laugh.

A HAPPIER END

DETAILS WERE A CASUALTY OF THE SYSTEM. INITIAL REPORTS of a deceased thirty-nine-year-old male, bald and running to fat, in a waterfront room of the Matsesta Microdistrict Party Select Hotel gave rise to the conclusion most feared and least anticipated: that it was Lavrentiy Pavlovich Beria who had conked out on his hotel bed mid-rub and tug.

Death wafted out of the Matsesta Microdistrict on the Black Sea breeze. The rumour was captured, boxed up, sent to Moscow, considered (but never contested), phrased and rephrased, and, finally, massaged for announcement on state media. By then the only true facts remaining were the sex, age and measurements of the deceased thirty-nine-year-old, possibly not even those.

Grief would be genuine only on the shores of the Black Sea, where Beria, as First Secretary of the Communist Party of the republic for seven years, had become a hero to the Georgian worker and peasant who had lived under his benign protection. For them, his death would be emotionally akin to the loss of a friend. Many years later he would lament to his executioners, 'Not dying in '38 was my missed opportunity. I was a great governor of Georgia. I die in '38, there are statues of me.'

In '38, when it was decreed that Beria had died, preparations were made for his friends to be called forward—not those here in the Select Hotel but the permitted ones, the leading scientists and state poets, the ballerinas and musicians, plus one representative worker and one intricately selected peasant. After a dignified period of rehearsals and rewrites, the boss of bosses, the General Secretary himself, the Unsinking Sun of Our Times, the Genius Leader of the Toilers of the Whole World, would issue a definitive statement to transform the grief of millions into a renewed defence of the Revolution. A state funeral would be outlined, sketches for statues recovered from planning files, and the Black Sea city of Sokhumi, where Beria had been raised, would be renamed in his honour: Beriagrad.

Black armbands would be knotted (not dusted off, being in constant use) and a minute's silence observed. Lavrentiy Pavlovich Beria, Georgian patriot and Soviet hero of spotless reputation, forger of metal, plougher of fields, feeder of babies, cultivator of life-saving mandarins, Father of the Soviet Florida and friend to all gymnasts, had perished in the service of the worker and the peasant. Gossips would trade their whispers, but Moscow would manage any hint of scandal out of existence. A faintly dissenting émigré voice, from Swiss or Mexican exile, might ask why a mere Caucasian grub with a shady secret police past should be so elevated; why a politics-obsessed regime raised these intriguers above the worker who spilt her blood on the factory floor and the soldier who gave his life for the Motherland. Why was one person valued above thousands extinguished by famine and struggle and petty crime and cancer and heart failure and stroke and infection (not to mention disappearance)? These cavils would be silenced as, for three days, from kitchen table to farmers' commune, the people grieved their loss.

And tens of thousands, scheduled for cancellation, would live.

But joy—or alas—this version proved as false as those rumours of that mad German prick planning to snatch Poland before year's end. Beria was alive! Beria was saved!

The deceased was not the local boss but a man who, if he was ever known, would be compulsorily forgotten. Vasil Anastasvili Murtov's death would be marked at most by a news brief in *Pravda*: a worker who had made one long-ago football appearance for his country passed away peacefully in his sleep, surrounded by his dearest friends, on the Black Sea coast.

Plans to commemorate Beria's demise would be packed in their drawers. Beriagrad would remain a fallback option.

Beria would demand sympathy not for his dead friend but for himself.

No photograph had ever been taken of Vasil Anastasvili Murtov aside from the headshot soaking up the last of his sweat on the stained identity card in a pocket of the Party tunic lying on the floor of the hotel room. The attending police chief, his eye on promotion, would undergo a moment of inspiration and report that First Secretary Beria had been the target of an assassination but miraculously survived. In his great wisdom, Beria travelled with a body double.

In time, the story of the failed assassination attempt would die its own death, and in the final wash-up it was impossible to deduce from the documentation whether any man, thirty-nine years old or otherwise, balding or not, running to fat or not, and any dark-haired woman or other person died in the Party hotel of the Matsesta Microdistrict on 1 July 1938. In fact (if such a formulation may so loosely be used), no such death can be found in the archives. Mistakes happen.

These alternative facts are not the end of the mistake. They are its beginning.

Part one
GEORGIA

FORTY DAYS TO LIVE

1

VASIL ANASTASVILI MURTOV AND ADAM ADAMASHVILI ADAMADZE sat in the black Emka on the lawn rippling from the basement of the shingled two-storey beach house all the way down to the Ureki seafront. Murtov had parked the car facing the house so they could be ready and undistracted by the Black Sea wind swells reflecting a sun that shone, dangerously, from outside the Soviet Union. Since 1937 you could be sent to the other world for showing too close an interest in foreign bodies.

The wind was building and swinging from the west. The midday onshores ruffled the pines. The black magnetic sand on the beach trembled beneath the gusts like a drying bedsheet.

Murtov was wearing a faded green state security tunic and blue trousers that had fretted in the crotch, a tear from wear. His hair was a tight number one military shave growing out in a horseshoe from ear to ear. He weighed ninety-two kilograms and was developing cellulite on his arse and middle, which Babilina had teased him about and, no matter how he starved himself, he couldn't shift. Chewing gum, the thinking man's snack, staved off his midday hunger. He unwrapped a stick and slid it between his lower jaw and the inside of his cheek, taking a moment to savour the dissolution of the sugar dust before the confection became a wad of tasteless fact. With the tip of his tongue he flipped it between the third and fourth teeth on his right-side jaw. Why he always began with the right side, every mouthful of every food, Murtov could not say. His comfort zone for food. In this job, in this life, if you couldn't forgive yourself one comfort zone you were truly fucked.

He glanced to the passenger seat. AAA had to be twenty-one max. His black hair was cut in a mid-fade with a solid quiff and some sort of bespoke design at the part. The smell of his hair oil filled the car. A scarred border of neck acne poked above the collar of AAA's embroidered red Ukrainian shirt, a garment in fashion among the Post-Revolutionary young who preferred it to the traditional Russian *kosovorotka*. They had begun wearing it when The Steel One's rush to rural collectivisation had starved millions of Ukrainian peasants in a war that was undeclared yet historically necessary. Omelettes break eggs, if indeed any eggs had been broken, which officially they had not. The fashion for the shirts was somehow both a celebration and a denial of the fiction.

AAA wore low-cut leather shoes without socks, and in the footwell his serge trousers rode up to reveal a racially ambiguous skin tone. In Pre-Revolutionary days, the first question Murtov's father would have asked about AAA was: 'Where's he from?' Hard to say; somewhere between Abkhazia and northern Asia, one of the Stans, or Jewish–Chinese with one Egyptian grandmother and another from Vladivostok. This kid had all eleven time zones in him. You couldn't tell anymore. More important: you couldn't ask.

Murtov checked his wristwatch. Too early to worry about time, but his blood pressure had been here before.

AAA spied Murtov's wristwatch before he could slide it back beneath his cuff.

'Pre,' AAA said.

Wristwatches had been banned after the October Revolution as an imperialist affectation. Workers told the time from the electric clocks on every street corner. It didn't matter if they had the wrong time; it only mattered that they were all wrong together.

'Better not get caught with that,' AAA added, condescension loaded with puritanism, the double-thick armour of Post-Revolutionary youth.

'Who by?' Murtov grunted. A shot of his eyes to the shingled house.

Murtov could not hide his wristwatch and AAA could not hide his face, upon which was written: *You old fools, you weary simpletons, enjoy your privileges while you can, your wristwatch is ticking . . .*

What was it friend Lenin had said? By the age of forty, an old Revolutionary has become an impediment.

Or was it friend Stalin?

AAA was a fidgeter. He fiddled with the radio knob, couldn't listen to more than ten seconds of Shostakovich before he quested for something else. Fresh out of Party academy, he knew the permitted music, and if he didn't know it he didn't want to. When he wasn't changing the radio station he was stroking the dash leather with its chrome and wood trim inlays, fingers sliding across the magnified glass of the tachometer dial as if they needed to substantiate what his eyes could not quite believe. AAA coddled the chrome shift knob in the shape of a hand grenade. Murtov didn't like AAA touching the shift knob; it was Pre territory. AAA hadn't even been born when Murtov was a family man of the wrong heritage and worried his life was over, when the boss had given him a new lease on that life. Murtov was reborn in October '17, which made him old. Since '37, old was as good as dead.

To clear AAA out of the gearstick zone, Murtov said, 'Check the glove box.'

Without removing his left hand from the grenade, AAA opened the glove box with his right. He slid out the in-built navigation set—compass, protractor, laminated map—and faked an appreciative whistle, the studied sarcasm of Post children. The new type didn't read Marx night after night until they got to the end, but absorbed his works in one-hour crib sessions. They had cast off the old Bolsheviks' self-denying purity and replaced it with a harsher purity of their own. They were physically cleaner than the shaggy ramblers of October. While educated, they were also insular; they cleaved to Great Russia. No more World Revolution; now it was Socialism in One Country. Unity, discipline, singleness of purpose: their ecstasies came from the perfect pursuit of Revolutionary *technique* more than the promises of a better world.

AAA took his leather-bound notepad out of his right breast pocket and wrote one word before putting the notepad away.

'Okay,' AAA said through an outward breath. He clicked the navigation set back into place and snapped the glove box shut. Murtov's right foot twitched on the swing-mounted racing-car accelerator pedal with six parallel rubber inserts. His hands gripped the three-spoke suede-covered steering wheel as if to stop himself going headlong over the horizon—*Fuck it all, I'm out of here.*

Murtov breathed.

'Sure,' AAA said, 'he goes round in a standard model, no way can he be seen in a Packard or a Mercedes, but . . . this luxury.'

AAA's fleshy nose, pulpy and large-pored, an overripe plum: the guy was growing something that would be repellent when—if—he got to Murtov's age. You didn't see noses like that on the young, like cancers, greedy life that eats other life.

'It's not for him,' Murtov said. 'It's for the worker.'

AAA's eyes challenged Murtov to reveal whether he was dumb or just playing at it. Murtov gave him nothing, not even a stick of chewing gum. Exactly what a dumb driver or a good actor would do.

'*Interesting*,' AAA said, or quoted. 'The boss chose the fit-out, or you enjoy the confidence of the Party?'

Murtov's eyes went to the outline of the notebook in AAA's pocket. Every decision a passage through a gate that locked behind you. The tension will kill us before the firing squad does.

'I enjoy the confidence of the Party.'

To enjoy the confidence of the Party was to carry its status day and night, rain, hail or shine, war or peace. To enjoy the confidence of the Party was to be recognised as acting, in every way, in its spirit. To enjoy the confidence of the Party was the highest aspiration for workers and peasants, even if it entailed sacrifice of personality. The sacrifice was half the fucking pleasure. In exchange, the bearer of the Party's confidence was entitled to the exercise of power. Murtov did not need to explain to AAA that his personal powers, his embodiment of the spirit of the Party, extended no further than his work vehicle.

AAA nodded, freer to commit to what he was about to say. 'I was just thinking, Soviet car on the outside, German on the inside, but you've got the aesthetic wrong. It's like, that'—he gave the grenade gear knob a condescending caress—'doesn't go with *that*.' His nose indicated the suede steering wheel. 'Just doesn't hang together style-wise, friend, know what I'm saying?'

Murtov gave a shrug. One generation in, they already had ideas about style. The thing about full circle was, it came around fast. Murtov could file this one away against AAA, if he needed it. If and when. He had notebooks of his own. And a smart prick wouldn't let the other guy see his.

'It's for the worker,' AAA said, 'but the *inside* worker, right? You. You practically live in it.'

'It's still just a kerosene tin on wheels.'

AAA's eyes went to the house. The shingles ran across the front verandah, crowned by a twin-gabled Black Sea–style slate roof. Across the sandstone-block basement level, pink camellias were in flower. From the front of the house, the lawn unfolded like a cresting wave, a sand dune knit together by soft couch grass surviving another arid summer.

'How long before we go up and knock?' AAA said.

'Hurrying him's only going to put you on the shit list.'

AAA, not pretending to listen, glanced over his shoulder at the enormous bunch of lilies on the back seat.

'Never seen that many flowers in one place.'

Murtov thought: a garden? Or maybe AAA had managed to race up the ladder without being sidetracked by gardens.

'Whose funeral is it again?'

'A fallen friend,' Murtov said.

'Not what's-his-name?'

When Murtov did not reply, AAA said, 'Oh, friend what's-his-name. He got cancelled, right? Then ended himself?' AAA nodded, pleased. 'He was *backward*.' The kid let the word fall with a thud. 'And what, the boss is delivering the flowers to the widow?'

'He's giving the eulogy.'

'What a friend,' AAA said, so genuine that his nose blushed. 'He always knows the right thing to say.'

Murtov chewed his gum. AAA changed the music on the radio. Murtov turned the sound down.

'He didn't always,' Murtov said. When he and the boss were schoolkids, puny furtive Lavrentiy Pavlovich Beria, brain the size of the Tsar's empire, vocabulary bigger still, bore conspicuous remnants of who he was and where he came from. He liked to use the precise literary word, only he got the pronunciations wrong. Like, he loved using 'albeit' (*tr: tum-tsa*), but he pronounced it 'al bite' (*tr: tsum-tsar*). The other boys burned him for that. Mocking a charity ward for his inadequacies was a foundation stone of Tsarist education. Lavrentiy Pavlovich, young Beria, Little Lavrushya, appeared to take it well, like this was the price he had to pay for being born with so much brain and so little breeding. He accepted that 'if there's one bucket of shit in the whole village, you can count on me to step in it', and their laughter was how he disarmed them.

Before he got them.

Murtov related some of this to AAA, who replied, 'We can be thankful that it is no longer permitted to bully a worker or peasant.'

Murtov halted at the trigger word. That notepad. But he went on, dumb is as dumb speaks, gesturing at the lilies. He recounted the story of when the chief of the Tsar's army and his wife visited their Sokhumi school district and young Beria was chosen for the subservient task of thanking the dignitaries and giving the lady a bunch of flowers.

'Flowers,' AAA repeated.

'Right,' Murtov said. Beria hadn't ever seen a bunch of flowers that big and didn't know if it was called a *sheaf* (*tr: GAR-si*), a *sheath* (*tr: gar-SI*) or a *wreath* (*tr: GAR-SI*). The other boys looked at the bunch of flowers like it was a landmine and told him that any of those words sounded right. Beria got up in front of the crowd and said, 'Madame Chief of Army, on behalf of our school, I would like to present you with this lovely . . . *reef*' (*tr: sar-gi*).

One of the boys said later that, given the choice of shovel, axe or mattock, Beria had taken his pick. Little Lavrushya finally lost it, charging at the other boy and ranting about how he'd 'get all of you Tsarist cunts, you wait'. To calm him down, another of the boys said, 'You did fine, al bite slightly fucking useless at the end.'

AAA nodded, his brow furrowed as if he was unsure whether Murtov's story had ended. 'Is that American chewing gum?'

Murtov pulled the crushed packet out of his tunic breast pocket and offered it. AAA shook his head. 'I didn't want any. I just didn't know you could get it.'

Murtov checked his wristwatch, openly this time. They risked being late for this funeral. He could send AAA up to hustle the boss and end the kid's glittering little career just like that.

'So your story has made me feel unsafe,' AAA said.

'We're not being recorded.' As he said it, Murtov was hit by a thought: maybe they were. AAA's generation, you never knew.

But no. He did know. This was his car. The only listening devices in here were Murtov's.

'You're wanting to reassert your subtextual power relations,' AAA said. 'So you've known First Secretary Beria since you were how old?'

'Nine. Elementary school, he moved into our house.'

'You're reminding me that you and the First Secretary go back before my birth, and there's a depth to your connection that a young friend like me can never hope to rival.'

Murtov recited the formula: 'I apologise if that made you feel unsafe.' And lighten the fuck up, kid.

'Apology accepted,' AAA said, for once unsarcastically. 'But tell me, this is when they had private schools? You were privileged to be receiving a visit from a decadent chief of the Tsar's army. You were part of the imperialist power elite. You were non-toilers.'

'The boss's biography is well known,' Murtov said. 'He was the son of an impoverished dissident. He received bourgeois charity and leveraged it to break the old order. He comes from a historic line of peasants.'

'And you come from a line of Tsarist bourgeois specialists,' AAA said, changing the music again—more Shostakovich—and giving the hand grenade a fresh grope.

'We're Georgian,' Murtov said. 'There was nothing special about being upper-class.' Georgia, with more princes per square mile than anywhere in the world. Once all the princes were liquidated, there weren't enough bullets left for the bourgeois specialists.

'It all turned upside down between you and friend Beria, didn't it?' AAA went on without hearing. 'One minute you were his protector, his benefactor's son, his bourgeois adoptive brother. He leveraged your inherited *blat*'—pull, patronage, privilege—'and flipped you over, defeated you like the skilled martial artist he is. And now you are ... what? His driver. His butler. His flunkey. Or "ancient retainer"—is that the correct word for Tsarist manservants? Whatever it is you are, friend. For him. For now.'

'Assistant Secretary,' Murtov said.

'One of the, what, four hundred and twelve ASs in our division?'

'A quiet life, friend.'

'Hiding in plain sight, I suppose. You intellectuals always know the right word.'

Murtov's neck stiffened. 'You won't find any intellectuals here. We never knew what the right word was either. It was just flowers to us.'

'Sure, believe that if it helps you live your quiet life and hold onto your access to *blat*. Better a hundred friends than a hundred roubles, eh, Murtov? You know, you were lucky to be able to join the Party when you did. It's a lot harder now.' In October days, the Party had welcomed anyone; now its door was open only to those with generations of peasant blood. Or those who could document it. 'But don't worry. Luckily for you, I don't look backwards,' AAA said, with the smugness of peasant privilege. 'I am on my way to the future. I'm learning from the ground up.'

'Up to where?'

'The *nomenklatura*, of course,' the young man said. The new men. In the masticatory way AAA pronounced it, he didn't need to affirm the obvious: Murtov's ineligibility.

Murtov remembered the banned poet's words: young men *who smell of dog and wolf*.

'We live in a time of science and enlightenment, progress and opportunity,' AAA declared. 'Every day, a gap opens for advancement.'

And every day, Murtov thought, a new man becomes a former man. An executioner wakes up as the victim. The young man who smelt of dog and wolf always thought he was the filler, never the gap.

'Higher the rise, harder the fall,' Murtov said.

'Yeah, safer to stay at the bottom.' AAA completed the street wisdom while giving Murtov a once-over, as if he had chanced upon that staple of Communist citizenry: the Great Soviet Coward.

'When you get into the *nomenklatura*, don't forget where you started,' Murtov said. '*The lowest of underlings can be more important than all the generals and marshals put together.*'

Murtov saw for the first time that AAA's eyes were a shade of mauve.

A wooden door slammed and their attention snapped out of the car. Friend Beria, only fifteen minutes late. Murtov checked his watch. Could have a problem with the traffic.

'And I thought you October types fought a revolution to get rid of bosses,' AAA said.

'A word to the wise,' Murtov said. 'Wherever you think you're going in future, right now you are an assistant to the flunkey with the spoilt biography. Don't speak until the boss has spoken, don't contradict him, and if he asks you a question say you're still making up your mind. Don't tell a lie but don't take the initiative. No matter how comfortable he makes you, don't speak first. Got it?'

'Sure, champ.'

'And when you've risen to the *nomenklatura* . . .'

'I know, I know. *The lowest can play tricks which all the big chiefs will be unable to undo.* I won't forget you, friend Murtov.' AAA gave Murtov's cheek a light touch, the softest of Georgian slaps. 'And you won't forget me.'

✱

The boss was reading from a leather-bound folder as he came down the sandstone steps cut into the grass dune. In his free hand he carried a roll of papers tied with string. In the crook of his elbow was a Thompson submachine gun.

Lavrentiy Pavlovich Beria stood at only 168 centimetres, a stroke of fortune given his ambitions. There was no room at the top for any man who towered over the boss of bosses. Tall men in the Kremlin walked with stooped shoulders. Beria wore his customary round-collared Georgian tunic, but today, out of respect for the funeral, it was dark charcoal, a stylish twist on black. The buttons were undone but, unlike Murtov, he had no gut. The lightness of the fabric betrayed an Italian origin to which only the higher cadres of the Party had access. Effortlessly stylish, permanently Revolutionary, the boss transcended Pre and Post. When Beria is eighty, Murtov thought, he'll have decreed it the new twenty.

The only sign of premature ageing was his baldness, though he had managed to recast this as a sign of youthful vigour. In the '20s, during his rise through the darkness, one of Beria's moves was to suddenly snatch at a man's hair, give it a nasty yank and terrify his victim into silence. Laughing, he would apologise, explaining that he had been testing for a toupee, and give his victim a slap in the face, the old Georgian play, and murmur, 'Now you will remember me.' They all did.

In 1931, the year he reached the summit of the Georgian government, Beria's own hair had failed suddenly and catastrophically. From then on, he tolerated only baldness in his inner circle. Beria would not be overshadowed on hair, the last fact of Georgian life beyond his control. As a consequence, baldness had become something of a cult in the wider Georgian Party. Young men and even women had shaved their heads in readiness for promotion to Beria's A-team until Beria had finally ordered, 'No more, you give me the creeps; you all look like you're fresh out of the gulag.' Still, he liked his intimates to look ready for the gulag.

AAA wound down his window, alert for instructions. The boss stopped on the lawn and turned his back to scribble on the document he was reading, then came towards the car, smiling with closed lips. His secret teeth were not so much stained as translucent. It touched Murtov, in a way, that Beria's square-cut mouth still harboured enough traces of vanity to remain sealed over those teeth. Murtov pondered his oldest friend's bland features, his physical ordinariness, his slight dampness, his nondescript poise, which hovered somewhere between self-satisfied efficiency and clerical humility. His small eyes hid behind a pair of round pince-nez that reflected light; a face like two holes in the open sky.

'Fuck,' Murtov said. 'Goose.'

'What is it?' AAA yelped, the sudden systems crash of his ideological shield giving Murtov the warm shot of rank-pulling pleasure that AAA had accused him of seeking by telling the story of the flowers.

Murtov's face wore the tightness of intrigue, but the good kind, the Leninist kind that had made the Bolsheviks the party of glorious wonderful victorious conspiracy. 'All right, listen closely,

Mr From the Ground Up. You are going to get out of the car. You are going to walk past him without saying anything unless he speaks to you, and if he does all you will say is that you'll be back in a moment. Keep your eyes down and do not look at him. Now. Go up the two sets of stone stairs to the front door. Don't go in the front door. There's a passageway up to the left of the house. Don't go to the end, but turn right at the next door, which is between the windows. A hallway opens out in front of you, but don't take that. Take the second door on the right, and then there is another door to the right, but don't take that. That's the bathroom. Next to that is the kitchen. Enter there, but before you get into the kitchen turn left into the pantry. There should be a box, about yay big . . .' Murtov opened his hands to illustrate. 'Bring it down.'

AAA's nose empurpled. 'The hell am I going to remember all this?'

'You went to the Party academy, didn't you? If the box I've described is not in the pantry, go back to the kitchen. It'll be there.'

'You can't send me into his house.'

'Nobody's inside and he doesn't lock the doors. The timber has warped; they haven't locked up for years.'

'He'll have guards armed to the teeth, it's gonna be like this fucking car.' *Russian on the outside, German on the inside.* 'Why are you doing this to me?'

'It's his holiday house.'

'I do not feel that this is a safe workplace.'

'If we run late, sunshine, you'll know the meaning of unsafe.'

AAA opened the car door. Outside, the boss's pencil was putting a dot on his last i. AAA turned back to Murtov.

'Go on, fuck off,' Murtov said.

AAA's face buckled. 'But it's First Secretary Beria's house!'
'Stop talking, start remembering.'
'How do you know exactly where everything is?'
'I grew up in it.'

Murtov watched AAA take the sandstone steps two at a time. The boss climbed into the back of the car, placed his folders and his submachine gun on the seat and rubbed his hands together.

'Nice flowers,' Beria said. 'A reef, right?'
'You forgot the gift.'
'That's what you sent him up for? I'm out of my head, got some serious news.'

They watched AAA emerge from the house, lopsided under the weight of the box.

Murtov knew he had made a terrible mistake. Something about that kid really gave him the shits, and out of vanity, irritation, whatever, he had slipped up. Fuck. The most dangerous thing in 1938 wasn't to be an ex-bourgeois intellectual Old Bolshevik. The most dangerous thing was to let on that there was more to you than met the eye.

'How's he going?' Beria asked.
'Where'd you find him?'
'Friend Natia.' Beria's deputy.
'Figures.'
'He all right?'
'Like the fucking October Revolution, boss.'

Smiling with his lips over his teeth, Beria chimed in with the old friends' punchline. 'Yeah, right: too soon to tell.'

II

MURTOV WAS MASSAGING THE EMKA, THE GLORIOUSLY FAMOUS and famously glorious GAZ-M1, the Soviet people's own kerosene tin on wheels, around the potholed coastal road. It was a good road, by Georgian standards, unlike the main routes which could only be negotiated in a tank. In the passenger seat, AAA's rapt expression spoke for The Promise of a Radiant Future; every pothole was a reason to celebrate the coming paved superhighways, every muddy ditch was a canal in the making, every brambly vacant lot was a future People's Park of synchronised gymnastics, parade practice and parachute towers.

They were making good progress to the funeral; Murtov had got too worked up about running late. Nonetheless, when they slowed behind a truck, Beria looked up from his reading to exclaim, 'Overtake, will you? Traffic rules are for peasants!'

Murtov made sure AAA saw him smiling. The boss was making a joke. In AAA's world, humour had been outlawed unless it was in the service of the state, but Beria's humour was in the service of Beria. Back in the 1920s, Soviet leaders had used only public transport and were paid ordinary workers' wages and lined up for food like everyone else. In Beria's free Georgia of the 1930s, a leader had a driver, an assistant driver, a cook, a gardener, medical and household staff, a fleet of cars and air transport, a home stocked with canaries, dogs, cats, a bear cub, nannies, grandparents, a deaf-mute aunt and a sense of humour. As all this wealth belonged to the Soviet state, it was permitted, no matter what these young puritans thought.

Clouds massed and the wind stiffened, dicing the Black Sea into whitecaps. Murtov sometimes dreamt about taking his family on a rowboat and ending up, through enthusiasm or forgetfulness, over the horizon. What used to be on the distant shore? Turkey? Bulgaria? Soviet maps no longer stretched that far.

He glanced into his rear-vision mirror. Beria was reading his *Cheka Weekly*, the *Weekly Digest of the Extraordinary Commission for Combating Speculation and Counter-Revolution*. He smacked his lips over the weekly disappearance quotas. Privately, Beria condemned the unhinged extremes of the purge prosecuted by the Moscow Police chief, Nikolai Ivanovich Yezhov, but he approved of the long lists in the *Cheka Weekly* because they relieved the pressure on his Transcaucasian republics of Georgia, Azerbaijian and Armenia. He ruled the south, he liked to say, with 'white gloves'. He styled himself as the protector of the Caucasians, based on his ability to keep the local arrest rate down. It took a secret policeman to stop the secret policemen. According to the most recent elections, 99.8 percent of the Transcaucasian population agreed with him.

'Only two thousand one hundred and ninety-eight former persons were created in the Caucasus last week,' Beria said. 'A full sixty percent below the USSR average.' He snapped the *Cheka Weekly* shut and inhaled the crisp air. 'Our unshaven mountains,' he said lovingly of the scenery, a description stolen from the former poet Mandelstam. As a proud Caucasian, Beria believed that everything worthwhile the Soviet Union produced had originated in the land of milk and honey and oil between the Black and Caspian seas. 'Look at the map,' he liked to declare. 'Caucasia is the centre of the world!'

In the front passenger seat, AAA was cradling the lilies. The kid cleared his throat and nodded at Murtov's chewing gum. To spare AAA the risk of dropping the flowers, Murtov placed a single stick onto his tongue. AAA thanked him with his mauve eyes.

'Faggots,' said the cheerful voice from the back seat.

With a shake of his head, Murtov reminded the kid: *Err on the side of silence*. The foundational principle of our system. Plenty of erring going on, that was for sure. Not one muscle moved in AAA's face. He even stopped chewing. These first days of employment in Beria's personal detail were a dangerous period: AAA had youth, he had hair, and he had a few centimetres too much height. Murtov, weary of losing his interns, was pleased by AAA's self-discipline.

Absently, Beria fondled his Thompson submachine gun. He had not employed armed bodyguards since a camping trip in the summer of 1935 when his personal security detachment had tried to kill him. The two men, from South Ossetia in Georgia's north, had been recruited for their stupid bravery and their quickness to fight without asking questions. These were perfect qualities for bodyguards if Beria should be confronted by imperialist holdouts, but feelings in South Ossetia ran stronger on matters of nationality than ideology. The two guards were employed under the 1935 Friendship of the Peoples cultural policy, and while the policy was intended to unite the diverse nationalities of the USSR under the banner of Marxism, it also gave the South Ossetians a perfect opportunity to remove one Georgian from the world, which, they believed, had to be an improvement.

One moonless night they perforated Beria's tent with gunfire. Their mistake was that Beria was not sleeping in the tent. Smelling a South Ossetian rat, he had swapped tents with Murtov, whom the rain of bullets somehow missed. Beria seldom slept, except to snatch a few hours for Revolutionary dreams; that night, he lay awake with Revolutionary suspicions. He sprang out of his tent with his Tommy gun and liquidated the two assassins. Feeling sorry for Murtov over the tent swap (he hadn't told him why, he just said he felt like a change), Beria awarded him the star-shaped medal of Hero of the Soviet Union. Ever since, Beria had dispensed with bodyguards and carried his own Tommy gun, arming Murtov with his personal TT-30 Soviet-made Tokarev pistol for display purposes, unloaded. The trainee driver, presently AAA, was equipped with a handgun that fired blanks. Beria inclined against unnecessary risks.

The boss was on to a new topic. 'Look, I love my kids to death, but it's got to be said: the boy's a moron and the girl's a cunt.' Noticing AAA's widened eyes, he continued, 'I'm not meant to say that about children of the Revolution, am I? But no Georgian has ever been able to make a persuasive argument without obscenities!

Okay, ruin our fucking traditions if you want. She's not a cunt. She's a bitch.'

Murtov cut his eyes at AAA, who was fixed on the whiskered scenery, chewing his gum. The kid wasn't mocking Murtov as the 'ancient retainer' anymore, not since he had found the boss's beach dacha exactly as Murtov had described, sparse and unpretentious and unchanged, the last unlocked property in the security state.

Checking his mirrors, Murtov overtook a hay wagon. 'Which one left the note in your folder?'

'Both,' Beria said. 'The moron because he wasn't listening when I told him I had no time for his bullshit notes. And the bitch because she was.'

'Anything important?'

'What do you reckon?'

Beria was known for his intolerance, shading into hatred, of young children. Murtov remembered when Beria's wife Nina had brought their newborn son into the office to show the female assistants. Beria had required, as a condition of marriage, that Nina promise not to have children, but twice she had betrayed him. He was chairing a meeting when Nina brought the boy in. With the assistants cooing over him, the baby boy let out a high-pitched squeal that penetrated into the conference room. The boss paused his briefing and said, 'Where's King Herod when you need him?' The bald men around the conference table sensed each other's mood like a flock of birds entering their flying formation, found safety in numbers, and released a chorus of requisite laughter.

Beria warmed to children once they reached puberty. He approved of Moscow's 1935 decision to make children as young as twelve eligible for the death penalty. 'At twelve,' he said, 'they're old enough.'

Now, on the back seat, he was waxing philosophical. 'In middle age you take stock of why you're doing what you're doing, you've been racing all these years without thinking about why, and when you strip back the fat and gristle, what you're left with is the next generation. It's all for them. What else is there? And the average Soviet citizen, they stop there. It's enough to know that they're doing it for their stupid kids. Their even stupider grandkids. Pass something on. A better world. Full stop, end of story. Only I've been asking the next question. Okay, I'm doing it for the children of Georgia. But *why*, when they're such a fucking waste of space? Mine are a waste of *two* spaces.'

Murtov glanced at AAA as if he, as a member of the Post generation, needed to justify the space on the front seat that he might be wasting right now. But AAA kept his gaze on the shoulder of the road, where landslips from recent rains were being dug out by crews of incarcerated kulaks. Murtov tried to block his ears to Beria's familiar diatribe against children. He contemplated the kulaks, stripped of their land, be it vast fields or, more likely, dismal little strawberry patches. Slaves of the state now, some glared balefully at the passing Emka. Beria had done his utmost to keep them out of the Siberian prison camps; Georgia needed free labour.

'Saying you're doing it for the kids,' Beria was going on, 'that's not thinking, that's bourgeois automatism.' Beria concluded his little oration with a shrug and a private smile that suggested he, alone in the workers' and peasants' paradise, had come up with the correct answer to the question of *Why?*

Having given his jaw a workout, Murtov spat his gum into a leaf torn out of his notebook. He'd read somewhere that chewing gum stimulated the frontal cortex. Frontal or some other cortex?

Anyway, it stimulated something. Higher functions. That was why the monkeys had taken up chewing in the first place. Eventually all that chewing turned them into men, and after a few millennia more chewing, Communists. But AAA didn't stimulate anything. He chewed one deliberate chew, then moved on to the next chew. He's as gorgeous as a girl, Murtov thought. Maybe I am a faggot. The boss can make the world up as he goes along.

'*The ABC of Communism*,' AAA said.

'Ah—it speaks!' said Beria.

'*The ABC of Communism*,' the kid repeated. 'Published 1918. It was mandatory in our school. There will be no more speaking of "my" children, only "our" children.'

'The fuck's he on about?' Beria asked Murtov.

'The selfless Revolutionary will break from Pre-Revolutionary ties such as religion and family, and blow up the shell of private life,' AAA went on. 'As Gorky writes, *The new structure of political life demands a new structure of the soul. In the future we are building, there will be no such thing as private family*.' He dared meet the boss's eyes. 'So you need not worry, friend.'

Murtov held his breath for AAA. It was a longer speech than Murtov had ever heard an intern dare.

'Fuck me, it not only talks but it's swallowed *The ABC*,' Beria said. 'I thought I was just having a whinge about my kids.'

The boss was back in his *Cheka Weekly*. Murtov was always telling his daughters, Get out of your books, smell the breeze, don't let the natural world pass you by. The one who really needed to hear it was Beria.

'So this funeral,' Murtov said.

'Fucking eulogy, I really don't have time today,' Beria replied. 'Hey, Vasil, what do you reckon? Buried or cremated?'

'You want us to stay and wait, or go and come back?'

'Serious. When the time comes, you want me to bury or cremate you?'

'Assuming you're not gone first.'

'Oh, we can assume that.' Beria gave a tight smile.

'Cremation man, myself,' Murtov said.

'You?' The boss wanted to hear from AAA.

'Burial suggests bourgeois religious mysticism.'

The boss took this in, then: 'Niche or scattered?'

Murtov shrugged. 'Same diff. You're only ashes, right?'

'Gotta choose,' the boss said.

'Scattered.'

'Friend?'

'Scattering ashes contravenes Georgian littering laws,' AAA said, adjusting his grip on the sheaf of lilies.

Murtov sought eye contact in the mirror—for parking purposes, he needed to know how long Beria would be at the funeral—but the boss was riffing.

'I'd prefer to be cremated and then scattered in a special place. Unlike what happened to my old man. You remember that, Vasil?'

'Sure,' Murtov said.

'See, friend,' the boss said to AAA, 'when my father died he didn't leave any positive instructions, only what he didn't want, so the rest was sort of left up to my siblings and me. He was an old peasant rebel, as pure as a Dostoevsky devil—not like my adoptive parents, eh, Vasil?'

Dostoevsky. An image of Beria when they were boys flashed into Murtov's head. Squeezed into the alcove under the stairs, Beria consumed Dostoevsky, mainly *Crime and Punishment*, over and over and over, like it was his Holy Bible. He re-read it until he broke the spine.

'Fortunately the apple didn't fall too far from the tree and I inherited my own blood,' Beria continued. 'Anyway. We had him cremated but one of his dying wishes was that he didn't want a niche in a fucking church wall.'

'Imperialist superstition,' AAA said dutifully.

'No, it cost twelve hundred roubles and he didn't want to burden us. What a guy,' Beria said without feeling. 'But he didn't leave an alternative, so when he was cremated, we were given the box, you know, and left to our own devices. Because I was the oldest, it came home with me.

'My siblings weren't the most decisive people at the best of times. Nobody came up with a solution. My brother Aghasi went back to where he was living and my sister Nyah took charge of the family humpy in Abkhazia. We didn't get together often. The next couple of Christmases I went to my brother in Petersburg, which had no relevance for the old man, so I didn't take the ashes.'

AAA mouthed to Murtov: 'Leningrad?' The kid was shocked. Even a Party chief wasn't meant to dead-name a Soviet city.

'We discussed it vaguely,' the boss continued. 'Like, "Why don't we scatter his ashes down on the black sands in Ureki, he loved it so much," or, "How about his favourite fishing spot up the Khobi River, that would be a fitting end." But these were theoretical conversations because we were having them in Petersburg while the old man was spending Christmas in his box in Georgia. So one thing led to another—or didn't—and nothing was done.

'The years went by. The Revolution came. I moved to a joint in Baku, then back to Tbilisi, then that gig ended and I moved away again. In the ten years after the old man died, I moved four times.'

Beria recalled his early adulthood like he was any worker shifting from job to job and house to house, instead of taking a series of ruthlessly calculated steps up the leadership ladder. Each new 'joint' was a more heavily secured residence in the government quarter of a new city. Murtov had seen him use this slang at workers' meetings; it had won him his reputation as a man of the people.

'But on the tenth anniversary,' the boss continued, 'my brother said, "Come on, let's get our shit together and honour the old fella. Let's scatter his ashes in the Sokhumi Botanical Gardens where he walked every day. Or he walked there once, didn't he?" So we settled on the duck pond. I liked the idea that the ducks might eat our father's ashes and recirculate them into the ecosystem. Do ducks eat ashes floating on the water? Dunno. But they shit out something.'

He was hard to stop in this mood, Murtov thought. Caffeine pills, amphetamine shots, cocaine, whatever he had stashed away in the beach house.

'So we set the date and my sister and brother are coming to Sokhumi. We're going to have a little ceremony, each of us says a few words, we chuck the ashes on the duck pond, then go get pissed. Good day, right? Only, the night before they arrive, I decide I'd better get the ashes out but I am fucked if I can find them. I've only moved into this joint about a year ago, so I go through the boxes that are still unpacked—this happens when you move a lot—and no ashes.

'And so I sit down and face up to the truth. *I wouldn't have a fucking clue where my father's ashes are. I've lost them.* So what to do? What do you reckon, friend?'

AAA chewed. 'Before my time, friend.'

'Good answer, you'll go far. So I visit this dumb-fuck Georgian Orthodox priest and he says, "Friend, children losing their parents' ashes happens more than you'd think. Our advice is to burn something else and put it in a consecrated urn. Which we can offer you at a small charge."

'I'm hemming and hawing, not because I don't think it's a good idea—it's a fucking genius idea, four hours before my siblings are getting in—but I don't want to be seen to be jumping at it too eagerly. I mean, it is fraud. Even more than the rest of religion. Fraud upon fraud. But the priest says, like he's reading my mind, "It's not really deception; what your siblings don't know can't hurt them, and it's not as bad as having to tell them you've lost the ashes. To God, it's all the same. And it's not like your father's going to care." This is the voice of experience, right. Fucked if I know why we didn't do away with all these priests, seems like a loophole in the system if you ask me, but Moscow reckons religion keeps the provinces quiet.

'Anyway, so I go for a walk and I'm feeling one inch tall and forgiven at the same time. Maybe that's the point of religion. Your problems solved for a fee. I return to the church and ask the priest what I should burn as a substitute, but after he's taken my money—the urn costs slightly more than a "small charge"—he acts all offended that I'm asking for more help and now he's off the clock. Like I might be asking him for some substitute person's ashes, you know, for an additional "small charge". I thought the Georgian Orthodox God might cop that, but no go.

'I try to burn a couple of branches in the backyard, but they're too fresh and wet, and besides there's a fire ban and some good socialist might report me. I'm running out of time. My siblings are due in an hour, and then we're off to the duck pond. I don't have a fireplace, but my neighbour does, so I knock on the door and thank fuck his wife's home. I don't know how to ask if I can scrape up a bagful of ashes from her hearth, but I've got no time to stuff around. She looks at me like I'm barking mad for thinking she's the type of woman who would leave cold ashes in her fireplace. She's not asking me what I need them for. But she does say if I want to look in her rubbish bin, last week's ashes are there. Only they're with the normal rubbish, the apple cores and food slops and coffee grounds and whatnot.

'Now she's looking at me with pure disgust as I shove my face in her bin. Sure enough, I find some ashes to scoop into the urn. I am not the neighbour she thought I was. Her husband was the Attorney-General; poor bugger got cancelled the next week.'

'Unlucky,' Murtov said.

'So in the end I've got enough of the ashes to make a convincing case that this here is the old man. I meet my brother and sister at the duck pond and we do everything as planned, blah-blah about Papa and his fishing and his, ah, love of ducks, and that's what it's all about, isn't it? The symbolism and the love or whatever, right?'

'The love,' Murtov said.

AAA kept chewing his gum.

'So we're about to do the scattering,' the boss continued. 'I open the urn and we each take a handful. And I'm thinking, Please God don't let there be a mutton chop bone or a peach stone. My heart's in my mouth. We pause over the pond, and now the worst thing happens.'

'Solid matter?' said AAA, enmired in the boss's tale. 'An unfavourable wind?'

'A fucking people's militia park ranger!' The boss rubbed his hands. 'He bowls up in his donkey cart, asks what we're doing, and it's pretty obvious. We're dressed in formal clothes, we've got an Orthodox urn, and we're throwing the ashes in that solemn ashes-throwing way.

'The ranger says he's going to fine us for littering. My brother and sister are looking at me, like, *You deal with this, you're the Party boy*, but that's not my style, friend, we're all equal, I don't pull rank. My brother and sister are pissed off at my democratic spirit, but so be it. I admit we're scattering our papa's ashes at his favourite place, and the militia guy is quite sympathetic, he says, "Yeah, people do it all the time, but they don't know it's against Georgian law. The law might be stupid," he says, "but it's the law." Maybe he recognises me, I dunno.

'And the fine's nearly two thousand roubles. *Two fucking grand!* My brother blows up, says we could have got a niche for two grand. As the ranger's writing the ticket, I say, "Just hypothetically, if these were not human remains but, I don't know, just dirt or ashes from some random fireplace, is it also littering?"

'He scratches his beard and says, "Well, I've never seen that, because why would people be throwing random ashes into the pond?" And suddenly he's seen straight through me. I say, "No reason, but what if they were?" And he says, "No, I don't reckon that would be a fineable offence."

'And everyone's looking at me to fess up. My brother, my sister, the park ranger who's sussed that I'm someone who enjoys the confidence of the Party. They're all onto me. Is two grand worth it? Or do I stick with my story? What they don't know can't hurt them and that. Except now I'm pretty sure they know.

'And I go, "Friend, that's a shit law. Two grand."

'And he finishes writing the ticket. And we're all laughing in the end because my sister says to the ranger, "*You* don't make the laws, but *this prick will one day!*"

'And we go and get pissed and talk about the old man, and Aghasi and Nyah don't say a word about the fine, we agree we'll pay a third each, and that's it. But I'm thinking the whole time, they know what I did, and it still can't hurt them.'

'Where are they now?' AAA said. 'Your brother and sister?'

Beria did not reply. Instead he produced a small jar from his pocket. It was filled with shrunken red peppers in olive oil. He dipped his index and middle fingers, drew out a pepper and popped it into his mouth. Pleasure watered his eyes. He offered the jar to the front seat and cried, 'From Mexico, condiments of friend Trotsky!'

Murtov drove the Emka into Batumi, the regional capital on the southern Georgian coast. The clouds lifted to unwrap a perfect summer's afternoon, the sun illuminating the grapevines on the steep slopes. The Emka handled the descending mountain road like a sleek lizard. The approaches were lined with reminders that happiness was compulsory: billboards with *Life has become better, friends, life is more joyous*, among other quotations from The Steel One, The Inspirer and Organiser of the Victory of Socialism. At the centre of an intersection was a statue of Pavlik Morozov, the most famous boy in the USSR, whose story had been taught in schools since his death at age thirteen. In 1932, during the forced collectivisation of agriculture, Pavlik had informed on his father, a rich peasant, for forging documents to cheat the state. His father was executed, but his kulak relatives took revenge, murdering poor heroic Pavlik. The relatives were then shot and the martyr Pavlik's story was told in verse, plays, song and opera. Rather than have him immortalised in one giant statue in Red Square, Moscow had commissioned the sculptor Viktoria Solomonovich to create thousands of life-sized statues of Pavlik for distribution around the country. The fable fused Soviet heroism with The Steel One's love of the gospel tales he learnt when he was a seminarian here in Georgia. As Matthew's book said, *He who loves his father and mother more than he loves Me is unworthy of Me*. Me, in this case, being the Party.

Murtov saw AAA's eyes glisten as the car paused in front of the statue in Batumi.

'Fun fact,' Beria said to AAA. 'Viktoria Solomonovich was killed when one of her statues collapsed onto her. Fun fact number two. This roundabout has just been cleared of a carpet of dead pigeons. They used to spend all night shitting on Pavlik's head. We couldn't have that, could we? So I had the statue electrified. Instead of cleaning shit off Pavlik's head every morning, the streetsweeper now just has to sweep up the dead pigeons. Don't say I haven't given the Georgian worker a better life, eh!'

Fun fact number three. The entire story of Pavlik Morozov was an official fiction written by Moscow. So Beria had told Murtov. But what AAA doesn't know, Murtov thought, can't hurt him.

'Sure you don't want one?' Beria was again presenting his jar of chillis. 'Oh come on, I wouldn't say they're from Trotsky if it was true, would I? That would get us all sentenced without right of correspondence!'

This time AAA accepted, laying the flowers across his lap and inserting his fingers into the jar as reverently as if into a font of holy water. He put the chilli in his mouth without removing his chewing gum. That's how nervous the kid must be, Murtov thought, as AAA's eyes bulged and his cheeks puffed. He gave one resolute bite but tears rolled down his face and sweat beaded on his neck. His nose glowed. He gave another dutiful socialist chew as laughter broke out from the back seat.

'It's all right, don't torture yourself!' Beria crowed, rubbing his hands with so much glee they might have caught fire. Murtov had seen him pull this prank on maybe one hundred victims. The boss gobbled these infernal things like they were sunflower seeds, he was hooked on them, but the real pleasure they gave him was when he could use them for a practical joke.

AAA spat the half-chewed pepper into his hand and stared at it.

'Fucking Christ.' He looked around the dashboard.

'No ashtray,' Murtov said. 'Germans mustn't smoke.'

'Nah, they do smoke, they just bury their ash in the ground,' said the boss, who did not tolerate smoking in his vicinity unless it was the boss of bosses himself with his disgusting pipe. AAA breached Georgia's anti-littering laws by throwing the remains of the pepper, embedded in his chewie, out his window. His eyes begged Murtov for a fresh stick of gum. Murtov handed him the packet.

Murtov turned the car into the grounds of the crematorium where, in the chapel, his oldest friend, still chuckling over his chilli stunt, was due to deliver the eulogy and present a sheaf of flowers to the widow of the acquaintance who had cancelled out of this life, just as, not long after disposing of their father's ashes, the boss's brother Aghasi and sister Nyah had. The boss delivered eulogies at their funerals too. Eulogies were a specialty of his. At Aghasi's funeral, Beria had told the story about their father's ashes, and how now, in the paradise created by our great friend the General Secretary, you no longer had to pay 'small charges' to churches. This was another improvement in the world, Beria said from the pulpit. Neither his brother nor his sister made forty.

'There, on the grass.' Beria pointed in front of the chapel. To AAA he said, 'Parking spaces are for peasants, eh?'

People in black shuffled by, making approving comments about how Beria got around in a Russian shitbox. The Emka had a front grille like a dog's face and its engine barked. Soviets, Beria liked to say: so quick to put down our achievements.

'So,' Murtov said, 'wait here or come back in an hour?'

'Wait here.' The boss took the lilies from AAA. 'I'm getting out as soon as I've handed over these weeds and said my piece. I've got to get to the office.'

'Nothing urgent?' Murtov said.

The boss hooked his finger inside his tunic collar, letting air in. 'There's word that he's coming.'

'*He?*' AAA squeaked.

Beria didn't hear AAA.

'Ah. *Him*,' Murtov said. 'When?'

'Nothing's confirmed, but I'm guessing it's the anniversary of him taking over the Party. That's only thirty-eight days away. And if it's something that big, he'll bring the whole shitshow: family, Politburo, half of fucking Moscow. He'll want to stay at the beach. For old times' sake, you know?'

'Are you certain?'

'Moscow has asked me to book out the entire waterfront, so it can't be anything else. If he wants it that way, I'm going to do better. Let's knock it all down and put up something brand-fucking-spanking-new. Let's knock his socks off. First time in a decade he's coming home; if that's not worth some serious demolitions I don't know what is. Make a statement about what we Georgians will do for our brothers and sisters.'

'You seem fairly sure.'

'If I've guessed wrong, what does it matter? But no, I'm not wrong.' Beria touched the security police insignia on the upper arm of Murtov's tunic. It depicted a sword striking a serpent. Looked at a different way, the serpent was strangling the sword. 'You know,' Beria said softly, as if to himself, 'I've never been sure which is us.'

A gelatinous silence filled the car.

'Thirty-eight days.' Murtov was the one to speak. 'It's a quick build.'

'Oh well,' Beria said, giving a slight hiccup as if regaining consciousness, 'I'm not worried about that so much as the excavations.'

'Excavations,' Murtov repeated.

'I'm the one who knows where the bodies are buried.'

'Actual bodies?' AAA whispered.

'Might need an ambitious young Post to get shit done,' Beria said. 'All those bodies.'

The mauve eyes dilated. AAA's nose pulsed like a maritime lantern.

'Oh, for fuck's sake,' Beria said. 'Trouble with you Posts, you can't see a joke coming until it's run you over.'

'Ah,' AAA said. 'Ha-ha-ha!'

It really is painful, Murtov thought, hearing one of the children of October try to laugh. They say we old folks are crushed by our fear, but they're the ones with more years of life to lose.

Beria leant forward and gave AAA a hard clap on his shoulder. Murtov saw the blush spread up from AAA's neck, darkening his olive skin like a bruise or a shaving rash, stopping at the base of his ear. The boss had let him in. The family stories, the trick with the pepper, and now the inside knowledge of what was coming. Flattered into submission, AAA had cast off his Post-Revolutionary arrogance. He was primed on Beria.

'I'm *so* not looking forward to this,' Beria said, shooting AAA a wink before hopping out of the car.

III

MURTOV COLLECTED BERIA WHILE THE FUNERAL WAS STILL under way, eulogy done and dusted, and dropped him at the central admin building in Batumi. AAA got out to escort the boss to level three, but before the elevator had arrived Beria came back to the Emka and handed Murtov his 'packet', the envelope containing a wad of roubles that Murtov received irregularly on top of his salary. The packet was triple its usual thickness, but this was neither surprising nor encouraging. Beria, having lived in the cashless world of the super-elite for more than a decade, had little grasp of the value of money, and the packet could as easily contain a few roubles as a few hundred. While Beria always handed it to Murtov with intense beneficence in his eyes, the packet was one of Beria's few gestures that meant precisely nothing.

Murtov drove the Emka into the overnight garage. After getting out he circled the car, pulling the four handles to check they were locked. Once he had inspected the undercarriage with a mirror, he left the keys with the attendant.

As an Assistant Secretary to the Central Committee of the Communist Party of the Transcaucasus, Murtov did not enjoy the private use of an official vehicle. He caught a trolley car to the railway station nearest his summer apartment. Inside the trolley car, passengers wore clean clothes and carried their hats on their laps, obeying a 1937 law that imposed fines for poor public deportment. He stopped at a closed dispensary where fifteen or twenty silent Party members were lined up. Shortages meant that if anything was for sale, the people's reflex was to queue. Queues were the best appeal a shop could make for more customers. People attracted people. If they didn't need the item that everyone was queuing for, they might need it in the future. Or they could on-sell it to the black market, which in Batumi was larger than the legal one. Being a high government employee, Murtov bypassed the line and went to the counter beneath the sign MEMBERS OF PEOPLE'S WILL SERVED OUT OF TURN, and proceeded to 'get hold of'—the word 'buy' was not in use—a non-prescription antihistamine draught. As he passed the line to leave the store, he felt younger Party eyes bore into his back.

He boarded a public bus to complete his journey. His commute time was one hour and forty-five minutes to cover approximately five versts, which he could have walked in one hour if he didn't mind being followed. Throughout, he carried the heavy carton AAA had fetched from the boss's Ureki beach house.

He arrived at nine o'clock at the two-bedroom apartment in a block the Georgian Party allocated assistant secretaries during the two summer months when Party headquarters moved from Tbilisi to the Black Sea coast. The building was a 1930s 'Stalinka', built for middle officials, with bas reliefs and columns on the outside and an unused internal courtyard. The foyer's ceilings were an exuberant four metres high. The corridor on Murtov's floor was filled with cooking smells from other residents, few of whom he had met. He used the communal bathroom at the end of the hall before walking to his door. The lights in the other apartments were off. Since 1937, most Party members had begun going to bed early; or, if they stayed awake, they lay in the dark listening for cars pulling up, wondering who was being visited tonight. He noticed a blob of red sealing wax on the door next to his, a sign that the apartment had been vacated. The occupant had worked in Beria's secretariat, though Murtov had not known him well. In recent evenings Murtov and Babilina had heard the man's wife berating him, a common feature of Party marriages since wives decided that a good scolding might diminish their husbands' self-confidence to speak loosely in their offices. Babilina would never do that, and, judging by the blob of sealing wax, it didn't work anyway.

The Murtovs' lights were on. The apartment was spacious, with large metal-framed windows overlooking a park and thick Georgian rugs covering the floorboards. By the front door were two leather overnight bags, each packed with a change of adult clothing. On the single bookshelf were the sacred texts: the complete works of Marx and Engels, Lenin and Stalin. Murtov noted that several of Babilina's English and French novels, her holiday reading, had been removed.

Ana and Melor were lying on a rug playing cards after a day at the NKVD summer school. Other girls at the school had names that had come into fashion in the 1920s: Iskra (after *Spark*, the Bolshevik newsletter), Kim (an acronym for Communist Youth

International) and Ninel (Lenin spelt backwards). Babilina had asserted that there was still a place for traditional Georgian names, which was good for Ana. By the time their second arrived, The Steel One's rule had been confirmed and Murtov insisted on naming her acronymously after Marx, Engels, Lenin and the October Revolution. Babilina had reluctantly agreed.

It was a name that Melor had lived up to. At school, defining herself in contrast to her sullen non-joiner of a sister, Melor was an enthusiastic member of junior councils, quickly earning the rank of 'October Child'. She now referred to 'Uncle Lenin' often enough for Babilina to remind her, tenderly and cautiously, that Lenin was not her real uncle. Melor had struggled to process that. Now she had begun speaking of 'Papa Stalin', and often asked both of her parents to tell her that her first word, like her friend Iskra's, had been 'Stalin'. Babilina said flatly 'It was not', while Murtov said, 'Your mouth was always full of cabbage, so anything is possible.'

Among all the Party elite schools, the NKVDs were the best resourced, and tonight the girls were wearing the school's uniform of electric blue knickerbockers and red vests. In the first years after the Revolution, uniforms and insignia had been forbidden as symbols of Tsarist inequality, but recently Moscow had restored the NKVD's blue cap, blue trousers and sword-and-serpent badge as well as medals for the military and badges for Party members. Soviet society was growing into its prosperity! Ana and Melor also wore red kerchiefs to signify their much-sought-after membership of the Young Pioneers, the Party children's club, though Ana wore hers as a bandana with a non-standard knot at her forehead. Melor wore hers correctly, tied at her throat.

'Hi, Papa!' they cried but did not get off the floor.

'And what did you do today?' Murtov asked.

'We learnt the alphabet and, guess what, I was allowed to write my letter to Papa Stalin!' Melor exclaimed. The letter was the first formal writing task children performed once they had mastered their basic alphabet. Their teachers gave them the paper and checked their lettering. The children asked Papa Stalin for presents and competed over who would give up the most years of their life for a day in his company.

'What did you say to him?' Murtov asked.

He noticed Ana rolling her eyes as her younger sister replied, 'I told him how handsome he looks in the photograph in our classroom and I thanked him for inventing the motor car and controlling the Northern Lights so I can sleep in the winter.'

'And what present did you ask him for?'

'To let me join the Komsomol Youth at fourteen and not a day later!'

'Good job,' Murtov said before going into the kitchen. He didn't have the heart to tell Melor that, as a descendant of non-toilers and bourgeois specialists, she might not find the Komsomol as welcoming as she was assuming, even after petitioning Papa Stalin personally.

The apartment had the privilege of its own kitchen rather than mere access to the communal one next to the bathroom. Though its furnishings were plain, it was clearly a dwelling for special officials. There were two telephones and the kitchen had running water. Babilina had refused Melor's pleas to invite her friends over; it was risky to let outsiders see your advantages. Melor had protested. Ana had understood, and said she had no friends to invite over anyway.

Murtov put his packet in a private place and laid Beria's box on the kitchen table. The stove was warm. He lifted the lid and saw a fire smouldering. He came out past the girls and went to the main bedroom, where he found Babilina propped against the headboard reading a foreign novel.

'Better not get caught with that,' he warned as he sat on the edge of the bed and removed his shoes and socks.

Babilina pulled a face. 'What can they do, sack me?'

It was a joke fresh in the telling but old in the undergrowth. Babilina had been a literature professor at Tbilisi's university when the compulsory retirement age was lowered from fifty-five to forty, a measure designed to clear out scholars who had come of age in Pre times. She, like Murtov, was thirty-nine years old, but she had retired without waiting for her pension. Cautioning her against such an attention-grabbing act, Murtov had signed her up for the Institute of Red Professors, but that proved another of his mistakes. Babilina carried 'the plague germ', as she put it: her family—school teachers, amateur playwrights and poets—had been exiled in the 1920s and scattered to the winds in faraway places like Ceylon and South Africa and Australia, where they still existed in theory, perhaps in reality. Babilina, who had inherited her family's oppositional temperament, objected to joining such a 'compromised bunch of suckholes' as the Institute of Red Professors. In any case, the institute was suddenly and inexplicably banned in 1938. Murtov had apologised to Babilina for acting stupidly, patriarchally, cravenly and, worst of all, uselessly.

Only by retiring—not being retrenched—did Babilina believe her quiet protest could register. To affirm her point, she had then committed the ultimate heresy. She had reverted to that relic of Pre-Revolutionary bourgeois decadence: she had become a homemaker. As she liked to remind Murtov, at least someone in the family was obeying historical necessity.

She lifted a pillow and laid it over the telephone on her bedside table. Murtov had been unable to convince her that the telephones did not contain listening devices.

'I don't want Melor to catch me reading this,' she said, splaying her book open on her stomach. 'We might have a little Pavlinka Morozova on our hands.'

'She told me about her letter to Papa Stalin.'

'That's not the half of it,' Babilina said. 'After she saw the sealing wax next door, I caught her throwing some of my foreign books into the stove. She left Marx, Engels, Lenin and Stalin, but everything else she was getting rid of. I even had to save my diaries.'

Murtov knew about Babilina's suicide note of a diary, which he could never convince her to stop writing. Her one concession to prudence was to record her daily life in handwriting so microscopic and words so erudite that an NKVD agent would need a strong magnifying glass and an improbable level of literacy to decipher it.

'I asked Melor what she was doing to my books and she said, "I'm saving us, Mama."'

'Might not have been a bad idea,' Murtov said.

Babilina poked out her tongue. *My children love The Steel One most of all, and me second*,' she said, quoting the wife of the poet Pasternak. 'My younger child anyway. She brought home a textbook and showed me very proudly how she had drawn a devil's horns and beard on the photograph of Tukhachevsky,' Babilina said, naming the formerly great Red Army general, the hero of the Civil War who had recently been redesignated an enemy of the people. 'She was ready to do the same to all the other former persons in the textbook. Instead I gave her white pieces of paper to stick over their faces. She asked me why she couldn't just draw on them. I said, "Today they might be former persons, but tomorrow they might be heroes again. These pieces of paper are removable."'

'You'll confuse her,' Murtov said. 'She's only working on her Bolshevik self.'

'Her Bolshevik self,' Babilina repeated. She dog-eared her book and put it aside. 'How's the new guy? Adam something?'

'Keen. Up himself. Typical Post.'

'Well, there's always hope for advancement when the man above you can disappear tomorrow.'

She held open her hand. Murtov's index finger traced a shape in her palm. 'I'm irreplaceable.'

'You and Stalin, the Soviet Union's last two irreplaceable men,' she said, deadpan. 'Oops! I forgot the no-joke device!' Babilina turned an imaginary switch at the side of her throat. Her lips formed a white line. 'You got an early mark?'

'The boss had something urgent so he left as soon as he'd read his eulogy.'

'Who was it for again?' Babilina asked, fortunately missing the more important part of his answer.

Murtov told her about the colleague who had self-effaced and then asked, 'How was your day? Oh. Here.'

He placed the antihistamine draught on Babilina's metal bedside table, painted brown like the wall panels to imitate wood. The ceiling had mould in the cornices but was spiderweb-free. She pushed herself up to kiss his forehead. The exertion strained her, however, and she slumped back against the headboard.

'You got hold of it yourself, or you had to *go to* him?' She used the phrase for petitioning the boss.

'Party privileges. Have you been able to do anything? The girls eaten?'

More than she had to fight her latest allergy, Babilina battled to suspend disbelief in this life they led; she suffered spells of feeling like she and Murtov existed as characters in some theatre. Their real lives were what they had grown up with: children of prosperous Georgian bourgeois merchants, fed each night by paid staff. If their parents needed to shield them from some dangerous truth, they armoured them with food, gifts and attention. That long-ago boy Murtov and girl Babilina had passed through their period of youthful rebellion and now dwelt inside a pair of amateur actors on the Soviet stage. Babilina had come to terms with it, she supposed. It was the price of survival; she paid it for her girls' sake. But what were the strains upon Murtov, who played this role not so much on a stage as on a high wire, partnered with the biggest actor of all, who might at any moment push him to his certain death? It seemed to Babilina that the longer Murtov walked that high wire, the further the beautiful boy she had fallen in love with receded into the past. He too was playing his role to protect her and their daughters, but the unpaid account was mounting. For years he'd only had to protect them from Beria; since '37, he and Beria had both been hunted by the Post-Revolutionary youth, egged on by The Steel One. The greater the danger, the less Murtov wanted Babilina to see it. How, she wondered, could *she* protect *him*? How to retrieve his soul from its internal migration, which went deeper and further with each threat it managed to survive?

'Actually, I've been on the telephone to the girls' summer school.' Babilina held up her book, which had an English title that Murtov could not translate. Babilina only read books in their original language.

Murtov struggled to make the connection between the book and telephone calls to the summer school until he recalled that they had gifted a copy of this same book to their children's teacher.

'Are we in trouble for giving her a bourgeois book?'

'Not yet,' Babilina said, noting his use of 'we' instead of 'you'. 'Though we may be later. I don't know. It's English but the author is a socialist. A coalminer, apparently. I'm only reading it now. And . . .' She puffed her cheeks and fanned herself.

Murtov, raised on Cyrillic, could not even pronounce the strange English name on the cover. 'I don't see why you should be worried. If she doesn't feel it's appropriate, she'll do what everyone does. Burn it.' With a flick of his head towards the room the girls were in, he added, 'Taught early in life.'

'No, she wrote to me the other day saying she was very appreciative of the gift and was about to start reading it. That it was from an imperialist country isn't an issue.'

'So . . . ?'

'Normally I tell you that you should read more, but . . .'

'I never read anything except Marx,' Murtov said in his Party voice, eyes to the ceiling.

'It's mortifying! It's full of . . . indecency! It's . . . I didn't know there were words for . . . Do you know what *titwanking* is?'

'I have heard talk.'

'Well, you might have in your NKVD locker rooms, but I don't want to be responsible for introducing it to our daughters' teacher who is . . . I think she's in her seventies. I had no idea, Vasil! It's been banned in Britain, but I thought that was for its socialist ideas.'

'You ought to read and clear everything first.'

'Be my own censor? I suppose you're right this time. *Frottage*. Have you heard of that?'

'Sounds French. Therefore decadent.'

'You might know what *reaming* is, given the company you keep. Oh, but of course, our good friend Lavrentiy Pavlovich has become so abstemious, so true to Stalinist prudery, he would have me before the firing squad if he knew I gave such filth to a teacher!'

Murtov, she saw, was making a calculation. Even in the bedroom, with a marital pillow over the telephone, he had to mind what he said. Caution was baked into him. Babilina's quip about the firing squad was a metaphor, an exaggeration, or so he maintained in his occasional arguments with her when she kept insisting that no, she meant 'firing squad' literally. He brushed her off. She refused to be brushed. Hence: arguments.

'I might spend some time with the girls,' he said. 'Did you say they'd eaten?'

'I spent the whole day on the telephone trying to talk someone at the school into getting it away from her without letting them or her know why.'

'You know, people say they will read a book in their thankyou note without intending to do so. She's probably regifted it.'

'To her sister,' Babilina said. 'Who's probably a nun.'

This time she was speaking figuratively. There were no nuns in The Steel One's Russia, not even in Beria's Georgia. Keeping the priests was concession enough.

'I got hold of the departmental assistant, a Post girl who seemed up for a bit of thievery. But she wanted to know exactly what made stealing the book necessary. I said, well, it contains some words that are not at all nice. She said, such as? And I couldn't bring myself to say *creampie*. Do you know what a creampie is?'

Murtov pushed himself to his feet. 'Do you want a glass of water to wash down that antihistamine taste?'

'One word of this slips out . . .'

'Do you want me to do something?'

Babilina's laugh descended into a wheeze. She patted her chest. Her long black hair was tied in a loose ponytail that fell over her shoulder onto her nightdress. With such tightly controlled rules on hair in his workplace, Murtov wanted to bury his face in the perfume of Babilina's rich bourgeois locks.

'Below your pay grade, my love. If my plot with the assistant backfires, yes, thank you, I might call on you, but I'd be in a camp by then. If I'm not here tomorrow, you'll know what's happened.'

The packed bags by the front door: real, not a metaphor or an in-joke.

'I'm sure you're making too much of it,' he said, kissing the crown of her head. 'If the boss wanted to do anything to us, he's had ten years as head of the Cheka and seven as governor. You have to see the good in him.'

'My love, you don't even know if you believe that yourself.'

As Murtov left the bedroom, Babilina called out, 'Perhaps he has only left us alone because he is playing a longer game!'

Murtov prayed that the neighbours had gone to sleep. But they never did. When the late-night cars came for them, they would try to buy their freedom with the words they had heard through the Murtovs' door.

Ana and Melor had stopped playing cards and lay on the rug like upturned insects, their limbs waggling as if uselessly trying to right their balance. The family dog, Nicholas II, a five-breed mongrel they had been allocated from a Party shelter, lay between the girls like a bolster pillow. Murtov bent to give Nicholas II a pat. Titwank, he thought, picturing that lovely old schoolteacher. Creampie. In his experience, you could never predict people's responses to transgressive imperialist material. She might give a yawn. Been there, done that.

'What're you Pioneers playing?'

Neither answered.

'Maybe you could do something together?'

Melor still did not answer, but after a sigh, Ana said, 'We are, Papa. We're playing dead.'

He continued to the kitchen. Had they been taught about the lowered age for the death penalty? Was that in their heads? He shoved the thought away. In the 'refrigerator'—the cool space between the inner and outer kitchen windows—he found cabbage he could chop and some Polish sausage that needed frying. When he had the ingredients heating, Murtov went back to the children. Melor was saying mean things to Ana, who was ignoring her. Melor was competitive and fundamentally a bad sport, with a habit of sabotaging any game she was losing. Ana was gentler and reserved, wishing to avoid confrontation, but every time she so much as scratched her nose Melor took it as a provocation. Murtov recalled what Lavrentiy Pavlovich had said about his children. *Moron. Cunt.* God help us, he thought, when these two are old enough to join the Komsomol.

Murtov breathed. This woman, these two children. Why else live? It wasn't as the boss put it. It wasn't a transaction; this amount of sacrifice for that amount of legacy. Beria spoke as if he had been swindled on a deal. Yet, as much as he disdained his wife and children, he frowned on divorce. When his male underlings talked about leaving their wife for another woman, Beria would advise the mistress to move to Moscow, where she could find a much better calibre of cheat. The mistresses always followed his guidance.

Murtov asked the girls if they cared to join him for sausage and vegetables. He was halfway through shovelling his down his throat by the time they slumped into their chairs at the little deal table.

'Dad,' Melor said, 'who was the first man? Our teacher asked us to go home and do research. Was it God?'

'Better not say that at Party school,' Murtov said. 'Where did you hear about God?'

'I asked Mum who was the first man and she said don't forget God.'

Christ, Murtov thought. Titwanking, frottage, reaming and God. The things Babilina was letting in. She might do more damage as a homemaker than she'd threatened as a university professor.

Murtov set about a three-minute version of the theory of evolution, from microbacteria to dinosaurs to mammals to homo sapiens to Communism. He was fairly certain that he was getting a lot wrong, but Melor kept pressing.

'Why so many questions?' he asked.

Melor looked at him with an adoring face that made Murtov aware of the existence of his heart.

'I want to make you forget to send us to bed.'

'Come here.'

Melor let him hug her so hard she groaned. He felt the shadow of Papa Stalin hovering, ready to muscle in. He opened his arms to include Ana, and, after untying her Pioneer scarf, she came to him.

'Papa, can we go to the Children's Theatre?' Melor asked.

'Of course. What is it you want to see?'

The Squealer!

He knew the play, a variation on the Pavlik Morozov story. *The Squealer* was about a group of children who, rescued from homelessness, worked as shoemaker's apprentices. Some stole shoes and materials and sold them on the black market. The hero had to decide whether to squeal and have his friends sent to prison, and spent much of the play hesitating over this dilemma. In the end, as he wanted to be a true hero, he squealed.

'Please, Papa? There are no tickets!'

'Let me see if I can go to someone.'

'Yay! Ana, he's going to get tickets!'

Murtov played a few rounds of cards before sending the girls off to clean their teeth. He was sitting at the rustic table, trying to do absolutely nothing, listening contentedly to them fighting in the bathroom, when he heard a movement.

'What's up?' he said. 'Can I get you anything?'

Babilina was wearing her dressing-gown. Half of her hair was pressed to the side of her head, giving her a comical asymmetry. Her face was wrinkled from her pillow, which she carried under her arm. She placed it on the telephone on the kitchen sideboard.

'You know it's illegal now to store food in the refrigerator,' he said. 'One-hundred-rouble fine.'

Babilina was frowning at the box from the beach house.

'Is this what you had to go back to the office for?'

Murtov shook his head. 'It's a gift for you, actually. From him. For taking me away more than usual during the summer.'

Babilina studied the box. 'He's been taking you away from me forever. Doesn't necessitate a gift.'

'You don't want to open it?'

'Where's it from?' she said dully.

'Does it have to be from anywhere? I believe it's made in Turkey.'

'Don't you play the smart-arse with me, friend.'

When he was 'friend', he was in trouble.

'It's from the beach house. Does everything from him have to be treated like it's booby-trapped?'

'It belonged to the deceased, didn't it? He ended himself and then they stole everything of value that he owned. And now that hyena in syrup pretends to reward you for your service, when this is really just making you complicit in the whole dirty business.'

Hyena in syrup: so spot-on it must have come from one of her banned poets. Murtov shook his head. 'Hell of a lot of dots you've joined.'

Babilina smiled sourly. 'I'm assuming that instead of doing something really unusual and out of character, such as buying a thoughtful gift, he's done something that is perfectly consistent. A spontaneous gift for working you like a forced labourer? That's what I call joining the wrong dots. My love, not even your children are as naive as you.'

Murtov followed Babilina's eyes through the window to the darkened park across the street. He saw two men in long coats and forage caps doing nothing much. It was no particular reason for alarm: once the families and twilight strollers had gone home, a 1938 Soviet night was ninety-nine percent men in long coats.

Babilina sneezed.

'*Gesundheit*,' Murtov replied with a quarter-smile: the only German word he knew.

'Fascist scum,' she said lightly, wiping her nose.

She had contracted their marriage on the assumption that her scepticism was several steps ahead of Murtov's blurry good nature. Her eyes were moist and her bottom lip trembled. Murtov acted as her guardian angel by sealing his lips. She accepted that. But how open were his eyes?

'So you haven't told me,' she said.

'Told you?'

'Why Lavrushya had to rush back to the office.'

'Didn't I tell you?'

'I know you want to protect us,' Babilina said. 'I know that you don't get out of bed each morning and serve your hyena for love of the Party. I know the pressure of what you see each day feels like it can burst your head and bleed from your ears. But listen. Vasil. He has more than one way of doing us in.'

'You give him too much credit.'

'What—are you going to tell me again that Beria is an instrument of historical necessity like everyone else? That he's not good or bad, he's just a cog in the mechanism? Is that what you think he is? I still believe that you're only *pretending* to believe that Marxist bullshit. You've known him too long.'

'Trust me.'

'How can I trust you when you are too scared to *talk* to me?'

'Come here.' He beckoned.

She sat on his lap, her hands limp on the tabletop. He created a part in her hair and kissed her temple, which was salty with her fever sweats. He murmured about the things he had heard in the car and the tale Beria had told about his father's cremains. He told her about waiting outside the funeral.

'Do you remember the Lavrushya we grew up with?' he said.

'The boy who graduated from his Dostoevsky and loved Dumas and Stendhal, Tolstoy, Goethe, *The Thousand and One Nights*?'

'The kind of books our daughter was throwing in the stove.'

'The books *he* still displays on *his* private shelf. And do you remember why we hitched our wagon to him when everything was in flames?'

'Because he was the only person left who had no fear. Of course I remember, Vasil. If this country has stripped me of my memory, I might as well give up. I mean, actually give up.'

'He had to leave the funeral and go back to the office because he might have a big job on,' Murtov said. 'A very big job.'

Babilina waited. Even though as Assistant Secretary he was forbidden from disclosing information to any individual, including and most of all his ideologically suspect unemployed-intelligentsia wife, Murtov told her.

'Big celebration,' he said. 'Anniversary of the Stalin ascension.'

'Old shitbreath's coming back to Georgia?' Only she, Babilina, spoke of old shitbreath and the hyena in syrup. In Murtov's opinion it was she, not Beria, who was the last Soviet to live without fear.

'Beria's going to demolish the Party rest homes in Ureki to put up a holiday compound, and he's going to get it done in four weeks.'

Babilina's eyes widened. 'Is that Pre weeks or Post weeks?'

The Revolution, in its general reinvention of reality, had not been too modest to overthrow time itself. The seven-day week, with a day of rest, had been deemed too inefficient for the purposes of the First Five-Year Plan, so the Bolshevik Party had reinvented the week as ten days with a one-day weekend.

'Forty days, give or take.'

'It doesn't sound any more sane when you put it that way. But why go to all that trouble? It's not even much of a beach, all that black sand.' Babilina used her customary insult, like a worn-out joke, to console Murtov for the past he had traded away in exchange for a future.

'Lavrushya has never spared any expense for his ambition, and this time it's not ambition, it's survival.'

'He'll never get it done in time,' she said. 'He's crapping himself, is that what you're trying to avoid saying? Shitbreath's coming, Beria's panicking. But what does it mean for you? For us?'

They listened. A Black Maria, the NKVD's van, crunched its gears. The girls had fallen quiet. One sleeping, the other eavesdropping.

Murtov shook his head. 'You know Lavrushya. If he can set a construction speed record to prove that one republic can make socialism work, he'll go for it. But it's a gamble.'

'And he's scared. He's feeling what everyone else feels.'

'I didn't say that.'

Babilina put her hands on each side of Murtov's chin and said, 'You do have something up your sleeve, right? You don't need to tell me what it is, I know. But you must have something. You cannot continue to use history as your guide, when history has reached its end.'

Murtov crossed his eyes and poked his tongue out of the corner of his mouth, his customary imitation of an uncomprehending madman. The conversation had reached its boundary.

'Those devils who survive by pretending they are insane,' Babilina said. 'You must have better than that.'

'We'll make it.' Murtov kissed her cheeks. 'Always have.'

Babilina ground her head from side to side, as if she had seen the end of a story of which Murtov couldn't get through the first chapters.

'If he dares to read the eulogy at *your* funeral,' she said, 'I swear to you I will deglove him on the spot.'

He wrapped her in his arms and subdued her next sneezing attack. 'I'm not planning to give him the chance.'

IV

THE MORNING DAWNED MILD AFTER A SEA BREEZE HAD BLOWN through the night. Murtov was wearing a grey state security tunic frayed tissue-thin in the armpits and collar. What remained of his hair was freshly shaven. He deposited the Turkish-made coffee pot on the weed-strewn verge outside the apartments. It would be taken before lunch, maybe by one of the coffee lovers in long coats.

He rode his bus and his trolley and then another bus to the Batumi office. On the trolley he started reading the Party newspaper, *Izvestia*. He noticed other passengers staring at him: it was a marker of status to have one's own copy, rather than reading the sheets of newsprint glued to the walls of buildings. Whichever your version, the main thing was to be seen reading it.

At the interchange shelter he found an unattended shopping bag. Wrapped in paper was a suit that, judging by the material, would have cost more than Murtov earned in two months, even with his extra packet. He went to put it back on the bench but the other queuing passengers said it would get stolen, so he'd better give it to the driver.

'Haven't you read *Izvestia*?' he said. 'Petty crime in Georgia is officially zero.'

The passengers were in no mood for jokes.

On the bus, the driver said, 'I'm in my first week.'

'You have to take it,' Murtov said. 'You're the driver.'

'It was in the shelter, not in my bus.'

'It is in your bus now. You can take it to lost property.'

'No such thing in fucking Beria's Georgia.'

'Can you get a move on, you sons of asses?' one of the passengers called out.

'Fucksake, we're going to be late!' another voice said.

'It might help if we knew what the time was,' said another, earning an appreciative if mirthless laugh from the others.

A new law aimed at reducing absenteeism had made it a deportable offence to be more than twenty minutes late for work. The fear was spread further by the fact that most of the street-corner electric clocks were broken or, worse, mendacious.

When Murtov turned to face the disgruntled ranks, they fell silent. He did not see himself as a heavy, nor was there any outward sign of the closeness of his association with Beria, but there was something about him. The driver took the suit.

✷

Two hours later, Murtov arrived at the garage for his assignment. The valet, an emaciated septuagenarian named Klitschko, told Murtov that he was instead to go to the third floor to meet friend Natia Meskhi.

In the elevator he patted down his rumpled tunic and breathed back his nerves. A summons from friend Meskhi was never good news. Maybe Beria's 2IC knew about the dumped coffee pot or the book Babilina had given to the elderly schoolteacher. Or the lost suit. Natia Meskhi knew everything. She had eyes in the back of her eyes.

She welcomed him cordially, coming to the foyer herself and ushering him not to the spartan workspace where she had a desk amid the rank-and-file staff—no status symbols for Natia Meskhi—but through a series of winding corridors. When she saw Murtov noticing that the nameplates had been removed from the doors of all but the most senior officials, she said lightly, 'Here today, gone tomorrow. We couldn't keep up with the pace of putting on new ones. And we Georgians are meant to be spared this nonsense!'

She took him into an empty office where plaid-covered sofas surrounded a circular table laden with coffee and a rack of teacakes. Hungry after his commute, Murtov ate two cakes before Meskhi had finished pouring his coffee.

'How are you finding friend Adam Adamashvili?' she asked.

Murtov hesitated. Meskhi was twenty-eight years old with two inches of mousy hair and a build and complexion like a suet pudding. She was clad in the usual embroidered Ukrainian shirt and trousers. Meskhi had not risen in the Georgian Party organisation due to looks or sex, or even youth, but she ticked the important boxes: she was phenomenally intelligent, single-minded and ruthless in the pursuit of goals that contributed to strategic aims. Her work ethic sometimes had the boss wondering aloud if she looked like she never went to bed because she never did. First to arrive at headquarters and last to leave, Natia was, in Beria's not entirely condescending description, a force of nature.

Like an earthquake, Murtov thought.

But she was making nice this morning and he was too seasoned not to play.

'I hope friend Beria has found him satisfactory?' she asked.

Natia Meskhi was an avid practitioner of what had come to be known as 'in-depth language', a form of Partyspeak in which words meant their exact opposite. For instance, when the secret police decreed that torture was illegal, the in-depth translation was that torture had become mandatory. When *Izvestia* forecast a 'peaceful university demonstration' against imperialist saboteurs, it meant a university department would be stormed and the intellectuals dragged away by their hair. It was a language of false bottoms. Meskhi was not asking Murtov for information about AAA; she was probing him about the boss.

'He's good, friend Adam is,' Murtov said. 'Ninety percent of the time.'

'Ninety percent of the time!' Natia gave a husky laugh and treated herself to a cake. She drank water from a glass embossed with her name, part of her office policy to minimise washing-up so they could save on water wastage and prevent any backsliding to a dehumanising class-based division of labour.

'Let me tell you something, Vasil,' Natia said. Murtov had never got used to someone several years his junior, born when Rasputin ran the Tsar's empire, addressing him as her equal. But Natia could pull it off.

'You know when you've had a friend all your life and you only see them on feast days, maybe big birthdays?' Natia said. 'Funerals and marriages? They're part of the furniture, always there, but you've never asked them a question and so they're a complete mystery? You're not even sure you know their surname?'

'You know my surname,' Murtov said. She knew just about everything about him and, for all he knew, everything about each and every Georgian. She was the one apparatchik, he feared, who might even be ahead of Beria. She impressed him as a prodigy so gifted, so far ahead of the game, that you didn't know whether it was safer to join her slipstream or to get out of her way.

'I'm not talking about you, Vasil; I mean my Uncle Bernard. He's thirty years older than me, very Pre. He's even older than you! He's one of my mother's cousins. I wouldn't be able to tell you the first thing about him.'

She can read your thoughts, Murtov said to himself, *you dumb fuck*.

'I didn't know what he'd been doing under the Tsar,' Natia was saying. 'So we got talking after my mother's funeral.'

'I was sorry to hear about your mother,' Murtov said. Natia's mother had recently cancelled out, leading Beria to declare a day of mourning in the office which was curtailed when Natia came to work expecting a normal shift. She wanted all Party frowns turned upside down.

'When everyone was transitioning from the funeral to the wake, Uncle Bernard and I somehow found ourselves in the same car,' Natia said, skating over Murtov's condolence. 'And I look at him—you know, the connections get kind of loosened up at your mother's funeral—and I see things afresh. I say to him, "Uncle Bernard, what did you do back when you worked? Nobody's ever told me." Uncle Bernard said, "It wasn't for polite conversation."

'So it wasn't just me not showing curiosity about a blood relative. It was an understanding. But he let it slip now, because—well, it was a long time ago and this was his cousin's funeral. What could it matter anymore? Uncle Bernard tells me that back in Pre times, he was a schoolteacher. I say, "Cool, where did you teach?" He says, "Mainly girls' orphanages." Then he goes quiet. And I say, "Mainly?"

'I won't beat around the bush,' Natia continued. 'Turns out Uncle Bernard taught in camps for the daughters of political prisoners they'd sent to Siberia. They had to do something with the children, right? So they put them in these "camps".' Natia raised her fingers in quotation marks. 'Like, I can talk about this to you, Murtov, because you fought in the Revolution, right, you're an Old Bolshevik . . .'

'Not that old.'

'Just saying, you'll know what this means. Someone my age, it's hard to grasp what could have happened in those camps. Young children of men sent away for plotting against the Tsar. What happens to the daughters of the lowest of the low? You tell me.'

Murtov shook his head. 'We all heard.'

'Could've been girls you knew, right?'

'But they did have schools.'

'Yes!' Natia said. 'They went through the charade of educating these girls in school hours before they did what they pleased with them. There were men—and women—running these places. I hope the Revolution dealt with them.'

'But your uncle survived.'

Natia nodded. 'A lot of Tsarist sympathisers and capitalists survived, didn't they, Vasil?'

'I don't know about that.'

'Anyway. I say, "Uncle Bernard, we've got to talk this through. We're not very tolerant, we Post-Revolutionary youth. In case you haven't noticed."'

Murtov threw up his hands, trying hard to convey carefree indifference.

'Uncle Bernard told me he was a teacher of literature. He stood at the front of a classroom and gave lessons. I asked him if he knew what was done to those girls outside school hours and he got up on his hind legs, all offended dignity, and said, "I taught them Tolstoy, Turgenev and Lermontov. These were proper schools." Uncle Bernard did know, or suspect, what was happening after hours—he could see the wreckage of these girls every day—but he didn't have any influence, he was just a professional Russian literature teacher doing his job.

'So I asked him if he'd "got to know"'—Natia's fingers must have been cramping up from all the inverted commas—'any of the girls. I mean, that's what anyone would want to know, right? Those places were playgrounds for sickos. It was a free-for-all, wasn't it? I wasn't embarrassed to ask him. But he went off about how the satisfaction in the job for a serious teacher was improving the lives of these damaged girls by teaching them the universal truths in Chekhov, the poetic technique in Pushkin, blah blah. How hard it was with poor resources, but he was a serious pedagogue applying his craft. The challenges of teaching metre and scansion and syntax to help girls forget they'd spent all night being buggered by Tsarist yobs.'

Murtov thought about the book Babilina was trying to get stolen from the children's schoolteacher. The last time he'd heard pornographic language twice in one week was pre '17.

'But so,' Natia went on, sitting forward on the plaid couch and tearing a cake in half—Murtov knew she was going to eat the second half too—'I'm burning for more salacious stuff. You know, did the girls give blow jobs for a rusk? I know the Revolution put an end to sexual depravity, but history fascinates me. Uncle Bernard loosened up just one notch and told me, "It was pretty much how you think it'd be: the guards were doing it but the really nasty stuff was done by the building contractors, the financiers and their cronies, the aristocrats on visits, sometimes members of the Tsar's own retinue. It was run like a resort brothel. Things were out of control." A hint of mist had got into his eyes.'

Murtov felt a spike of anxiety for Uncle Bernard.

'And so I'm getting *really* curious,' Natia said. 'And he seems vulnerable, open, with the nostalgia and the funeral and that. So I go in for the kill. I say, "Come on, Uncle Bernard, you're telling me you didn't get a piece?" I'm on the edge of my seat now. We're pulling up at the municipal hall where my mother's wake is. Uncle Bernard pauses to thank the driver and unclip himself and get out of the car, and I think I've blown it, I've terrified him into silence. I'm not trying to trap him; I genuinely want to know.

'But as we're about to move into the hall, he draws himself together and says, as if he's giving his plea at the Revolutionary Trials—you know, the old "I was only following orders" . . .' Natia paused for Murtov to nod his acknowledgement then continued: 'Uncle Bernard says, "I was totally disciplined. For ninety percent of the time."

'And I crack up. I say, "*Ninety* percent of the time?! What the fuck, Uncle Bernard! Rasputin himself was totally disciplined *ninety* percent of the time. Those Fascist sadists in Germany are totally disciplined *ninety* percent of the time. Attila the Hun was a real charmer *ninety* percent of the time!"

'All Uncle Bernard says is, "Ninety percent of the time I was disciplined. And you'd better stop laughing, we're at your mother's wake."'

Natia blinked encouragingly at Murtov, as if helping a dull pupil with his lesson.

'So AAA . . .' he said. It had never hurt Murtov to be slow with Natia. Behind the curve was a warm and dark place to hide.

'Don't talk to me about the ninety percent,' Natia said. 'It's the other ten percent that tells me what I need.'

AAA was hers. AAA was Post, AAA was multiracial, AAA was a pure Natia mole. What was her message about AAA's other ten percent? In his confusion, Murtov didn't know if Natia was warning him as a friend or warning him *off* as an adversary.

An electronic buzzer sounded through the office for the First Secretary's daily ten a.m. briefing.

'Guess we're both busy,' Murtov said.

'Hm.' Natia nodded to herself, as if assessing whether they were busy or not, and ran a hand over her brush-like hair. 'What I'm trying to say, friend Murtov, is that I know you are going on a special assignment later today, and AAA is not permitted to accompany you.'

Murtov shrugged. When you are clueless, say nothing. A policy that had got him to his fortieth year.

'Look, I won't pretend,' Natia said. 'It fucking pisses me off that friend Beria still employs you as his personal buddy-in-chief with an Assistant Secretary title. How you have known each other since you were little boys in Pre times, you're some kind of childhood teddy bear he still keeps to cuddle, right? There is nothing more backward and imperialist than this fucking "boyhood friendship" *blat*, this special little club of yours.'

'I was born again in October '17,' Murtov said.

'You fought in the Revolution, didn't you?'

'Alongside Lavrentiy Pavlovich.'

'Ah—but on which side?' Natia grimaced. 'People of my generation are outraged that you and your type are still free to walk the streets. You don't even bother cooking up a new set of identity papers saying you were born a peasant—what a normal person would do. You're so brazen, but there it is, you still get to hang around. What I struggle to accept is the ten per cent of the time when'—her lip curled in distaste—'I am not getting the information I need. That's what I'm trying to tell you. It's all in the ten percent.'

Murtov said, 'So which car am I taking?'

'He wants you in the morning briefing. You fucking men. I thought the Revolution had put an end to your shit.'

The second buzzer sounded, in intermittent bursts, to summon Beria's men and their shit within one minute. Natia stood and dusted crumbs off her front.

'Old mates who govern Georgia. It's like a joke he's playing on his own country.'

She was speaking out as a woman, Murtov thought, but in her in-depth language she was flaunting her strength. Only the mighty could talk so freely about the boss. Nothing Natia did was unplanned. So young to be so strategic.

She picked up another cake and bit on it. Murtov ushered her through the door, an overhang of his bourgeois courtesy. She declined and made him go first.

'Eh, friend,' he heard her say. A bubble rose through his gullet. 'We know Babilina's spreading seditious literature. Don't worry, she's already a former person at the university so we can't sack her, can we?' Natia found this so funny she had a coughing fit after inhaling cake. 'Just make sure it never gets up to ten percent.'

V

CHEEKS PINK FROM THEIR TETE-A-TETE, MURTOV FOLLOWED Natia through the secretariat office, where the labour of processing in-boxes into out-boxes was proceeding with Georgian efficiency. The boss was standing over a young female typist, massaging her shoulders. The girl could not have been more than fifteen. Beria gave Murtov an eye-bobble in the direction of Natia and came after them into the conference room, shutting the door behind him.

The dark-panelled walls were decorated with gas lamps, small paintings depicting peasants and soldiers, and a large portrait of The Steel One. The carpets still harboured the odour of stale tobacco. The boss had banned smoking in the office upon his ascension from chief snoop to chief executive. Seven years, Murtov thought, and the stench remains.

Standing, Beria surveyed the faces around the table: head of state security Vsevolod Merkulov, head of secret police Evgenii

Dumbadze, head of Party security Sergei Kruglov, head of internal affairs Sergo Goglidze, and the brothers Kobulov—Amayak and Bogdan—whose titles were unknown to Murtov but were both involved with security. Beria cheerfully nicknamed Bogdan 'The Samovar' while Amayak was 'The worst man God put on the earth'. Titles didn't matter. This group's qualification for being Beria's A-team was having befriended him during the Revolution. Through his rise from Chekist to governor, these stocky meatballs of men learnt when to laugh at his one-liners and when to pretend they could help him run the Caucasus. Whether they feared him or were awed by him or simply loved him, probably all three, they carried out his orders like switch-operated machines. They were idiots, Murtov thought, but they possessed high Beria IQ: their brains contained tumblers that spun and locked on to what he wanted from them.

'*Buenos días, amigos!*'

Beria's favourite movie was *Villa Villa!*, about the Mexican Pancho Villa. He too fancied himself chief of a hard-riding bandit posse. Even now that his public image had been moulded from mobster to governor, he sometimes had a projector set up in this room so he could view the movie with his gang; he roared his approval during Villa's murders as if watching a comedic documentary. This conference room was Beria's playground, his theatre. Murtov took a seat at the furthest end, beside Natia Meskhi.

'So what are we buying, what are we selling?' The boss began the meeting with his customary capitalist parody. He drew a jar of his peppers from a pocket of his light Italian-fabric tunic. 'Oh shit, where's Ketevan?'

Anticipating the summons, Beria's personal secretary and minute-taker, a rusted-on bureaucrat who had survived Tsarist,

Menshevik and Bolshevik rule so ably that Beria joked she would even outlive him, appeared with her notepad. Now in her eighties, Ketevan Nozadze measured two Berias in size, thanks largely to the sweet treats he slipped into her purse in return for the complete discretion she had shown all her masters. Beria liked to say that she had swallowed a bank vault. Ketevan, who flirted ceaselessly with Beria, told him to stop paying her such outrageous compliments.

Ketevan looked for a seat at the conference table. 'Well,' she said, 'I might as well go on your knee.'

She manoeuvred herself towards Beria, who laughingly fended her off.

'Oh, I'd only break you.' Ketevan retreated to a beautiful leather couch by the wall behind Beria, comfortable in the knowledge that she was the only Georgian permitted to address him so frankly.

Ketevan in place, attendance recorded, the minutes of yesterday's meeting approved and signed, Beria asked for updates. Notwithstanding the Soviet Union's pride in workforce gender equality—Beria often boasted that having Ketevan and Meskhi as 'my two right hands' made him a suffragette—the Georgian Politburo was resolutely macho. When dealing with economic or organisational problems, the posse spoke as if they had been in hand-to-hand combat with reactionary elements.

Murtov followed the proceedings with the banned poet's words in his head. *Around him a rabble of thin-necked leaders, fawning half-men for him to play with. They whinny, purr or whine as he prates and points a finger, one by one forging his laws, to be flung like horseshoes at the head, the eye or the groin.* For all their status in the republic, these baldheads were too terrified to sleep at night without powerful sedative drugs or enough alcohol to fell an ox. Georgia's rulers they may be, but Murtov could hear whinnies, purrs and whines. At any given conference, one of the chiefs was within millimetres of bursting into tears and half-a-dozen others were breathing shallowly. Only the Kobulov brothers, who had no updates to deliver, sat in calm silence, scratching their balls.

Beria listened with narrowed eyes, nodding as if selecting from a buffet. Who would he eat today? Which fuck-up? Which career eavesdropper? Which of these backstreet accidents he'd put in control of Georgia? In turn, they read out figures on factory output, agricultural volumes, energy generation, collective farm populations, military equipment supply, transportation on-time rates, progress on the modernisation of hospitals and school retention levels, not having a fucking clue what they were saying except that their numbers were fictions that would put Dostoevsky to shame. The men in charge knew it and the man in charge of them knew they knew it. They weren't here for their capabilities; they were here for his amusement.

'I don't know what it is you actually do,' Beria interrupted Goglidze's report on energy. Murtov heard collective breath being held and smelt droplets of piss soaking into serge trousers. 'But somehow the republic needs you.' The boss rubbed his hands; perhaps this was going to be one of those days when he crucified no-one.

To Kruglov he said, 'One thousand three hundred new entrants into the labour farms!' As nobody in the room knew whether that was a good number or a terrible disappointment, again there was an intake of breath. 'Good man!' Beria clapped. Kruglov's face poured itself back into its pouches; he was safe.

Since Lenin, the first law had been: 'Who whom?' Who is us and whom is them? You had to get used to not knowing if, by dinnertime, some illiterate NKVD fuck had got your name wrong and you had been shifted from the *Who* column to the *Whom*s. Your innocence was no protection. Quite likely, your innocence was your crime.

There was a knock on the door and the very young stenographer Beria had been massaging asked Ketevan to please inform the First Secretary that he had a telephone call from Moscow. As this was the single permissible reason to break his conferences, Beria was already on his feet. 'Don't go,' he said to the room as he skipped after the typist. 'I haven't finished with you lot.'

Minutes passed and nothing was said. The cautious optimism that had developed with Beria not tearing strips off Goglidze and Kruglov ebbed out of the room.

When the boss returned, his face was crimson and the veins in his temples bulged. A call from Moscow meant an order from the General Secretary, usually conveyed through Sergo Ordzhonikidze, Beria's Georgian mentor, now the People's Commissar of Heavy Industry. Beria did not relay the order to the meeting. They didn't need to know. They only needed to clench their buttocks.

He grinned nastily as Dumbadze finished his update on production from Georgia's chemical factories.

'You know what a great chemist I am?' Beria snapped. 'I can transform a head of department into a piece of shit, and a piece of shit into a head of department.' He zeroed in on Dumbadze. 'Where did you get that human being look? Have you lost weight?'

'Er . . . p-put it on, actually . . .'

'Why did you miss budget? Why are you allowing so much *blat* go on under your unsightly nose?'

Dumbadze stammered, 'If there are any shortfalls I will explain them at tomorrow's conference.'

'*At tomorrow's conference,*' Beria repeated. 'You think you're still going to be around? Is that why you always put things off till tomorrow? You think you can string me along, you think I'll have forgotten?'

Dumbadze began to speak but Beria swatted him away and turned on Goglidze. 'You, you've got nothing. Why does the actual head of energy send you here in his place?'

'Lavrentiy Pavlovich, I . . . I only give you the official figures provided by staff. I cannot help the typical shortcomings of the bureaucracy.'

'Horseshit,' Beria snapped. 'I know better than the *bureaucracy* what the figures are, certainly better than you do, so I'm wondering what the point of you is.' He turned to the Kobulov brothers and asked, 'What is the point of Goglidze?'

They gave nonchalant shrugs. Natia Meskhi had once told Murtov her nickname for them: 'The Rhetorical Brothers', because their function was to receive the boss's rhetorical questions.

'You.' Beria tilted his chin at Natia. 'Haven't heard much from you, have we? Think you can sit quietly below the radar?'

Nods around the table from six men jostling to get below the same radar.

'I can report,' Natia said, reading from her folder, 'that homelessness in Tbilisi is now zero.'

'Homeless? Losers,' Beria said. 'Tell me something I care about.'

'School entry for infants, which is now to take place at four years instead of five, has reached one hundred percent of the eligible population.'

'You go on about kids because you can't have any,' he said. 'I told Goglidze here not to breed anymore, but he couldn't keep it in his pants, could you, dickbrain?'

Murtov saw Goglidze tense up even more, which he'd have thought was physically impossible.

Beria said, 'I moved you into a smaller apartment with two other families so there wouldn't be room for you and your slut to keep polluting the Georgian population with your pathetic genes.'

Goglidze began to croak an explanation but the cat was only fooling with a mouse. Beria cut him off. 'What else, friend Meskhi?'

Natia held her nerve. 'We have reports that forest fires on the northern border have now killed thirty people on both sides, mostly Ossetian labourers.'

'Good. More losers. No crop damage? Just forest fires?'

Natia gave Ketevan an almost imperceptible nod. Ketevan's pen paused. Natia didn't want to go on record confirming one thing or the other. Murtov noted with interest that Ketevan took nods from Natia.

'Well, we're not a social service,' Beria said, though from what Murtov knew, as he looked around at the faces concentrating fiercely on the leather tabletop, a social service was what the Georgian socialist government was supposed to be.

Natia went to her next item. 'The Georgian republic's liaison with our sister Transcaucasian states of Azerbaijan and Armenia—'

'I know what Transcaucasia is,' Beria said. 'Who's the liaison again?'

'Friend Levan Kapanadze,' she said.

'That fucking Jew? Isn't he dead?' With this, the boss leaned back in his chair, opened his copy of *Our Achievements*, the journal founded by the novelist Maxim Gorky to publicise, well, their achievements, and put his feet on the table, presenting his posse with the leather soles of his English-made brogues.

'We have been able,' Natia continued, 'to see the consequences of the new labour law from Moscow freeing up the return of small traders to the fields of shoemaking, tailoring, hairdressing, plumbing, carpentry and upholstery. This, we expect, will alleviate shortages in consumer items.'

'And does the "law",' Beria sneered from behind *Our Achievements*, 'allow them to put these consumer items on general sale?'

'As you know,' Natia replied, 'the Moscow labour law only permits them to make specific sales to customers on request, not to open up shops.'

'And how is the shoemaker expected to sell the customer a shoe?' Beria's voice asked.

'Ah. The law requires that the customer bring the shoe, plus any materials required to repair it.'

'Which I presume that the customer hasn't got. Because that's why the customer has come to the *shoemaker* in the first place.'

'I'm just telling you what the law allows,' Natia said.

'Fucking good law it sounds like,' Beria's voice said. 'Fucking big change it'll make to the shortages.'

Silence followed as the leaders of the Georgian Communist Party and government waited for the First Secretary to speak, fart, anything.

Beria pushed out a mean laugh. Cautiously, the others followed: first Merkulov, then Dumbadze, then, in ranking order, the rest.

'Come on!' Beria said. 'You don't laugh, you don't eat!'

Forced laughter, one of the more painful Soviet sounds, continued until, after an eternity, the voice behind the journal said wearily, 'Oh, fuck off the lot of you. Come back when you've made life better and more joyous.'

The chiefs retreated with downturned mouths betrayed by the bright eyes of relief. Beria threw at each of them, like a final show of contempt, a fat packet bulging with roubles. They had got off lightly; a call from Moscow could trigger incendiary rages. They filed out of the conference room and fanned away to their offices to yell at their staff.

As Murtov was trailing out, Natia murmured: 'And he wonders why they're so useless.'

From behind him, Murtov heard: 'Oh, V, stay a moment, will you? Shut the door?'

Murtov shut the door, remained on his feet and looked at his oldest friend's shoes.

'Yeah, they're all geniuses, as faithful to me as family, but not one of them would I have a cup of tea with. I s'pose you can't choose your brothers.'

Beria slapped *Our Achievements* on the conference table and laced his fingers behind his head. Murtov waited and thought: have a cup of tea.

'God strike me pink, Vasil, what a pack of cunts. Every morning it's the lot of them sitting on the fence, crapping their daks, and once they know what I've decided, oh yeah, then they're all in. What a charade. Anyone who believes Georgians are so laidback and free-wheeling, we're not a bunch of living corpses like the Russians, ought to walk in my shoes for a day. Where's our precious fucking larrikin spirit? Nobody gets a thing done. It's always *the bureaucracy's* fault, it's always "sorry, *they* won't let me do it". So it lands with me. Gutless lazy hens, the lot of them.'

'Governance issues,' Murtov said.

'It makes me sick. I want to protect Georgia from the worst of it and make this place a stand-out republic, don't I?'

'You are the best thing the Georgian people have going for them.'

'And I'm a fair dinkum leader, I'm not just a dirty Chekist.'

'You've proven that over seven years, Lavrushya.'

'You know me, V; maybe only you. It's not so bad here, is it? I've given the Georgians good harvests, and I've protected them from the worst of the shit pouring out of Moscow. Those psychopaths, Yezhov and his gang—they can't get at us. I can see it in here.' He tapped the *Cheka Weekly* on the table. 'Georgia's the one working economy in the USSR. We've only lost a few thousand Party officials, and that's because I've put my neck on the line. We are a proud nation and we fight for our corner, and you know why?'

'It's because we have you.'

Beria waved a hand as if he'd had a gutful of flattery. 'It's because I don't fill their heads with gibberish about Marx and Lenin and historical necessity and base and superstructure. When I see a textbook, I reach for a fucking match. In Georgia, we recognise that what drives a man is love of country and love of his friends, love of his loved ones! We are the republic of love, aren't we, V?'

'We are, Lavrushya.'

'Right, right.' Beria was calming down. He ate one of his chillis. 'Fucking Moscow, they're doing my head in. All the little yes-men are scared of me, I can feel it.'

'I'm sure they just respect you,' Murtov said.

'No, they're shit-scared. They've begun to suspect that I'm The Steel One's heir apparent. Fuck, where have I gone wrong?'

'That doesn't sound like a bad thing.'

'It's the worst thing!'

'Well, maybe they don't really think of you that way.'

'You know what the trick is?' Beria said, his eyes closed. 'I'm smarter than all of them, smarter than the old man too. The trick is not letting anyone else know it. I have to join the cult where we all believe in the Supreme Genius of Humanity, the Experienced Proletarian Commander, the Theoretician of Genius and Organiser of Collective Farm Construction.'

'And he is,' Murtov said, with a quick glance at the portrait on the wall. It showed no sign of hearing.

'It's not that he doesn't have a brain,' Beria continued his dangerous line of thought, suicidal if anyone other than Murtov was listening, 'but his intelligence is limited to an uncanny understanding of the physics of human power. He fancies himself a carpenter, you know that? Just like old mate he grew up worshipping at seminary school. He understands people like they're wood and nails and screws: who's soft, who's hard, who you can hit on the head, who you can turn to penetrate into the soft stuff. There's a craft in that and he uses it brilliantly, I'll give him that. But the Soviet toiler deserves better, that's all I'm saying. It'll take more than a carpenter to get us to the Communist paradise.'

'Your work in Georgia is appreciated, I'm sure.'

Beria's eyes popped open behind their glass disks. 'But that's exactly what I've got to avoid! All I need to do, until my moment comes, is stop them from seeing my capabilities! And that's why I'm so worried about this fucking visit. I'm being set up.'

'They want you to fail?'

'They want me to succeed! If I fuck it up, then that's good for me, it shows them I'm just an over-promoted policeman and they don't have to worry about me.'

'So you want to make a mess of it?'

'No! Or not so badly that I cruel my chances of getting to Moscow.'

'So you do want to succeed.'

'Not that either! If I make too great a success of it, Yezhov will have me shot.'

'So what do you want?'

'This task is some river I have to cross. What's on the other side? Recognition? Ordination as the heir? That's the end of me. Is it something else? Worse, better, who the fuck knows? It's the not knowing—*how much* should I mess it up, *how much* should I make it a success, where's the fulcrum point, what's the best strategic outcome—that's what's driving me insane.'

'I don't know how I can help you.'

Beria cackled a little feverishly. 'Of course you can't help me, you chump. Oh, V, you're always good for a laugh. No. I only asked you to come back because . . . See that couch, the leather one?'

Murtov looked at the studded three-seater which still bore the imprint of the Ketevan rump. In Murtov's mind, it held the status of an elephant in this room: back in '21, in the Revolution's aftermath when the Bolsheviks finally managed to seize recalcitrant Georgia, it had been pilfered by Beria's Cheka from the Murtov family house in Sokhumi. The sofa whispered between Murtov and Lavrushya, unheard by anyone else. As a free-spirited boy, Murtov had jumped all over it. Murtov's parents had sat on it to drink champagne and play cards in the evenings, as had his grandparents before them. Little Lavrushya, their charity ward, had never so much as touched it. When the Murtovs had enjoyed its luxury, Little Lavrushya had watched from the shadows.

Murtov had invited him to come play; his parents had invited him to come take a sip of wine; but Little Lavrushya said no. Always no.

'You want it?' Beria said.

'Do I want it.'

'Don't repeat me, I've had enough of that. I ask you in good faith: do you want it? It's serviceable, considering it's Russian-made. I believe it dates from Tsarist times.'

Weirdly, though Beria never forgot anything so personal as this couch—he never forgot anything—he seemed to be offering it to Murtov like just another 'packet'.

'It weighs a fucking ton,' Beria said. 'One of these days Ketevan's going to break it in half and it'll be a cunt of a thing to get out.'

'Why?' Murtov said.

'I'm over it. Oh, I get it, your pride and all that, blah blah. Okay, let me sell it to you.'

Murtov did not know what to say. 'You'll sell it to me?'

'Are we in a cave?' Beria smacked the side of his head. 'All I hear is a fucking echo.'

'How much?'

'I don't know. Ten thousand.'

Ten thousand roubles! Murtov began to think that this was the purpose of the conversation: Beria did remember the significance of the couch—of course he did—and this shadow play was his way of letting Murtov know that he could not be let out of morning conference without a nick in his flesh.

'I don't have anything like that,' Murtov said. Please, he thought, let me be right about Beria and money. Let him forget how much he has given me in my packets.

'You're interested, though?' Beria rubbed his hands eagerly. 'Okay, it's yours for three hundred. And I won't negotiate any further.'

Now the price was so low it was an open insult. 'I . . . I'll think about it.'

'Don't think too long.'

'But . . . why?'

'Well,' Beria said, with a glance that was somehow both sly and panicked, 'I understand Babilina wasn't too impressed with the coffee maker.'

Murtov flushed. The men in the long coats. The coffee maker on the kerbside. Or worse—Beria had heard. Through the telephones, through the cobwebbed cornices. Unthinkable.

'And rightly so,' Beria went on. 'I apologise; it was an afterthought, it showed insufficient respect. But this couch . . . this is really something.'

'I don't think Babilina wants any gifts.'

'Please don't upset me,' Beria said. 'I know it's tough with her losing her job, and two girls still to raise . . . What are they—eleven, twelve?'

He knew how old they were.

'You and Babilina need all the help you can get. I don't forget my old friends, V.'

Sometimes Beria's pince-nez felt like laser beams, super-weapons from the future.

'And how are the girls?' Beria said. 'Children always enjoy a nice piece of furniture to play on. Uncle Lavrushya hasn't forgotten them.'

Beria's smile moved towards the squeaking door hinges.

Murtov said, 'Shall I get Ketevan to convert the minutes of the meeting into executive orders?'

From the door, Natia Meskhi watched the two men with half a smile.

'I was about to ask the same thing,' she said. 'Do you want a transcript?'

'Fuck, that's all I need, my only two competent people ganging up on me,' Beria said with a showy sigh. 'No executive orders. No minutes. Best to keep them guessing. Okay, conference over—what's next?'

VI

NEXT DAY, AS NATIA MESKHI HAD FORESEEN, MURTOV WAS driving his oldest friend through a complex sequence of checkpoints, changes of car and clues to still more secret locations, a shedding of two anonymous vehicular escorts, following orders issued from the back seat. The weather was brightening after a murky morning. The boss had dispensed with his tunic and was wearing a white round-collared shirt that showed off chest and shoulders impressive in a man of his age. A traditional Georgian *Svaneti* hat sat like a pet cat on his lap.

'Left here,' Beria said.

Murtov turned left.

'Any reason for the secrecy?' Murtov glanced into his mirror. Uncharacteristically, Beria was gazing out of the window, taking in the rural scenery. His hands, instead of autonomously rubbing themselves together or flicking through his folders, lay open on his thighs, parenthesising his hat as if he were relaxing on a country drive. But Beria did not do relaxation and he did not do country drives.

'You don't tell me all your secrets either,' Beria said airily.

Murtov said nothing.

'The couch?' Beria added.

'Oh. Babilina was sleepy with her allergies. I didn't raise the subject.'

Beria offered a less-than-interested sniff and said, 'That fellow the other day. The funeral.'

Murtov met his pince-nez in the mirror.

'He did cancel himself.'

Murtov's oldest friend was not Lavrentiy Pavlovich Beria but the glassy reflections that accrued between them. He waited for the boss to elaborate.

'He was caught at Sokhumi trying to board a freighter for Turkey.'

Murtov was surprised. So firmly was maritime traffic controlled by Beria's people, smuggling oneself aboard a Black Sea freighter was tantamount to jumping in front of a train.

'He was caught with dirty pictures. Pillar of the Party, respectable elder, and boom, the guards check his bag and the game's up. Young girls. And worse.'

'Worse?'

'He didn't have a valid visa.'

'There was intelligence?'

Beria nodded. 'Meskhi authorised the search. Pity. If it had got to me, I could have done something for him. Not about the visa, but maybe I could have confiscated the pictures. But you know what she's like. Crimes like these, there's no half-measures.

She presented me with the information as a "courtesy", can you believe that? All I could do for him was keep it out of *Pravda*. Broken man. No surprise he took the exit. If he'd resisted, they'd have arrested his family.'

After another silence, Murtov said, 'He could only save his family by ending himself.'

'This is the world we live in,' the boss said helplessly, sinking back into his seat. 'Who says the Soviet system doesn't allow free choice?'

'Did the girls in the photos have any choice?'

'Oh, choice. You should see them,' Beria said, gazing dreamily at the landscape.

'And you delivered his eulogy.'

'One of my best. You still need directions?'

By now Murtov knew where they were going. He thought about how the person looking at those photographs for gratification was as guilty as whoever created and sold them. All the scum in together. At least collectivisation worked somewhere.

'My point is,' Beria said wearily, 'Meskhi knows too much before it gets to me. That's why all the secrecy today. I don't want her knowing everything.'

'She knows I'm taking you somewhere but she doesn't know where.'

Beria pressed against the bench seat and whispered in Murtov's ear: 'Is she still with us, or has she flipped? What about the kid she's given me?'

'Flipped to who?'

Everyone whispered in Georgia, but they whispered to stay out of Beria's hearing. What did it mean that Beria was whispering too?

On the outskirts of the town of Gori, Murtov swung the car into a sealed estate, the gate opening as the guard checked the vehicle. Murtov slowed to the ten-kilometre-per-hour speed limit and eased into a parking space on an avenue of single-storey villas painted a Tuscan earth colour with bougainvilleas climbing the walls. Beria had rebuilt Gori, The Steel One's birthplace, into an imaginary Italian resort.

'I figured we were coming here,' Murtov said, unclipping his seatbelt. 'Why not tell me? You reckon I'm suss as well?'

Beria's face had moved out of the rear-vision mirror. Murtov heard the static of his hands rubbing together. 'I need to have *something* up on you.'

Like it was only one thing.

The day had changed its mood again and light rain was falling as Murtov and Beria stepped into the portico. Before Murtov could ring the bell, the door opened from the inside.

An elderly man, grovelling like a butler, gas lamps shining off his liver-spotted scalp, showed them into a spacious living room furnished with Georgian rugs, two thickly stuffed sofas, a glass-topped table, a bookshelf and a radio set. In the bookshelf were the complete works of Marx and Engels, Lenin and Stalin, plus an up-to-date set of *Our Achievements*. On the whitewashed wall was an Orthodox cross.

'That drizzle!' the old man said, like someone who went outdoors.

Beria abandoned himself onto one of the couches like an overgrown teenager. Murtov perched on the other.

'You live like the last of a thousand-year line of imperialists,' Beria said. 'While the worker and the peasant continue to toil.'

The elderly man bowed his head, a mass of keratoses. He wore a cream cable-knit V-neck and loose synthetic slacks. 'We with spoilt biographies subsist at the pleasure of the workers' state,' he said as he went into his kitchen before emerging with a tray holding a wine jug, three glasses and a plate of *khachapuri*, a yeasty bread filled with grated cheese and egg. One of the glasses, containing water, was for Murtov.

Beria took his little jar out of his pocket and chewed a pepper.

'You really are an old queen,' he said before pouring wine into the two remaining glasses, Georgian-style, right-handed and close to the body to avoid spilling a drop. 'You've been baking.'

'Special occasion,' the old man said, maintaining his obsequious demeanour, taking the least-comfortable chair, an antique carver.

'But not special enough to replace that thing with a portrait of The Steel One.' Beria raised his eyes to the crucifix.

'Ooh, I've done even better!'

From a leather portfolio beside his chair, the old man produced a half-completed charcoal sketch of a young, or youthlike, Beria.

Beria nodded with a small smile. 'Not a bad likeness. I'll let you off just this once. Next time, I'll see it up on the wall instead of *that*.' He blew a raspberry at the crucifix. 'Otherwise I'll think you are an irredeemable enemy of the people.'

'Nobody is irredeemable,' the old man said. 'There are no enemies once a man crosses the threshold of his friend's home. Yes, I have been cooking.' He poured more wine and nibbled at the most burnt of the *khachapuri*. 'Not often I get a visit from the brass. How are you, Lavrushya?'

A silence fell at the childhood nickname. Beria paused with his wineglass at his lips and then tossed it back. 'I treat you well, don't I, Anastas?'

The old man produced a copy of *Izvestia*. 'Here, just today, I read in an encomium to Governor Beria that he was'—Anastas unfolded the newspaper to the relevant page—'*a homeless child of a peasant family persecuted by the Tsar, almost lost to a life of juvenile delinquency, but taken in by the Bolshevik underground Party orphanage and reformed by an education in Marxism–Leninism.* My goodness, Lavrushya, have you outlawed memory itself?'

Beria gave an equable shrug. 'We live in a new age with new perils. One adapts.'

'The gift of memory is all that separates us from the animals, our miraculous ability to reverse time and relive the past.'

'Don't worry, I remember enough,' Beria said with thin lips.

Anastas slapped his knees. 'Well! As long as you don't forget who actually raised you, I won't take it as a personal insult. I can keep a secret too! Now. Let's eat!'

Beria deflated. He was too busy to eat. But a Georgian did not refuse a meal. With a long-suffering sigh he got up to sample Anastas's private bathroom.

Anastas went to the kitchen, where Murtov heard him humming happily while finishing his preparations. Murtov picked up a book from the glass-topped table. It was about the Dinamo football team, the NKVD's club for which Murtov had dreamt of playing before his career was cut short. So, he thought: the old man had beaten a full retreat to an inner world of sports, baking and card-playing. It was the logical end ever since he had traded critical helpful information for a fast-tracked placement in this rest home-cum-prison for non-toilers who might still be of use to the Party. For the fifteen years of his incarceration in this gilded cage, since Murtov's mother had passed away from a heart attack, Anastas had been of continuing utility to Beria. He maintained a disciplined veneer one hundred percent of the time. When his housekeeper was deported because her husband had been shot for espionage, Anastas had carried on from one day to the next as if she never existed. You were never too old to adapt. 'If it happened,' he liked to tell his precious only son, 'it was necessary.'

Murtov went into the kitchen. It had an oddly comforting urinary smell.

'How are you?' he said.

'All the better for seeing you.'

Anastas grasped Murtov's hand. Murtov squeezed his father's, dry as a document.

The toilet flushed. Anastas Murtov wiped a tear from his eye.

✣

Beria and Murtov sat at the glass-topped table while Anastas served lunch: *kapati*, a Georgian sausage; *pkhali*, a mix of vegetables, herbs and walnuts; *lobio*, a kidney bean salad; *badridzhniz khizilala*, an eggplant caviar; and the refreshed clay jug of Georgian wine poured into a *kantsi*, a wine horn that Anastas, remaining on his feet, raised in a toast.

'And they say the Soviet Union is suffering a famine,' Beria said. 'For a former person you live pretty well, don't you?'

'As *tamada*,' Anastas said, taking the role of toastmaster, 'I salute the prosperity of the Georgian people. As the tale goes, when God was allocating all the parts of the earth to its peoples, the Georgians were too busy having a feast and missed the deadline. God was about to leave them without a country, but the *tamada* toasted God and his creation of beautiful food and wine and rivers, and God was so happy he let the Georgians have the last spot left, which he had been keeping for himself: his paradise.'

Beria raised his wine, Murtov his water.

'Precisely,' Beria said. 'To Stalin.'

'And to our Georgian leader Lavrentiy Pavlovich, who has steered us through the hungry years and preserved our bounty of food and drink!' Anastas said, refilling his horn and throwing it down in one gulp. 'To a great governorship! Food is, after all, the world.'

'I like the single continuous Georgian line, *tamada*,' Beria said. 'From God, via The Steel One, to myself. Well done.'

After a period of silent but determined eating, Beria said, 'There is a new atmosphere. New people. You know what's been going on in Russia. I am not sure I can protect the Georgians forever. Year zero is coming.'

'Year zero!' Anastas said with a complacent laugh. Before Murtov could stop him or kick his shin, the old man went on, 'I keep telling you, the old generation is dying out before it can pass on its wisdom. What do we bequeath the future if we depart in silence?'

'I'd prefer you bequeath nothing but your silence,' Beria said coldly. 'You have no idea how many enemies I have or what angles they could attack from.'

'Now, now!' Anastas said. 'The Stalin Constitution of 1936 specifically lifted restrictions placed on sons due to their fathers' class origins—you are both free, regardless of my spoilt biography!' He was back on his feet, raising his refilled wine horn. 'I wish to tell a story.'

'Please no,' Murtov and Beria both muttered.

'It is about the young man whose friends kept disappearing in this madness. One after another they vanished. Soon the young man realised that he was the common link. He didn't know what he had done wrong, but it must be his fault! Now everyone avoided him. His family, even. His isolation was worse than death. When he could no longer stand it, he cancelled himself. It was the only way he could protect his loved ones.'

'Your point?' Beria said.

Anastas's wine horn was still raised. 'Drink.'

The young men drank.

'My point is what Georgians understand and Russians do not: without the love of family and friends—love of country, love of those who brought you up, those who love *you*—there is no life, neither past nor future. Socialist principles can never replace love.'

No wonder Georgians drink so much, Murtov thought: it licenses them to forget what they've said. Even when they are not drinking, they still say they don't remember.

Beria said, 'I can do without you being shot just yet.'

Once they had finished the last of the wine and the eggplant, Beria said, 'I came to ask for your help.'

It was not unusual for the most powerful figure in the republic to go secretly to his disgraced and imprisoned benefactor for aid. Beria's brain was a search engine for usefulness. At the age of nine, he had been sponsored, mentored and adopted by Anastas Murtov after his own father had been jailed for attempting to kill a government official, and his mother, left with three young children and no means of support, had brought her eldest to the wealthiest merchant in Sokhumi and uttered her plea: her child genius was destined for greatness if only he had a father to give him a start in life. Compassionate Anastas Murtov had dived into the role: he housed Lavrushya and put him through elementary and secondary school, university and residency in Baku. Anastas used his high-level contacts to secure the boy a position in the Menshevik Party, the socialist faction that governed Georgia from the fall of the Tsar in 1917 until 1921, not knowing that Lavrushya was by now working undercover for the Bolshevik insurgency. Anastas's charity was simple and traditional: the Murtovs were a family of several generations' wealth and this boy was a rising young man of formidable talent. Even with everything that had happened since—uprisings, civil war, famine, Five-Year Plans, collectivisation, depression, repression, the passing of Madame Murtov—Anastas gave himself personal credit for seeing the potential in the boy, for opening the pathways for this young mastermind to become a Great Man.

Among his other contributions, Anastas had also taught Lavrushya how to win at cards. All you needed was opponents who were too scared to accuse you of cheating.

'I received a call from Moscow,' Beria said. 'We are to receive an important visitor.'

Beria needed advice on details of engineering and development, organisation and logistics, etiquette and conduct in a manner that must necessarily remain confidential. He could not, of course, reveal to his staff that when it came to hosting the General Secretary of the Communist Party of the Union of Soviet Socialist Republics, he was all at sea. His lack of savoir faire haunted him. For Beria to show off his Bolshevik coarseness was all very well in front of a Georgian audience, but not when the boss of bosses was around. Coarseness was *his* trademark and nobody was allowed to compete.

The Steel One ran a Tsar's court, so for guidance on behaviour Beria needed a Tsarist mentor. Only the Murtovs knew how far behind he always, always, fucking *always* felt himself to be.

Beria had flattered Anastas by 'going to' him. Now the old man knew about the coming visit, a kernel of inside information more precious than gold, he was on his game. Vasil Murtov was reminded that, behind the daffy exterior, his father knew exactly which end was up. Beria needed him. The effects of the alcohol fell away and Anastas got to work, instructing Lavrushya crisply on the interior design of the imperial quarters, protocol, how the program of commemorative proceedings should unfold, and how to handle a Tsar's nuanced needs. Anastas was delighted to prove his continuing worth to the lad he still considered, in the secret recesses of his imprisoned memory, his protégé, his own personal creation.

'But can it be done?' Beria asked.

'Let me tell you a story,' said Anastas.

Beria's fist closed, but he exhaled and nodded.

'Don't be cross with me, it's a short one. On the first anniversary of the Revolution, they had forgotten to build a platform for Lenin to make his speech. There were no carpenters or builders' labourers to hand, only a barracks of imprisoned intellectuals and professionals. Whites! Tsarist loyalists! The night before the anniversary, bonfires were lit, and those enemy intellectuals got to work and finished the platform before sunrise. Even if they were doing it for the man who had put them in prison, they took pride in their work. Anything can be done if your workers believe they are doing it for a higher purpose.'

'So you think we can do it,' Beria said.

'To prove that we Georgians can do anything, we move mountains. But when The Steel One arrives and you give him a bouquet of flowers,' the old man said with a tender smile, 'mind you don't call it a "reef".'

Out of the corner of his eye, Murtov checked on Beria's reaction. Had Anastas gone too far? No, the boss was rubbing his hands and laughing at the old joke, though not as merrily as Anastas.

Beria asked Murtov to fetch his folder from the car. Murtov came back a few minutes later to find Anastas and Beria bent over the blueprints for the new buildings at Ureki. Murtov saw the rosy flush of relevance in his father's cheeks. Behind the clueless geriatric lay a still-sharp player; but behind the still-sharp player was a vain fool. The old man did not realise that usefulness was a non-renewable resource; he was diminished by what he handed over. Now he had less to offer than an hour earlier. He had not caught up with the zero-sum ways of the new.

'You always wanted to be an architect,' Anastas said.

'But you sent me to oil engineering school,' Beria replied.

'If it was good enough for my son, it was good enough for you.'

Murtov saw the slip coming before Anastas spoke. Beria showed nothing. Murtov thought about what his father had said, that memory can reverse time. If only he could reverse it now, by just a moment or two.

'And we became revolutionaries instead,' Beria said. 'But all's well that ends well. Now I'm the architect of all Georgia. No degree necessary. Take that, you silly old bourgeois cunt.'

'Oh Lavrushya!' the old man giggled and went out to the kitchen to pour some celebratory vodka. Murtov, his arms suddenly leaden with anxiety, propped himself on the table.

Beria had all he needed. He followed Anastas, saying, 'I really don't have time.'

But the old man responded, 'Nonsense, you're never too busy for the best drop in the village.'

Anastas might have been on the crest of a new story but it remained undelivered. Murtov heard a rattle, like a handful of marbles bouncing on a hard surface, then a fleshy slap on the polished parquetry floor.

Murtov went to the kitchen. Anastas was folded in an L-shape between Beria's feet and the sideboard. He whimpered softly and held his jaw with his left hand. His right was clutching his trousers.

Dropping to his knees, Murtov picked up his father's head and rested it on his thigh. 'Papa,' he said, 'I keep telling you this floor wax is too slippery; it's a hazard at your age.'

Anastas was searching his son's face. Murtov closed his eyes.

After long consideration Anastas said, 'I'm slipping over all the time.'

'Come on, on your feet,' Beria said, nudging Anastas's ribs with his toe. To Murtov he said, 'Poor old duffer.'

Murtov was helping Anastas to his feet as Beria went to the table to gather his papers. Murtov still could not meet his father's eye. His nostrils twitched and he saw the stain spreading on the crotch of the old man's trousers. On the floor were the four buttons from his fly. The sound of them falling to the parquetry was the rattling Murtov had heard. An old Chekist trick: a man whose hands are occupied with holding up his trousers cannot defend himself.

Murtov sat his father at the table. He gave him a kiss on his forehead, turned and followed Beria out to the car.

Once they were on the move again, Beria said, 'So you enjoyed catching up with Papa?'

Murtov replied, 'Stalin is my papa and I have no need of another one.'

Beria laughed, on and off, all the way to Batumi. Occasionally he popped one of his chillis. Then he began laughing again.

VII

THE PLANE TREES IN BATUMI'S NEWLY OPENED PARK OF CULTURE and Rest offered shade from the hottest day of the summer. Babilina and Murtov were walking Nicholas II. She had fought off her allergies with the help of the medication he had got hold of in the closed pharmacy.

Today was Metalworkers' Day. Children played in the park's sandy lanes; the reassuring smell of horse manure hung in the air from the novelty pony rides. There was a busy ferris wheel and an outdoor bowling alley. You could be forgiven for thinking The Steel One hadn't realised what was going on here. The Georgian people owed Governor Beria. In public, during the daytime, there was no Terror. Loudspeakers played marching music and workers on holiday appeared to be stepping in martial time. Everyone together! In the designated Agitational Corner of the park, a public demonstration was underway. The Party speaker received cheers as he announced new production records, unveiled the latest achievements of Soviet aviators and polar explorers, and, rousing the greatest applause, stated his pity for anybody so unfortunate as to be living outside the people's paradise. The happiness was infectious; from the edges of the audience, armed NKVD personnel quietly made sure of it.

Murtov had been given an afternoon off, the boss requiring only AAA to drive him to Ureki, where demolitions were starting. AAA appreciated the improved status in being permitted to drive the boss without Murtov supervising, and Murtov appreciated every spare hour with Babilina.

'You can trust the kid?' she said.

'No, but I could do with a break.'

Babilina knew that Murtov would be working extra shifts once Beria's hectic energy gathered pace. This afternoon was a respite from what was to come. Excitable Nicholas II, who wore a canvas halter to stop him from pulling his walker's arm off when he saw another dog, lunged for a coloured ball that a young child had dropped. The alarmed mother pulled the child away.

'It's not a muzzle, it's a halter,' Murtov said to the woman, as if she should know the difference. 'He doesn't bite.'

As the woman, casting a frightened look at Murtov, hustled her child away, Babilina said, 'You're the one who needs a muzzle, my love.'

When they reached the free canine area, Murtov removed Nicholas II's halter and began throwing him his own ball. Nicholas II did not bring it back. He found a particular satisfaction in chewing his rubber balls to shreds, which left him puzzled about no longer having anything to chase. Murtov shouted, 'Let it go, Nikita, you moron!'

Censorious dog owners scowled at Murtov, who replied, 'Nicholas II is a moron!'

'What's up your nose?' Babilina said.

'Nothing.'

'Which kind of nothing? Is Lavrushya beginning to go bad?'

'I don't know what you're talking about, Babi.'

'Old shitbreath's arrival messing with his mind?'

Murtov shook his head slowly.

'Oh well, I wouldn't be surprised,' Babilina carried on. 'Even he's got to be vulnerable to the Vozhd.'

Babilina understood the importance Beria was placing upon making a good impression on the 'Vozhd' (shitbreath now insisted on being called Leader like that mad prick in Germany). It wasn't in Beria's nature to grovel, but she knew him well. Fear and hope would do their work on him: fear of failure, hope that he would win promotion to the Moscow Politburo. She had always found Beria's restless ambition tiresome and destabilising. He was such a child! The little boy who had dreamt of creating eternal cities still burnt brightly; he had never aspired to the role of effective but unpleasant provincial Chekist, though that was clearly where his gifts lay, in her view. 'Moscow accepts my results while holding its nose,' Beria complained on the social occasions when she could not avoid a conversation with him. He wanted to be taken seriously. 'If you're not in Moscow,' he informed her, 'you're camping out.' Tough shit, she thought; he wasn't the first Georgian to believe he had grown too big for his homeland. But Beria could not quite know what was waiting for him in Moscow. High office or the firing squad? Either one would serve him right. The more his heart strove towards Moscow, the closer he felt its hot breath.

Babilina was indifferent to Beria's fate. All she cared about was how his self-devouring ambition would recoil upon her girls.

Murtov untied a canvas faeces bag from Nicholas II's leash. Nicholas II took his shit, but the grass was overgrown and Murtov lost the exact location. As he was searching for it, she saw him step in it. The shit dissolved into the tread of his boots, which he wiped on the grass, spreading the menace. The state was issuing fines for ignoring dog shit, but also for proliferating it.

Nicholas II ran after another dog's ball. Babilina stood over the crouching Murtov. 'Not your day,' she said.

Murtov had his boot off and was trying to pick Nicholas II's orange-tan shit out of the tread with a stick.

'I'm not taking his coffee pots, and as for your long-lost family sofa, Lavrushya can shove it up his arse.'

'Three hundred roubles,' Murtov replied. 'It's a steal.'

'Isn't there zero theft in Georgia? I read it in *Izvestia*.'

Babilina thought she could see what her husband couldn't. She'd known Beria for almost as long, having gone to school in Sokhumi with both boys. She had been surprised and disturbed by how Murtov respected his creepy adopted brother, whom she had sniffed out as a manipulator and sadist. There was something not quite right in the two boys' sibling relationship that she could never—to this day!—penetrate. The ensuing years convinced her that her initial suspicions about Beria were, if anything, lacking in imagination. His schoolboy viciousness had been a rehearsal for times that suited him. He leapfrogged everyone in the local Cheka; almost overnight he rose to the top. Meanwhile, she and Murtov became intimate during the Revolution, when as teenage rebels intoxicated on scientific progress they joined the uprising against the brutality and random injustice of Tsarism. Murtov had dubbed her his 'dream conspirator', meaning that she was his ideal and that he could not quite believe she existed. They were perfect for each other at a time when utopia seemed within their grasp. During the Revolution Murtov had proven himself brave, both physically and in the strength of his principles. They married in the Communist fashion—that is, not marrying but becoming de facto spouses under the Code on Marriage and the Family, one of the Bolshevik Party's first laws, which pulled the rug from under superstitious, backward, Church-sanctioned unions and validated truly free love. By then, with so much action and excitement speeding up time and crowding out the space for inner reflection, it was too late for her to probe Murtov's deeply strange connection to Lavrentiy Beria. Things between the adoptive brothers had been somehow fixed in the privacy of the Murtov home, and then the Revolution melted a seal across that inner chamber.

The Revolution also fixed the three of them in time; her bond with Murtov, having promised so much, had never quite been allowed to grow up naturally, she felt, once it had become the property of the Party and Murtov the property of Beria. Just when property had been abolished! She and Murtov did their best to fence off some privacy for love, but soon they had children, which, instead of buying them more intimacy, added to their lives a new layer of anxiety. Since the late 1920s, when the regime sank its claws into private life, the struggle to raise a family had become intertwined with the game of survival. Not only they but their little girls were now in the Party's hands. Beria's hands. If she were honest, she could not accurately put her finger on how Murtov *did* feel about Lavrushya. It was not quite blind loyalty and naivety—even if she often accused him of this—but nor was it her clear-eyed disgust; it lay somewhere in between, amid unexplored folds of complexity and contradiction. Perhaps it was this mystery in her husband that kept her fascinated with him. Though she occasionally wondered if she was living in false hope.

'I'm not taking that couch,' she said. 'Lavrushya is trying to fob it off on you, to imprison you in the past, to remind you of what you are.'

'Oh, that's all a fog to me.'

'You're so full of shit.'

Murtov gave Nicholas II a stomach rub. A little way away, two other dogs were grappling in a ditch, one of the unfinished parts of the Park of Culture and Rest, a boating pond of the future.

Murtov met her eyes. 'You have to trust me.'

'And you need to give me more to work with.'

What did those eyes know? What was that mind up to? This fucking Revolution, she thought.

As a desperate antidote, like she was administering an injection of other worlds, she spoke some lines of Emerson, her favourite American, on friendship.

'Let him be to thee for ever a sort of beautiful enemy, untameable, devoutly revered, and not a trivial conveniency to be soon outgrown and cast aside.'

Yes! This was the thing her husband could not articulate about his friendship with Beria. They were wrestlers, combatants in Georgia's favourite sport, each trying to turn the other over in an erotic embrace, a mutual invasion that only ends when one concedes to the other. Beria would never concede to Murtov, of course. That had always been clear. She hoped that Murtov had not conceded to Beria either; only that Beria thought he had.

Or was this more wishful thinking?

Emerson did little for Murtov, who remained impassive. Her poor translation into Georgian, perhaps. She said, 'You can hide all you want, my love, but no amount of fear can destroy your feelings. And even if those feelings are to be wiped out in this generation, they will come back to life in the next.'

She cast her eyes to Nicholas II, who, having tired of the adults, had found a younger playmate in Melor.

'I have tickets for *The Squealer*,' Murtov said.

Babilina's heart sank a little at Melor's enthusiasm for following every Party fad. She turned white. In a low growl that made Murtov duck his head as if flinching from a blow, Babilina said, '*He* has tickets. Well, that's not going to happen.'

'So I'll be disappointing them and him.'

'Disappoint away.'

'He's under incredible stress,' Murtov said. 'I'm worried about what's building up.'

'Every Georgian should be worried. But I am telling you, whatever you are brewing, he is not getting within a country mile of our daughters. Your daughters, Vasil. Not Beria's, not the Party's, not the Revolution's. *Your* daughters.'

THIRTY DAYS TO LIVE

VIII

MURTOV ACCOMPANIED MELOR AND ANA WHEN THEY TOOK their lute and bagpipes to the centre of Batumi and spent an hour and a half playing for the people. The local Party had been in a flap over whether street busking for money, a traditional activity in holiday-time Batumi, was not an imperialist/capitalist vestige, but the provincial Soviet had allowed some re-emergence of economic liberalism to allay shortages. In this case, it was a shortage of Georgian cultural product. Murtov's appearance in the back of the room at an emergency session had sealed the matter; when local officials saw Murtov, they saw Beria.

One of the reasons Beria was popular as First Secretary of the Transcaucasus was his habit of relaxing Bolshevik ideology to accommodate cultural customs. Ana's bagpipe-playing reminded Georgians that they were a wild and lyrical folk, untameable like the Celts and the Basques, an outlaw people united in their love of this baffling instrument, as if their very ears heard a unique frequency. We are not a miniature Russia; we don't have to ape those meatheads. So: busking with bagpipes.

Since the opening of the busking season, Melor and Ana had been performing at this busy corner of Gogebashvili Street by the sea port. Ana blew her bagpipes while Melor improved her skills on the *panduri*, a three-stringed lute, playing nationalist melodies and children's songs, even some Christian hymns. Murtov stood to the side as they opened with Melor's favourite patriotic song, 'Ever Higher'—'*We were born to make fairy tales come true*'—before moving onto the optimistic Soviet rhyme: '*An Eastern juggler/ Planted plump pips on Sunday/Which came up palaces on Monday.*'

Babilina sometimes joked that the girls would soon be earning more than their parents. The joke had worn thin as the reality dawned: Ana and Melor made more roubles in an hour than Murtov received in a week, and Babilina was jobless. If it weren't for having to go back to school in Tbilisi at the end of August, the girls could become the family breadwinners. The girls weren't motivated by money. Melor did it out of patriotism and Ana, whose purposes were often more opaque, did it perhaps for love of music. Though they had been socking away thousands, Babilina had been taking them on shopping trips with five or ten roubles apiece. She was determined to teach them self-reliance: how to shop, how to cook and do their laundry, how to live without parents.

As their busking chaperone, Murtov also had a role. The sea port was a high-value site, and some veteran musicians did not take kindly to a couple of cute-as-shit Party elite blow-ins scooping the pool. There was supposedly a buskers' pecking order, though when Murtov made his presence known, the competition melted away.

Sometimes joyous Georgian pedestrians would dance to the girls' music but forget to donate coins—until they saw Murtov hovering. When a pair of ancient ladies, clutching their throats with emotion, interrupted the two angels to tell them how they used to do a bit of singing themselves when the churches could operate more freely, Murtov had to step up and tell them that they could hire his daughters for conversation another time. The old ladies emptied their purses. There was something about Murtov.

Murtov did not like himself in this role. The girls were making the most beautiful traditional Georgian music you'd heard in your life, and there's this brick shithouse loitering like their pimp or, worse, their admirer. People said to each other, 'How proud would you be if you were their parents?' Murtov, overhearing this, wearing his friendliest grin, sometimes said yes, he was proud to bursting, but grinning at strangers was not a strength of his. They turned white, put coins in the *panduri* case, and beetled off.

In two hours on Gogebashvili Street, the girls made more than five hundred roubles. They finished their session with 'The International', Ana frowning over her bagpipes while Melor sang the climactic words: *'We shall build our world: a new world!'*

After driving the girls home, Murtov drove with AAA to take the boss to a grimy six-storey apartment building in the regional city of Kutaisi. The preparations for what was being called the 'Stalin gala' were keeping pace with Beria's breakneck schedule. The original thousands of kulaks deployed for re-educational labour had been too slow, too apathetic. So Natia Meskhi had mobilised squads of shock workers from the factories, the athletic elite powered by amphetamines and fanatical belief—in the end of days, in the beginning of days? No difference!—to work around the clock constructing accommodation on the Soviet scale for the guest-in-chief, his retinue of family members, senior Party personnel and their entourages, plus ancillary staff including chefs, food tasters and housekeepers.

The faster the project was moving, the more volatile Beria's temper. He had the chief architect sent away when his drawings named the central building 'The Big House', which Beria interpreted as a subversive joke. By the time it was explained to Beria that the architect simply hadn't known what 'The Big House' meant, it was too late to bring him back. Beria named the structure 'The People's Temple of the New' and replaced the architect.

Murtov and AAA waited outside the Kutaisi apartment block. Murtov had parked the Emka under a line of liquidambar trees in the deserted avenue bisecting central Kutaisi. Fortunately parking was not a problem. Aside from a pair of babushkas chatting on the pavement, Kutaisi's citizens were either indoors or had fucked off in search of sunshine.

AAA asked Murtov how his morning had been.

'My kids busk, I keep an eye on them,' Murtov said.

AAA nodded. 'How old are they?'

'Twelve and eleven.'

'Almost women then.'

A cold bubble of silence.

'Nowhere near it.'

'Yeah, well, the nuclear family is so retrograde; my sole duty is to the Party.' AAA fiddled with the gearshift.

Murtov considered reminding him that Beria himself had children. But then, Beria was not the best model.

He looked through the windscreen to the mossy grey-green converted office block. Kutaisi was so nondescript in its architecture that Georgian film-makers used it as a generic urban landscape, a city that looked like any city. A city of the future, the boss called it.

Two hours thirty-three minutes—Murtov checked his watch—they had been waiting. It was the third-last Saturday before the summer solstice, a still afternoon with high cloud cover, the humidity heavy between skin and clothes. Time was a patient beast, as hungry and methodical as the Party itself.

'Getting bored?' Murtov said. When AAA did not reply, Murtov went on, 'Last guy in your job was ordered to wait outside a building to record when a resident came and went, and who visited him. Days go by, not a peep. The target never left, nobody visited. Now and then the curtains parted and the target looked out at him. Our guy started thinking he was the one under surveillance, and the target was making notes on *him*. Drove him spare.'

Murtov waited for AAA to ask what had happened to his predecessor. But AAA said nothing.

'You want me to open the windows?' Murtov said.

AAA's eyes had settled on the building the boss had entered with his jaunty step two hours and thirty-four minutes earlier.

'I'm good,' AAA replied serenely.

Life is upside down, Murtov thought. Time is wasted on the young while agitation is wasted on the middle-aged.

'Are you?'

Now AAA noticed him with those mauve eyes, scandalously pretty if you took them in isolation. *If*, then *but*. *Who*, then *whom*. Nothing in isolation.

'What do you mean, am I?'

'Are you *good*? Or are you merely comfortable enough that you don't need me to crack the windows? Are you saying that you are *good*?'

'You all right, friend?'

Murtov broke open a pack of American chewing gum. He folded the foil over the end and offered it to AAA, who shook his head. His predecessor never recovered from those days waiting outside a building, not knowing if he was watching or being watched, if he was Who or Whom. Last Murtov heard, he was living in a hospital.

Murtov said, 'I'm *good*.'

'Aside from the obvious.'

'The obvious.'

'Why you do anything.' AAA lifted his eyes towards the building across the road and the anonymous blocks beyond.

'Oh, we do it all for the Revolution.'

'Lavrentiy Pavlovich said you Pres are all doing it for love of family but you don't know why.' AAA smirked like he had just stepped on Murtov's head to climb a rung of the ladder. He took the packet of chewing gum out of Murtov's hand. *Lavrentiy Pavlovich*, yeah, right.

For Murtov, after a morning watching the girls play their music, joy's tide had gone out, leaving mudflats, stinking rubbish, rotting weed.

'You've got a father, too, don't you?' AAA said. 'Tucked away somewhere?'

Murtov stiffened. AAA had changed since being elevated to driving *Lavrentiy Pavlovich* alone and picking up his laundry. The kid was relaxed, almost condescending towards good old Murtov.

'That generation wore themselves out, didn't they?' AAA said. 'Fixated on material comforts. The spark has gone, life is behind them.'

AAA did not mean *them*. He meant *you*.

'For my generation,' AAA continued, 'the present is nothing but a preparation for the glorious life to come. We do our exercises in the morning, and then go out to accelerate the Motherland's progress towards our shared goal. We tear down the rubble and build Communism. Then life will begin.'

'The boss is the same age as me,' Murtov said. 'The Steel One is even older. Be careful which rubble you want to tear down.'

'Oh, the miracle of our leaders is that they are men of the future,' AAA said with stars in his eyes. 'They retain their youthful activism. Speaking of whom . . .'

Across the road, the boss emerged. He glanced in both directions. His pince-nez, holes in his head. He was carrying his raincoat over his arm, concealing his Tommy gun. Whatever had gone on in there must have been recreation, Murtov thought. Or not recreation; Beria didn't do recreation as such. But the recreational kind of work. The boss skipped across the road.

Murtov wrapped his used gum in a torn piece of today's *Pravda*. He threw the newspaper under AAA's feet, opened the glove box and carefully placed the wrapped gum beside the navigation set.

As Murtov drove, his eyes monitored the rear-vision mirror. The boss was smiling privately. He hummed Tchaikovsky, always a sign of an uplifted mood. He was not flicking through his work papers or chewing chillis from his jar; whatever he was digesting from the past three hours was filling him up. Murtov had an odd feeling in his stomach, the habitual warmth and sense of safety when things had gone well for Beria mixed with a foreboding implanted by the same.

Murtov slid his eyes right. AAA was gazing out the window, expression unreadable. Him and his *Lavrentiy Pavlovich*.

The boss's humming had no tune, no musicality, nor any self-consciousness of the fact. Only through his willpower was it Tchaikovsky.

As they waited at an intersection, Murtov remembered the boss's anxiety that Natia Meskhi might be white-anting him, presumably using AAA. What then to make of AAA's cockiness? Murtov's conversation with the kid had led him no closer. He was no good at this intrigue business.

When the boss finished humming, AAA turned on the radio. By chance it was the same Tchaikovsky: something from *Swan Lake*.

✿

Evening was falling when they arrived at the boss's next appointment, back in central Batumi. Murtov parked where Beria told him, on the pavement in front of the new extension to the state art gallery. The boss finger-combed his imaginary hair and checked his see-through teeth in the mirror.

'Right, come in with me. I'll need backup.'

Leaving his Tommy gun in the car, Beria climbed the stairs into the building, Murtov in front and AAA behind. A gallery director type with a chocolatey forelock performed the kowtowing. Beria glanced about restlessly, as if looking for someone, and restrained what must have been a niggling urge to grab a handful of the gallery director's flop. The director was the worst combination of smallness and largeness, a servant in an emperor's uniform, who deserved every mouthful of the shit he was eating from Beria's hand. The gallery director's future, Murtov knew, would depend on the boss's mood an hour from now.

The main hall was wall-to-wall women of a certain age: glamorous Bolshevik plutocrats, a couple of Civil War veterans in wheelchairs. Caucasians took pride in their plumage. Good socialist *blat*, brightly coloured.

Murtov took AAA aside to stand in a corner like what they were: goons. He breathed chemical hair products in floral disguises, the new craze for *eau de cologne*; his eyes stung from so much jewellery and white teeth. In Pre times, an event like this would have been a fundraiser for haute bourgeois wives, not even aristocrats, just climbers with money; tonight it was what you would call a Party power dinner, organised by the Georgian Soviet Wives' Movement. In the 1920s, these wives had gone into hiding. But now, in Beria's new Georgia, prosperity was back. Femininity was in fashion; Beria himself had ordered the distribution of European dresses and perfume to replace the sexless, classless, Revolutionary olive-drabness sent down from Russia. Wasn't beauty the first step to universal fulfilment and the end of scarcity?

A laugh tinkled through the room, imitated from actresses in the latest approved motion pictures. The Wives' Movement exhorted young peasant women to become engineers, aviators, soldiers and activists. None of the women in the room were engineers, aviators, soldiers or activists. They were rich housewives with a gift for breaking and entering. They had decked the banquet room with red tablecloths and optimistic slogans, proclaiming victory over the hungry years. *Life has become better, friends, life is more joyous!—J. Stalin.* You had to hand it to the elite; they had a knack for finding themselves on the winning team. Had *they* ever suffered hunger? Murtov couldn't sneer at them. Wasn't he the beneficiary of the same magic trick?

Beria took a glass of Georgian champagne and mingled. Murtov was familiar with the mask: every muscle, every fold of skin on the boss's face was focused on the fascinating information he was receiving from his present interlocutor, while the reptile sensors, visible only to Murtov, were casting their net.

The important people sat for a meal of *ikhvis chakhokhbili*, a duck stew with walnuts, and *khinkali*, dumplings in broth. The tables overflowed with 'deficit goods' to which ordinary Georgians had no access, such as American ketchup. By recent decree from Moscow, the United States and their ketchup were the Soviet Union's new best friends.

There was plenty of vodka, which Moscow was producing in great quantities. The Kremlin had ordered it as a taxation-raising measure to fund an urgent build-up of the Red Army. The vodka wasn't designed to keep the population drunk; as Beria said, drunkenness was just a convenient by-product.

Once the mains were digested, the gallery director played *tamada*, raising his *kantsi* to The Steel One. He even made a toast to the ketchup, translating from an imported advertisement: 'In America a bottle of ketchup stands on every restaurant table and in the pantry of every housewife. Ketchup is the best, sharp, aromatic relish for meat, fish, vegetables and other dishes!' There was no irony, no art, only applause.

The director–*tamada* poured another horn and turned his attention to Beria. 'We salute our leader from a long line of peasant blood who has risen from the people!' He commented on the newly purchased artworks that were 'making Batumi the jewel of

Georgia, and Georgia the jewel of the Soviet Union'. This gelded milquetoast played the role of a Beria trophy, being paraded like Spartacus before Caesar's wife. Everyone else in the room? They were next.

Rubbing his hands, Beria walked to the podium. He seized the microphone and spoke in praise of the Wives' Movement's achievements in 'the realisation of the vision dictated from Moscow'. He did not mention the impending visit—this was not the place or time for an excess of 'Long live Stalins'—but Beria was tumescent with his plans, an Uncle Frost who knows he has a gift to leave under the New Year's Tree.

'I am flattered by our friend's description of me,' Beria said with a nod in the general vicinity of the gallery director, 'as one who has *risen from the people*. But I want you to know that he is incorrect.'

The gallery director's face suddenly merged with the whitewashed wall behind him.

'I,' Beria said, 'have risen *together with* the people.'

Beria's character had numerous faces, but inhabited each with total sincerity, which allowed him to knead frightened souls into the shape of his will. At events like this, when he had a roomful of terror at his feet, he was at his very best.

Murtov cast his eyes over the desert of applauding pelts. He made private speculations about possibilities and threats and checked AAA, who stood at brisk attention.

'Enjoying yourselves?'

Friend Natia Meskhi wore loose serge trousers, beaten-up boots and a Ukrainian shirt not tight enough to reveal either curves or their lack. A dowdy finch among apex parrots.

'Ninety percent of the time,' Murtov said.

Natia allowed a smile. 'How about you, Adam?'

'The other ten,' AAA said.

'I'm sure this one will work out better than his predecessors,' Natia purred to Murtov. 'He might even outlast you.'

'Good luck to him,' Murtov said.

'So—keeping an eye out for the enemy within?'

'The usual,' Murtov said.

'Have you ever wondered'—Meskhi leant close to his ear—'if the enemy could be within *here*?' She gave his chest a light tap. 'Ever wondered if that's where the waverer is really hiding out?'

Murtov moved half a step away. 'Are you a member of the Wives' Movement, friend Meskhi?'

'Not my thing, really.' She gave him a smile in in-depth language. He might evade her for now, but she knew her little poison dart had hit its mark.

Beria's speech was followed by an art auction that raised eye-watering sums for the education of workers' and peasants' children. Since the denizens in the room had moved their snouts from their masters' trough to the state's, they were required to be charitable. Natia observed in a low voice, 'In Pre days, charity used to be a point they were making, to elevate themselves, but now the point is made by the Party.' She noted that the Wives' Movement was distributing fuck-off expensive thankyou charms to each table setting. She wondered how many of these ladies were going to be hanging an artwork purchased with the double-tax-exemption of a Party expense. 'You play this system right, you can actually make money on the deductions. Get the state to pay for all your luxuries.'

'It's the people's money in the end,' Murtov replied.

Natia gave him a pert smile of reassurance. His secrets were safe with her, she was saying, which put Murtov in a lather: *Which secrets? Why her?*

The final auction item—a portrait of Beria himself sitting in the purchaser's own home, to be painted by the famous Charkviani—fetched seventeen times Murtov's annual salary.

'All for a good cause,' Natia said. Murtov clocked that she preferred swapping sly murmurs at the side of the room to the chore of making small talk with VIPs whose innermost secrets she already had on file. 'Exciting changes are afoot, yeah?'

Murtov shrugged.

Natia put her mouth to his ear. 'Great opportunities for Melor and Ana.'

There was something about Natia: she could stir him up in ways he had forgotten he was still prone to. This is 1938, he told himself. It's only fear. It's only terror.

'All this freedom,' Natia said. 'Georgia really is doing well.'

'Thanks to friend Beria,' Murtov said.

'Of course, it hangs by a thread. If something goes wrong with the gala—or even if it goes well and he is promoted to Moscow—for Georgia at any moment it might go *pfff*!' As she mimicked the vanishing of all this prosperity, Natia beamed. 'Nothing is guaranteed, is it? For Georgia, for him—for you or your girls!'

She wished him a good evening and inserted herself into the Wives' Movement. She reminded Murtov of Rikki-Tikki-Tavi, the mongoose who defeated the cobra. Babilina had read him the story by the imperialist Kipling. It was prohibited now, even though it had no frottage or reaming.

Beria's gaze flickered Murtov's way. Murtov replied with a hint of a nod and said to AAA, 'The one in the dark blue suit with the backcombed bob—three o'clock—head of the trustees of the children's hospital. Go stand three metres to her right in a direct line to the exit and clear the way to the car.'

He watched AAA glide shark-like into position. Murtov stepped through the crowd, which was in after-dinner disarray among the circular tables. As Beria stopped to talk to the chair of the trustees of the children's hospital, Murtov closed in.

'Congratulations on your winning bid, Franja,' Beria was saying. 'We've known each other so long and you've never had me to your home. I've heard so much about your granddaughter.'

The trustee, a woman of between sixty and sixty-five years in Murtov's estimate, squinched her eyes in a heavily fortified smile. 'Oh, friend Lavrentiy Pavlovich, we'll do the sitting in my office—my staff will be honoured.'

Murtov's blood began to fizz. He made brief eye contact with Beria, whose nostrils were flaring.

'So you still won't let a peasant boy into the family sanctum,' Beria said, shaking his head. 'Old habits die hard.'

'Not at all,' the trustee said with a wave of her hand, practised in dismissiveness, though the jewellery fluttered with nerves. 'Business and pleasure should be kept separate. I'd rather my home was a refuge from work.'

'Of course,' the boss said with a slight bow. 'Your family's safety must come first.'

'I wasn't talking about my family.'

'I know *you* weren't.'

Now Murtov saw the first twitch in the cheek, the doe isolated from the herd.

'What was that?'

There was a thrilling intimacy to her question. She and Beria had cut straight to the core.

'Your granddaughter is doing very well in our Komsomol trainee program,' Beria said. 'Rosa, isn't it? Fourteen: such a promising age.'

Though the trustee's body was secure in her resplendent cladding, her flesh was dissolving.

'Please,' she whispered.

'I don't know what you're pleading for,' Beria said. 'We're just at a lovely charity event.'

'The Party is Rosa's whole life,' the trustee said. 'And she is just starting out . . .'

'The Party will look after her,' Beria said. 'But there is only so much I can do for her in the formal surroundings of your office, where all eyes are on me.'

Without another word he shouldered past her in AAA's direction. Murtov picked up the tang of her dread. Beria paused at the threshold of the room as the art gallery director stepped in his path to grovel. In a flash, Beria reached out and ripped at the man's floppy hair. Out came a hank of fallen-aristocrat brown. 'Sorry, champ, you needed something to remember me by,' Beria said, watching the hair float to the floor before turning back to the blue-suited woman who was now by Murtov's side.

'Well?' The boss started for the exit.

Murtov did not need to lay a hand on her.

AAA, waiting outside, opened the car for them. To Murtov he mouthed, 'What the fuck?'

Murtov let no expression trespass on his features, nor words escape his lips.

✿

During the ten-minute drive to the seafront apartment block where the head trustee of the children's hospital lived for the summer months, the boss asked AAA to tune the Emka's radio to the station which played some of the late-romantic orchestral music his guest enjoyed. AAA found the station.

'Now that I think of it, I have seen your granddaughter play cello in the Georgian Communist Party's in-house symphony orchestra,' Beria said fondly. He extolled Rosa's musical skills. He chewed a pepper and offered the woman one. When, hand trembling, she reached for his jar, he withdrew it and patted her cheek and said, 'No, Franja, you wouldn't like it; I just wanted to see if you'd say yes.'

Murtov brought the car to a halt outside the apartment block. Beria told him to wait for one hour. He asked AAA to come upstairs.

'No,' the woman gasped, but the boss was already out of the car.

Murtov waited one hour and fifteen minutes according to his wristwatch. He read *Pravda* and rested his eyes, staring out the window at the Batumi harbour scene—fishing boats, ferries, leisure craft—that would present such a splendid view from the top floor.

After the hour and fifteen minutes, AAA and the chair of the trustees came out of the building. Beria was not with them. In the car, Franja clutched the doorhandle but her hand would not hold still and her eyes would not focus. Soon Murtov's concentration on the harbour view was arrested by the sound of stifled sobbing. He kept his eyes averted. The woman deserved the dignity of weeping unseen.

Some time later, Beria bounded out of the building, opened the car door and, with exaggerated courtliness, escorted the chair of the trustees back inside.

'You okay?' Murtov said to AAA.

The younger man's eyes were damp and his nose was blushing. 'What the fuck?' he said. 'What the fucking fuck?'

'Charity jubilees,' Murtov said. 'You'll get used to them.'

AAA looked at him with horror. 'You really don't have a clue, do you? Or you're the best fucking actor in the USSR.'

Before the conversation could proceed, Beria was back in the car. He did not speak, so neither did Murtov or AAA. All the way back to the garage, AAA kept having to make as if he wasn't wiping moisture from his eyes.

IX

BABILINA WAITED FOR MURTOV AT THE STALIN SPORTS PARK IN Batumi. The girls were playing football with other children from the NKVD summer school. It was a grey blustery afternoon and she stood, arms crossed, in the shelter of a toilet block overlooking a vast plain of marked-out fields. Other NKVD mothers stood at a distance, occasionally casting wary glances her way. Nobody else was as close to Beria as her husband; nobody else paid the price.

She watched the girls kick a football with their schoolmates. She took care that Ana and Melor didn't grow too obsessed with one activity. For Ana it was music. For Melor, it had become worshipping Papa Stalin. In the football game, Ana had the grace and skill, the sweet timing, but was disengaged. Melor was all uncoordinated energy, chasing the ball to where it had just been, never seeing where it was going next. Their teams were divided into Reds versus Whites, goodies against baddies. Ana wore white. Melor cried if she was not chosen to wear red.

Babilina recalled Vasil and Lavrushya at the gymnasium back in Sokhumi. Football was all the rage in Tsarist days, then it had disappeared with the world war and in 1917 was banned by Lenin, who also banned chess for being too bourgeois. Games for games' sake, like art for art's sake, were imperialist decadence. Under The Steel One, 'shock brigades' of chess and football coaches had organised five-year plans to re-educate players, and the games had crept back, first in outlying republics like Georgia, then in the centre. Which was surprising, she thought, because The Steel One still hated them and he didn't allow many activities that he hated, or even liked. But with religion severely restricted, the masses needed another opiate. The NKVD funded the Dinamo club and the trade unions funded Spartak, while the other workers' bodies and the military funded their teams. Now, all of a sudden, you had children playing.

Sport could help you forget. Except, all those years ago, you couldn't ever forget Little Lavrushya. His cruel streak was obvious to girls, but boys like Vasil respected his cleverness. On the field, Beria would hack at opponents' legs and nudge the ball with his hand and cheat in every imaginable way . . . and he knew how to get away with it. Where Babilina saw Beria's cheating as a weakness of character, Vasil admired it as a strength. 'Lavrushya gets shit done,' was his version. Beria seemed furtively to admire Vasil's alpha-male athleticism, his ability to leap above the pack and head the ball into the corner of the net or to curve it with his boot around a wall of defenders. When Vasil ran he was a gazelle. Beria, who moved like a beetle, must have been flattered to be Vasil's brother in those times, though he took care to hide it.

When they turned sixteen only the dumb shits were still playing sports. Lavrushya took up debating club and mock trials and student council and theatre. Brain not body. He could see what was coming.

Lavrushya was never much to look at. Girls didn't like this strange boy who chose stubbornly to wear his adoptive family's cast-offs while his mother subsisted in some far-off Abkhazian barn. His father had disappeared. The girls in debating club, smart and strong and dominant, didn't appreciate Lavrushya's move onto their turf. He would have loved to be loved. Vasil tried to steer girls Lavrushya's way, but none was interested, and if they were, Lavrushya didn't fancy the ones who could be pushed towards him. He wanted the unattainable ones, whose status reflected his idea of himself. In debating club, he tried to win them over but his stronger impulse was to punish them. He would explore special, strategic harm, by pressing a little button of insecurity when they least expected it. He did it with a smile, so nobody could quite perceive his cruelty until after it stung them. He would organise the vote for one of them to be school captain or debating captain. But first, they had to fear him.

Then the Revolution came and he was on the winning side, that odd little cult of misfits and psychopaths who followed Lenin. With his Georgian enemies now at his mercy, Lavrushya was too smart to simply destroy them. He built alliances with those who had hurt him and then he put them under his heel. Babilina knew The Steel One's famous and fearsome words: 'To choose one's victims, to prepare one's plans minutely, to slake an implacable vengeance, and then to go to bed . . . There is nothing sweeter in the world.' But Lavrushya left his implacable vengeance unslaked, dangling it over them, a threat he could use and keep on using.

Lavrushya: still that paranoid and alienated teenager; so many years later, still living beneath the stairs and cooking up his vicious, byzantine, sadistic plots of revenge. Babilina often wondered about his marriage. He had found his beauty queen, his Nina, during the heady days of October and then locked her away in Tbilisi. Babilina seldom saw Nina or their children. Babilina shivered; she did not like to speculate on what happened behind Beria's closed doors.

A beggar came through the toilet block, hand out. Babilina gave him a few roubles. The NKVD wives in their long coats ignored him. Babilina watched him drag himself away. Poor beggar. Beria's beggar.

On Babilina's walk to school in Sokhumi when she was a girl, every day there was a beggar on a corner. She sometimes gave him a coin. One day she was joined by Vasil and Little Lavrushya, who ignored her and went on grandly declaring his intention to be an architect, to create cities 'where I know where everyone lives'.

When they came to the beggar, Vasil gave the man a kopek. Lavrushya scoffed. He held a coin in front of the beggar's hand, and the moment the beggar reached for it, Lavrushya pulled it away. When Babilina chastised him for his cruelty, Lavrushya said, 'You know nothing. We, the beggar and I, have an understanding as equals. Tomorrow, I will show you something.'

The next day, Lavrushya took Babilina and Vasil behind a tree where they could watch the beggar. When people ignored the beggar, he ignored them. But when people gave him a coin, the beggar would simper away with his thankyous and then, once they had moved on, spit at them. 'See?' Lavrushya said. 'The beggar hates anyone who gives him money. Giving him a kopek shows only your bourgeois weakness. I have seen him spit at you. But he won't spit at me. By taunting him, showing him the money and then pulling it away, I am showing the beggar that I am wise to his tricks. I know his game, and I am not falling for it. He and I, we respect one another. We shall be equals under socialism.' It was the first time she had heard a schoolmate speak of socialist ideals.

✿

Melor came off the field to ask Babilina if she could bring her friends from the Red team home. Babilina was making an excuse for why she couldn't when Murtov arrived, an hour late.

'Can't I bring them?' Melor pleaded with her mother.

'I'm sorry, darling.'

'Looks like rain,' he said. 'Melor, why don't you go back to the game before it pours?'

Melor looked at Murtov. 'You and Mama want to talk about bad things?'

The rule: no 'talk about bad things' inside the house, no 'talk about bad things' in front of the girls, no 'talk about bad things' where anyone might hear. With a theatrical huff, Melor ran off to rejoin her friends.

'What game is he playing now?' Babilina asked Murtov.

She did not need to elaborate. There was only one *he* in their lives.

Murtov couldn't look at her.

'They're going to miss this group,' Babilina said, her eyes on Ana and Melor and their football pals.

A few paces away, at the edge of the toilet block, two men wearing blue forage caps and long coats had materialised. Babilina waited until they moved away.

'So he's building his great temple,' she said. 'For the Vozhd. Moscow will come in with their entourage and have the big anniversary, they'll reward him with promotion and he's off. What about us then?'

'What about us?'

'For fuck's sake, Vasil.'

The two men in blue forage caps had come back into hearing range. The overcast sky turned to rain and Babilina, a commanding note in her voice, called the girls in.

Murtov had to make some telephone calls from the kitchen. When he had finished, he found Melor and Ana in their rooms performing a spring clean. Babilina was doing the same in the main bedroom, stuffing clothes into charity boxes. A pillow lay over the bedside telephone.

'But we're here for weeks more,' he said.

Babilina said nothing.

'Babi? Why did you say the girls would miss their friends?'

'I've been thinking about Lavrushya and that beggar. You remember?' She spoke without looking at him, continuing her work. 'Old shitbreath is going to throw him a coin. And the moment his back is turned, Lavrushya will spit upon him. I don't want to be there when that happens.'

'You think he'll spit on Stalin?'

'You are walking straight into it and taking the girls and me with you.'

'I know what I'm doing.'

'So you say.'

Babilina, her lips a white line, turned back to her job. She felt him watching her as she folded and stacked the old clothes. He loved to tell her that he admired her supple adaptability between the simplest and most complex tasks. She could parse Pushkin one minute, and the next fold tablecloths like the most experienced babushka.

'Stop standing there and give me a hand, will you?'

Murtov's hands fumbled the clothes like giant mittens.

Babilina stopped folding. 'You always ask me to trust you, but you won't give me the least inkling what you have in mind.'

'You know why.' His eyes were on the ceiling, on the cornices, on the lamps, on the pillow over the telephone.

'I know *why*, but I never know *what*. So I have to make my own plans, and *you* will have to trust *me*. This?' She indicated the packing cases. 'I'm getting ready.'

'You're getting ready,' Murtov echoed.

'Trust me,' she said. '*I* know what *I'm* doing too.'

'You have a plan.'

'My love, we've all got to be ready for the beggar's response.'

TWENTY-FIVE DAYS TO LIVE

X

IT WAS ONLY WHILE DRIVING TO THE BUILDING SITE OF THE People's Temple of the New, where an army of shock workers and former persons was transforming the Ureki beachfront into a residential complex worthy of the boss of bosses and all the other bosses, that Murtov realised he had not yet seen it, nor asked himself whether Beria had a reason for keeping him away.

During the frantic twenty-four/ten preparations for the event that would 'make or break' him, Beria was not sleeping. When he wasn't supervising the building works, he was accepting invitations to schools, Party summer camps, musical performances, charity luncheons and sports days, to officially open events and mingle with the thousands of children at play. For a driver, he used only AAA.

AAA had clearly been rattled by Beria's visit with the chair of the trustees of the children's hospital. Murtov had seen this cycle before. Mistrusting his new drivers, Beria made them witness certain events and so prepared their arrest warrant.

On the last day of May, Murtov had been summoned to drive the boss to Ureki. He waited in the Emka outside the waterfront bolthole where Beria was entertaining the governor of the Georgian People's Reserve Bank, a distinguished economist famed for her conservative stewardship of monetary policy and for the gracious loveliness of her two granddaughters, who were ballerinas.

AAA came out of the building first. For a long time he sat in silence beside Murtov. Finally he raised his damp mauve eyes. 'Is this what happened to your other 2ICs?'

'I don't know what you're talking about,' Murtov said.

'That's interesting,' AAA said with a bitter nod. 'You "don't know", or you literally don't know?'

A part of Murtov wanted to steer AAA to safety. The larger part of him wanted to keep AAA as a buffer. Same as all the other 2ICs.

'We live in a workers' paradise,' AAA said with catechistic determination.

'If you say so,' Murtov said. 'He's coming.'

Beria, who did not look as if his stress had been relieved, ordered Murtov first to the old princes' palace compound on a hilltop in central Batumi.

An advance party of senior officials had arrived from Moscow to inspect the building works. Leading the delegation was friend Sergo Ordzhonikidze, who was staying in the compound. If not the second-most powerful man in the Soviet Union by rank, 'Dear Sergo' had, during the 1920s and early 1930s, been the one member of the inner circle whom Stalin did not regard as a complete and utter drongo. Sergo was also the only other Georgian. A tall, concave, weary man with prinked hair, an earthbound moustache and sagging eyes, Sergo had sponsored Beria's rise in the Caucasus. But after showing an odd reluctance to join the purge of 1937 with the requisite efficiency, Sergo was no longer thought to have The Steel One's ear. Beria's Moscow informants told him that the inner circle was being dominated by a younger, more driven individual, the supreme chief of the NKVD Nikolai Yezhov, who had all the other Politburo members competing to set and meet ever-increasing quotas for arrests, expulsions and deportations. Numbers of counter-revolutionary heads on spikes comprised Moscow's new metrics. Members of the Politburo anticipated what Vozhd would want next, and, instructed by Yezhov, they worked towards it. The Steel One might speak of 'wreckers' in the Ukraine; Yezhov would produce a list of ten thousand Ukrainian enemies of the people; in response, the Commissar for the Ukraine, Nikita Khrushchev, 'worked towards' the leader by presenting Yezhov with a list of twenty thousand, now safely liquidated.

Dear Sergo Ordzhonikidze, no stranger to brutality, did not trust Yezhov and had decided to recuse himself from this newest purge. Beria had continued to play nice to Dear Sergo's face, and sympathised outwardly with his mentor's complaints that The Steel One now 'only spoke the language of brutality'. But in recent months, Beria had sniffed change. Dear Sergo was on the way out. His being packed off to check on Beria's building works might be another sign of his impending irrelevance.

'I've noticed something strange about Dear Sergo,' Beria said to Murtov as they drove into Batumi, commencing this conversation as if after a brief pause. 'He's even more lugubrious than usual. God, he's a downer, I don't know how much longer Moscow will put up with him.'

'I trust he will issue the necessary development approvals,' Murtov said.

'He's looking over his shoulder,' Beria said. 'I did hear a rumour'—he leant over the padded rim of the front seat—'that the dwarf has also come down.'

The dwarf: Yezhov. 'You did say you wanted someone with clout,' Murtov said.

'I haven't seen him at the building site and none of our people saw him get off the plane. Maybe he was packed into a suitcase.'

'Well, that would make friend Ordzhonikidze nervous,' Murtov said.

'Where did you hear the rumour?' AAA asked, his first utterance since the boss had got into the car.

Beria leant back in his seat and stared out the window. It was an indiscreet and stupid question. You never asked the boss where he picked up his gossip.

They did not discuss the dwarf further. Murtov had never met Nikolai Yezhov, a man whose tiny stature was said to be in inverse proportion to his thirst for blood. Yezhov had personally sent to the other world so many thousands that 1937 had been nicknamed Yezhov's Thing (*tr: Yezhovshchina*). The Year, like a Chinese Year of the Rat, belonged to Yezhov as much as 1917 belonged to Lenin, and as much as every other year belonged to Stalin. The stories were so frightful that even Murtov, who regarded such tales as bedtime spine-chillers to scare adults into becoming children, paid attention. Yezhov was said to douse cats with kerosene and set them alight for his entertainment. Until Yezhov, you had to have done something wrong for the security police to knock on your door. Until Yezhov, the men in long coats arrived at your house with hours up their sleeve to verify your identity, to sit and chat, to go through your things, to test you out, to talk about your past, even to share sweets and cigarettes, and they told you not to take too many of your possessions to the cells because you would be released in a few days. But when Yezhov took charge, the night visitors didn't bother checking that they had the right target, never mind whether you'd done anything wrong. They just barged in and snatched you. If they made a mistake and took the wrong person, good—that meant they could come back and take another. You were helping them fill their quota.

'Why doesn't someone tell Stalin??' the people cried, thinking Yezhov had gone rogue. But that didn't seem to help. Yezhov had to keep running and running, killing and killing, until he, like all the executioners, eventually became a victim. As Beria said in one of his lighter moods, 'Only death wins in the end.'

If I was Dear Sergo and the dwarf was shadowing me to Georgia, Murtov thought, I would be shitting myself too.

'Left here,' the boss said at the first checkpoint of the palace district.

'We're not picking up Dear Sergo?'

'What, you reckon I'm insane? If the dwarf is here, the last person I want to be sharing a car with is old friend Ordzhonikidze.'

'I just thought . . .'

'Nah, he's still at Ureki,' Beria said. 'We have a more onerous duty.'

Murtov drove the Emka up the sloping driveway and through a second checkpoint into the courtyard of a residence built for a Tsarist nobleman, surrounded by well-tended gardens, converted into a Party officials' boarding house. Beria's posse—Merkulov, Dumbadze, Kruglov, Goglidze and the Kobulov brothers—lived on the first and second floors. Beria sometimes remarked that if he ever needed to purge his own Politburo, he would only need to poison the one water tank.

Beria entered not the mansion but a small wooden annexe, originally a gateman's lodge. In the people's republic, there was no such thing as gatemen, only armed security detachments on rotating shifts. From this humble lodge, clinging feebly to Beria's arm, emerged its occupant, eighty-one-year-old Ekaterina Geladze, a shrivelled figure known to the boss as 'Keke' and to the people of the USSR as the Mother of the Nation. Clad in traditional Georgian mourning attire, a black smock-style dress and headwear with lace fringe, she gave an irritable farewell to her two companions, shrivelled ravens who raised their hands gravely and evaporated inside to pray for her soul.

Beria eased Keke onto the back seat of the Emka. She groaned in cinematic pain. The boss strapped on her seatbelt. Murtov started the engine and took the northern coastal road to Ureki.

'I haven't been to the peninsula for I am trying to think of how long,' Keke said. 'Oh, look at the sun, what a lovely day. Our glorious tropical Georgia.'

'Look on a map and the Caucasus is the centre of the world,' Murtov said.

'Or a good place to disappear someone,' Beria muttered.

'Isn't this magnificent, so lush and fertile! My Soso is wise to come down here for a rest. He must be exhausted.'

Keke's continual dead-naming of her son sizzled with danger in Murtov's ears. Her body odour filled the car like a gas attack. With a nod, Murtov permitted AAA to crack his window.

Keke eyed Murtov in the rear-vision mirror. 'You grew up in these parts, didn't you, dearie?'

Murtov's neck tensed. He had driven the Mother of the Nation many times but was not privy to how much Beria had told her about his origins. Murtov, who lived in the shadows, had no official personal biography.

'We both rose with the Georgian people, Vasil and I,' Beria said.

'What a fine thing for sons to remain in their childhood places. Soso gets so very homesick!'

Beria slid into his usual surly adolescent funk whenever he had to look after Stalin's mother. *Pravda* lauded The Steel One as a faithful and attentive son who visited Keke on his periodic Georgian holidays. All Georgians knew of the 'radiant love between the Great Mother and the Great Leader'. *Pravda* had informed the public that Keke was 'cordial and lively . . . seems to light up when she talks about their unforgettable reunions. "The whole world rejoices when it looks upon my son and our country," she was quoted as saying. "What would you expect me, his mother, to feel?"' The truth, which got right up Beria's nose, was that the 'Georgian holiday' was a fiction and Stalin had not seen Keke since the 1920s. When he visited the Black Sea at Sochi for his annual summer rests, securely across the border in Russia, Stalin issued strict orders that his mother not be told he was anywhere near Georgia.

Their progress to Ureki was soon halted by a traffic jam.

'Look at that: how lovely to see children out,' Keke said.

The Mother of the Nation narrated each moment as if the valve between her eyes and mouth had broken down with age, and what entered her head as visual input needed immediate exit as verbal output. Murtov pitied her. She took irrepressible pride in her son, could not shut up about how wonderful he was, how successful, how loving, how perfect in every way. It pained

Murtov to hear the poor old thing talk like this about a son who so neglected her, until he realised that her admiration and Soso's neglect were bound together. A less perfect son would not be in such high demand. Indeed, it was an *honour* for Keke to never see him. Soso was a once-in-a-generation hero and it was Keke's privilege to sacrifice her needs to those of millions, to the radiant future her son was wearing himself out building.

'Mmm,' Beria said at intervals.

Murtov often wondered how much Beria could swallow of this maternal gush. It was Beria, farmed out as a child by his own mother, who bought Keke her name day presents and made sure she was taken to church; Beria who had her attended by the best medical staff; Beria who housed her, under his budget, in the meagre lodgings she chose for her martyrdom. Beria it was who translated the letters the Kremlin sent her, written in Russian, always ending with, 'Mother, may you live ten thousand years.' Beria brought the well-wishers, with their flowers and fruit, who wanted to thank her for giving the world the great Stalin. It was Beria who sat with her and suffered the shrine to the absent Soso that Keke's dingy room had become, photographs and memorabilia decking every wall like the sanctum of an unhealthily obsessed fan. If the Stalin cult of personality had its ground zero, it lay in that gateman's lodge where a mother worshipped the son who was too important to see her.

And Beria, whose mother had sold her house to pay a family to take him, played the role of son.

Keke narrated on the traffic, the government shops and their signage, the weather, the interior features of the Emka and whatever else swam through her vision. Beria was genuinely indifferent to her, reading his papers and occasionally concurring. He really was like a son.

'Look at that,' Keke said. 'Those poor men, they look so hungry.'

The traffic had stopped against the flow of a convoy of prison workers from Ureki. Construction on the people's temple was running so tight that more gulag inmates had been shipped in. The regime to which Keke had, literally, given birth was not one to express sympathy for those dirty, gaunt, grizzled faces gazing defeatedly out of military trucks. Murtov wondered how many had been hunters, idlers, sportsmen, equestrians, heads of ancient family lines; he wondered if they were defenders of their privileges, the worst of the old order, or just ordinary folk caught in the wrong place, wrong side, wrong time. Who whom? Too late to ask. Their prison uniforms stripped them of individual distinction. They had been allocated their spoilt biographies. Their working lives had started, as Beria liked to say, better late than never. It struck Murtov as a fresh surprise how, after twenty years of the Soviet security organs, and now Yezhov's Thing, there could be any old capitalists left. His father seemed to be the last preserved for display, a (just) living, (just) breathing testament to Revolutionary clemency.

'Look how frail they are,' Keke said. 'Almost cripples.' Then she paused. 'Like my poor Soso, with his withered little arm.'

Murtov was glad that the wraiths in the trucks could not see through the Emka's one-way glass—not because of what they might think of Keke and Beria in the back seat but because of what they might make of him in the front. Vasil Anastasvili Murtov, the only son of wealth attending the people's temple without chains on his ankles.

'You remember that time at the beach, how weak he was?' Keke said.

Beria, scowling into his leather folder, did not respond. She was referring to an incident she had not witnessed; in fact, she was repeating a fable Beria had told her.

She tapped Murtov on the shoulder. 'Beria's son went into the waves at Batumi. Soso, who cannot swim, was so frantic with worry that he stood there crying for the boy to come back. Once the boy was on dry land, Soso scolded you, as his father.' She turned to Beria. 'Didn't he? He was so worried, he really couldn't believe a boy could swim. Just because *he* can't.'

'He's Stalin, he could swim across the Black Sea if he wanted,' Murtov said.

'Yes, he probably just doesn't want to,' Beria said.

Keke began to complain of how tired she had been feeling, and why did she have to be dragged out here when Soso had not yet arrived? Still, she was looking forward to 'catching up' with 'Dear little Sergo Ordzhonikidze' after so long.

Murtov showed his credentials at the Ureki checkpoints. A series of banners materialised along the roadside, portraying the boss of bosses in authoritative poses. The Lenin cult had been largely eschewed in the 1920s, the early years of Stalin's ascent to power. But things had changed in the 1930s, Lenin's image reappearing universally with The Steel One at his side. Here in Stalin's homeland, Beria was pushing it hard, leaving Lenin out altogether. Murtov worried. Would Stalin want to be so exposed? Didn't he prefer to be at Lenin's shoulder? Lenin was a handy human shield, never more so than long after his death. You never knew when Moscow's mind had changed and what was yesterday encouraged, even enforced, was today a capital crime.

The sight of so many versions of her offspring, multiplied and larger than life, plunged Keke into reminiscence. 'Isn't he beautiful? Do you know,' she said to Murtov, 'when he was born, his father's first words were, "It's a girl!" And then he fell over, passed out cold. I thought it was the sight of blood, but no, he had been over-celebrating.'

'What will the Vozhd think of the banners?' Beria said.

But Keke could not be diverted. She spun a chain of interlinked tales about Soso in his infancy: the time Soso got lost in a market, the time Soso was bashed by a classmate in church school, Soso's heroic surmounting of his mediocre early intellectual development. None of what she was saying could be repeated in public, but the Mother of the Nation enjoyed impunity inside the car. Murtov sensed her sly relish at how much she was infuriating Beria.

'I'll be honoured to give a speech at Soso's gala dinner,' she said. She tapped her head. 'I have been making notes.'

Beria chewed so hard on a chilli that his back teeth clicked. Murtov noticed patches of sweat at his collar and armpits.

'Are you worried about what I would say? I think I'll correct the record about my pregnancy.' With Beria plunging deep into his notes, Keke addressed Murtov: 'As you probably know, Soso's father was a violent man whose first love was vodka. He never overcame the torments of his upbringing. We were poor and downtrodden. We lost our first two children.' She crossed herself and wiped her eye; it was as dry as a stone. 'When I fell pregnant a third time, my husband was adamant that we could not afford a child and it would be doomed to a life of adversity, just as he had been. He was a traditional husband, accustomed to his word being law. If he had no authority anywhere else, he could assert it at home. He said we would be doing the child a favour if we terminated the pregnancy.

'This came as a shock to me, as our religion forbade abortion. Things weren't as they are now . . .' She paused for Murtov to acknowledge the fact that abortion was not only legal under Bolshevism but free of charge. 'It was against the law and against his beliefs, and yet he urged me to terminate. Now listen, this is the story I want to tell the world.'

Keke leant forward, giving Murtov an eye-watering waft of underarm.

'Soso has recounted this as an episode of his tenacity, even before his birth! I stood up to my husband and refused to end my unborn child's life. My opportunities for independent action were few and far between, and this was the time I said "No!" to that man. I said, "I am going to bear and raise this child and you are going to be a father whether you like it or not!" Ironic, yes? That Soso should be a survivor of a homicide attempt? Like our Father in heaven, I've always said. As He survived Herod, Soso survived his own father.' Again she crossed herself, Orthodox-fashion. 'Well, that is not quite how it played out, I am here to tell you. The truth was that his father did want a child but *I* was the one who wanted the abortion. I thought my child, if he survived infancy, would be cursed by that man's blood. I wanted to defy his hopes for a family line. Ha!' Without waiting for interruption, she continued: 'In defiance of his wishes I set off for the woman in our village who did such things. Being illegal, this took some organising and all the kopeks I could scrape together. But I was determined to leave that man and commence a life of hope and peril as a free woman.

'The first step in my liberation would be the medical procedure I was on my way towards when I was knocked down by a horse cart. I was out cold. I did make it to a doctor, but not the one I had planned. I spent two weeks recovering from a broken arm, a concussion and lacerations. My husband only visited me once, and he was drunk and furious at me for endangering our unborn baby. Needless to say, he never found out where I'd been going. As I convalesced, I had time to think. My emotions were in turmoil. I suffered such extraordinary pangs of guilt, the Lord led me to a reversal. How could I have thought of killing my unborn son? The Lord had sent that horse cart as a sign: even in my womb, Soso was determined to live, no matter what his mother and the people of the town and their horses threw at him. I was powerless to resist. I rose from my bed as determined as before, only now to bear and raise him. Plus, I'd done my dough. The abortion woman wasn't offering a refund. And as it turned out, my husband passed away from drink not long after Soso was born, and from then on it was just my boy and me against the world . . . Oh my lord, what has she done with her *hair*?'

They were at the final checkpoint, where Natia Meskhi was standing at attention. Many women cropped their hair short when Moscow was coming to town. It wasn't the Vozhd they had to fear, but his son Vasili, the hangers-on and extended family members, the battalion of entitled young Muscovites on the prowl. Plus, if the rumour was correct, the dwarf was lurking. You did not want to be a woman of the remotest attractiveness when the dwarf came.

Bottle-green-uniformed Moscow NKVD men were running mirrors under the car and inspecting the boot, which Murtov opened. He and AAA presented their identity cards, a procedure from which the boss and Keke were excused. The Mother of the

Nation clutched Beria's arm and expressed her astonished admiration for a ten-metre-high banner showing her son with a faraway gaze, as if overseeing an infinite military parade.

'Fucksake!' Beria hissed from the side of his mouth, unable to swat away her hand in front of all these Moscow personnel. 'I've brought you out for the day, can't you give me one moment's peace?'

'Now, now, no need to be like that.' Keke smiled. 'We're all friends.' Far from offended, she glowed with triumph.

'You know you're not indispensable,' Beria said.

'I am the Mother of the Nation!'

'Don't assume I can't appoint a replacement.'

AAA didn't know where to look. He gave Murtov a concerned glance.

'Oh, I do love when you quote my Soso,' she said, giving Beria a pat on the hand.

Don't assume I can't appoint a replacement was one of the leader's famous quotes, uttered to Lenin's widow, Nadezhda Krupskaya, whenever she was annoying him. 'I am Lenin's widow!' Krupskaya had declared. The Steel One had shot back: 'Don't assume I can't appoint a replacement.'

The story was horseshit, of course. Beria himself had invented it for the official history he had published about the rise of the Georgian Bolshevik Party. Keke knew it was Beria's invention too.

Murtov piloted the car at walking pace along the unpaved seafront track he had spent much of his childhood playing on. He smelt the resin of the pines, the salt of the Black Sea, the metal of the black sand. The summer clouds hung low and pregnant with rain. He saw the scale of the blasting that had taken place under the boss's supervision. The temple for Keke's son and his entourage would sprawl across five estates, a series of interlinked pavilions and villas growing to a point of climax at the last block, where a monument to stonemasonry, wearing a necklace of floodlights, uplights and downlights, a brand-new structure of unprecedented grandeur and size, would mushroom on the very site of the beloved unlocked dacha in which Murtov had spent his summers and Beria, more recently, his weekend retreats.

'Goodness,' Keke said, so taken aback by the size of it that she let her daffy-old-grandma mask drop. 'You lot won't stop until you've outdone the Tsars, will you?'

Murtov followed the guards' directions to a crudely paved turning circle. Beria took Keke's arm and they emerged from the car to beam for official photographs against a background of banners bearing The Steel One's image. Beria smiled warmly at Keke, who assumed the posture of Mother of the Nation.

After parking the car, Murtov walked towards the site of the people's temple. Edging down the lawn, digging the sides of his leather-soled boots into the slope so he would not fall, clad in a military tunic—he was famous as the only member of the Politburo, outside Stalin himself, permitted to wear this as his everyday uniform—came Sergo Ordzhonikidze, third in line to the leadership of the USSR.

Beria was right. His mentor, with slumped shoulders and limp moustache, looked as though the life had been rattled out of him.

When Dear Sergo saw Keke Geladze, whom he had known since boyhood, his tired eyes melted and he opened his arms. Beria went to the photographer to make sure the angles were right. Sergo and Keke stood side by side, not touching, Sergo looking like a Georgian bishop and Keke a parishioner, their faces solemn for the image that would be carried back to Moscow as evidence that the people's temple was being approved according to the standards The Steel One would expect.

While this was taking place, Beria followed Murtov's eye up the grass dune to the ghost of the home where they had shared their happiest memories.

'I didn't tell you?' Beria said.

XI

WHILE WAITING FOR THE OFFICIAL PROCEEDINGS TO FINISH, Murtov returned to the Emka, which was parked in an open patch of dirt where, during his childhood, had stood a little shop and, on feast days, a fair with donkey rides, an Armenian freak show and a mule-drawn merry-go-round. The NKVD men patrolling the car park were wearing the colours and badge of the Moscow secret police, not the Georgian division. While Murtov pondered what this meant, he was accosted by Natia Meskhi.

'Like the do,' he said, nodding at her newly shaved head.

'I can get you sentenced without right of correspondence for commenting on my personal appearance.'

Like a turtle, Murtov retracted his neck into his collar. 'We used to call it paying a compliment.'

'You used to do a lot of things.'

'I was flattering you.'

'Flattery will get you wherever I say.' Natia ushered him to another black Emka. 'Mystery tour.'

The car left the compound and pulled onto the Batumi road. Murtov told himself not to panic. The question was not whether he was being kidnapped, which was a routine occurrence in the workers' and peasants' paradise. The question was for how long, for what purpose, and would it hurt. Did Beria know? Was Beria behind it? Murtov hoped so. He took heart from the fact that the spring harvests had been and gone. From reading the *Cheka Weekly* he had deduced that kidnappings peaked each spring as a distraction from poor grain results. You really had to watch yourself at harvest time.

'Can I ask where we're going?' he said as the Emka turned in the direction of Kutaisi.

Natia let a smile hover on her lips. 'Yes,' she said.

'. . . And?'

'Yes, you may ask.'

Trouble, trouble, everywhere.

'I am getting the idea that the First Secretary doesn't know about this,' Murtov said.

'Poor man; it freaks you out if Lavrentiy Pavlovich isn't privy to your latest bowel movement. Don't worry, he has AAA to drive him back. He really doesn't need you.'

'I'd like to contact my spouse if I'm going to be late home.'

'The destruction of a holiday dacha that was so important to you,' Natia continued. 'So much history, blown up just like that. I can't imagine how it must feel. Of course, I don't want to imagine it, because that would be to put myself inside the head of a bourgeois reactionary whose family prosperity was based on capitalist-imperialist theft from the people. But I'll allow that it was a long time ago, and it's your boyhood, and you must be prey to sentiments that sit in your heart, outside the reach of the struggle.'

'That's one way of putting it.' Murtov wasn't taking the bait. 'That house held just as many memories for the boss.'

'He was the one who ordered its demolition.'

'Which is proof of his devotion to the struggle.'

Natia rolled her eyes. 'Yeah, yeah, and I suppose you think you've been put on other duties for the last couple of weeks so that you wouldn't see what he was doing?'

'I hadn't thought about that.'

'Well, once you do think about it, I can tell you it's bullshit. He wasn't protecting you. He really does not give a fuck how you feel. But yes, you're right, if he can send a signal to Moscow that he is willing to destroy all that is dearest to him to make the General Secretary's stay in Georgia just that little bit more comfortable, then that signal will be duly noted.' She looked him in the face. 'But don't forget, he doesn't give a fuck about *you*.'

'Where are we going?'

'You have no need to worry,' Natia said. 'It'll be totally fine, and Babilina won't be fretting. We've told her you won't be home.'

She waited for Murtov to respond, but when he remained silent she said, 'You know, when I first met Beria I thought he was the embodiment of evil. I really mean that. In my sheltered existence as a Pioneer and in the Komsomol, I'd never come across anyone who made me think, ah, so that's what human evil looks like. I found him irresistible, to be honest, because his attention was addictive. He would creep up behind me at my typewriter, and first thing I knew his hands were on my shoulders giving me a massage. At other times he would take me into his office and show off his collection of coins, his fountain pens, his watches, his first editions of rare books. I felt privileged. If he was breaking socialist rules, this only enhanced his charisma. He *made* the rules! He had a limitless capacity to make a young person feel special. But what he gave, he took away. One minute he was buying you gifts or showing you his sanctum, and the next you would say hello in the corridor and he would freeze you out as if you didn't exist. He didn't realise that young staff like me took everything he said to heart, we remembered it forever, whereas for him it was like throwing chaff to pigeons in the park.'

'That's not evil,' Murtov said.

'At one of my first executive conferences I told him I had been offered a promotion to the Party secretariat in Baku by the commissar for Azerbaijan, friend Bagirov. Now, I knew that friend Bagirov and friend Beria went back a long way, they'd been close since the Revolution, so I had nothing to fear. Or so I thought. But Beria was incensed. He said, "I know all about your arrangement with Bagirov. If you go to Baku, you will never come back here and I will destroy everything that is precious to you starting with your family." I burst into tears. He sat back, chuckling away, and his toadies were laughing with him. I was so upset, not because he was such a prick but because he was a Bolshevik and Bolsheviks were meant to be better than this.'

'You reckon that's evil,' Murtov said.

'Well, no. That was just misogynistic and manipulative. He had his pets, and the rest were slaughtered. I'd been dropped from the club. Later that day, at a meeting, there was no space for me. I said to Ketevan, "What's happened to my space—isn't the seating meant to be in alphabetical order, you know, B for Beria, D for Dumbadze, G for Goglidze, through to Merkulov and Meskhi?" She said, "The alphabet's been changed." I said,

"Permanently?" She said, "The only permanence in the Georgian alphabet is that B comes first." In the office, everyone avoided me like I had the plague. You know who was the first person to say a kind word to me?'

'I can guess.'

'Right. I had had forty-eight hours to consider the only important questions remaining to me—whether I will slit my wrists, shoot myself or take pills—and then I get an invitation. He gives me the legendary one-on-one long lunch, the top-shelf wine and vodka and food and service and then the two of us are talking all day and into the night. It's like a seduction without the fucking. Not once did I have the guts to ask him what was going on, why he'd torn me down and was now doing *this*, and to this day he's never explained. It seems he just had a passing fancy to shred me, expose my weaknesses, remind me who was in charge, before restoring my privileges. He was toying with me because he got his jollies from it. And this was the final step of my initiation.'

'You have a low threshold for what you think of as evil,' Murtov said.

'I haven't got to the evil yet. Once I was established in the executive committee, I saw him doing it to others. You know his eye for detail, his work ethic. Whether it's major strategic questions or deciding between a rubber or synthetic O-ring in the plumbing in the staff kitchen, he's across it. He can commit any outrage against ideology—and he's worse than a fucking Tsarist, you know—yet he gets away with it because he's so fucking competent. You know that most of the people up the top can't even tie their shoelaces. Their only qualification is their obedience and willingness to do literally anything to save their necks. The Revolution merely replaced corrupt Tsarist *charkas* with corrupt Bolshevik *charkas*. The machine only keeps running thanks to the tireless competence of a few individuals. Like friend Beria.'

Murtov digested her indiscretion: how could she speak so seditiously? Who was protecting her? Then he figured it out. *Charka* was a Russian term of abuse for Georgian hillbillies.

'So you're not Georgian, you're Russian,' he said. 'I knew there was something not quite right about you.'

'You hen! You son of an ass!' Natia laughed and continued in her perfect unaccented Georgian: 'Trained by the NKVD in Moscow. But I've come to love your Georgia. It's the General Secretary's home ground, so you have to understand Georgia if you want to understand the Party. But it's also a vulnerable point. Too many people here knew him when he was a young Revolutionary. And too many people know that he made some questionable choices.'

Murtov stiffened. It was reckless, even if Natia was travelling under some protective Moscow armour, to traverse this ground. To mention that The Steel One might have taken the other side during those confusing years when a new month brought a new Revolution was a taboo punishable by . . . by what, Murtov didn't dare guess. He knew, and Beria knew, enough about Stalin's 'questionable choices', not least because good old Keke talked about them so freely. Fortunately nobody paid any attention to Keke. In the rest of the Soviet Union, you risked being sentenced without right of correspondence if you so much as dreamt of Stalin's pre-1917 past unless it was word-for-word from the official history. You did not so much as whisper his dead nicknames, Koba or Soso. But here in Georgia—a country so proud of its outlaw heritage that there were still streets named Housebreakers'

Way, Larcenists' Lane, Pickpockets' Road and Solicitors' Street—the old bandits delighted in stories about their man Koba. So close to 'Cobra'! What a legend he was! If you looked closely in some Georgian alleys and taverns, the posters with the slogan *Life has become better, friends, life is more joyous!—J. Stalin* had been faintly defaced so that they read *Life has become better, friends, life is more joyous! for Stalin.* The NKVD could not track down and eliminate every local who remembered the former Georgian. Impossible. So Stalin's zombie past, which would not die, had to be controlled.

'The General Secretary knows he has a ticking time bomb in the Caucasus, so he needs a local boss who can keep it in check,' Natia continued. 'That's why Beria is tolerated. The Vozhd can trust him—or no, he can't trust him, but he *has to* trust him, principally because Beria has stains on his own record. He made his own questionable choices. The Vozhd thinks this balances things out and Beria can hold the home territory for him. Because Beria's here in Georgia, he is close to the Vozhd's weak spot, which gives him awesome power and also puts him in constant peril.'

'Still, not exactly evil,' Murtov said.

Natia gave him a narrow-eyed smile, as if assessing him for the first time. 'You have a unique connection with him, Vasil. You don't see the full person. He's the prince and you are his fool.'

'Flattery will get you as far as it got me,' Murtov replied with a grimace, pulling at his collar to let some air in. 'What am I needed for?'

'You'll see,' Natia said with a final smile and a curiously girlish brush of her fingers along his forearm.

The transit was conducted, like Murtov's most recent trip to see his father, as if they were being followed. Thirty minutes out of

Ureki, Murtov and Meskhi transferred to a second black car. After an overly complicated inland drive, the second car dropped them at a third, which delivered them to a street in Kutaisi from which they walked two blocks. As they arrived at the same greenish grey six-storey block where Murtov occasionally brought the boss, he realised that Natia Meskhi hadn't finished her story, hadn't got to the real evil.

XII

A HAND AT A THIRD-FLOOR WINDOW DROPPED A KEY. MESKHI unlocked the building and spoke a code to an NKVD guard to enter the elevator, which climbed to a spacious reception room. A bank of telephones sat on a desk. Three filing cabinets stood against nicotine-stained timber panelling. Covering the floor was a Georgian carpet. The gas wall lamps were moulded in the shape of thrusting Communist workers. Murtov smelt burning copper wire. In his head was the NKVD's unofficial motto: *Give me a man and I shall make you a case.*

'One warning,' said Natia, who retained her teasing humour. 'We tell people before they meet friend Yezhov: he has a very, very big head.'

It was always this way, he thought: they kept you guessing and finally let it drop casually, like you were meant to know. He was here to meet the USSR's chief of internal security.

'You need an ego to get to the top,' Murtov said.

Natia lowered her eyes into a private smile. 'I mean his actual head. Sometimes people get hypnotised by the size. So don't freak out.'

Murtov was pondering just how big it could be when a voice called 'Enter!' from behind the oak door adjacent to the reception desk. Murtov and Natia went into a room much the same as the first: same style of carpet, same iconic gas lamps, same size desk, same smell of burning wire. Natia closed the door behind them.

'Here,' said the voice from under the desk.

Murtov saw the crown of a blue NKVD forage cap move along the desk blotter. It swayed and bobbed like a puppet. Natia giggled through her nose.

'Surprise!'

The manifestation that jumped out was pleased with its joke. Friend Yezhov, showing a set of large yellow teeth, shuffled around the desk, not hiding his famous limp or his famous gammy left leg; Yezhov was famous, too, for dancing the *golpak* on that leg in front of full ballrooms. His flaunting of his gimpiness was a shining example of Soviet grit. He offered Murtov his hand, which felt like a fish fillet, almost glutinous, and ushered his guests to a leather sofa. He took a padded settee, angling forward eagerly with his boneless hands clasped in his lap.

'Half the time when I pull that stunt, they shit themselves because they're scared of laughing!'

The chief of the organs, the poisoning dwarf, was the smallest adult Murtov had ever laid eyes on. Beria had described him as 'four feet of unexploded dynamite'. Murtov felt a burn of pity for the little boy of eight or nine when he realised he had hit his peak.

Yezhov's head wasn't that big. Murtov would say it was a normal adult-sized head. But it did look full of itself, beaming with great cheer and self-assurance on that toy-like frame. 'Yezhovye' meant 'hedgehog' in Russian, and since the beginning of the Terror the country was said to be caught in the hedgehog's gauntlets. Murtov found him more like a large-eyed, swollen-headed bat.

Murtov's eye accidentally met Yezhov's, but both slid away like partners in a complicated folk dance. There were two types of Soviet officials: The Steel One, who believed that if you did not look him in the eye you were plotting against him; and all the others, who could not maintain eye contact for fear of discovering that you *were* plotting against them. Conspiracy, the Soviet Union's national sport, could get you all the way to the Moscow Politburo, Beria liked to say, but once there you had to stop plotting or else that was it, you were done.

'Yes, gawk away at the dwarf, Vasil Anastasvili,' Yezhov said, grinning to light up the room, outshining the gas lamps and a long-necked desk light that cast him in partial silhouette. 'Don't think I take offence. But don't think I don't, either! I much prefer if you gawked at a *person of small stature*. How are you anyway? Something to wet your whistle?'

Yezhov made no move to the open drinks cabinet behind his desk.

'Thank you, friend Nikolai Ivanovich,' Murtov said. 'I don't partake.'

Yezhov slapped his knee. 'Call yourself a Georgian? I thought you *charkas* were the champion drunks of our workers' paradise!'

'Alcohol never liked me,' Murtov said.

'Couldn't say the same about your boss, eh?' Yezhov said. 'Why, I've seen friend Beria in action in Moscow. You know, the old man loves to get his people pissed as newts. It's his nightly entertainment.

He distrusts teetotallers as much as Caesar distrusted thin men. You should see what he does to Molotov. But your Beria's capacity is astounding. The old man has poured grog down his throat to see how long he can hold out, and he's never broken him. Sometimes I think it's a Beria superpower: he can still backstab on five gallons of Polish vodka. But I've noticed he prefers your pissy Georgian wine. Must be a *charka* thing.'

Murtov bowed his head, as if sharing Yezhov's admiration of Beria's superpower.

'You Georgians have much to be proud of,' Yezhov went on. 'You haven't just given the world the greatest hero of all time. Friend Meskhi tells me Kutaisi, which I thought was a complete shithole, was the home of Jason and the Argonauts and the Golden Fleece. Sheep's fleeces being used to sieve grains of gold from the rivers! No wonder you all think you've been kissed on the dick by a rainbow! Oh, and'—Yezhov sat back, crossed his little legs and laced his hands casually at the back of his head, armpitting Murtov—'my condolences on the beach dacha. I understand it had great sentimental value for you.'

'It is the Georgian workers' house.'

'And peasants,' Yezhov said, wagging a finger. 'Don't forget, workers *and peasants*.'

Murtov hoped that the agony of polite conversation was over. This little man was the 'directing organ' himself. He stood by The Steel Pen as it hovered over the lists to pass sentences without right of correspondence, whispering into The Steel Ear who should live and who should die. Yezhov breathed The Steel One's very air. Last year, during the height of Yezhov's Thing, Stalin made a speech proclaiming him 'a flame burning the serpents' nests' and 'a bullet for all scorpions'.

'Now, business,' Yezhov said. 'We are conducting what you might call a fact-checking exercise. In preparation for the General Secretary's visit, we must be scrupulous about the accuracy of all relevant information. I'm a bit of a stickler for facts myself, wouldn't you say, friend Meskhi?'

Natia tittered. Murtov had never heard such a girlish sound from her.

'So what we're doing,' Yezhov continued, 'is cross-checking our collated biographies of the General Secretary's *charka* hosts against eyewitness reports. And if friend Beria has had one constant eyewitness, who has seen everything worth seeing, that witness, my dear Vasil Anastasvili, is you.'

'Not everything,' Murtov said, his throat dry.

'Not everything! Love it! Don't you, friend Meskhi?' Yezhov clapped his child's hands, tawny-coloured with thick black hairs between the knuckles. These were the hands that kept the NKVD's most precious collection: the bullets recovered from the brains of the leader's personal enemies and engraved with their names. A Zinoviev bullet, a Kamenev bullet, a Bukharin bullet, one day perhaps a Trotsky bullet. The newest was the Yagoda bullet—Yezhov's own predecessor, shot this summer. Soon, Beria had forecast, there would be a Yezhov bullet. Who then would own the collection?

'Friend Murtov, please don't be afraid. Our intentions are entirely benign. We are Party members, we are equally loyal to the Vozhd, this is just a process. The eternal Soviet labour of filling out forms for archives where they will never see the light of day. A process, yeah?'

Murtov nodded, his neck cramping. The first and final rule of facing an interrogation during Yezhov's Thing was to accept everything, oppose nothing, and cross your fucking fingers. Sometimes all they wanted was some roubles for your compulsory national bond, your loan to what Babilina called the 'shakedown state'. Murtov wondered if his salary deductions had been made.

And then there was the Georgian method of taking interrogations: make as if you are insane, denounce people who are already dead.

'First . . .' Yezhov leant nearer, as if to bring his head so close to Murtov that he could cancel their disparity and reduce them to a pair of skulls. Murtov smelt Yezhov's breath, the same burning copper wire scent that wafted through the office. 'The home at Ureki,' Yezhov said. 'I'm very interested in the history—before it's lost forever, yeah? I understand that our mutual friend moved in there with your family at the age of, what, twelve?'

'That's not right,' Murtov croaked, uncertain of everything about this conversation except that it would not end well.

Yezhov seemed pleased. 'Friend Meskhi, this is why I told you we need fact-checking! Now, Vasil Anastasvili, set me straight.'

'He moved in with us at our main home in Sokhumi. Ureki was the second home. And he was nine.'

'Goodness, a big house in town *and* a holiday dacha—what a blessed childhood.'

'Lavrentiy Pavlovich was born a peasant in Merkheuli, which I'm sure you know,' Murtov said. 'His father had joined the 1905 revolution and shot dead a Tsarist policeman. Lavrentiy Pavlovich's mother, who became a widow . . .'

'No need for chapter and verse,' Yezhov cut in. 'I just want your own family's involvement.'

'Lavrentiy Pavlovich was a gifted child but his family had nothing,' Murtov recited quickly. 'My father Anastas Karvelashvili was on the school council. He became aware of the Beria family's brilliant but penniless son and offered him everything he could ever need.'

'Very generous,' Yezhov agreed. 'But—with respect—get fucked.'

Murtov swallowed. He needed a drink.

'You know as well as I that Beria's family weren't 'penniless'. They had a farmhouse and a few acres, which they were forced to sell so that Little Lavrushya could move in with your family and attend your gymnasium school. Anastas bankrupted Beria's family, burning all of the kid's bridges so he had nowhere to go back to.'

'I don't know if that's right. Why would my father do that?'

'Because he's bourgeois Menshevik scum! No offence. And how's the old boy hanging? So to speak.'

'Fine,' Murtov said tightly. A mental image came to him of his father under house arrest, curled up, winded, the buttons of his trousers scattered on the kitchen floor.

'Whether you knew about the price your father extracted is not my concern. I mean, what else might he have demanded from Beria's mother? She was a single woman!'

'No, I . . .'

'Just joking, but who knows? Interesting to speculate, yeah? I could cook up theories all day. Anyway. Friend Lavrentiy Pavlovich moved in. I presume he was offered the full status of a family member?'

'All the privileges of a son of the house,' Murtov said.

'But he had to sleep in an alcove under the stairs, yeah? Not even a bedroom. And your father made him work like a house servant.'

'Lavrushya was offered a bedroom next to mine but he refused it. He preferred the alcove. My father begged him to move upstairs, but Lavrushya—friend Beria—had a . . . particular determination . . .'

'We're all aware of his *particular determination*,' Yezhov insinuated.

Murtov burrowed on, hoping to get to the end and out. 'When he graduated from the gymnasium, he wished to study architecture. He dreamt of creating cities that would elevate the human soul. He spent his evenings drawing elaborate plans for apartments with shared dormitories and bathrooms with separate alcoves for marital liaisons. Architecture as social engineering. He thought through every last detail. But my father was sending me to Baku Technicum to study oil industry engineering and he wanted both of us boys to enjoy the same advantages.'

Yezhov raised an eyebrow. 'It was your father's decision?'

'Lavrushya had an . . . unusual relationship with my father.'

'With you too.'

'That's a matter of perspective,' Murtov said.

Yezhov's smirk was circus-clown grotesque. 'We'll get to your *perspective* in a sec. But just going back. Our information is that when Beria refused to go to Baku, your father went back to Beria's mother. Made her beg him to go.'

'My father was in his thrall. He would grant him anything.'

'Except his dearest wish to be an architect.'

'Cities in the sky were a boyhood dream, not a serious ambition for a young working man.'

'Anyway. He has been able to fulfil that dream as the leader of the Georgian Soviet Socialist Republic, has he not? That must give him the greatest satisfaction, knocking down all those tired old towns, putting up socialist paradises.'

'Of course, friend,' Murtov said.

'I wanted to be an architect too, only I never had the opportunities.'

Murtov lowered his head in mute sympathy.

'You'll wish I was an architect. Ha! But anyway, moving on. Let's go back to how he really was as a boy,' Yezhov said. 'That's what I'm interested in. You *charka* mobsters are so big on clan loyalty, it's a neurosis. There's one Georgian I know who retains the most supreme incompetents out of nothing more than familiarity. Clan loyalty is a wonderful trait but it has its downsides. Who was our *Lavrushya* loyal to?'

Murtov shook his head. 'He was a loner. He had a nickname in school: the Detective. Whenever items were lost and a reward was offered for their return, Lavrushya had a knack for finding them.'

'The Detective,' Yezhov repeated, nodding. 'That's good; I haven't heard that.'

'But he never accepted the reward. He just found the item, returned it to the owner, and melted away. He was accused of stealing the items in the first place and planting them so that he could be the finder, but he shied away from any kind of thanks or approval.'

'Perhaps being known as the Detective was reward enough,' mused the chief of the secret police.

'It was clear that he had . . . mixed, complicated feelings . . . for the bourgeoisie. But he did not always make things easier for himself. He was ostracised at the gymnasium. He felt the other boys and girls looked down on him, he had a reputation as a cheat, and he was picked on for his . . . ways and his . . . appearance.'

'Ah, the ugly duckling?' Yezhov said with feeling.

'Boys are cruel. They—we—had girlfriends and good prospects, and Lavrushya was not treated well. But he was smart. If he was drawn into a fight, he was not big or strong enough to win a straight-on wrestle, but he knew how to inflict what you might call strategic pain.'

'Strategic?' Yezhov perked up at the prospect of information about pain.

'He would jab them in the eye, or push them against a corner of a desk to injure their backs. He didn't overpower them, but he did enough to ensure that they didn't try it on again.'

'Interesting,' Yezhov said, steepling his fingers. 'I know he practises martial arts.'

'I have seen him throw General Kulik himself onto the ground.' Realising that the dwarf might be offended by this boast that Beria could outfight the bulkiest marshal in the Red Army, Murtov bit his tongue, literally.

'But what about you? You were one of those bourgeois boys, right? What was it that glued the pair of you together?'

Murtov paused. Was this the trap? Yezhov had got him going, he had lured him in through his weakness for remembering the past. Better not to have any memory. Nostalgia would get him one day, Babilina had repeatedly warned him. He looked at Natia for help but her face was avid for Yezhov's next move. The burning copper smell stabbed its way up Murtov's nose like a length of wire.

'I can see a lot running through your mind, friend,' Yezhov said gently. 'Don't stress. There are no traps, there are no wrong answers. It's not 1937 anymore,' he added in a tone of mild regret. 'See, the General Secretary is a great fan of old mate. We all are. The Party has plans for friend Beria. So you will understand our curiosity to see what makes this prodigy *tick*. The Vozhd is fortunate to have you here as a resource. Your information—*you yourself*—are valuable to the future of the Soviet Union, Vasil Anastasvili. But it's all good, you're going to get home to Babilina tonight. Or at worst, tomorrow morning.'

Murtov had never felt more scared than when Babilina's name tripped off Yezhov's wettened lips. The more Yezhov assured him that this was a harmless chat, the more a minefield of wrong answers stretched before him. But what did you do when you were forced into a minefield? You closed your eyes and took one step, then the next.

'I only ever offered him my love and friendship as a brother, and then my loyalty as a Bolshevik,' Murtov croaked. 'Could I have some water please?'

'No water here,' Yezhov said with a raised hand. 'Only vodka.'

Murtov nodded and, with a gasp of thirsty delight, Yezhov directed Natia to pour three shots. Murtov remembered something Beria had told him about 'Iron Felix' Dzerzhinsky, the Cheka's founder. Dzerzhinsky, known to be a complete whackjob, 'took *physical pleasure* from interrogations'. Murtov could see Yezhov quivering as he downed his drink Russian-style, splashing it all over his front.

Natia brought a glass of vodka to Murtov, who took a deep breath and threw it down his throat. It didn't quench his thirst but it steadied his nerves. Yezhov asked Natia to leave the bottle at his feet.

'I gave him love,' Murtov said.

'But surely he was in awe of you!' Yezhov said, pouring himself another shot without offering the bottle to Murtov. 'Your status as his rich brother, your prowess as a football player. Oh, how I love games!' He drained his glass and clapped. It was well known that when Spartak, the trade union club, played their arch rivals, the NKVD-sponsored Dinamo, the Spartak team bus's tyres burst on their way to the ground and their players arrived late after a maximum of security checks. After Yezhov became head of the NKVD, the Spartak football hierarchy began disappearing: first their director, then their coach, then their captain. Then their key players would collapse with stomach ailments during games. 'Didn't you represent Georgia Youth against Russia?'

'Only once,' Murtov said.

'I was there, can you believe it?' Yezhov said with a misty smile. 'The roar of the crowd as you walked onto the field. Two thousand people in the new stadium in Tbilisi sounded like one million on Red Square. I remember that noise like it was yesterday, like a wave of fluid beneath the earth, erupting in a geyser!' He illustrated with his tiny hairy hands.

Murtov remembered the noise better than the game . . . other than his mistake, which he had never stopped remembering.

'A one-nil defeat,' Yezhov said. 'But your proudest moment was also your greatest shame, I suppose. You played well—the Russians were superior but you kept them out—until the final minute.'

'I suppose you were there to support Russia,' Murtov said with a dry cough. He faltered, unable to continue.

Yezhov helped him remember: 'When you back-passed to your goalkeeper but didn't see the Russian player ready to intercept. Friend, I feel your pain! Nobody understands like I do, the loneliness of the villain of the piece. But take solace,' he said with a flash of his eyes at the snickering Meskhi. 'You were very good for ninety percent of the game.'

Murtov shook the memory away like a dog shaking off water. The villain of the piece? A bad back-pass versus the liquidation of half the Bolshevik Party and three in every four Red Army officers? *Fucking nostalgia, it'll get you every time! Focus!*

Yezhov was pouring himself and Natia another glass. Murtov was glad he didn't have to refuse. It had been how long since the last time he drank? Wasn't it after that very football match? Yezhov must have known this. In Yezhov's Thing, coincidences had been outlawed.

'You were shamed publicly,' Yezhov said. 'You let your country down. Nobody would come near you or even look at you. Only one lad had the courage to offer you his hand in friendship, right?'

'It's true,' Murtov said. The solitary person to offer a warm gesture of consolation was Lavrushya. He came to Murtov in the dressing room and embraced him in front of the others. It was the first time in the eight years they had lived together, gone to school together, shared holidays together, that Lavrushya had shown Murtov real friendship at risk to himself. There was something about Murtov's humiliation that opened Lavrushya's heart. Then they had gone out and drunk for three days, at the end of which Murtov discovered that he could never drink again, while Beria discovered that even titanic quantities could not disable him.

'Your football days were over,' Yezhov said. 'All your schoolboy heroics, gone with one back-pass. Yet for you and Lavrushya, that was a fresh start.'

'Sport and recreation can be a formative influence on youth,' Murtov said. 'But it is ultimately a bourgeois deviation popular among the British imperialist class.'

'Don't get yourself in trouble!' Yezhov exclaimed. 'You know that your boss still kicks a ball every morning, does his judo drills, lifts weights in his studio with mirrors on the walls . . . Not an image I want in my head! He promotes sport and recreation among the Georgian young, as you well know! I hope you're not saying he's cultivating imperialist habits?'

Murtov bit his cheeks, thinking: Landmine! 'I was happy to leave sport behind me. Our Revolutionary days were coming.'

'Oh don't worry, I won't tell. I'm more interested in friend Beria's kindness at that moment, when you failed so spectacularly.'

'It was a turning point.'

'And perhaps it secured your safety,' Yezhov added. 'Considering what followed. Now: the dynamic between you changed at university in Baku, yeah?'

'The boss grew in confidence. And yes, I . . . I suppose you could say I shrank.' Murtov's fidelity to the past was uncontrollable, like a bubble of air pushing to the surface. Yezhov knew it and was coaxing it out.

'You call him the boss,' Yezhov said. 'All very tight, aren't you? The *charka* way?'

'I apologise. There is only one boss.'

'Yeah, another *charka*.' Yezhov showed his teeth. Murtov's stomach plummeted. If Yezhov was speaking so freely about the Vozhd himself, it could only mean one thing. Murtov would not be allowed to leave this room.

'Please!' Yezhov said. 'There is a little boss in every district. I am intrigued by how this reversed dynamic was revealed during the Revolution.'

'In Baku we joined a group that read socialist literature and circulated pamphlets.'

'The Bagirov cell, mentored by Dear Sergo Ordzhonikidze. And of course friend Bagirov is now Party chief in Azerbaijan and Dear Sergo is in the Politburo. You mobsters.'

'Lavrushya looked after me. I was the son of non-toilers.'

'And you still are. And he still does.' With the vodka, an edge had crept into Yezhov's tone. 'He was a particularly gifted conspirator, yeah?'

'He saw opportunities before anyone else,' Murtov said. 'Others in the group would be arrested when leaving meetings. Lavrushya got us out separately, by a different door. He knew what was going to happen. He and I would take long walks on the streets of Baku, a tough city in those days. You could die on the footpath and nobody would notice you were dead until they robbed your body. Lavrushya took this in his stride—he was incapable of being shocked—and he talked of how exciting it would be if you were a security officer, to have the power over life and death, to arrest and search anyone at your will. It is no secret that he was motivated by the desire for total scientific command over circumstances and the elimination of luck. A very socialist principle.'

'I suppose this was what he liked about architecture,' Yezhov said.

'So did that nutjob in Germany.'

Murtov heard Natia's sharp intake of breath and wondered if mentioning the German was permitted. Hadn't Yezhov said he wanted to be an architect?

'So friend Beria admired the Tsar's secret police,' Yezhov said. 'You know, we heard rumours that he was playing both sides, informing on us for the Tsarists and on them for us. You and he were loitering in Caspian Sea boathouses in Baku listening to gossip from the revolutionary dockworkers and sailors, then passing the information to the enemy. And you both joined the imperialist army.'

'We spied only for the Bolshevik Party,' Murtov said. He felt surprisingly calm now that he had finally been accused of something. They had never spied for the other side. If such a thing were even half-suspected at the higher levels, he and Beria would have been sent to the other world in 1917.

'Once you were in the army, your bourgeois credentials must have come in handy for you both,' Yezhov said, glassy-eyed from his fourth shot.

'Lavrushya was clever,' Murtov said. 'Every day he saved my life.'

'What was it about him that you identified as leadership material? I mean, there's nothing in his appearance that screams "leader".'

Murtov openly appraised the NKVD chief's stature. 'Is there ever?'

'Ha ha, got me.' Yezhov took the joke. 'So what was it?'

'He could keep secrets. Anyone else, starve them a few days, threaten their family, and soon they were giving up their information. Not Lavrushya. He kept everything tight.'

At the mention of torture methods, Yezhov again sharpened his attention. 'Terrible! So primitive!'

'Yes,' Murtov said cautiously. 'Terrible.'

'We're so much more scientific now. Come on, indulge me. Play my true-or-false game. Okay? Here goes. I belt you in the genitals with a sandbag until you rupture.'

'Friend . . .'

'True or false? Do we do that nowadays?'

'Uh. False.'

'Nope, true! Needles under the fingernails?'

'False, friend.'

'Come on! You're not trying! Standing you on your tiptoes against a wall for two days, taking a broken chair leg to your kneecaps whenever you falter. Pure fatigue, you know, is like a truth serum itself, it poisons the internal organs. Do we do that?'

'No. Ah. False.'

'True again! Something in your answers tells me I'm producing the wrong emotions. Now. Friend Murtov. I now dunk your face into a spittoon furnished by a full regiment of productive NKVD droolers. True or false?'

'False, friend.'

'You're no fun,' Yezhov said with a sigh. 'We get a confession rate of ninety-nine percent from that one.' He poured a vodka. 'Now. Where were we? Ah yes. Lavrushya. In the Revolution. Why you found him so attractive.'

'I wouldn't say attractive.'

'But you committed to follow him, yeah? How come?'

'He was strong as iron and three steps ahead in dangerous times,' Murtov said, eager to move the conversation back to the events of twenty years ago. He realised he was giving Yezhov what he wanted, but he had to get away from that true-or-false game. 'We were bonded by our suffering. We were arrested here in Kutaisi and went on a hunger strike. We were sentenced to death together . . . we vowed to die as brothers with our heads high . . .'

'Wow, the dynamic really had changed,' Yezhov interrupted. 'What genuine Revolutionaries you were. But tell me something. I can kind of understand what you saw—see—in him. But once you met Babilina, you had something to lose.'

'Friend, I cannot . . .'

'Speak about Babi, sure, I know. But you've got to trust me, Murtov, I already know all I need about your little "marriage".'

Murtov considered a number of responses, but if he heard Babilina's name from Yezhov's lips one more time, he did not trust what his body might do.

'For the offspring of non-toilers, you and she really bought into the cause, didn't you! Following The Code on Marriage and the Family! Full-on Bolsheviks! We Party members get a bad rap, don't we? Bad husbands and wives, bad mothers and fathers. But you two are like me and my beloved Genia. We behave just like old-fashioned Pre-Revolutionary loving husbands and wives and parents. Isn't that a bit weird, that we would reject marriage and yet form a tight little *loving* family?'

Murtov said nothing. It was well known that Yezhov was a rampant sado-masochistic homosexual and that his beloved Yevgenia maintained a stable of lovers.

'Moving on,' Yezhov said, to Murtov's relief. 'My focus is friend Beria, not your personal life. You had to stay on his right side, and he rewarded you with his protection, which you really needed now that you had something to lose. Your need for his protection grew more and more essential when you had your daughters and he rose in the Party. But here is my question. Why *you*? Why should Beria be so loyal to you, when, let's face it, he has been loyal to nobody else? His Achilles heel is well known: he despises people. He might do a lot for The People, but we know how much he loathes *people*. He despises us Russians, he despises the Party members he has to work with. He despises everyone who is weak and easily manipulated—which means pretty much everyone. I suppose the only person he doesn't despise is The Steel One. I hope so, for his sake. But Stalin is Stalin. Why should Beria show this singular feeling, which runs against the grain of his entire character, for *you*? Why adopt you, when he resisted being adopted by your father? Is it just a *charka* gangster thing?'

It was not as if Murtov had never asked himself this question. Babilina asked it, one way or another, every day they placed their lives in Lavrushya's hands.

Murtov closed his eyes. 'You might struggle to believe this, Nikolai Ivanovich, but I believe in the socialist future. I believe in the measures that must be taken to defend the Revolution. I believe in what you yourself, friend, have had to do, cutting into good flesh to remove the bad. I believe that Communism holds out hope for all. I believe the Vozhd is leading us on the scientific and rational and enlightened path by which humankind can leave slavery and war in the past. When has any movement ever, in history, gathered in one place with a specific plan to transform humankind for the better? How could anyone with an awareness of historical necessity miss such an opportunity?'

Yezhov was silent. Then he began a slow, excruciating handclap.

Murtov kept his eyes clamped shut. He could not bear the size of the man's head.

'Bravo, well said. So the strength of your idealism is proven by the distance you have travelled. You could have chosen your privileges but instead you took the great flight of faith, you chose Bolshevism. You loved Lenin and you love Stalin. *You love Beria*, even to the last day when nobody else could possibly love him. I get it now. You place your life in his hands, and he protects you because he needs to have one centre of idealism left on his cynical, self-interested, over-ambitious journey. You are his good luck charm. You remind him of childhood, for you are still a child yourself. You might be just one of Papa Stalin's one hundred and seventy million children. But for Beria, it is as if you are his only son.'

It was more than that, though. Murtov remembered the day they first met Stalin, in a conspiratorial Bolshevik gathering in Tbilisi in 1921, when the Reds, having defeated the Whites in the Civil War, still had to bring Georgia across. Murtov sat in the front row with Beria, whose bespectacled eyes were fixed on the rough, mumbling, inarticulate schemer making a complete mess of his speech. Although Georgian was Stalin's native tongue, he insisted on speaking in his heavily accented Russian, which made him sound both pretentious and crude—ridiculous! The Georgian audience laughed at 'Soso', imitated his speaking voice and his dangling left arm. But Beria was the first to rush up and coat him in the syrup of his compliments. Beria turned to the audience and cried, 'With The Steel One we shall uproot and destroy the weeds and plough Georgia throughout!' He began applauding. Even though only Murtov and a few others followed, it saved the event from being a complete debacle and Stalin was visibly grateful to this young glassy-eyed enthusiast. Later, Murtov asked Beria why he had committed himself to such a loser, and Beria said, 'I have heard so much about him and now I see what the mystery is. The mystery is that there is no mystery. He is built of nothing but *will*, and that is why we are going to back him to the hilt.' Murtov asked why, in the looming battle to succeed Lenin as leader, Beria wouldn't give his support to Trotsky, who was an intellectual in the Beria mould. Beria said, 'That's why I'm backing Stalin. Who wants to be the second-smartest guy in the room?'

'What are you thinking about?' Yezhov interrupted Murtov's suicidal musings. 'Honestly, now.'

'Honestly? I want to go to the toilet and I want to go home.'

'Both in good time,' Yezhov said with a show of his yellow horse teeth. 'But see, you still don't understand. You declare your loyalty to your brother and your conviction to the Bolshevik cause. Good for you.' Now he leaned forward again, so close that Murtov's eyes stung from the synthetic beeswax in his pomade, and said in a low voice, 'But we in Moscow don't want you here.' Yezhov tapped Murtov's forehead. 'Intellectual convictions can change. And we don't want you here either.' He tapped Murtov's chest. 'You can always have a change of heart. We want you'—he reached down and gave Murtov's balls a rough squeeze—'*here*. Your fears will remain until the day you die. That's where we want you.'

Murtov tried to shift away, but Yezhov held on until he was satisfied.

Then he tilted back into his settee and said, 'I think we have almost finished cross-checking the known facts about your *boss*. Since the Civil War, he has been prominent enough not to have too many secrets from us. And a word to the wise, friend Murtov. I know you like reminiscing, but don't get too caught up in the past. The Society of Old Bolsheviks has been banned. And you know what else? Memoirs. No more memoirs. Not published, not spoken, not even in here.' He pointed at his temple. 'So try not to remember too much, eh? Not when there's so much glory to look forward to.'

He nodded to Natia, who passed him a file from which he read. '*As a reward for loyalty to the Vozhd in his struggle with the traitor Trotsky, Beria was recruited into the organs to suppress opposition in Azerbaijan.* And he was a good Cheka leader, wasn't he? He improved prison conditions, he replaced the bed rolls with proper mattresses and the buckets with proper toilets. In interrogations, he treated intellectual suspects as his equals, laid out the evidence and persuaded them that they would get twenty years either way so they might as well sign. I can respect that.'

Murtov blinked back the tears that threatened to run down his cheeks.

Yezhov resumed reading from the file. *'As head of the Georgian security police, member of the Georgian Central Committee and then Party leader in the Transcaucasus, friend Beria was instrumental in securing peace and prosperity'*—he looked up—'for you clansmen anyway. He has been a staunch supporter of the Vozhd in these testing recent years, and I must register my personal thanks. He showed his loyalty after the unfortunate accident that befell friend Mogilevsky.' Yezhov gave a little smirk. 'Solomon Grigorevich Mogilevsky, Beria's last obstacle in his rise to head of Transcaucasian internal security, was so unfortunate to die in that mid-air plane explosion. Beria delivered a fawning eulogy: "I cannot believe it, I do not want to believe it, I will never again hear the soft voice of Solomon Grigorevich!" Ah, what soaring rhetoric.'

Yezhov went back to his summation: *'This intelligence, loyalty and capacity for work is why we have entrusted to friend Beria the preparations for the auspicious anniversary visit of 1938. Of all the republics in the union, Georgia is the most favoured by sound scientific leadership. Friend Beria's book,* On the History of Bolshevik Organisations in Transcaucasia, *enlightened the world on the Vozhd's previously hidden contribution to the success of socialism in his home region, and has since become a bestseller on five continents. Friend Beria must also be commended for thwarting the assassination plot against the Vozhd during a previous visit to Georgia, personally arresting the conspirators and providing evidence he had single-handedly gathered of their fiendish Trotskyist intentions.'*

Yezhov put the folder on the carpet by his settee and contemplated Murtov like a cat sizing up its canary. 'A glittering career indeed. Since his elevation to the Central Committee in 1934, we in Moscow Centre have admired his many gifts. You must be proud, having gambled on him. And he credits you with saving him from the Ossetian assassination plot in 1935. Quite a bond you two share.'

'It wasn't such a gamble.'

'Sure it wasn't.'

Murtov bowed his head and thought of Babilina and the kids. 'I can go now?'

'Course you can,' Yezhov said. But he was pouring himself a fresh drink. The shot glass looked like a tumbler in Yezhov's hand, and only shrank to its correct proportions when it approached his mouth. 'Just one thing,' he said, clapping his hand against his oversized forehead. 'I nearly forgot: the girls. Passionate football players, yeah? And what first-rate musicians they both are!'

'No,' Murtov said thickly.

'I haven't asked a question yet.' Yezhov took on a new, peppery tone. 'Tell me, what do you make of this thing he has for . . . females of a certain age?'

'I don't know about that.' The bubble inside Murtov turned to a ball of ice. They always left the ambush until last, when your brain had checked out of the building and was considering the public transport timetable.

'Come on, we know what he's been doing,' Yezhov said with a flick of his eyes towards Meskhi. 'All those daughters and granddaughters.'

'The more bourgeois the better,' Meskhi said. She had a full-body hunger about her. This was what she was here for. This was, maybe, what Murtov had been brought here for. Forget 'fact-checking'; if he listened to the in-depth language, they were out to get the boss, if not tonight then some day soon. And if it was Yezhov out to get him, that meant Moscow. Probably. Murtov could not discount Yezhov moving alone against Beria. But it was more likely that whatever Yezhov was doing, he was working towards The Steel One.

'May I?' Murtov nodded at the vodka.

Glee showing on his voluptuous lips, Yezhov poured. Murtov downed it.

'The history, if you will,' Yezhov said.

'Friend Beria has been married to Nina since the '20s. He met her when he was imprisoned in Tbilisi for Bolshevik activities during the Reds' victory over the Whites. She was the sister of his cellmate Gegechkori, and she faithfully came and visited—'

'Oh, please!' Yezhov interrupted. 'Don't insult me, yeah? We know how he met Nina. He tried to pick her up off the street, as he was doing prolifically from his first day in the Cheka. We know he was confronted by her brother Gegechkori, who was a Red Army lieutenant. We know that Beria then arrested Gegechkori and that Nina came to plead for him. We know that Beria raped her and because she was such a good sort he couldn't bring himself to let her go, so he imprisoned her. We know that when it suited his career to have a wife, he chose his prisoner. We know that they have two children and that Beria keeps her in Tbilisi. If we needed your tired official version, we wouldn't have asked for the pleasure of your company. True or false, friend? What we want is the *truth*.'

Murtov closed his eyes. The vodka was weighing on him. 'He did not imprison Nina. She was a staunch young Bolshevik. This is all documented. They married because he was moving to Baku to work for the Party.'

'Fuck off!'

Murtov opened his eyes to see that the head of the NKVD had smashed the vodka bottle on the arm of his chair, spilling the last of its contents onto his uniform. Thick shards of glass lay on the carpet and on Yezhov's lap. Incandescent, he swept them away. They flew all over the room. Froth decorated the corners of his mouth. Natia Meskhi was bug-eyed, willing him on.

'My question is, do you really believe the fictions this man has created around his past?' Yezhov's voice cracked. 'Or are you just playing the game?'

'You are confusing me . . .'

'You are choosing, friend, to protect the Soviet Union's most prolific rapist!' Yezhov thundered. 'We know about his sultan habits. You Georgians fancy yourselves such knockabouts, you swashbuckling sailors and pirates; you're all so *real*, aren't you, compared with us phony Russians? But who's the real phony, yeah? The great puritan Beria. The great wise governor who makes them lie face down on his desk and pull down their underwear for him. He stands on their necks and horsewhips their buttocks. He only stops when they lose control of their bowels. True or false, Murtov? True or false?!'

'False. All false.' Murtov looked at Meskhi. AAA, the waterfront apartment. The hospital trustee's granddaughter. AAA. 'I've never seen that.'

'Fuck off,' Yezhov said again. 'You saw it when you were at school. Beria's revenge on the nice bourgeois girls. They didn't want him, but he managed to scare them enough so they would avoid you too. Can you really not have thought about this?'

Murtov remembered his first girlfriends. How did Yezhov know this shit? It was true that girls had suddenly stopped seeing him, for reasons he could never work out, after he had introduced them to Beria. In Babilina, Beria had sensed the impassable. But maybe he had spared Babilina because by then he believed he had broken and house-trained Murtov.

'I don't know,' Murtov said.

'Don't be so fucking thick,' Yezhov said.

'I suppose you don't even believe he murders his interrogation suspects,' Natia added.

'Admit it,' Yezhov said. 'He scares the living shit out of you. That's all your precious *charka* brotherhood is about.'

Murtov said nothing.

'And you were so chatty before.' Yezhov snarled. 'Such a fucking loyal friend to this fucker who has spent his *entire life* humiliating your family. He retains you as his personal lapdog. In revenge for all your father did for him, he has imprisoned him and used him and belittled him and, as you well know, just to remind your old man who's boss, finishes any meeting with him by punching him in the face. *This is so you remember who I am.* Another of your noble Georgian traditions. Don't pretend you don't know, you pathetic creature. Look at yourself. Do you have any pride? You dare call yourself a socialist!'

'Hey, at least he's been kept alive,' Natia chipped in nastily. 'Bourgeois scum like the Murtovs, you know, most were gone by '21. I can't believe how well the Murtovs live. I can't believe they *live*.'

'Well, it enhances the savour of Beria's revenge,' Yezhov said to her in an analytical manner, as if Murtov were no longer in the room. 'As long as this idiot is on hand, poor little Lavrushya can keep jerking off over the obstacles he has overcome.'

'Psychologically, it makes sense.'

'Speaking of the dark tunnels of the human psyche,' Yezhov said grandiosely, 'there are some Murtovs he hasn't dealt with yet.'

Yezhov and Natia inspected Murtov. They were enjoying themselves like a pair of pals torturing a cat after a long day at work.

'How about the Conveyor?' Yezhov said. 'Now the Conveyor, that's got a hundred percent success rate. The Conveyor will have you confessing you're the Queen of Spain. Let me tell you about—'

'True!' Murtov cried. 'True!

With trembling hands, Murtov crossed himself. *What the fuck*, he thought. His hands were doing things beyond his control.

'I've been wondering the same as you,' Natia said to Yezhov. 'Is he really an idiot or does he just put it on for self-preservation? Now I know.'

Yezhov was shaking his head in apparently genuine pity.

'He doesn't fool me with his false "true",' he said and turned to Murtov. 'Answer me this, Vasil. How much does the Soviet state weigh?'

'I don't understand. Please.'

'No really, how much does it weigh? If you add up every car, every truck, every piece of machinery. Every rifle, every pistol, every bomb, every aeroplane. How much?'

'Friend, I don't know why you ask me this.'

'Every house, every office block, every government building, every piece of gravel in the roads. Every brick that comes out of the kilns. How much?'

'What do you want from me?'

'Every one of the people. Every friend. Every bite of bread and every lump of shit.'

'I don't know.'

'Let me ask you this,' Yezhov said. He was inclining forward again. The second vodka was dragging the skin on Murtov's face towards the floor. Yezhov's child-sized hand reached forward and tilted up Murtov's chin. 'The weight of all the Soviet state, everything you can think of weighing, is on one side of the scales. And here, on the other side, is you. The Soviet state on one side, and little Murtov on the other. How dare you think you can withstand it? How?'

'I never did.'

'Good. So. Here's the thing. Here's what I'm getting at. Lavrushya still has one last score to settle with you.'

Murtov's head shook itself.

'They love their music,' Yezhov said with great tenderness. 'Bagpipes, *panduri*, good patriotic socialist songs. Busking on the streets—for money? That right, friend Meskhi?'

'Children's street hooliganism and mischief can attract arrests and heavy fines,' Natia said. 'Even twelve-year-olds are subject to adult prosecution. They can get picked up any day. Doesn't matter who's looking after them. The law's the law. Legally, twelve makes you an adult.' Her eyes were piercing Murtov.

'Ah, this Soviet world,' Yezhov said sympathetically. 'So many laws, so little legality.'

'You said it, friend,' Natia replied.

Yezhov's eyes had not left Murtov. 'You know why the Vozhd dropped the qualifying age for the death penalty to twelve? So he can execute children? No. That would be silly. It's so we can tell you we can. And we're seeing if it can work even better than the Conveyor.'

'Nice,' Natia said.

'And what was poor little Lavrushya doing when he was twelve?' Yeshov said. 'The age Ana and Melor are now? He was sleeping under a stairway and eating scraps like a servant.'

'His choice,' Murtov gasped.

'His family had sold their barn to pay your father, who had no need of their money but took it anyway. Beria's mother vanished to some nunnery to pray for her son's soul, which speaks of a profound guilt and shame on her part. Talk about a spoilt biography! He hated both sets of parents, his natural ones for their stupidity and his adoptive ones for their greed. And at twelve he'd just discovered ways of hurting children to get what he wanted from them. Which, as it turns out, was—*is*—not inconsiderable. Babilina's right, V. He's only keeping you until he gets the girls. Ana first, and next year Melor.'

'You lie, dwarf!' Murtov whispered. He gave zero fucks what he called the chief of the NKVD now. He was already dead. His head went on shaking itself. Again, somehow, some devil was picking up his hand and using it to draw a cross on his chest.

'Well!' Yezhov announced with a smack of his hands on his thighs. 'I'm serious. I really would prefer *person of small stature.*'

Murtov was drowning in fear. But . . . He shook himself again. He must not give up. He hadn't been hurt. This wasn't brainwashing and it wasn't torture; it was chess! He had to keep his wits about him for the next move. For his girls! He remembered, all of a sudden, something Beria had said about Yezhov's Thing: that the Terror was purely historical necessity. It wasn't an accident brought about by Yezhov's bad nature. If it wasn't the dwarf, it would be someone else. It had to happen. It was mechanistic. It will only be over, Beria said, when that other historical necessity, world war, arrives again and they begin to ask how many people they need to keep. The Terror started of its own accord, and it will finish of its own accord too. Calling it Yezhov's Thing is pure propaganda. Yezhov, as an individual with free will, is null and void. And if he is nothing, if he belongs only to the imagination, then he can be resisted.

Yezhov shook his head slowly, with a tragic air. Again, he gave the impression of reading Murtov's thoughts.

'You, friend, are dead meat. But how does death feel? Like shit! So maybe you're not dead. Death wouldn't feel so bad. Come on, V. Show me you're alive.'

Murtov hurled his empty vodka glass at Yezhov and screamed, 'Dwarf!'

Even with that enormous head as a target, just a couple of feet away, Murtov's eyesight was too blurry and his arm too wooden. The glass's hard base struck the filing cabinet and it bounced onto the carpet, intact. Or had it passed through Yezhov's head? So Murtov might be dead after all. A ghost, like Yezhov.

The dwarf steepled his hairy fingers, his tale finished, appraising his victim.

'Person. Of. Small. Stature,' he repeated, singsong. 'Be careful with your words, old mate. This is your last reminder.'

'Shit just got real, eh?' Natia Meskhi said with one of her snickers.

Yezhov rose from the settee to his feet, not a great distance, and nodded to Meskhi, who slid a hand under Murtov's arm and steered him upwards. Yezhov and Meskhi had drunk most of the bottle before Yezhov had smashed it, but they seemed stone-cold sober while Murtov was wobbling about and coughing up gouts of bile.

'And they say I'm low-born,' Yezhov said. 'What's that joke? A good Bolshevik doesn't throw up on the floor, a good Bolshevik throws up on himself! Friend Murtov, just remember one thing for me, will you? For all your *charka* ethics, you might be forgetting the one Georgian gangster virtue that Papa Stalin has given us as a nation. If one member of the family is guilty, then all of you are. Russians are prone to forget about family ties. It takes a Georgian to remind us.'

Yezhov placed a hand on Murtov's shoulder and pulled him down so they were eye to eye. Yezhov kissed him, soft and yet also hard, on the lips.

'That's from the Vozhd. In thanks. He will appreciate the information. You know, he's always caught in a bit of a bind: he doesn't want the people to be able to express themselves freely, but he's also obsessed with finding out what they are thinking. That's why he needs the NKVD. We do his social research for him. If it's bad news, we're the ones who have to pass it up the line. So—I give you his thanks.'

'What do you want from me?'

'We'll let you know,' Yezhov chirped, slapping him on the back. 'Good chat, V. Have a great weekend.'

XIII

IT WAS NEARLY DAWN BY THE TIME MURTOV ARRIVED HOME ON a trolley car doing the rounds of Batumi, collecting workers for early shifts. He shivered in his coat, a reaction compounded by the pre-dawn chill. Two apartments in his corridor had new wax seals over their doors.

The girls did not wake but Babilina was slurping cups of samovar tea.

'My love.' She cradled him in silence. Murtov wished he could hand her his heart: terror, sorrow, shock, but most of all guilty relief that he had come out of Kutaisi alive. Yezhov had dizzied him, whirling his thirty-nine years against the walls like sludge in a centrifuge. Murtov could not cry; his insides were scoured.

Per normal NKVD practice, Natia Meskhi had given him a non-disclosure agreement to sign on his exit. Telling Babilina would doom her to certain death. Fuck you, Murtov thought.

He poured more tea from the samovar, placed a pillow over the telephone, and told Babilina everything.

After hearing him to the end, Babilina said, 'So they've been hearing us.' In a high-pitched voice, she cried, 'Hello, friend Yezhov, and go fuck yourself!' Then she crossed her arms and stared at the floor. 'I've been telling you Ana and Melor can be snatched any day. Now Yezhov knows it. He's going to make us wish we were never born.'

'I am also worried about my father,' Murtov said. 'He has witnessed too much.'

'What can you do?'

'See him. Warn him. I don't know.'

'So you go warn him. What can *he* do?'

'It doesn't matter. I have to go.'

When Melor and Ana rose a short time later, Babilina told them they were having a few days off from summer school. Ana asked if they could busk; Melor asked if they could see their friends. Babilina said a temporary state of emergency meant they had to stay at home.

'But why isn't Papa staying at home?' Ana said.

Murtov, having had an hour's rest, was readying to leave.

'Your father helps make the rules,' Babilina said.

'Nonsense!' Melor replied. 'Only Papa Stalin makes the rules.'

Murtov hugged the girls, rang the office and told them he had taken ill and would need the day off. Beria had, oddly, made no inquiries about his disappearance from Ureki.

He caught a bus, another bus, a trolley and a train before walking five versts to the secured estate outside Gori. He had a plan for how he would talk his way in, but it was unnecessary. The gates were wide open and unattended. He walked up an avenue between identical villas in their Tuscan colours until he came to the cul-de-sac where his father lived.

His hand, that rogue instrument, made a cross on his chest.

At the end of the cul-de-sac was an ambulance. Its light was not rotating. The ambulance officers were chatting casually, smoking Russian cigarettes. The vehicle's door was open. Inside was a body under a white sheet.

Murtov had no powers of resistance. The emotions that had earlier run dry flooded through him and he sobbed like a child.

Out of Anastas's villa came a number of men in the belted bottle-green overcoats of Yezhov's Moscow NKVD. At their tail was a tall, stooped figure in a Red Army uniform. He approached Murtov with his hand extended. 'I am terribly sorry,' said Dear Sergo Ordzhonikidze.

Murtov recovered himself in the presence of the great personage and tried to converse like a Bolshevik. The People's Commissar of Heavy Industry said he had been intending to pay friend Anastas Karvelashvili a social visit, but found the old man unconscious on the back patio of his villa. A watering can lay by his side. 'Natural causes,' Dear Sergo said with his undertaker's mouth, his undertaker's eyes. 'The luckiest man in the country, but still . . .' He nodded compassionately and sighed as if he could not, after all these years, take one more death.

'Why?' was the first word Murtov spoke.

Resembling a grim reaper who had been worked to exhaustion, Sergo said, 'Death wins in the end. Our task is to be ready.'

'Friend commissar, why were you visiting my father? What is he to you?'

Dear Sergo's self-possession could not conceal a tic beneath his eye. 'I have known him for two decades, friend. When I was involved in installing Bolshevik rule in Georgia, he gave us great assistance, and we had kept in touch.'

'He never told me.'

'None of us knows everything about our father,' Sergo said, placing a hand on Murtov's shoulder. Murtov noticed that he was carrying something flat tucked under his arm. Sergo turned it away, but not before Murtov glimpsed what it was: a framed portrait in charcoal of a young Beria.

Dear Sergo's retinue were getting into their vehicles and the ambulance men were being given their orders when a gleaming Emka cruised into the cul-de-sac. Sergo's car passed it on its way to the exit. Out of the Emka jumped Beria, attended by AAA.

'Was that Dear Sergo? What was he doing here?' Beria asked. 'My god, what a terrible shock.' He fixed a mournful face upon Murtov. 'If it has happened . . . it was necessary.'

Beria turned towards the villa and set about his work like the boss of a state-owned funeral service.

Three hours later, Murtov was driving Beria's Emka to the Georgian capital. Beria sat in the back, AAA in the passenger seat. Beria had judged that 'the best thing' for Murtov was work, and he had plenty on. Murtov, made passive by the momentousness of events and the intimidating efficiency of the senior Party figures, was carried along as if in a dream.

'We'll take care of the funeral,' the boss said lightly.

AAA made a note in his pad.

'You needn't worry about a thing; the Party will cover the costs. We'll put on a big show in . . . maybe not Tbilisi—you won't want to drag everyone away from their holidays, not with the gala coming up ... Let's have it at Batumi cathedral! Your father was such a devout man, we can at least put on a few bells and smells for him.'

'Ah, friend?' AAA looked up from his notepad. 'The Holy Mother of God Cathedral?'

'Why not!' Beria clapped his hands, then began vigorously rubbing them.

'The Orthodox cathedral has been converted into a laboratory for the development of high-voltage electronic devices,' AAA said.

'You think I don't know that? We are the Communist Party of Transcaucasia! We will reconvert it to the Holy Mother of God! Nothing is too much for Anastas Karvelashvili, to whom we owe ... such a debt!'

While AAA made detailed scribbles and Murtov drove, Beria mused about 'how many funerals I've been attending'. They hit a logjam. Former persons were fixing the road.

'This traffic, it's killing me,' Beria said. 'What do you do if you're stuck behind a hearse, friend? Overtake, or stay behind? My brother-in-law is a hearse driver. I saw him in traffic recently, all the mourners queued up behind him. I ordered friend Adam to overtake, but out of respect for the solemnity of the occasion, I did not acknowledge my brother-in-law. The next time he saw me, he accused me of being up myself. Priceless!'

Beria took his jar out of his pocket. He offered a chilli to AAA, who chewed it as dry-eyed as if he had been munching these things all his life.

Beria's eyes met Murtov's in the rear-vision mirror.

'Battle on, V.'

Murtov did not say: *My father just died, cunt.* Instead he said the second thing that came into his head. 'I spend my life in this car.'

AAA clapped Murtov's shoulder. 'That's because you're a driver, friend!'

Murtov pressed the accelerator. The Emka's response was characteristically unemphatic.

'I get it,' Beria said. 'We all get stale. Why, do you remember the late twenties?' When Murtov did not say anything, the boss turned to AAA. 'I was dead sick of being a spy, you know what I'm saying? I'd been running the organs throughout the Transcaucasus, a big job but unsatisfying. Mostly just rooting out terrorists and keeping things quiet. Oh, I was making a difference in small ways. When I settled the uprising with the Adjara Muslims, those savages up in the hills, we made a difference, didn't we, V?'

Murtov gave the faintest of nods.

'They were hiding in bushes and taking pot shots at Georgian police, army, civilians,' Beria said to a receptive AAA. 'Not a full-scale insurgency but they were a pain in the arse. The local military couldn't deal with them, so we went up and met their leaders. Do you know what the morons wanted? For their wives to wear veils and their daughters not to go to schools.'

'The socialist government had banned the veil and made the schools open to girls,' AAA said approvingly.

'Not in the hills we didn't,' Beria said. 'We were trying, but they kept fighting us. Was it really worth losing control of the region just so that we could see Muslim girls' faces and give them an education before they went off to cook for their husbands? You had to be pragmatic. And Georgian socialism is tolerant of religious traditions. So I said, "Fuck it, have your veils, keep your stupid girls at home. If you clowns want to stay in the Middle Ages, be my guests." The uprising was settled there and then.'

Sealed with the execution of the leaders of the Muslim tribes that Beria hadn't negotiated with, nicely entrenching Georgia's new Adjara friends with their unshaven hills, their girl-slaves and their now-enlarged flocks of sheep.

'So there were moments of achievement when I ran the Cheka,' Beria went on, 'but being chief of the spies is limiting. My soul was aching for architecture. I still wanted to be a student, to live that life! I had spent my youth securing the Revolution. So the next time Dear Sergo was back home, I said, "Friend Ordzhonikidze, commissar, Dear Sergo, I am bored with spying. I want to create cities. I want to leave a mark." You know what he said? He said, "You *are* leaving a mark." I replied, "But is it a mark if it must be invisible? I do not create; I eradicate." Dear Sergo asked me what I wanted. When I told him I wanted to go back to architecture, he consulted with The Steel One, who didn't want me in a university, no. He appointed me Governor. "You are too old to be a student, Lavrushya," Dear Sergo told me. "A revolution needs soldiers, not architects."

'Ah, I was soon to turn thirty-three, the age of Christ's death—too old to be a student, just right to be crucified! I was invited to Moscow and elevated to the Central Committee. They *hated* me. I was the archetypal Johnny-come-lately. Molotov, The Hammer, said, "Don't only monkeys come from Georgia?" And so I knew what they really called the Vozhd in their minds. They think we *charkas* are apes. Georgian mafia. Brutes. Animals. It must humiliate them that they are under our thumb. They said, "Nobody knows you, how can you be on the Central Committee?" I said, "Look at your boss. We primates get shit done!"'

With his chilli-stained fingers he enumerated his achievements. 'We have improved literacy, kindergarten attendance, the emancipation of women everywhere except among the Adjarans. We crushed the black market. We mechanised the coal and manganese mining in the Caucasus. We started the oil boom in the Caspian Sea that underwrites the future strength of the entire USSR. We manufacture entire products end to end, the only one of the republics permitted to do so, when all the others are only allowed to manufacture parts and send them to stinking Moscow for final assembly. We broke the rule of servitude! We've turned the swamps into irrigation channels and converted our agricultural output into high-yielding citrus fruit and tobacco. Mandarin oranges! We created the Soviet Florida! We've given the Georgian peasant both collectivisation and prosperity, far ahead of anywhere else in the union, and we reward him with the health spas we have built on the world's loveliest coast.' This from a man who had never seen any coast other than those of the Black and Caspian seas. 'We did it, didn't we, friends? The Soviet Florida!'

'Sure did,' AAA said.

'Sure did,' Murtov said, eyes on the road.

To AAA, Beria said, 'I wanted you to know that your boss isn't just an *intriguer*.'

'All Georgians praise your greatness, friend!' AAA was nearly soiling himself with enthusiasm. 'Under your governorship, the doubters were destroyed!'

Beria waggled his finger. 'Haven't you read my *On the History of Bolshevik Organisations in Transcaucasia?*'

'Numerous times!' AAA simpered.

'Then you would know that excess nationalistic pride is anathema to me. True, Georgians are fortunate, but we owe our fortune to the General Secretary's wise stewardship. He has never shown his Georgian countrymen any favouritism and nor should he. We are one union under Marxist–Leninist–Stalinist socialism. And I don't like suckholes. Left here, V.'

Murtov pulled the car into a driveway with a security checkpoint. He was numb, deaf, half-blind. He had barely listened to a word of Beria's insane stump speech. He drove up a lush trail to the forecourt of a residential building with pillars and pediments in the neoclassical wedding-cake style Beria had inflicted upon Tbilisi.

When Murtov parked, AAA went into the house with the easy familiarity of one who had been here before. Beria stayed with Murtov.

'Why are we here?' Murtov said.

'It's where we're putting up Dear Sergo before he leaves. I need to talk to him.'

Murtov turned around to see if there was anything he wanted.

'I'm sorry about Anastas,' Beria said. 'He was my father too. I'm feeling just as sad as you.'

Murtov lowered his eyes.

'Take the car back to Batumi,' Beria said. 'Keep it as long as you need. I'll organise my own return. You'll want to spend time with the girls of course. And you'll have start on the funeral arrangements.' He gripped the back of Murtov's neck. 'Make sure you don't lose the ashes!' He reached for the doorhandle, then paused and said, 'They're coming for me, aren't they?' He studied Murtov for long enough to make a sweat break out below Murtov's nose. 'I know they've got to you.'

Murtov began to speak but Beria raised his hand. 'You of all people should know that not much goes on without my knowledge.'

There was nothing for Murtov to say.

'Are they setting me up?'

'I . . . I don't know, Lavrushya. They didn't tell me.'

Beria inspected his fingernails. 'What *are* they telling you? That I'm planning an assassination attempt when he comes to Georgia?'

'Why would they say that?'

'It's what I would say if I were in their shoes. You wait: if they want you to get me, they'll sell it to you as the only way to save *him*.'

'It was just . . . fact-checking. Nothing bad.'

'"Fact-checking"? That sounds very bad. But tell me: was it only Yezhov?'

Murtov tried to swallow but his throat was sandpaper. Beria was testing him: he never asked a question to which he did not already know the answer. It would cost Murtov nothing to shop Natia Meskhi. And yet something trapped her name behind his lips.

Beria's spectacles reflected Murtov. The front door of the neoclassical mansion opened and closed. From the corner of his eye Murtov saw Sergo Ordzhonikidze, the weight of heavy industry on his shoulders, dragging his feet down the steps with an apologetic half-smile, AAA at his flank. Dear Sergo's strong head of Soviet hair was a reminder of the limits of Beria's domain.

'Just Yezhov,' Murtov said. If Natia was still alive and at her office desk the next morning, he would know that he had made the right choice. He didn't know who he feared more, Natia or Beria. Murtov heard Babilina: *You always have to bet on both horses.* Advice, or accusation?

Beria leant over the bench seat and whispered, 'You watch, V. I'm going to fuck them up. They won't know what's hit them.'

Now Beria turned to the approaching Ordzhonikidze, put on his most delighted grin, allowed his hands a last quick rub, and opened the car door.

TWENTY DAYS TO LIVE

XIV

THE FUNERAL OF ANASTAS KARVELASHVILI MURTOV WAS brought forward to fit into Dear Sergo's stay in Georgia. The People's Commissar of Heavy Industry had approved the ongoing construction work for the Fourteenth Congress of the Georgian Revolutionary Committee for the Construction and Maintenance of Transcaucasian Light and Medium Industry and Public Housing. 'Stalin Gala' tripped more easily off the tongue.

Beria's order for the reconversion of the Holy Mother of God Cathedral had AAA working day and night, but the young man beat the clock with the help of shock workers personally holding up tapestries in the nave to obscure the electronic equipment. As a reward, AAA was permitted to shave his head. He had begun wearing shoes without heels and stood scarcely taller than the boss.

The invited congregation was larger than expected for a former person under house arrest, but Beria wanted a good turnout to honour Dear Sergo's presence. As a special favour, Beria permitted the bereaved son to drive the Party Emka to his home, collect Babilina and their daughters, and be excused from logging the petrol consumed from the closed garage. 'You'll want to keep the girls fresh,' Beria told Murtov.

Melor sat in the front seat of the Emka, playing with the accessories. Ana was in the back seat holding Babilina's hand. That very morning, Ana had come to Babilina in tears. Babilina drew out of her that she had a 'tumour' and was 'going to die'. After some persuasion, Ana showed her the swelling beneath her right nipple. Ana burst into tears again. She knew it wasn't a tumour. Babilina's heart stopped. She couldn't interpret whether Ana's sobs were nostalgia for the end of her childhood or dread of what lay ahead.

When they approached the church Murtov, dressed in a dark grey formal tunic, pulled over and asked Melor to sit in the back.

Melor pouted. 'Why?'

Babilina said, 'Because even the children of Papa Stalin sit in the back, my love. Sit in the front and people will think you are showing off.'

She had kept the girls at home since Murtov's return from Kutaisi. It was all she could think to do. If they busked or went to school or the park, they could be snatched in public in an NKVD 'accident'. It wasn't as if the apartment was any kind of sanctuary, but at least, in Babilina's desperate, boxed-in logic, Beria's men would have to fight her for them.

Today, Murtov had asked his girls to comfort him at the funeral. Babilina was given no choice. 'We will be bringing them to Beria,' she told him. But Murtov was on another planet and she couldn't abandon him there.

They were running a little late and the parking was a nightmare, with the Beria and Ordzhonikidze entourages having taken the best spaces. Murtov grew agitated but Babilina assured him that the service would not begin without him. 'It might,' he replied.

The event turned out to be less a funeral than a Party conference. The front row was occupied in ranking order by Sergo Ordzhonikidze, Beria, Merkulov, Goglidze, Kruglov, Dumbadze and the brothers Kobulov. A Georgian Orthodox priest was allowed a few minutes before Beria seized the pulpit and delivered a résumé of his own achievements. There were internal elections coming up and, even though the result was fixed, it was incumbent on the candidate to make a democratic show, particularly in front of Dear Sergo. Buried in the speech were some words eulogising 'the reformed non-toiler' Anastas Karvelashvili Murtov.

The Murtovs shared the second row with two bodyguards and the Beria family, down from Tbilisi: wife Nina, son Sergo and daughter Guranda. The moron and the bitch were neatly dressed and polite to those seated around them. Babilina was surprised by Nina Beria's gaunt, sucked-in cheeks and grey hair. Next to the ebullient boss, Nina seemed drained of vitality, a Whom yoked to a Who.

At the end of the service, Sergo Ordzhonikidze offered the Murtovs his long-faced sympathies. Melor, conspicuously impressed by a Moscow Politburo member, handed the commissar a letter to pass to Papa Stalin.

Gleaming in Sergo's reflected glory came Beria, who cradled each of the girls' hands lengthily in his. 'My sincere condolences on your loss,' he told the girls, neither of whom had known their grandfather. To Babilina he murmured, 'Poor Vasil is not himself.

To be honest, I don't know if he will ever recover. Please accept my invitation to my apartment any day, any time. Your girls will be in need of a father figure.'

Babilina was too shocked to respond.

'Uncle Lavrushya,' Melor said, 'Mama told me you don't have tickets to *The Squealer*?'

Beria got on his haunches. 'Far from it! Your mother must have been misinformed. For you, my dear, front row. And how about you, Ana? Are you interested in *The Squealer*?'

Ana had moved closer to her mother.

'Georgian girls mature so early, don't they?' Beria said with a sentimental air. He gave both girls a pat on the cheek and moved on, sticking close to Dear Sergo.

Only Party officials and the Murtovs travelled to the wake in the Batumi Town Hall across the square. Beria sent his wife and children on their way. Babilina sneaked a couple of vodkas from the uniformed waiters while Beria made another interminably perky speech in which he extolled Dear Sergo, who was soon to turn fifty. Babilina thought he looked seventy-five. She was quietly fascinated by Dear Sergo, whose nickname was not bestowed with the customary Georgian sarcasm. Old shitbreath himself had genuinely, almost pityingly, dubbed him 'Dear' due to his reputed unwillingness to 'take severe measures' against enemies of the people. Babilina wondered what it took for a man with compassion to survive. She could see what it cost her husband: Dear Vasil, who stayed alive by walking through life with his head ducked. But how could you refuse to kill if you were one of The Steel One's own henchmen? Wasn't a dead heart the number one qualification? What did Dear Sergo have? She had a chance to exercise her curiosity—made more frank by the second vodka—when he approached her.

'My sorrow for your loss,' Sergo said from his great height.

Babilina *curtsied*. What the fuck? Other than playing a Chekhov girl on stage as a child, when had she ever curtsied? It was a gesture from imperialist days, submissive, improper for a worker-to-worker interaction, and she wished she could have stopped herself.

'We have met on previous visits, friend commissar,' she said. Another ill-disciplined blurt! What, vodka aside, had come over her?

'I remember.' Sergo's eyes, alone in that stricken face, smiled. 'When friend Lavrentiy Pavlovich and your husband first moved to Tbilisi in the twenties, you were beginning your teaching career. I trust you are still employed at the university in Tbilisi?'

Babilina blushed as she produced the Bolshevik formula: 'I am working on my self.'

Unlike other high officials, Sergo listened. 'You and your daughters have to be careful of all these skunks.' His eyes settled on Beria, who was entertaining one of his secretaries. 'The loss of self cannot be a partial thing. The Russians have done it to Georgia. To our social bonds, to our persons, to our selves. We thought we were giving a little of our self away, but they took everything.'

'The Russians?'

He fixed her with a smile of profound dejection. 'You know what the great historian Karamazin said when he was asked to describe Russians? *They steal.* That is all there is to say. You can only work on your self if it has not been stolen.'

Babilina was tongue-tied. In a desperate attempt at small talk, she said, 'So friend, do you think there will be a war?' She gave a nervous laugh that she tried to disguise as a cough. War with Germany was a permitted subject. Or was it? Fuck! *Was* it?

Ordzhonikidze's moustache lengthened but this time his eyes did not smile. 'No, there will be no war under friend Stalin. But the struggle for peace will destroy millions.'

Why was this towering figure confiding in her, speaking such unspeakable words? Why was he making her a witness? If she and he were dragged out by men in leather coats, she would not have been surprised. But as she hung there in frightened silence, her hands reaching instinctively for Ana and Melor, more important people came up behind Dear Sergo and soon Beria spirited him away.

She watched them, the People's Commissar and his protégé. What was the bond between this last kind man in Stalin's Politburo and, of all people, Beria? Maybe Sergo still saw the awkward but proud loner whom, she feared, Vasil also saw. In spite of, what, thirty years of evidence to the contrary?

She pursued a waiter until she got another vodka out of him.

Now Beria surfaced at her side, as if from her thoughts.

He bowed. 'Friend Babilina.'

'Lavrentiy Pavlovich.' She took his hand. With his pince-nez and square mouth, he looked even more like an office clerk than most office clerks did, certainly the Georgian ones. In fact, he had beaten Stalin in erasing his origins. No matter how he tried, The Steel One still looked Georgian. Beria, on the other hand, resembled nobody from nowhere.

'Vasil looks terrible,' Beria said.

'He works twenty-four hours a day for you, ten days a week. He has just lost his father. How do you expect him to look?'

Beria gave her an amused nod. 'Man's soul finds peace when he immerses himself in work. Work allows us to avoid thinking of . . . unpleasant things. Speaking of work,' he tweaked the subject with a sly smile, 'how's the foreign literature business going?' She wondered what he was insinuating about her departure from the university . . . or could he know about the book she had given the girls' teacher?

'Oh, you have forgotten more about books than I will ever learn,' Babilina said. 'I heard you appointed yourself chairman of the judging committee for the Stalin Prize for Literature?'

'Deputy chair,' Beria said. 'Professor Fadeev, your former supervisor, remains chair. There were so many poor outcomes from that committee, I felt I owed it to the Party to step in. Ensure some integrity of process. You wouldn't believe what I found,' he said, moving closer to her and adopting a confidential air. 'These academics, they weren't reading the books they were judging!'

'Scandalous.'

'To be honest, who could blame them? Slab after slab, thousands of pages of dreadful Party-line tosh. Kill me now. But so, I had to have my fun. I would read a passage at random, then go into one of these judging sessions and ask the professors what they thought of such-and-such a scene in such-and-such a book. They were shitting themselves trying to cover up the fact that they hadn't read a line. Then, finally, your Professor Fadeev said, "Oh, come on, friend Beria, put yourself in our place. You'd choke if you had to fill yourself with so much shit."'

'Sometimes Professor Fadeev forgets himself,' Babilina said.

'I laughed till I nearly died. "Fadeev," I said, "that's the first intelligent thing I've heard you say!" Ah, good times.' Beria wiped his eyes and took a jar from his pocket. 'Pepper?'

She shook her head, breathing deeply to subdue the explosion inside her. She must stay composed and strategic, keep her mind on what was coming next, and assess Beria not on his moral qualities but as an adversary whose actions were purely political. If you keep your cool, she told herself, it is possible to outflank him.

'What fun you can have with literature,' Beria said. He must, she thought, know about the pornographic English novel. 'Ah! Just what I have been waiting for!'

The musical performance was beginning. Melor and Ana had taken their positions on the stage and began to play Georgian folk songs. Beria had insisted on music, as a salve for the grief of their grandfather's death.

'You know,' Beria murmured in her ear, 'a future is coming when we will no longer be speaking of "your" children or "my" children, only "our" children'. *The ABC of Communism.* I highly recommend it. It's a dark horse for the Stalin Prize.'

With a flick of his tail, he glided away. Beria was more than two-faced, Babilina thought. He had as many faces as there were minutes in the day. He was talking with Ordzhonikidze now, unwilling to be upstaged by a pair of girls. Yet, as she observed the choreography of the Important Men, she saw how Beria managed to manipulate the space around him so that he could keep his glass-disc eyes on Ana and Melor.

Babilina cursed herself for exposing them to this atmosphere. Why did Vasil have to ask them to come? But she couldn't have left them alone in the apartment either. And she couldn't leave Vasil alone with all of this; although, she thought as she watched him float around, he might as well have been on the moon.

Now, that sinister Natia Meskhi slinked up beside her and made a tired joke about the bagpipes: 'And they say that there is no torture in Georgia.'

THE FIRST FRIEND

When was it *ever* going to stop? All the constant fucking intrigue, it was doing her head in. Men like Beria were born for intrigue. Conspiracy was their gift. Maybe, notwithstanding their baloney about being great governors and organisers, intrigue was their *only* gift. It was their inheritance from Lenin, the Jesus Christ of intriguers. They loved it, they lived for it, they got drunk on it. People like herself and Murtov had dreamed of a Communist future. Then, betrayed by the Stalinist present, they embarked on their internal migration, only desiring to keep their families together and snatch some happiness from today. Let the conspiracy flow past and not catch them in its wash. She wanted silence and blankness and peace. But this intriguers' torrent was never going to let her find firm ground underfoot.

She looked grimly around the hall. If it was not Georgians obsessed with Beria, Beria, Beria, it was the others, all the way up to Dear Sergo's level, obsessed with Stalin, Stalin, Stalin. She remembered something chilling that Ana had said to her a few days earlier. The girls' class had been learning about microbes. Once Ana learnt microbes were everywhere, she began to see them in her clothes, her food, on her parents' skin, even in the air she breathed. She cried, 'Mama, I can't drink water! All I can see are these tiny living creatures!' Babilina had thought that no, Ana wasn't learning about bacteria, she was learning how to be a Soviet citizen.

Beria! That microbe, alive in the water and the air! And here he was, up on the stage having his photograph taken with her daughters! How had she let that happen? He was hugging Ana. Babilina wanted to rush up and snatch her away, kick him in the groin. But of course that would bring on the direst consequences.

Beria had less respect for Party wives than any other form of human life.

She focused on the stage as if to control events with her eyeballs. Beria had released Ana, thank heavens. The girls were rushing to her with thousand-rouble notes in their fingers. Even Ana was smiling. Melor had theatre tickets: *The Squealer*, of course. Murtov drifted behind, maudlin and distant. She enveloped him with her arms, even in front of the dignitaries.

The People's Commissar of Heavy Industry and his retinue, including Beria and his retinue, swept past in the direction of their cars. Sergo paused to kiss Babilina on both cheeks. He pumped Murtov's hand, ruffled the girls' hair and asked if Georgian musical instruments weren't the best!

Ana said, 'No, the best violins are made in Germany.'

Instead of the requisite reply—Soviet violins are the best, send the dissenter to the other world!—Ordzhonikidze smiled. 'Well, I shall give orders to our violin makers in Moscow that ours must come up to German standards, and when they are, you will be given the first.'

Ana replied quietly, 'I don't play the violin,' and Sergo was unable to contain a quack of laughter.

Then he came to give Babilina another kiss, or so she thought, but instead he brought his enormous moustache close to her ear.

'You deserve a future. You will be a great loss to the Soviet people.'

Babilina pulled back, but Sergo kept hold of her hands and searched her eyes.

What was this—language or in-depth language? This was a mate of Stalin's, one of that gang of thugs, the masters of terror . . . what could he possibly mean?

To her stricken confusion, he brought his moustache back to her ear. 'Sometimes the enemy within is that same self that you are working on. If that is so, you must find a way out.'

As he withdrew, Babilina mouthed: 'And so must you.' It came out like the curtsy. She had no control. She didn't know if Dear Sergo understood her. She didn't know if she wanted him to.

Beria ushered Dear Sergo and the official party through the town hall doors, which were engraved with heroic scenes from Georgian history. Behind them trailed the ghoulish Natia Meskhi. Bizarrely, that ominous pudding had tears in her eyes as she beheld Babilina, Vasil, Melor and Ana, and blew them kisses.

'What a beautiful family,' she said before following Beria and Ordzhonikidze to the cars.

Part two
RUSSIA

FIFTEEN DAYS TO LIVE

XV

'THAT'S IT, V, WE'RE COOKED. I CAN'T THINK MY WAY AROUND IT.'

The boss gazed gloomily out of the sealed Pullman train at the nothingness north of Rostov. They were two days into the three-day train journey to Moscow. They had presented their internal passports to a frightened-looking conductor at Tbilisi terminal and boarded a 'soft' carriage—'first class' and 'second class' had been prohibited, so the cars were defined by whether their seats were upholstered leather or hard wood.

Skirting the Russia–Ukraine border near Donetsk, Murtov looked out at the wheat-farming peasants bent double under their sheaves (*tr: GAR-si*). It mildly surprised him, after the enforced famines, that there were any Ukrainians left. Perhaps these peasants were Russians brought in as replacements.

A film had fallen over Beria's eyes. He sighed more than spoke: 'Why would you bother?'

This glimpse of vulnerability, humanity even, was a red light for Murtov. In Beria's unguarded moments you needed even more than usual to be on your guard.

Beria had said little since his summons had arrived, a telegram from the General Secretary himself, signed 'Ivan Vasilievich', Stalin's code name after his hero Ivan the Terrible. He urgently wanted to talk to Beria face to face. Beria assumed it was bad news—'What else could it be?'—and two days and nights of sullen brooding on the train had only deepened his foreboding.

'The dwarf will have found some piffling security shortcomings in our preparations,' Beria told Murtov yet again, as if by repeating information he might persuade it to change. 'The gala will be called off and all our renewal will have been for nothing.'

Murtov thought: renewal of my home. *Your* home.

'That's the best spin I can put on it,' Beria said.

'What's the worst?'

'That I will be sent to the other world.' He regarded Murtov. 'Don't worry, they won't disrespect you. You're my first friend. They'll shoot you too.'

Beria went back to contemplating the steppe. He was not a pessimist by nature, but sometimes he needed to talk himself into a state of utter despair to create a slingshot for his fightback. Hadn't he promised Murtov he was going to fuck them up?

'I can't afford to be away,' Beria said, drumming his fingers on the window and looking hatefully at the peasants. He had micromanaged the miracle of Ureki, the lightning construction of Stalin's seaside temple, right down to his invention of a new way to transport former persons to the work sites. Beria had figured out that you could maximise the number of prisoners in a truck by seating them with their legs in a V-shape, each man's groin squashed against the tailbone of the man in front. It satisfied and amused him to see capitalists, kulaks and Whites in 'my V-chain'. He claimed to have got the idea from the name he called his one true friend.

Finishing the temple had now been left to Natia Meskhi. For all Beria cared, he could have left Stalin's mother in charge. The gala was doomed.

Since boarding the train, Beria had gone without sleep. The more fatigued he grew, the more frantic his anxiety, clicking over like an infinitely repeating number. He went to the bathroom to inject himself with amphetamines. When he came out, he railed against his 'useless posse': Merkulov, Dumbadze, Kruglov and Goglidze, even the brothers Kobulov. Each of them might flip over to Yezhov (he mentioned neither Meskhi nor AAA). Beria vowed wildly to have his entire Georgian Politburo cancelled—if he managed to survive Moscow.

'Whatever else I have achieved I have been unfailingly loyal to the Party. I have not done a *thing*!' He smacked his hand against the wooden fold-out table, then wrung his hurt fingers.

There was no calming him. This was what Babilina was always warning Murtov about: innocence was the worst crime you could commit during Yezhov's Thing. Innocence gave your accusers licence to use their imagination, which was far more dangerous than facts. Beria, by convincing himself he was innocent, was driving himself mad.

'You are a victim of your achievements,' Murtov said. 'You are too efficient, too honest, too hard-working, too . . . *good*.'

'Ain't that the truth, V. Ain't that the truth.'

'But we don't know anything yet. You might have been called up to receive a surprise Order of Lenin.'

'That's not a good thing! When he's decided to give you the chop, he first showers you with medals. The moment you relax, you're done. Your crime is your ingratitude after he gave you so much.'

Murtov wiped his face, trying not to give anything away. 'You've left friend Meskhi in charge. Two weeks ago you didn't seem so sure.'

'Oh, I don't think I told you.'

Murtov shook his head. There was no such thing as *I don't think I told you*.

'Yezhov tried to get at me through Meskhi,' Beria said. 'He mailed her an arrest warrant to serve me.'

'Yezhov sent Natia an arrest warrant for *you*?' Murtov blinked.

'After your father's funeral. When Dear Sergo left.'

'What happened?'

'Yezhov had promised Meskhi my job. She came straight to me. There it was in black and white: a real arrest warrant with my name on it!'

'What was the offence?' Murtov asked, trembling.

Beria took his jar from his pocket and picked out a chilli. 'I didn't even read it. What he didn't account for was that we are strong together, we Caucasians. Natia knew she had better prospects as my 2IC than if she had me knocked off. Who wants to have your head above the parapet at the moment? Yezhov miscalculated, typical of that midget intelligence. She came straight to me and asked what we should do.'

He doesn't know Natia is Russian, Murtov realised. He's fucked. One tiny crack in omniscience and the whole thing comes down. First rule of the NKVD.

'I called Moscow and spoke to Dear Sergo, as well as Khrushchev and Molotov. That's three of the Politburo I can trust to make sure the old man knows what Yezhov's up to.'

'They helped? But what if—'

'What if the old man is behind it? Sure. Yezhov is Stalin's pet. But for the rest, there's safety in numbers.'

'How could they persuade the General Secretary to overrule Yezhov?'

'They can't. But I reminded them to tell him that my Stalin Prize for Literature committee has awarded him first prize for his *Collected Works* and it's being announced today. The vanity card is always a good one to play, remember that.'

'So we'll be okay? If he's called Yezhov off, why are you worrying so much?'

'What makes you think I'm worrying?'

Murtov didn't know what to say. Beria had flicked a switch from despondency to a bizarre overconfidence. The amphetamines always fucked him up.

'I can trust Natia,' Beria said. His glasses flashed. 'She saved my life.'

Murtov slipped in and out of sleep. Beria was wired, calculating, playing multiple chess games inside his head and cheating in all of them. Moscow Fever was taking hold.

Once Murtov woke to see Beria fossicking in his black leather travel bag. He fished out his duty revolver. As he was not allowed his Tommy gun in Moscow, he had brought the side-arm. When he saw Murtov's eyes on him, Beria pointed the gun, giving Murtov a violent start. Then he turned it against his own temple.

'*Lavrushya!*'

With a delighted cackle, Beria pulled the trigger. It clicked against his head. He 'fired' again and again, amused to death.

'Don't worry,' he said. 'Georgian roulette: no bullets. But we'll load it before we go into the Kremlin.'

'They'll search you.'

'Really? The First Secretary of the Central Committee for all of Transcaucasia? I guess they will. If he's planning to have me arrested, I suppose he'll take precautions. Pity. I wouldn't mind offing the old cunt.'

Murtov checked the carriage to make sure nobody, no steward or guard, had heard this crazy talk.

Beria chuckled away. 'Stop fussing like an old woman! No, I'd never shoot The Steel One. But to play ball with him, you've got to be as fucked up as he is. I remember once when he visited Sochi, he didn't want anyone to know. The only person I told was Nina, who I brought because he drools over her so much. When he found out that I wasn't alone, he gave me his ball-freezing stare and said, "When I give an order it must be obeyed to the letter." I thought he was going to have me sent to the other world right there. But then Nina cosied up to him like a kitten and he was all sweetness and light. I've never seen anyone so schizo. It was a useful lesson. The successful leader is the one who keeps everybody guessing. When all this shit blows up in his face, it's going to be "bad Yezhov". He'll turn around on a kopek, you watch. We just have to make sure we're still alive.'

Beria stroked his gun. 'If I get in a room with friend Yezhov, on the other hand . . . Nah, I'd prefer to throttle him. A bullet is so impersonal, don't you think? Almost rude.'

When they stepped out of their soft car onto the platform in Moscow's giant Kazansky railway terminal, they were met by Yezhov himself, limping at the head of an NKVD detachment. The place smelt of soot and cooking fat. Overhead, elaborate stonework walls opened into an atrium showing the starry night and a crescent moon. Crowds watched from the ticketing lines, but a security cordon kept them at a distance and the cavernous terminal rang eerily with their silence.

The dwarf stood on tiptoes to plant kisses on Beria's cheeks. One of Yezhov's green-uniformed guards slid in and took Beria's black travel bag to load into an American Packard waiting at the entrance. No Soviet Emkas, not even if they were German on the inside, for the Moscow elite. Murtov didn't think Beria had been really serious about shooting Yezhov, even less Stalin himself, but he was relieved to see the revolver taken away.

'That is a welcome kiss from the General Secretary,' Yezhov said. 'And *this*'—he gave a sharp jab to Beria's right kidney, causing him to leap—'is a howdy-do from the NKVD. Good trip?'

Murtov was permitted to ride in the same Packard as Beria and Yezhov. He first bent beneath the vehicle and checked for explosives. 'Old habits,' he said to Yezhov's raised eyebrows. The higher wheelbase of the American car made it easier to clear. Inside, the Packard was spacious, with soft leather seats and cotton lace curtains drawn across the windows. Assisted by roadblocks in their favour, they glided through the streets of Moscow, where Murtov had only been twice, as bodyguard to his oldest friend. Workers poured out of a subway station and, on the boulevards by the Moskva River, hung from overcrowded street trolleys. Murtov didn't like the place: Moscow was down at heel yet also full of its importance, like those up-themselves Russians.

'Don't forget what they say about Moscow,' Yezhov said. 'Easy to get in, nightmare to get out!'

Murtov saw St Basil's Cathedral and thought of his girls; even if they were trained not to recognise churches, their eyes would be on these ice-cream spires. Whatever Communism had done, it had never given the human race a building like this. Beria often said St Basil's should have been destroyed in the Revolution. Only Stalin, that superstitious sentimentalist, defended the cathedral. Deep down, Beria said, The Steel One was still the seminarian, his mother's son.

Yezhov showed Murtov no glimmer of personal recognition. Another good sign was when the armoured Packard drove past Dzerzhinsky Street and the Lubyanka prison, the Big House. Maybe Yezhov's friendly welcome was genuine.

The Kremlin came upon them. On top of its walls were floodlit red stars made of rubies expropriated from churches. The Packard turned through the Spasskaya Gate, the driver giving a password to the guard before the great iron gates swung open. Murtov couldn't resist a swell of awe at Russian power. You could feel it in Yezhov's more punctilious demeanour towards the uniformed guards.

When the car stopped, Yezhov asked Beria if he had prepared.

'Prepared?'

'Nobody told you? You're addressing the Central Committee first thing tomorrow.'

Beria shook his head in confusion. Murtov had seen this before. Whenever he entered the Kremlin courtyard, Beria lost his self-esteem, his control, his cynicism. In the face of all this *architecture*, he became the would-be student.

'Christ, the staff are incompetent,' Yezhov said. 'You haven't written your speech?'

'Wh-what speech?'

'Your acceptance, what else?' Yezhov said, giving him a too-hard slap on the cheek.

'What am I accepting?'

'Don't tell me they haven't told you *that*. Congratulations, Lavrushya. You have been appointed my deputy: 2IC of the entire NKVD. Big job! Maybe have a nap before you get to work, yeah?'

With a high laugh, Yezhov gimped away. In the vastness of the courtyard, he resembled an ant.

XVI

AS ADOLESCENTS AT THE SOKHUMI GYMNASIUM HIGH SCHOOL, Murtov and Beria teamed up for scams. There was the one where they talked two Armenian boarders, sons of princes, into paying them for French tutorials. Neither Murtov nor Lavrushya knew a word of French, but the Armenians knew even less, and they got away with it for six months. Then there was their side hustle in smuggling spirits from Tsaritsyn in Russia to sell on the Sokhumi black market. They had the grog transported through the checkpoints by an old lady they paid to put the bottles in a coffin and sing devoutly, '*Spiritus, spiritus!*' as she passed the guards. In their scams, Murtov was always the front man, Lavrushya always the brains.

Best of all was when Lavrushya wrote Murtov's examination papers for him. It was mutually beneficial: Murtov was stretched for time with his football and social commitments, while Lavrushya lurked in his alcove under the stairs. Murtov offered to pay him, but Lavrushya's satisfaction lay in fooling people. Payment would have cheapened it. Murtov could not get him to accept a single rouble. The only worry was that the essays would be too well-written and betray Murtov with grades of A or A plus, but Lavrushya was clever enough to modulate his proficiency to Murtov's B-minus level, even to forge his handwriting.

When the Revolution turned the tables and Beria became the boss and Murtov the assistant, Lavrushya asked Murtov to write *his* speeches. It wasn't that Murtov was any good, but the job was time-consuming with all the necessary facts and figures. Beria would polish the speeches once Murtov had researched and produced his usual B-minus. The boss said he liked their plainness; it was not in his interest to be too rhetorically flamboyant. And their in-depth purpose, to remind Murtov who was whom, was served.

Murtov's first important writing task had been at the 1934 Seventeenth Party Congress in Moscow, Beria's first national-level appearance. His speech bragged about his economic successes as Party First Secretary of Transcaucasia and won him election to full membership of the one-hundred-and-twenty-strong Central Committee of the Communist Party of the Soviet Union, one level down from Stalin's Politburo. Beria's jubilation showed how he valued being seen as more than a provincial Georgian personage.

Beria's—or Murtov's then Beria's—book *On the History of Bolshevik Organisations in Transcaucasia*, now read by adults and children in most countries of the world, was a bold revision of momentous events which had been wrongly construed to minimise Stalin's influence in the region, particularly from 1917 to 1921. Stalin had complained of the 'rotten liberalism' prevalent in previous histories, prompting Beria to embark on the rewriting project himself. (Stalin's best friend Sergei Kirov had refused the commission, declaring that he was 'a man of action, not a cocksucking writer'. Kirov was murdered a month later, so there was an opening.) Beria wished to prove he was both man of action and cocksucking writer. He ordered Murtov to ghostwrite the book, typed out from spoken discourses Beria delivered over many late nights. Upon publication, Beria became a cocksucking scholar, a cocksucking man of letters: his cocksucking name was on the cocksucking cover!

The book was so vast, Murtov in turn commissioned a Georgian academic named Bedya to help. Beria knew little of Bedya's contribution, but he complimented Murtov on his improved style before personally delivering his bound manuscript to a grateful Stalin.

✿

Beria and Murtov were put up in the House on the Embankment, a set of giant apartment blocks diagonally across the Moskva River from the Kremlin. They were given a flat in Block 12, reputedly the best, where the children of the Politburo, even Stalin's daughter Svetlana and his son Vasili, resided with their nannies, servants, cooks and housekeepers. Beria's allocated apartment had seven rooms and an enormous balcony, double-thick walls, telephones, a solarium and running hot water. There were armed NKVD guards stationed permanently on each landing.

In their plush oversized suite, decorated with gilt wallpaper, a portrait of The Steel One in each room, paintings of Revolutionary scenes and framed prints of the Soviet Constitution and Lenin's finest speeches, its ceiling cornices moulded with fairies and cherubs, an overtired Beria ignored Yezhov's advice to take a nap and monstered Murtov to convert their eight-hundred-page book into a four-minute address to the Central Committee. Mainly Beria wanted to correct what he remembered of its mistakes. Murtov sat at the writing desk with its brass inlay and set up a typewriter provided by the staff.

'The first edition said Stalin was not in Georgia between 1919 and 1920,' Beria said, pacing the fine carpet while Murtov, at the writing desk, tried to keep up.

'But he wasn't,' Murtov said. 'It's well documented that he was leading the fight against reactionaries and wreckers in the Moscow region and Poland.'

'Not anymore he wasn't. He gave me a specific note after publication that he was in Georgia *continuously* to counter the Menshevik threat.'

'How could he have been in Georgia while also in Moscow and Poland?'

'Doesn't matter,' Beria said irritably. 'And while we're at it, we can no longer acknowledge any of the old Georgian Bolsheviks as having played a role in the Revolution. *Charkas* remind him of his beginnings. Fucksake, the book said Peter the Great and Ivan the Terrible were descended from Georgian kings. I thought he'd be happy but he said, "I don't still stink of Georgia like you, Beria; I'm Russian now." I had to tell him the mistake was my staff's fault. Sorry, pal.'

'Ah, his actions during the Revolution . . .' Murtov, flustered, was pulling at his earlobes and trying to bring Beria back to the speech. 'Where would this come?'

'It *won't* come in my speech!' Beria exclaimed, as if spelling out the obvious. 'What has to come is its repudiation. I must specifically say that Stalin is leading a new Revolution by the Young

Bolsheviks against the Old. It's of critical importance to repudiate the past *because* of its inconsistencies!'

'How old is he?' Murtov asked. He was puzzled. Wasn't The Steel One's sixtieth birthday being celebrated with great fanfare in Red Square in the coming December?

'He's young,' Beria snapped.

'But he's older than the Old Bolsheviks he's rubbing out because of their age.'

'You can make him twenty-one for all I care, as long as he's a Young Bolshevik!'

Murtov typed, feeling the double pressure of getting the speech written and stopping the boss from melting down. After Beria's three manic days in the train, his reprieve—a promotion! A speech to the Central Committee!—had, far from cheering him up, sent him into a new tizz. Perhaps he didn't believe the good news. It had come from Yezhov, after all. Perhaps Beria believed he was being tricked into writing this speech as a confession? It was a trick Beria himself had pulled. Murtov, from what he had seen of Yezhov, wouldn't credit him with that kind of brain. But Beria did not know Yezhov. Beria only knew Beria. And what he would do if he was in Yezhov's shoes was to trick Beria.

Around it went.

By the end of the evening, they had a document. It was three times longer than it was meant to be but Murtov, exhausted, would not have the energy to edit and retype it until the morning. As he collapsed into his obscenely grand yet undeniably comfortable four-poster bed at around two a.m., he heard his oldest friend hammering the keys.

The last thing Murtov was aware of as he closed his eyes was a soft male voice in the corridor outside the apartment.

'Come on, let's go home, we've got enough for the night.'

But his Russian was not good, and he was drifting off, so he might have imagined it.

✻

Murtov woke at six and Beria was still typing. When the time came to dress and go to the Central Committee, Beria took a bath, from which he emerged with an energy as fresh as the cologne he was splashing on his just-shaved bald head.

'Fucking collar and tie,' he said, constructing a knot in the mirror. At parades in Georgia, Beria wore round-necked folk tunics, but in Moscow, where the members of the Central Committee wore military and other official uniforms, 'Stalin only ever wants me to look like a mafioso.' Beria hated it, but he obeyed.

While Beria was complainingly retying his knot, Murtov read the speech. It praised The Steel One relentlessly for his youthful mastery of the Transcaucasian domain. It bulged with gratitude and flattery. Honestly, Murtov thought, Beria could have banged this out off the top of his head in five minutes. What a fucking night.

Murtov read about crowds in Tbilisi breaking out in spontaneous applause from their balconies on the day the 'Stalin 1936 Constitution', which gave the Vozhd absolute power, was proclaimed.

'Hang on,' he said in alarm.

'What?' Beria was having another go at his tie.

'The Stalin Constitution can only fit into your narrative if it took place two years earlier, in 1934, before the release of your book.'

'Why's that? Fuck these knots. Can you do them?'

'Because your book was "inspired by" the Stalin Constitution.'

'Okay, I've got enough on my hands here. Fix it, will you?'

Murtov crossed out '1936' and replaced it with '1934', relocating Stalin's most famous constitution to two years ahead of its time. It felt as easy as moving a chair from a dark corner into a nice patch of sunlight. Murtov watched Beria fussing with his tie and thought of the NKVD's precept about obtaining written confessions: *Fabrication with a view to publication*. If it was written, so it would be.

Murtov was almost too tired to go to the visitors' gallery in the Great Palace to listen to Beria's speech, but he was wide enough awake to hear the boss solemnly invoke 'the visionary Stalin 1934 Constitution, far-sighted and ahead of its time'. Murtov inspected the Politburo for their reaction.

Stalin aside, the big guns were in attendance: the Politburo members Molotov, Khrushchev (the only two baldheads in the crew and, not coincidentally, the Russians with whom Beria enjoyed a modicum of rapport), Mikoyan, Malenkov and Voroshilov. Kaganovich, the one Jew in the Politburo, was displaying shaven cheeks and moustache to replace his beard; the rumour was that Stalin had cut it off himself, declaring, 'I'm sick of having a rabbi in my meetings.' Beside Kaganovich was Yezhov, who must have been sitting on a monstrous cushion to get his face above the railing, and beside him was Dear Sergo Ordzhonikidze, who gazed down mournfully upon Beria like a father who has arrived at the day when his son has outstripped him, yet instead of the pride he'd anticipated he feels the cold wind of his obsolescence. All applauded Beria's rearrangement of the Stalin Constitution from 1936 to the more convenient 1934.

After Beria's speech, Stalin made his entry. Murtov's eye was magnetically drawn to the General Secretary. The portrait expanded into three dimensions and became a man; or did it? The idea of The Steel One was projected into every citizen's dreams and nightmares; here now were the flesh and the blood, the skin and the hair, the *man* who slipped into the presidium with as little fanfare as if he were just another delegate, to take his seat. Could so much history, geography, philosophy, art and literature be contained in one human body? And weight: he thought of what Yezhov had said about how much the Soviet state weighed. Could all of that incomprehensible weight be collected in one human frame? This was the fascination of looking at him: you were almost watching yourself performing the complex and futile mental task of separating Stalin from 'Stalin'. You never had a hope of seeing the man as a man; nor could you stop trying.

Beria often described Stalin as 'unexpectedly yellow'. His skin was the colour of weak tea with milk: the famous 'Kremlin complexion' rarely touched by sunlight. He had his mother's head, the cubic skull of a Georgian peasant. The pockmarked face was bracketed between the majestic brush of greying hair and the rich, darker-toned moustache. Like that head case in Germany, you could portray the Vozhd as a walking moustache. Two mad pricks going mo-to-mo across Poland. Europe's destiny hung between a walrus and a toothbrush.

Stalin sat while General Voroshilov, the People's Commissar of Defence, made a short and incoherent speech. Stalin scrawled notes until he decided Voroshilov should shut up. He issued a bobble of his eyebrows. Voroshilov, midway through a rambling sentence, gratefully declared: 'Friend Stalin has the floor!'

The Central Committee rose to their feet and began an ovation of such duration and volume that Murtov sensed an uneasy competition; it was known that the first member of the audience to cease clapping, even if compelled by age or infirmity, would be noted. The applause went on, unflagging, as the portrait walked to the podium. He moved with a light foot: Stalin had Russified himself by will, but there was a telltale Georgian fuck-you fluency in his body language. Murtov understood him as an actor who was contracted to fulfil his never-ending obligations: he was the least free man of all, enslaved by 'Stalin'. Beria had told him that Stalin always locked his door when he slept. 'It's not that he's afraid of being killed; he has his bodyguards to prevent that. It's that Stalin must always be Stalin, and if anyone sees him asleep, not being Stalin, that would be the end of it.'

Stalin wore a military uniform that, unlike the Near Year Trees of medals standing around him, was only decorated with one modest Hero of the Soviet Union medal on his left breast. While the applause went on, he stroked his moustache with the dull patience of a man waiting for his bus, and occasionally raised a hand to stop the clamour . . . but this motion instead triggered a re-crescendo, a mass celebration of the one moment in their lives when the people were allowed to disobey him. Finally his fingers folded over in a signal of *Enough—and this time I mean it*, permitting the delegates to resume their seats. Even then, some still competed to be the last standing and clapping.

There was something surreal, almost impossible for Murtov to believe, in Stalin being an actual man who breathed the same air as him. But here he was. Murtov knew the stories of The Steel One materialising in a Moscow metro carriage on his own, no bodyguard, to ask a worker how her day had been and what he could do for her. One of these workers had replied, 'I'd love to look round the Kremlin.' Stalin arranged it. Whatever the propaganda value, the deeper impression was of disbelief: was The Steel One really *there, in real life?* You had to pinch yourself.

Murtov was unable to focus on the speech. Stalin was a shortish man, but taller than Murtov recalled, and his vocal tone was high and clotted, as if his voicebox was located not in his throat but somewhere near his gall bladder. The theme of The Steel One's speech was 'If Tomorrow Brings War'. He spoke of the current situation as 'breathing space' before the next step in World Revolution, socialism's final victorious clash with capitalism, which for present purposes wore a German uniform. He projected the historical inevitability of mankind's crossroads between peace and enlightenment and progress on the one side and fascist barbarity and death on the other. He spoke fighting words, with a kind of machismo bolstered by his Revolutionary warriors sitting behind him, their middle-aged sag corseted within their fine tunics. He spoke of sacrifice and courage, drawing attention not to the privations faced by the Soviet people but to the great polar explorers and aviators such as Babushkin, whose aeroplane had recently crashed, killing all on board; Stalin ordered the display of Babushkin's ashes in Red Square to remind the people of the ultimate sacrifice they would soon be called to make.

After its hypnotic rupture in the passage of time—Murtov could not say whether Stalin's speech went for thirty minutes or three hours—it came to an end. The ecstasy of applause went forever. You could build another St Basil's out of this sound. Murtov owned a gramophone recording of a previous Stalin speech; its eighth side consisted entirely of applause.

Approximately half of the Central Committee—the chosen ones—poured into black cars and were driven a few hundred metres to the Kremlin's banquet hall for a stand-up drinks party. Beria told Murtov, in the car, that the only purpose of the shift was to 'show the fuckers who's Who and who's Whom'.

Murtov and Beria followed a gleaming guard across the courtyard past the Tsar Bell and the Tsar Cannon. Each was the biggest in the world, and neither had ever worked. Another officer, saluting them with a click of his heels, guided them through a cavernous foyer to an elevator which opened, two floors up, into a carpeted corridor. Murtov felt he was in the cleanest place in the universe. If anyone lived here, he must have guards following him to polish every surface he touched. The officers were dark-haired, whereas on Murtov's previous visit they had all been blond: a change of fashion due to The Steel One's current hostility to Germany. Murtov asked Beria where all the blonds had gone. 'Don't worry, V, they're not in Siberia or anything, the blond wave is being held in the cells for when he flips again.'

In the banquet hall, waiters with plates of oysters, caviar and vodka outnumbered the few dozen guests. In niches on the walls, bright red stars, miniatures of the giant ruby ones atop the Kremlin, illuminated the invited insiders, all men.

Beria clutched a copy of Stalin's *Collected Works* in embossed Georgian printing on high-grade Georgian vellum, enclosed in a tooled Georgian leather binder. It was quite a souvenir of the occasion and he was extremely keen to present it to the Vozhd.

Stalin held court amid his cronies, who were listening as eagerly as opera fans meeting their idol. When he received a glass of champagne, Stalin gripped the waiter by his shoulder and toasted 'The People'. The waiter turned white and spilt champagne on his shirt. Stalin made a joke and laughed; the others followed dutifully before The Hammer, Molotov, toasted the Vozhd's brotherhood with the common folk.

Beria muscled his way in. Stalin straightened his back, shook Beria's hand, and introduced himself with the comically unnecessary: 'Stalin.'

Although barred from the circle, Murtov was near enough to see Beria brush off the insult—as if Stalin could not recognise him!—and present the book. Somewhat embarrassingly, he urged the great man to read it 'whenever you are in need of solace or reassurance about your place in history'. Beria made a point of gazing directly into Stalin's yellow stare. Yezhov, who was at, or somewhat below, Stalin's armpit, shot Murtov a surreptitious eye roll.

The General Secretary received the gift graciously and palmed it off to an aide without looking at it. Murtov was close enough to hear his words. 'When I appointed this young Beria as Party First Secretary of the Transcaucasus, the Old Bolsheviks'—Stalin cut his eyes side to side in warning, as if any of them might be decreed Old—'told me he was too inexperienced, that he was just a lowly Mingrelian swot of dubious loyalty who'd spent the Revolution playing both sides . . .' Stalin paused and gave Beria the kind of smile that made you think, just momentarily, that this opinion was the leader's own. Then he continued: 'But his insignificance as a personage convinced me that, unlike others, he was less interested in promoting himself than in *doing the work*.'

Involuntarily, Murtov's chest filled.

'While others just push paper'—Stalin again swept his yellow eye around his inner circle—'Beria solves problems. He is a true Bolshevik. Don't believe anything they tell you about his consorting with the Mensheviks and the capitalists in the twenties; that was all done on my orders and with my knowledge. When I visited the mountains of western Georgia in 1924, someone had anticipated that I might appreciate a holiday house. Some little fairy had an army of White labour—the only White army remaining, eh'—he waited for the laughter—'build the house for me in record time. I was informed that the little fairy was this boy here. This true Bolshevik!'

Stalin presented Beria with a signed photograph of himself, the personal gift he chose for select recipients.

'Since that first visit,' Stalin went on, voice like a coffee grinder, 'I have made sure that Beria takes care of business for me in that little part of Russia which calls itself Georgia. He is *effective*. I take you fools out for Sunday walks around my dacha and you do a little dainty weeding. But friend Beria, he is out there with an axe! No tree is too large for him to chop down! If I want information, friend Beria will develop it!' Stalin was roaring with laughter now. 'But fucksake . . .' He turned squarely on Beria. 'Lavrentiy Pavlovich, lose the pince-nez! You look like fucking Trotsky!'

The applause was started by Beria himself, rapt that Stalin had called him by his first name and patronymic. The entire Politburo duly followed, even a wry-looking Yezhov, and Murtov was startled to hear, around the room, the applause spread like a contagion among those too far away to have heard the leader speak. Murtov was clapping as lustily as anybody. The Steel One had spoken the words 'Lavrentiy Pavlovich'. They would live.

✿

Towards the end of the evening, as he wilted under the fatigue of the three-day train journey, the panicked preparation of the speech, the tension and release of its success—for crying out loud, the fatigue of being in Moscow in 1938—Murtov was trying to catch Beria's eye. He knew he would not be allowed to depart before the boss, but the boss, surrounded by back-slappers, was in no mood to call it a night. He had put his pince-nez in his pocket, so he could not detect Murtov's hints even if he wanted to.

'The man of the hour,' said a voice from the vicinity of Murtov's rib cage.

'Friend Nikolai Ivanovich, you must be pleased with your new deputy.'

'My new deputy, working towards the Vozhd, yeah?' Yezhov said, as if telling some joke for which he was holding back the punchline. 'And how are you, friend Vasil Anastasvili? Looking forward to the move to Moscow? How will Babi and your two . . . *young ladies* . . . feel about that? I'm pretty sure my new deputy's family will prefer to stay in the Caucasus.'

'I do not make presumptions,' Murtov said. He'd have been happier if Yezhov believed he was an orphan bachelor with no friends or family.

'Big move,' Yezhov said, 'but due recognition for all Lavrushya has done in Georgia for the Party.'

Murtov bowed his head; if the dwarf's attention was drifting away from Babilina and the girls, Murtov was going to step out of his road.

'I mean, having been down there myself, I can't help being impressed by the daily praise in the newspapers, the front-page photographs, the portraits by the Georgian artists of the country's favourite son that I saw *everywhere* . . . Our friend'—he nodded towards Beria—'is responsible for all this appreciation?'

'You will have to ask him,' Murtov said. 'I can't be privy to all of friend Beria's achievements.'

'No, of course, your memory is not that vast,' Yezhov said, nodding as if anyone watching them would think they were discussing what a warm summer Muscovites were enjoying.

'Is that a problem?' Murtov asked.

'A problem. Well, there are problems and there are problems.'

'Are there?'

'I don't know, Vasil. You tell me.' Yezhov gave him a twinkle of a grin. 'When I was in Georgia, I heard all sorts of things. Rumours that old mate Beria was, let's say, not quite as deferential towards our immaculate Vozhd behind closed doors as he is'—Yezhov lifted his little arm to take in the banquet hall—'in public.'

'I don't understand,' said Murtov, who understood all too well. Yezhov wouldn't need to prepare a fresh network of informants in Georgia. Every second citizen was already an NKVD 'reliable', a freelance snitch who bought and sold snippets of gossip like rabbit pelts in the marketplace. The price could rise and fall irrespective of the truth. The trade in information was the Soviet Union's finest experiment in free markets, reflecting the excesses of both capitalism and socialism.

'What I'm saying . . .' Yezhov leant into Murtov's armpit. Murtov lowered his ear. 'What I'm saying is, I have a bad feeling about the General Secretary's personal security if he goes to Georgia.'

'But the Moscow NKVD takes complete charge of his security,' Murtov said. 'None of us, none of Beria's men, will be permitted anywhere near him.'

'I just have a feeling in my waters,' Yezhov said, 'and I always trust my waters. I think there is the strong possibility of an attempt on his life if he goes down there.'

'*If?* You mean there is some doubt about his going to Georgia?' The boss would absolutely do his block.

'Yes—I mean *no*, of course not . . . well, not at this stage,' Yezhov said with poorly acted vacillation. 'Not after all the *preparations* friend Beria has made.'

Yezhov could make a soap bubble sound double-edged, but the way he said 'preparations' was triple-edged, as if *preparations* implied that Beria was intricately laying down plans for an assassination. Or a false-flag 'assassination', another Soviet speciality. Murtov's mind raced. Had Natia Meskhi been privy to something that she'd passed on to Yezhov? Was Beria acting in conspiracy? He would have to be, to plot such a thing. With whom? As he'd shared nothing with Murtov, it would have to be a senior person in Moscow. Murtov looked for Beria and saw him talking with Sergo Ordzhonikidze.

But this was the problem with Yezhov. He got your mind racing ahead of itself.

'What are you telling me?' Murtov said.

Yezhov patted Murtov's hip. 'I'm telling you that if our General Secretary were in any danger, the course of world history could be sent in a dark direction indeed. A catastrophe for all mankind, for eternity. Just think on that a little.'

'I don't need to think.'

'If the leader should pay this visit to the Caucasus, it would serve him and world history very well if a responsible person were to keep a close eye on friend Lavrentiy Pavlovich. A very close eye.'

'You're worried that friend Beria, who has just been promoted to the deputy leadership of your NKVD for the whole of the Soviet Union, is going to . . . allow a lapse in security?' Murtov whispered. 'Am I hearing this correctly?'

'You might be or you might not be, friend. All I need is your solemn vow that you will protect the leader of the free world *against any foe.*' Yezhov leant close. 'I told you I was giving you a chance. This could be it, V: your opportunity to fuck that piece of shit up like you've always wanted to.'

Murtov hoped that his glassy expression could pass for consent. It must have, because Yezhov gave the flesh above his hip a hard tweak and told him to pass on his best wishes to 'Babi'. As he watched Yezhov dissolve into the crowd, Murtov thought, this is exactly what Lavrushya told me would happen next.

XVII

'FIVE STARS FOR THAT ONE.'

Murtov had finally got Beria back to the House on the Embankment. Beria, bringing the expertise he'd gained by planting more listening devices in more rooms than any man alive, pronounced himself satisfied that there were no bugs. Now they sat in carver chairs at the window overlooking a darkened Moskva River. Beria drank vodka and chewed chillis. Murtov sipped black tea.

'Think so?' Beria said.

'Your finest hour. The grand things the General Secretary said about you.'

Murtov hoped he could wash away the taste left by his conversation with Yezhov.

'He's so ugly,' Beria said.

'Yezhov?' Murtov blurted out the first name on his mind.

Beria shook his head. 'Was he there? I didn't look low enough.'

'Who then?'

'Who do you think? That skin is so poxy, you want to bog it with plaster. But how could you match that tint? That nicotine yellow: the eyes, the hair, even the tunic. It's all yellow,' he added, as if 'yellow' was the colour for all the discontent in the world, the colour of jaundice, the colour of toadying.

'He did call you Lavrentiy Pavlovich.'

'*So* ugly. No wonder he is so pure in the sack department. It's meant to set him above the others, but I think, honestly, no woman would have him, not even a prisoner. And the hair,' he concluded. 'All that fucking hair, but if you're up close, it's quite thin. It's an *illusion* of hair.'

Murtov sipped his tea.

'And *that little part of Russia which calls itself Georgia*. You hear that? What a shithead. He stinks of BO, you know? Same as his mother. The privilege of getting close to Stalin is to discover that he doesn't get his clothes laundered. Fuck I hate this place. It's all about scratching backs, knowing who's in and who's out, who's got which office and which car, who's the first to laugh when he cracks a joke. And what he said about my glasses? Tomorrow pince-nez could land me in the gulag. Quotas have to be filled. The other week Yezhov was having fuckers arrested for wearing the wrong type of hat. You don't have to tell a joke about Stalin to get arrested now. You only have to smile at overhearing one. They're literally running out of people to get rid of. Soon they'll begin arresting tables and chairs.' Beria poured himself a fresh vodka. 'What time's our train?'

'Six.'

'Please let it be a.m.'

Murtov nodded.

'I came off that Pullman wishing I would never have to step inside one again,' Beria said, 'and now I can't wait to get back on.'

'I know how you feel. I miss Georgia.'

Beria shook his head impatiently, to convey that Murtov was also missing the point.

'And in a month we've got to move to this shithole,' Beria said. 'That's so Stalin, to demote a man upwards.'

'But . . . it's an enormous promotion,' Murtov heard himself say. 'Deputy chief of the NKVD.'

'All of that teasing about me playing both sides during the Revolution, consorting with the Mensheviks, having a bet each way, being such an expert interrogator behind closed doors, "chopping down trees with my axe"—it's in-depth to let me know that they have a file on me, they'll decide how long I last. You didn't swallow it, did you?

'You know what Dear Sergo was telling me?' Beria went on. 'Last week, when Yezhov came back here from Georgia with his "report" on preparations—oh yeah, he was there, like I said he was—Stalin told him he was promoting me to Moscow. Yezhov said I would make a very good People's Commissar. Stalin said, "No, I can't put another Georgian at the top . . ." Hey, you can't say the old boy doesn't have a sense of humour. And then he told Yezhov what he was planning. Yezhov flipped out. He knows what's what. I'll be given two years to get rid of him and blame him for the purges, and once that's done I'm next down the chute.'

'It's your first national role,' Murtov said weakly.

Beria shook his head so firmly he nearly threw his pince-nez off his nose.

'Boss of all the Transcaucasus, and now in this madhouse under Stalin's eye. How's that a promotion?'

Murtov dearly wanted sleep—only four hours remained until they had to leave for Kazansky train station—but Beria needed to crap on all night about Stalin and Yezhov and how he treasured his 'meaningful life' making Georgia the greatest of the Soviet republics. He was protesting too much, Murtov thought. Then Beria narrowed his eyes and said, in a lower and cooler tone, 'I did see you talking with someone very, very diminutive.'

Murtov was so tired he felt he was in the end stages of an interrogation. He remembered that Beria had claimed not to have seen Yezhov.

'Yes, and you were right,' he said.

Beria's shoulders slumped. Above all his other hatreds, sometimes what he most hated was to have been right.

Murtov continued: 'When you told me that Yezhov would imply to Stalin that his visit to Georgia might imperil his personal safety? You were right.'

'Fuck that fucking fucker.' Beria's glasses flashed at Murtov. *'Fuck!'*

'He told me that Georgian terrorist elements might be planning a coup, and . . . and that I should keep an eye on you.'

Beria now laughed heartily. 'He's a piece of shit.'

Murtov didn't know if 'he' was Yezhov or Stalin. Probably both.

'I've heard it all now,' Beria said and moved towards his bedroom. Murtov at last had something to be grateful for.

Beria stopped in the threshold and cleaned his pince-nez with a handkerchief. He put his glasses back on and took a chilli from his jar. 'But if I'm such a threat, why not just have me shortened by a head?' he said, using one of Stalin's favourite phrases. 'Why is Yezhov letting him come to Georgia at all?'

'I'm not sure he is,' Murtov replied. 'He kept saying *if* the Vozhd's visit goes ahead.'

'What, he'd let his mother down?' Beria laughed bitterly.

'I'm just repeating what Yezhov told me.'

'You know what?'

'What?' Murtov croaked. He couldn't take another thing. He just couldn't.

'The 1934 Stalin Constitution,' Beria said. 'It's genius. You are a true writer, V. An engineer of the human soul.'

'It was necessary in the circumstances.'

'Just don't claim credit for it. If you breathe a word to anyone, I'm sorry but I'll have you cancelled. Unless the mistake is discovered and I'm blamed for it. Then you may take credit for the speech, and I'll have you cancelled again. What's the quote from Medici? "We are nowhere commanded to forgive our friends." The old boy loves repeating that. He thinks he made it up.'

With a wheezy laugh that betrayed, finally, his fatigue, Beria closed his bedroom door.

XVIII

THE THING ABOUT STALIN'S MOSCOW WAS, IT NEVER ENDED. Sometimes that was its design: you were taken to the outer limits of your endurance, to be told that you had only just begun.

Permanent fucking Revolution.

The call came at four o'clock in the morning, an hour after Murtov went to sleep and an hour before his alarm clock was set for him to pack their things for Kazansky terminal. The ringing telephone startled him from florid dreams. Stalin's personal secretary, Poskrebyshev, was telling him that Beria had received the great compliment of an invitation to Stalin's Nearby Dacha, at Kuntsevo on the outskirts of Moscow.

'When he comes to take up his position with the NKVD?' said a disorientated Murtov, who was finding the phone call hard to disentangle from his dreams.

'A car will collect yous at five.'

Poskrebyshev was a stupefyingly ugly man with a face that looked like it had been sculpted with a boot heel. It was said that when Stalin first met Poskrebyshev, he exclaimed, 'My god, man, you don't even look like a human being. You'll terrify people!' He hired him on the spot.

'A.m. or p.m.?' Murtov asked, but the line had gone dead.

Beria's ability to brush up clean and controlled, whether he had slept or not, no matter how much he had drunk, was another of his special gifts. He donned his mafioso suit and tie. He was silent during the drive to Kuntsevo, suspicious of the driver. He hinted that Murtov might be able to put in a call to Babilina, but Murtov wouldn't know what to tell her. Were they being held back for a day? A month? Forever?

The car snaked past the new Moscow Metro stations, those glorious socialist churches, and, more glorious still, the Palace of the Soviets, which remained a rubble-strewn building site but existed in the minds of every citizen as a structure higher than the Empire State Building, crowned with a statue of Lenin three times taller than the Statue of Liberty, a final proof of Soviet enormity. This dim dawn, urchin children were fishing in the flooded foundations.

After a crawl through the inner city, the car raced along the Government Highway, a pristine asphalt surface manned by traffic police blocking the side roads and waving through the bullet-proof Packard.

After covering six versts at high speeds the Packard turned down a narrow lane and was stopped at a barrier bordered by fir trees. Beyond was another checkpoint at a five-metre-high fence with observation slits, then a final checkpoint at a barbed-wire barricade. They proceeded a few hundred metres through a fir forest with fruit orchards and a roadside watermelon patch before the driveway bisected a rose garden and entered a turning circle around a stone-walled carp pond. Smoke from the waiting drivers' cigarettes billowed out of ten or fifteen parked Packards. Beyond the pool was a plain dark-green villa surrounded by searchlights.

'Here we go,' Beria said.

After a body search they entered a small, unadorned vestibule and handed their coats to a cloakroom attendant. To the right was an open door through which Murtov saw a corridor leading into darkness. In front was a wider corridor to a spacious conference room, in which Murtov could make out portraits of Lenin, Gorky and the famous actor Kachalov. 'How he loves the Russian people,' Beria said from the side of his mouth, 'only Kachalov's real name is Chverubovich. Belarusian scum.' He gave Murtov a last sardonic glance, as if to say, *Not even Stalin gets one past me*, and led the way through a tunnel of security staff.

The study throbbed with rowdy men: Politburo members plus some others Murtov didn't recognise. Overhead hung a simple unlit chandelier. Two leather armchairs sat in one corner, either side of a polar bear rug with open jaws, which the revellers took care not to trip on. The Vozhd's desk was an immense steppe topped with green baize and illuminated by a brass-shaded reading lamp. No papers, only a bank of telephones. Behind was a plump leather-covered swivelling armchair and a tall strongbox. Murtov couldn't help registering that the office had no windows, not one. Persian tapestries hung from the wall behind the desk. The other walls held an odd collection of pictures. Stalin could have surrounded himself with the cream of Russia's art galleries, but pinned to the panelling were crudely scissored photographs and cartoons from magazines, their edges curling. The requisite portrait of The Steel One, hanging between two tapestries, was modest in size, an almost reluctant concession to the fact that no Soviet room was excused from the obligation. This particular Stalin, Murtov noted, was a mediocre rendition of a smiling youngish Vozhd brimming with the innocent optimism of the First Five-Year Plan.

Due to the lack of ventilation, the air was humid, warm and rank with competing flatulences. Beside the twin armchairs was a buffet of fatty Russian meat dishes. It wasn't doing much trade. Most of these men were not allowing food to distract them—'In Moscow it's eat and you get beat,' Beria liked to say. On small circular tables at each end of the buffet were bottles of Georgian wine and Russian vodka. Though the Polish was better, and they all drank it in private, in Stalin's presence the vodka was Russian-only.

There were no waiters. It was help yourself to your drinks, and they did. Murtov estimated thirty men were in the space, drinking and smoking and shouting to be heard. He sensed a unique Kremlin mood: the uninhibited genuine jollity among men free to carry out acts of extreme violence. It was immediately apparent that this was not an early start but a late finish. Beria, in for a kopek in for a rouble, poured a large vodka and downed it with barely a wince.

Stalin's cronies were celebrating Dear Sergo's fiftieth birthday. The Steel One's nose had been put out of joint by all the attention paid to Sergo on his visit to Georgia, though he said his displeasure was not on his own account—he was above petty jealousy—but because he had saved up a surprise party here in Moscow.

Invited only as an afterthought, Beria was taking his snubbing in his stride, throwing back a second breakfast vodka and trying in vain to make Dear Sergo smile. Murtov stood close by Beria's side. The most inebriated Politburo members—Khrushchev, Zhdanov, Voroshilov and Malenkov—linked arms and broke out in the old Tsarist anthem, a song forbidden everywhere but here, where Stalin's ambition to be ranked alongside Ivan the Terrible could be openly acknowledged. Stalin nodded graciously, swaying in time with the singing. Beneath the clamour, Beria said to Dear Sergo, 'Sing about Catherine the Great! She was fucked by the nobility whereas our leader has managed to fuck the entire country.' At last, Dear Sergo's moustache curved upwards.

Murtov moved away from Beria and stood between an NKVD agent and the giant known as Vlasik, a Moscow street brawler and Chekist tittle-tattle who held the exalted position of personal bodyguard to Stalin, with the rank of army major-general. Murtov and Vlasik watched the party without speaking.

Much of the conversation was about that mad German prick and his seizure of Czechoslovakia. General Voroshilov had heard word that the western allies, who had been aligned with Russia in the last war, were ganging up to sweet-talk the loony into turning his attention eastwards and wipe out the Bolsheviks.

Stalin held the centre of the circle, dressed in a plain military-style tunic of fine dark-green cloth. In this, his safest place, he seemed shorter. His pockmarks were accentuated in the lamplight and his body odour radiated. The Politburo had the same BO stink, as though everything about him became a fashion trend.

'That headcase doesn't even reckon we're human,' Voroshilov said. The Steel One appeared to be thinking of something else. When he did speak, they all paid close attention to his quick gestures, his sly little gobbets of laughter and his precisely measured body language.

He was sceptical about Voroshilov's theory. 'I've begun to think that he hates the West more than he hates us,' he said. 'We'll be all right. When someone's as batshit-crazy as that guy, you just spin him around and point him in the other direction. His strategic problem, and our edge, is that he wants to kill *everybody*.'

General Voroshilov turned pale, wondering how parroting Stalin's official anti-German line had got him into this mess. He scurried off for a drink.

Stalin drank vodka mixed with a splash of Georgian wine. Beria was at the smorgasbord when the Vozhd threw his non-withered right arm around his shoulder and said, in Russian rather than Georgian, 'Listen, Beria. Friend Yezhov has given me some second thoughts.'

'About?' Beria asked in Georgian, through a grin as forced as a kulak with a train ticket.

'The old sentimental journey. Too risky, he reckons,' Stalin said in Russian.

'You're kidding, right?'

If Beria's outburst did not cause the room to quieten, it was only because he had spoken in Georgian.

But now Stalin silenced the room himself, exclaiming irritably, 'Speak Russian, friend!'

Stalin only ever called him 'friend' when he was angry, 'Lavrentiy Pavlovich' when showing him particular favour, 'Beria' at other times.

Murtov saw Dear Sergo move quickly towards Beria and Stalin. Those in the leader's immediate proximity were, even under the burden of their drunkenness, freezing in apprehension. Had that Georgian twerp just defied the Vozhd?

'I love to kid, as you know, Beria,' Stalin said with an eerie yellow warmth, 'but it's out of my hands. Yezhov doesn't think he can keep security watertight. My heart yearns to visit the Georgian peasant in our glorious countryside, but the NKVD won't let me.' He added in Georgian: 'That German loony we're all so worried about is mad as fuck, but you know as well as I do that there's fifty madder than him on any Georgian street.'

If Murtov wasn't mistaken, Beria's chin quivered. It was rare for a group of rivals to see his boss actually, visibly, crack. But then Beria spotted Yezhov across the room, grinning and toasting him silently. Beria's face hardened and he bunched his shoulders as if to launch himself.

Dear Sergo, sober as a troika of judges, pushed through to Beria, nimbly evading the tripping hazard of the polar bear's jaws, and put him in a mock headlock.

'Now, now, don't ruin my birthday,' Sergo said, with the face of a man whose birthdays had all been ruined. 'If the General Secretary can't make it to Georgia, he can't make it. Unless . . .' Sergo released Beria's head and rubbed his thumb and forefinger down the wings of his moustache. 'Unless Georgia steps aside and permits friend Yezhov to take total control. That should be theoretically possible, shouldn't it, Lavrentiy Pavlovich?'

Beria said sulkily, 'I don't see why we can't just put on extra Georgian security. It's not like we're short of men.'

'You could,' Sergo said. 'But I agree with the Vozhd.'

'I was never disagreeing with him!' Beria cried. 'Only with that dwarf!'

'Don't make me put you back in my headlock,' Sergo continued. 'It's my birthday. Now. A firmer hand from Moscow would be just the insurance policy we need to keep the visit on track. You've done so much work, you wouldn't want to jeopardise it out of Georgian pride.'

'Sure, do what he wants,' Beria said, looking at his shoes like a schoolboy.

'It's not a matter of what the General Secretary wants,' interrupted Yezhov, who couldn't resist crossing the room to see if he could keep the conflict alive. 'The future of the nation is at stake. I really don't think the Vozhd should risk it.'

Stalin pursed his lips and nodded, weighing the evidence shrewdly before agreeing that yes, he was the future of the nation.

'What about,' said Sergo, demonstrating his legendary skills as a mediator, 'Moscow appoints a temporary new Party secretary for the Transcaucasus, in recognition of friend Beria's promotion to his new position in Moscow? This new appointment can increase the numbers and bear full responsibility for the safety of the visit.'

'Splendid proposal!' Stalin said with a clap. 'And you know,' he added to Sergo, 'it is a Russian tradition never to say no to the birthday boy!' He spoke in Georgian—a funny way, Murtov thought, to invoke a Russian tradition.

It was Yezhov who looked disappointed now. He sincerely didn't want Stalin's trip to go ahead. 'Fucksake, Sergo,' he said. 'If I were you, I'd prefer never to have been born.'

'But who could it be, this new Transcaucasian supremo?' Stalin said, taken with the idea of a new appointment, enjoying this moment which, patently, he had staged from the outset. His eyes ranged over the room, then came back to Sergo. 'Why hadn't I thought of this? You are Russian and Georgian both, a Muscovite and a Caucasian. The perfect man to take charge of the region and give Beria a bit of a rest while he prepares for his move to Moscow. I would be ever so grateful, Dear Sergo, if you and Yezhov would safeguard the future of the nation on this dangerous mission.'

Murtov saw Beria's mouth tighten. His eyes, behind his glasses, were beyond penetration. He only had to choose which insult to take more personally. There was Yezhov's insinuation that he couldn't protect Stalin. There was the risk of all his work—the demolition of the Ureki shorefront for his temple to Stalin, all the image-making and construction and grovelling and fucking spadework—coming to nothing if the visit were called off. And now there was the humiliation of Sergo, that burnout, that shadow of his former self, being sent to babysit him.

'What do you think, Beria?' Stalin said.

Beria bowed his head. 'As you wish, friend General Secretary. Now if you don't mind, I need to visit the little boys' room.'

'See if you can't flush away those Trotskyite glasses!' Stalin called after him, to general amusement and relief.

Murtov accompanied Beria, who did a sweep for listening devices. Murtov put his back against the bathroom door.

Beria stood at the white porcelain urinal. As was his custom, he undid his belt and fly, peeled open his trousers, and pissed with his hands on his hips. It was well known that he liked to take a good look at other pissers. Murtov, having noticed that young AAA was hung like a python, had warned him never to pee at the same time as the boss. 'If he sees *that*,' Murtov said, 'you'll be out of here before you can do up your fly.'

'Jesus, Mary and Joseph,' Beria said now, buttoning up, removing his glasses, washing his face and looking in the mirror. He pulled down on his eyelids as if to tear his face off. 'Did you see how he did that?'

'It was a set-up,' Murtov said, not because he'd seen it coming—he hadn't—but because that was what Beria wanted to hear.

'Fucking *Sergo*. My so-called mentor.'

'You'll manage it,' Murtov said. 'They can't get anything past you.'

'It's always some machine, some anonymous *they*, isn't it? Someone says, "But you're Stalin, you can do anything." And he points at the picture on the wall and says, "I'm not Stalin—*that's* Stalin!" He wants us to think the machine works with or without him, a self-operating historical necessity, an algorithm where not even the guy running the show is responsible.'

'Historical necessity is why we joined the Party, Lavrushya.'

'We can make it good again, V. Jesus, did you hear what he said about yearning to visit the Georgian peasant? He hasn't seen a village since 1928. Look at how lavishly these pricks live here. They mock me for working so hard to balance my budgets, because to them, accountability doesn't exist. They're *sick*! Yezhov, fucksake. And as for . . . Don't get me started on Dear fucking Sergo.'

'You never know whose side he's on,' Murtov agreed.

'I've told you I love you, haven't I?' Beria came up and pinched Murtov's ear. For an instant Murtov thought the boss was going to kiss him on the lips. 'You always give me what I need.' He now slapped Murtov on the cheek, unnecessarily hard, and led him back to the party.

Yezhov was entertaining the Vozhd with animated impressions of people in the room and offering cruel morsels of gossip about their personal lives. They hated Yezhov, but there was one rule: if the Vozhd laughed, you had to laugh, especially if the joke was on you.

As Beria merged into the group, Yezhov turned on him, not to imitate him—Beria's colourlessness made him impossible to mimic—but to number his characteristics on his hairy little fingers.

'Boring, obsessive, secretive . . . Did I say boring?'

This got a weak laugh, so Yezhov upped the ante. 'He does hate being left out of things. Wasn't at all happy about the late invitation, were you, Lavrushya?'

Beria bristled but said nothing.

'That's why I'm bringing him to work under you,' Stalin said to Yezhov, his yellow eyes on Beria. 'He can make you a bit more serious, and you can help him lighten up. You'll be good for each other!' He clapped like a matchmaking babushka.

'But I'm still allowed to have him liquidated if he's *too* boring?' Yezhov said.

'Oh, but he will ferret things out for you,' Stalin said. 'Remember the time I lost my pipe in this very office?'

'I do!' Yezhov sniggered. 'By the time you found it behind the couch, friend Beria had already extracted full confessions from three suspects!'

Stalin bellowed with laughter, and Yezhov stood on his toes and smacked Beria hard on the shoulder. 'Oh come on, you're in Moscow now, *Detective*—you have to learn to take a joke.'

Murtov saw Beria flinch at the schoolyard nickname and calculate who could have told Yezhov. Fuck, fuck, oh fuck.

The attention shifted away from Beria. Murtov followed him as he walked over to Sergo, who was looking as though he would rather be getting his fingernails pulled in the Lubyanka than continue this birthday party.

'You had every opportunity to defend me against that shrimp,' Beria said in Georgian. 'You have been my mentor and my inspiration. What's happened, Dear Sergo? What have I done to you?'

Sergo looked at him with fathomless melancholy. Murtov understood all that was necessary. Ordzhonikidze was fried. Turn the stove off, he's finished.

'Never mind what I've done. It's what they have yet to do.'

'But that's why I need you,' Beria said. 'Even now . . .'

'I'll be got out of the way down on the Black Sea.'

'But you were the one who suggested it.'

'It was my role in this pantomime.'

'I've . . . I've built you your own villa at Ureki,' Beria said in a small voice. 'I thought you'd like it.'

'Oh sure, just me and Stalin, the only ones with our own villas,' Sergo snapped. 'Why do you think none of the others asked for their own? Your special favours are used to discredit me. And you know it!'

'I am only working towards the Vozhd,' Beria said, but Sergo interrupted him.

'Let me tell you what's coming your way, Lavrushya. Yezhov has already started removing anyone who might have a connection to you in the NKVD, both in the Transcaucasus and here. Not inviting you here—and then inviting you so late, just so he could savour your humiliation—you think this is the worst moment for you, but it is just a taste of things to come.'

'You can't leave me alone here,' Beria said. Murtov observed that his tone was uncharacteristically genuine.

'You've done it to yourself,' Sergo said with sudden acrimony. 'The big hullabaloo you made of my visit. The banners, the newspaper articles, you knew he would hate that. My own villa.

And you have the hide to ask for my protection now that you realise you're out of your depth.'

'My Dear Sergo, I don't know who has put this into your head . . .'

'You have ruined me, Lavrushya. A black cat has crossed between me and Koba.' He was risking one of Stalin's dead nicknames.

'Dear Sergo, friend, I—'

'I don't want you to call me your friend, Lavrushya. You have not been worthy of the name.'

Beria looked dumbfounded.

'When you come to Moscow, your one asset will be the Georgians you can surround yourself with. It doesn't matter that they are idiots; they are Georgian idiots. But you don't see that. You don't see anything.'

Murtov was stunned to hear such a character assessment. It was wrong for Sergo to say Beria didn't see anything. In fact, Beria's greatest endangerment to himself was that he saw *everything*.

Beria took Sergo's elbow, gently, and turned to Murtov. 'Vasil, you look dead on your feet. You take our car back to our suite and have a rest while we sort out which train we're taking back to Tbilisi. Friend Ordzhonikidze has clearly had enough, and so have I. I'll see him home.'

Murtov began to protest, saying it was his duty to look after the boss at all times in Moscow, but Beria brushed him off. 'You want me to think only of myself? Ensuring Dear Sergo's wellbeing is my overriding duty.'

Before Murtov could argue further, Stalin announced that he wanted to play *tamada*. He turned to the sideboard to fill his glass.

Murtov saw how hunched his back was, the vulnerable wrinkled nape of his neck.

Stalin turned back to the attentive crowd and raised his glass. 'Let us drink to the memory of Vladimir Ilyich, our leader, our teacher—our all! *Bitter!*'

'*Bitter!*' They toasted in the Russian style, the bitterness of the memory of Lenin's death sweetened by the bond of solidarity he had left them.

Stalin turned to an automatic record player and put on a Georgian folk song called 'Suliko'. He generally forbade 'nationalist deviation', but he had imbibed enough to make an exception. He danced the Georgian *lezghinka*, not too badly for a drunken cripple of sixty. He sang along, completely out of tune: '*I sought my sweetheart's grave, but could not find it.*'

Then, in the musical spaces between verses, he said, 'Poor, poor Zinoviev,' or, 'Poor, poor Bukharin,' or, 'Poor, poor Kamenev'—lamenting the Revolutionary friends whom he had ordered Yezhov to liquidate. Astonishing; Murtov didn't know what to think. Then Stalin danced in front of Ordzhonikidze and sang another verse of the song, followed with, 'Poor, poor Sergo . . .'

There was a horrified silence. Nobody knew where to look. Murtov knew in a flash that he should not be here. He was almost running to the exit when Stalin stopped dancing and said, 'Age has crept up on me. I am already an old man.'

There was a chorus of disagreement. 'Nonsense! You're holding up marvellously, you dance like a youngster!'

The Steel One exploded into a rage, ranting that they had all wanted to kill him—Zinoviev, Bukharin, Kamenev, Trotsky, all the Old Bolsheviks—but he had got them first.

Murtov did not stay to hear the end of it. He was taken back to the House on the Embankment by the same driver who had brought them to the Nearby Dacha. Back in the suite, he lay down. Despite his agitation, he fell immediately into a dreamless slumber.

XIX

IT WAS SOME FOURTEEN HOURS BEFORE MURTOV AWOKE. HE didn't know where he was or how he had got here. He stumbled from his bed into his wardrobe and relieved himself before he understood he was not in the bathroom. He staggered about in the darkness of the room, pulled open the curtains and gradually reacquainted himself with the sequence of events. He was in Moscow; he had escorted Beria to speak to the Central Committee and meet the General Secretary; there was the reception in the Kremlin; there was Kuntsevo and the postponement of their return; then, nothing. Was the hole in what came after, or what had gone before?

Remembering that he had fallen asleep without guaranteeing Lavrushya's whereabouts, Murtov made for the salon. To his great relief he found the boss sitting primly in his tunic with the round Georgian collar, looking fresh and rested, writing at the desk.

'You look like you've been hit by a truck,' Beria said without glancing up.

'I had gone so long without sleep—'

'Yes, yes. I'm writing a letter.'

'I . . . I don't know about the train,' Murtov said.

'Our return is delayed another day.'

'Oh.'

'You will be wondering why.'

'More appointments?'

'You might put it that way,' Beria said, signing his letter, folding it neatly, slipping it into an envelope and handing it to Murtov, who read the name: Zinaida Ordzhonikidze, the wife of Dear Sergo.

'All right,' Beria continued in the same brisk tone. He placed a chilli on his tongue. 'I had to write to the widow.'

'The *widow*?'

'You can't miss a day in Moscow, that's for sure. Dear Sergo cancelled out last night. Terrible tragedy. Overdose of sleeping pills. I took him home and he seemed well enough, just the usual morbid depression, nothing to be alarmed about. Apparently he went to his study after I left him, and . . .' Coolly, Beria motioned taking a drink.

Murtov couldn't believe Lavrentiy Pavlovich was speaking with such breeziness about Dear Sergo. He clapped the side of his head. 'I'm . . . I'm in shock.'

'Oh, I'm in shock too,' Beria said with little effort at conviction. 'Normally a "suicide" in this place is in-depth language. But no, I got the call when I arrived back here. This one's a bona fide self-effacement. Quite surprising to me.'

Murtov was still gaping in disbelief.

Beria flicked his chin at the letter in Murtov's hand. 'Be a good fellow and run that downstairs to the messenger service, will you?'

✿

For another twenty-four hours in Moscow, Murtov floated in this twilight state, increasingly certain that he had indeed been drugged at Kuntsevo. He couldn't remember getting back to the House on the Embankment. Something must have happened to leave him with headaches and gluggy movements, a slowness to react. The world spun past him.

Beria was his usual clean, effective self, and after his letter was sent to Sergo's quarters in the Kremlin he decided that they needed to visit the widow.

The Ordzhonikidze apartment was heavily guarded, and it took some time to get in. Sitting around a plate of cakes in the salon were Stalin, Khrushchev, Poskrebyshev and The Hammer, along with Yezhov and a handsome middle-aged woman in a headscarf whom Murtov recognised as Zinaida Ordzhonikidze.

All but Stalin and the widow looked up to register Beria's arrival with the clumsy Murtov in tow. Yezhov rolled his eyes and murmured, 'A rouble short, a day late.'

Everyone other than Stalin's bodyguard, Major-General Vlasik, was seated, so Beria was exposed like a man on a podium. He bowed deeply to Zinaida. 'My respects, madame. A god has fallen. One of the great heroes of the Revolution. My father, my guide, my soulmate. Life for the Soviet people will not be worth—'

'Steady on, pal,' Yezhov warned, seeing that Stalin was growing impatient with this encomium. The Steel One did not like to be outshone, even by the hero lying dead in the next room.

'Of course.' Beria took the hint, bowing his head. With a glance at Zinaida he said, 'Sleeping pills, I hear?'

'Fucking idiot,' Yezhov said. 'Show some decorum.'

Beria looked around in confusion.

'He sentenced himself without right of correspondence,' The Hammer said. 'Nagan service revolver.'

'Sleeping pills?' Yezhov said with an angry glare at Beria. 'Can't wait to have you as my deputy, *Detective*.'

Beria's chin was trembling. In Georgian he said, 'I cannot believe it, I do not want to believe it, I will never again hear the soft voice of—'

'Oh, spare me,' Sergo's widow said, also in Georgian. She sprang to her feet, walked over to Beria and slapped him in the face. In Russian she said, 'You rat, you denounced him. You probably put the gun in his hand yourself. Nobody saw him alive after you left . . .'

'I only gave him something to help him sleep,' Beria stated, hands raised, backing towards the doorway where Murtov stood, bewildered. Zinaida's accusation could not be true. Beria might have white-anted Sergo, he might have undermined him and gone behind his back and formed alliances against him and isolated him, he might have resented Sergo being sent to babysit Georgia for him, he might have double-dealt and spoken with forked tongue and played on Sergo's paranoia, he might have subverted and manipulated . . . but he would never have denounced him to Stalin. It was tactically unsound. The risk of it backfiring on himself was too great.

Murtov had a flash of insight. These Moscow people had come to a widow's room of grief, only a wall away from where their great friend and her beloved husband lay warm in his deathbed, his brains drying on the wall, and the first use they had made of the occasion was to get at Beria. They played for keeps, this lot, they really did.

'Now, now, everyone's upset.'

Stalin's clotted, Georgian-accented voice tranquillised the room.

He stood and went to the bookshelf. Stalin, it was well known, made a beeline for the bookshelves in any home he visited, and woe betide you if yours departed from orthodoxy. He genuinely believed that if everybody just made the effort to read more Marx and Lenin, they would reach the rationalist paradise. He believed in books and writing like an Islamist in his Koran. He took poetry seriously enough to send Mandelstam to his death. He slid out Gorky's 'The Girl and Death', little more than a pamphlet.

'This contains a more powerful weapon than guns or pills,' he said, weighing it in his hand. 'Love triumphs over death.'

He replaced the story in the shelf and said to the room, 'I won't have discord while we are mourning our Dear, Dear Sergo. Just calm the fuck down, okay, *friends*? Now. Let us learn what we must from the tragedy. Whenever a citizen takes his life, he is sending a message to the state. "See what you made me do!" So what did we make him do? What was poor Dear Sergo's final message to us?'

He glared around the room for effect, not for an answer.

'These past two years, Dear Sergo played the good guy, didn't he? Refusing to fill his quotas, making the rest of us look like skunks. I admit I was jealous of his popularity. But with his death, he has told the state what, tragically, he could not tell us in person. He has said, "You are spreading harm around you."'

Again he paused to challenge the faces.

'We must respect his memory by listening to his message,' Stalin said. 'What is needed now is not to look into someone's eyes to see if he is our friend, our true socialist brother. That is no way to judge character. We must begin once more to ask what he has *done*. This is how, in our last moments, we will all be judged.'

Murtov heard the intake of breath at the catechistic tone, as if he had done what his mother wanted and become a priest after all.

'To honour Dear Sergo,' Stalin went on, 'I will undertake my visit to our shared homeland. It is the least I can do for him. We owe him our tribute. You,' he said, turning to Beria, 'will be in sole command of all proceedings, all logistics, all security.' Stalin beckoned Beria forward, extending his clasped hands.

Beria went down on his knees. He gave Stalin his bare neck.

'Now is the time for healing, not quarrels. Lavrentiy Pavlovich, go home and prepare this great commemoration of our fallen hero. I depend on you. For the rest of us,' Stalin concluded, now addressing Zinaida, 'we will pray in the Soviet night for those we have lost.'

As a staff goon, Murtov did not presume to join the Vozhd, the widow and the People's Commissars who bowed their heads in prayer for those they had lost. Beria was on his knees. Such was the emotion, even General Vlasik was praying for Dear Sergo. Only one of Sergo's friends was not.

Yezhov was barely suppressing snorts of laughter. Of all the people in the room he could have chosen, his eyes were squarely fixed on Murtov.

Part Three
GEORGIA

SEVEN DAYS TO LIVE

XX

WHEN HE ARRIVED IN BATUMI, MURTOV DID NOT TRAVEL straight home. He knew it was treachery, of sorts, not to hasten to Babilina and the girls, to sink into the embrace of their love and, if little else, reassure them that he had returned from Moscow in one piece. But, in that crack in time between the frenzy he had witnessed and the maelstrom that was coming, Murtov needed, just for a moment, to disappear. In the Soviet Union it was very easy to *be* disappeared. But to seize the verb from its passive form, to vanish by your own free will, was virtually impossible.

Carrying his suitcase, wearing his Party tunic and leather shoes, a Georgian *Svaneti* hat on his head, he walked from the Batumi transport terminal to the beach. It was a bright, breezy mid-morning and the sun glimmered off the shifting facets of the chopped-up Black Sea. The strand was deserted apart from a cluster of workers picnicking on the coarse black sand, taking some respite at the end of their ten-day week. Murtov removed his shoes and walked down the beach. He did not want to hear the happy shouts, nor attract comment. *Look, a man has come to the sea to disappear himself.*

He stripped to his underwear, closed his eyes and allowed the onshore breeze to scour him. He had to cleanse himself of Moscow before his skin grew over its ingrained muck. He breathed slowly, expelling Russia. He took a step towards the water, looked from side to side, and said aloud, 'Fuck it.'

Georgia's sea had taken him in like a loving mother all his life. He stepped out of his underpants and threw them on his folded work clothes. Let them shoot me for immorality.

Floating on his back, Murtov contemplated the infinite blue dome. The Steel One would occupy outer space one of these days. He had secret teams working on rockets, satellites and flying saucers. But until then, none of them would see Murtov's naked body making the shape of a star.

He righted himself, trod water, and breaststroked out to sea. What if he kept going? Where had he ever been? It seemed an oversight, given his advantages in life, that he had never left his animalistic rut between the Caucasus and Moscow. For a few months of the war it looked like he would make it to the front, until the Tsar fell and Trotsky signed the surrender. Other than that, Murtov had been nowhere and, it struck him, he knew nothing. Funny to be pigeon-holed as Pre, over-experienced and corrupted by capitalism, when you had seen so little of the world. He had not even been to the far shore of this Black Sea. What if he just swam? A Soviet defector steps out of the sea in Turkey, wearing nothing but his state secrets. What would they make of that? Imprison me as a madman, an imposter with no means of self-identification other than my fantasies? Not much different from the life I am living.

He focused his eyes on the pine trees along the shore, the ochre tiled roofs, the hazy mountains. Nowhere else in the world could be as beautiful, he thought, and then he remembered the days when Lavrushya, in his earliest days as First Secretary, had cruised this water in a Party speedboat. Murtov had come too, initially to waterski and fish and swim with his oldest friend, but then, after his first year in office, Beria had ordered Murtov to go with Merkulov, Goglidze and Dumbadze in a separate security craft, a heavier vessel. One day, Beria had been on the water with the brothers Kobulov, the security craft some distance behind, when a school of swimmers from the Dinamo Sporting Club splashed by. Beria spotted a swimmer he knew: an older lady who had retired from the Tbilisi ballet and commenced work as a fitness instructor. Beria wanted this woman and a couple of the girls on his speedboat. The Kobulovs objected, saying they planned more drinking and fishing, but Beria commanded the woman and girls to board the speedboat and, when the brothers kept complaining, summarily pushed both into the sea. He sped towards the horizon with his new passengers. The Kobulovs, neither of whom knew how to swim, would have drowned if the security craft had not rescued them. 'And this is how he treats his friends,' he remembered Merkulov saying to Goglidze, before they saw Murtov listening and fell silent once more.

Short of breath—he had rested only fitfully on the train—Murtov turned to stroke back to his clothes, to Georgia, to the Soviet Union. To Babilina and the girls. To Beria.

Ducking under, Murtov kicked through the depths until his short wind brought him back to the surface. *Lavrushya, Lavrushya,*

Lavrushya. Like one of Ana's microbes. Would Murtov ever be capable of thinking about anything else? His father had brought them to this sea as a family, in the days when they owned the dacha at Ureki. Anastas had sat in a folding wooden chair on the beach and read a book, playing the dignified paterfamilias to disguise the fact that he could not swim. Murtov's friends—they always brought schoolfriends—would splash about. Begrudgingly, Lavrushya had allowed himself to be dragged to the beach, but he would not go in the water. He sat stiffly beside Anastas on an unrolled towel, under a broadbrimmed hat, in long sleeves to protect himself from the sun and from being seen unclothed by the girls, and made his usual point of refusing membership in the Murtov family. Had Lavrushya always hated them for trying to include him? Were these beach trips, from Lavrushya's point of view, acts of gratuitous cruelty? Was this hatred he nurtured as a boy so potent that it had propelled him for all these years, all the way to Moscow?

As he paddled to the shore, Murtov tried to remember what his mother had been doing on those days. She did come swimming, in a rubber cap and a lengthy, dark blue one-piece swimsuit. He recalled her giggling as her face bobbed above the waves. Some people find cold water hilarious. She couldn't speak for laughing. It was one of his clearest memories of her.

She would always return to the beach before the children. She would walk back up the sand in her swimsuit, a daring deed of self-exposure. Murtov's father would be buried in his book. What was Lavrushya seeing when Murtov's mother walked up the sand, still giggling, fresh from the salt water, tottering on the rocks and pebbles, bending over for her towel, rubbing herself dry? What would this have conveyed to the hate-filled child in his long sleeves, long trousers and hard shoes, bought for him by the property his natural mother had sold?

Murtov scrambled onto the beach. The black sand rolled underfoot like ball bearings, causing him to slip and fall, the waves now pushing him and now sucking him back. He felt ungainly in his nakedness and wanted his clothes.

By the time he was dressed, on the grass path, sitting to put on his shoes, Murtov felt simultaneously renewed and spent. Swimming in the sea was never something he regretted. But the voices in his head, the questions, had also been rejuvenated; it seemed that Beria had taken a refreshing swim along with him, and now that Murtov was ready to resume his life, so was his tormentor. It was Georgia's most successful tyranny, more complete than the Revolution itself.

Inside his shoes and socks Murtov's toes could feel the magnetic sand. It adhered to his arse and his back, refusing to leave him alone. Only in the Soviet Union, he thought. Even the fucking sand follows you around.

The girls had complained so much about not being allowed to busk, Babilina had them play their instruments inside the apartment while she pretended to be their audience and threw them coins. Murtov found them in this activity when he arrived. Nicholas II sat by Babilina's side, chewing happily on the remnants of a rubber ball. Murtov went to his secret place and put away the thick packet Beria had thrown him at the end of the train journey. Babilina seemed preoccupied with her independent life; it was always so when he had been away.

Even though Ana's chest was hurting and she had forsaken her bagpipes to sing, she and Melor still performed beautifully. In Moscow there was no busking. Tears came to Murtov's eyes as he watched his girls perform their music.

He wasn't imagining it: their songs had become more warlike. Melor sang 'March of the Happy-Go-Lucky Guys': *'When our country commands that we be heroes, then anyone can become a hero . . . If our enemy decides to start a battle, then we'll leap to defend our Motherland.'*

At the end, while Ana packed up, Melor sang 'The Sportsmen's March': *'When the time comes to beat the enemy, beat them back from every border!'*

'What's wrong with you today, Papa?' asked Ana.

Murtov shook his head. Ana understood: talkative children could be terribly dangerous.

'Can we go to the park?' Melor asked.

Ana added: 'Nikita will make you happy again.'

'Yes,' Murtov said. 'Yes, let's go outside.'

'You go ahead,' Babilina said. 'I have some things to do.'

Holding the girls' hands, Murtov walked bravely into the open air. Perhaps he had been over-anxious. Georgia was not, after all, Russia. But, passing a statue of Pavlik Morozov, Melor practised her Pioneer marching and chanted the Red Army slogan: *'Pioneers, be prepared—always prepared!'* Even in the summer schools, even here in Batumi, war was coming. When Melor saw faces look at her from apartment windows, she sang, *'Window-watchers, home-sitters, shame on you!'* Ana refused to step in time with her.

Once they arrived at the park and Melor ran off to find a game, Ana said to her father in a serious tone, 'You have to do something about her. This environment—it's not good for young children.

She is always talking about the great Pavlik.' When Murtov did not reply, Ana shook her head and said tersely, 'Mama is right, Papa: it is enough to speak to you, too much to expect you to act.' Then she walked off to pick wildflowers.

Murtov negotiated the release of Nikita's rubber ball and sent him bounding across the grass. He watched the other dogs converge in a social melee, blessedly innocent of the brewing storm. Despite the sunshine, he shivered.

Perhaps the animals did sense something. A German shepherd barked furiously whenever Murtov came into sight.

'I'm very sorry,' said the owner, putting a muzzle on her dog. 'It's your Party tunic. It sets him off.'

'An anti-Communist dog? It is a German shepherd, after all.'

'N-no, I didn't mean that, he's n-n-not a fascist, and the breed, w-w-we had no choice, we were given him . . .'

'Joking,' Murtov said.

The owner offered a weak smile before pulling her dog away. Murtov watched her sadly. What kind of world had they created where people feared for their lives because of their dog's ideology?

'Hey.'

A warm arm snaked between his elbow and his side. Babilina's head rested against his shoulder. He kissed the dark crown of her hair, imbibed its smoky fragrance.

'Be careful, I've got another allergic reaction.' She gave her eyes, red and running, a wipe with her sleeve. 'And conjunctivitis.'

'Something must be going around,' Murtov said.

'I think I'm allergic to 1938.'

They watched Ana wrestling Nicholas II's ball away before he could shred it. Other kids came to pat the dog or kick their footballs. Murtov and Babilina waited for the children to move away; you couldn't know if somebody else's kid would rat you out.

Babilina brushed her hair from her face. 'Was it bad?'

Murtov summarised Moscow. He told her about Beria's paranoia on the painful train trip, the surprise of his appointment to the NKVD as Yezhov's deputy, his speech to the Central Committee, the manipulations and mind games that followed in the Kremlin, the party in Stalin's dacha at Kuntsevo. He told her what he could about the death of Sergo Ordzhonikidze, which she had read about. *Pravda* reported heart failure. Murtov felt as weary as if he were reliving an entire year.

He noticed that Babilina was listening not with curiosity so much as measuring his words against some inner matrix.

'Enough about Lavrushya,' she said. 'How about you? Were *you* there?'

Murtov gave a half-shrug. 'I see the inside of buildings and cars. I couldn't tell you the first thing about Moscow.'

'Uh-huh.' She nodded, again giving him that uncanny sense that she was feeding his words into a calculating machine. 'And how was the return trip?'

Murtov thought about those three days. It was entirely different from their outbound journey. Beria had succumbed to a slumber so deep that Murtov could not rouse him for meals. Murtov watched him drooling down his chin. He understood why Stalin never let himself be seen sleeping. Beria, not playing 'Beria', was so defenceless and trusting that Murtov felt almost tender, their brotherhood renewed. He saw the boy in the sleeping face.

Then, feeling that he could be in deep trouble if he was caught, he pretended to tinker with his wristwatch.

Beria woke full of plans for his final weeks in Georgia. Paramount was completing the Temple of the New. Now that he had been given full responsibility, with Sergo 'out of the way' and Yezhov 'neutered', he was determined to achieve 'total perfection' in the gala, and absolute security 'in every shadow and every corner of the Georgian republic'. He had 'got the message', he said, about threats to the General Secretary. Eliminating every possible risk would mean, effectively, a breakneck purge of the Georgia he had created. 'Nothing will be left to chance. The General Secretary will remember this as the happiest week of his life.'

'That should almost be possible,' Murtov said.

Beria flared up. *'Almost?* A word that must be eradicated from the lexicon!'

The boss was focused on the gala, certainly, but the chess player in him was readying for Moscow. He would take with him 'a trusted cadre of advisers' to shield him against Yezhov, and even plot a counter-offensive against the inevitable white-anting.

'God help us if there's ever an actual war,' Babilina said, hearing this.

'The Vozhd believes Germany's ambitions lie to the west.'

'Well, he would know,' she said, frowning her way back into her own thoughts.

'And what made you so busy this morning?' he asked.

'Oh,' she said with a matter-of-fact sigh, 'I've finished packing up the household. Clothes, books, the children's toys, everything is now in boxes.'

'It might be weeks before we move to Moscow.'

Babilina's mouth formed a white hyphen.

'Moscow,' she repeated. 'Moscow is coming to us, isn't it?'

'The gala?'

'Let's walk further,' Babilina said. 'We're too close to those people.'

'The children or the adults?'

'Both. Let's watch Melor.'

They crossed the dog park to the sports fields where Melor was running herself ragged trying to keep up with the other players. Murtov took Babilina's hand, but finding it cold and unresponsive he let it drop.

'I mean,' she said at last, 'it's the bloodbath. We've been able to avoid it for so long.'

'Yezhov's Thing has been difficult, of course,' Murtov said with a formal air, 'but he has little influence in Georgia. Lavrentiy Pavlovich has successfully kept him at bay. And word is that the Yezhov purge is ending. We think that Sergo's death will be the last straw.'

Babilina shook her head emphatically. 'Your rose-coloured glasses, even after all these years. Or are you protecting me from knowing anything at all?'

'I don't know about that...'

'Oh, Vasil, open your eyes! Lavrushya *is* the next Yezhov. They'll turn him back into a spy and an executioner, what he's best at.'

'He has been best at governing this place.'

'Not for them he hasn't. No more Big Beria. He's got to be a Little Stalin.'

She had been talking with former colleagues in the university. Professor Bronstein, her old supervisor, had been disappeared. Stalin was wanting to make a final move on Trotsky, who was in exile over in Mexico; to finally cancel Trotsky and 'Trotskyism, whatever that is'. Trotsky's dead name was Bronstein, and Stalin had ordered the sentencing without right of correspondence of every Bronstein in the Soviet Union, whether or not they were related to him. Beria's police, led by Kruglov, had been busy rounding up the few dozen Georgian Bronsteins. 'The snag was, one of the local NKVD tasked with the job was himself born Bronstein but he'd changed it to Bronkovich,' she said. 'He was lining up a firing squad when he came face to face with his own father: my Professor Bronstein. The NKVD Bronstein refused to have him shot. A blood orgy followed—the whole village was wiped out—on Kruglov's orders, which means Beria's orders. True story.' She wiped her running nose. 'They won't let Georgia remain . . . relaxed . . . If it ever was. God help us. Now Sergo's gone, anything can happen.'

Her emotional tenor was heated but her assessment was rational.

'There's worse,' she said in a small voice, glancing to each side. 'The kids' music teacher? The one I gave the book to?'

'Oh. Titwanking.'

Babilina's distress halted his attempt at levity.

'The young member of staff we got to retrieve the book. She read it and took it to the principal, who reported it to the NKVD. The teacher . . .' Her voice cracked and her lip trembled. 'This beautiful old music teacher was taken into interrogation with the Kobulovs. They blindfolded and questioned her. She said, "You have covered my eyes but my hearing is as good as ever." You know what they did? They belted her ears. She is now deaf. *Deaf!* That's what Beria's Georgia is becoming. A place where they steal the hearing from elderly music teachers.'

Unable to say more, Babilina thrust out a letter written in a child's crude scrawl. Murtov read it through moistening eyes.

'*I, Melor Vasilievna Murtov, renounce my father, a former bourgeois, because for many years he was a parasite upon the people, and I am severing my relations with him.*' He handed it back to Babilina.

'So what? It is the standard formula. They are all made to do it as a writing exercise. You know this, Babi. It's not real.'

'But she kept it in her folder.'

Even as Babilina took the letter from him and scrunched it in her fist, her hand was shaking. Murtov looked around the park, ostensibly for anyone listening, but his eyes were drawn to the tips of the poplar trees swaying in the wind. He had as little control over events as he did over the sea breezes.

'It's a good thing you've packed up,' he said finally. 'We have to be prepared for the move to Moscow. The transfer will take place soon after the gala and—'

'I need to tell you something.' Babilina took his hands. 'The day of your father's funeral, when we were at the council hall, I had a conversation with friend Sergo.'

'Ordzhonikidze?'

'He told me we had to get out. He knew what was coming. It was too late for him, but he genuinely cared, and he warned me that for our survival . . .'

'Wait.'

Babilina was shaking her head, her eyes on the turf where Nicholas II had dropped what was left of his rubber ball. Laughing, Melor and two girlfriends were approaching. A little way off, Ana was sitting alone, her arms wrapped around her knees, looking at the ornamental clouds in the sky.

'You don't get to tell me to wait anymore,' Babilina said. 'I have always put you first, Vasil, but . . . but I need to put our daughters first.'

'Babi.'

'It's all changed,' she said. 'They used to send the men away and leave the families alone. Now they're sending the families too. The Terror isn't finished. It's spreading to the clans. They're doing it Georgian-style.'

'I have a plan.'

'Vasil's Five-Year Plan,' she said drily. 'For years I have believed in your plan, even if you were too protective to tell me what it was. I know that this is not your fault. I have seen what fear does. It eats out your brain. Your eyes go glassy and you won't talk to me, you just tell me to trust you, and I let you hypnotise me just as Beria has hypnotised you. But, my love, listen to me. Please listen. Whatever your plan is, you must ask yourself if it is merely a state of mind and a product of the Stalin algorithm and not really a plan at all. Your sense of a plan saves you from anguish, from the plague of emptiness, of time slipping away, of not knowing what is going to happen to us. Do you understand what I am saying? We are not *we*. We do not *do* things. We are Whom, and you are kidding yourself to believe you are one of the Who. We blow along on the wind and hope we do not end up eaten by the machine. We are not even people. *They* are not even people. Didn't Moscow show you that? They are just as much mindless bacteria as we are. The only remaining expression of *Who* is what Sergo did to himself. Death eliminates all problems. Sergo knew that. No man, no problem.'

'I don't know . . .'

'There is no other action Sergo could have taken!' she cried. 'And Lavrushya? Once a man has decided who dies and who lives, he becomes another microbe for the great vacuum cleaner to suck up or not suck up. It will go on accepting human sacrifice until it runs down. This is all that your plan, or Lavrushya's, or even old shitbreath's plans amount to. I have been thinking a great deal, with so much time on my hands, and I wonder if anyone's 'plan' is anything but a fairy tale. Your plan is . . . to have a plan. I have trusted you. It's taken a mighty lifetime of love. That is what you have asked of me, and I have given it willingly. But now . . . *I* have a plan.'

'But . . . when you have given up all faith in plans, how can you have faith in your own?'

Tears lacquered her face. 'Because the risk in trusting you has become greater than the risk in leaving you.'

'What *is* your plan?'

'I told you before, my love. You just have to trust me.'

'Babi. A few more days . . .'

She did not give Murtov the chance to cover himself in further ignominy. Instead, she picked up Nicholas II's shredded ball, threw it as hard as she could in the direction of the football players, and jogged off in pursuit of dog and ball, with Melor and the little girls larking after her.

XXI

THE VIRTUE OF SHAPE-SHIFTING, OF TURNING ONESELF INTO a substance more liquid than solid, to flow into gaps and cracks, was, in Murtov's experience, the essential personal quality required for survival. Persons with rigid outlines would, sooner or later, be redeployed to the other world. Babilina had been born with such outlines, just as Murtov had been born without them. He wondered, during the nights after their quarrel in the park, when he slept in the Emka in the basement of the regional headquarters in Batumi, whether he had passed from solid through liquid and become mere gas.

But then morning arrived. AAA—showing off his baldness, shaved daily to ward off an insistent dark shadow—would join Murtov in the vehicle, they would be given an assignment, and he became three-dimensional again. He was just stupid old Murtov,

Beria's lapdog, a bourgeois relic like his father, kept on the payroll as long as he was useful.

His native space was the car. His form took the shape of the driver's seat. The design of the steering wheel, the stitching of the upholstery, the eye height of the dashboard and the size of the replica hand grenade on the gearstick, the racing-car style accelerator pedal, were built around his dimensions. Or was he now built around the car's? It no longer mattered. The car at least proved that he existed. But Babilina was still right: he was a blob of *homo sovieticus fluidum*. Is this what it really means when they *liquidate* us?

The boss and Natia Meskhi were silent during the morning's ride from Batumi to Kutaisi. Murtov, out of his head with tiredness, drove as if in a dream. Once the boss and friend Natia left the car and went into a municipal dental hospital in Kutaisi, AAA began speaking.

'You know who they've gone in to see?'

'Dental check-up,' Murtov said.

AAA bulged with the barely suppressed delight of inside information. 'Sergei Bedya. Former engineer of the human soul.'

Murtov showed none of the reaction AAA was seeking. Bedya was the academic historian Murtov had enlisted to polish Beria's blockbuster *On the History of Bolshevik Organisations in Transcaucasia*. The fact of an outside collaboration would be dangerous if it reached Moscow, and you could never trust academics. Bedya might well have been boasting to colleagues that he wrote the book.

'Never heard of him,' Murtov said. 'He's having a dental check-up?'

'Terrible teeth,' AAA said, flashing his glowing smile. 'You know the intelligentsia: they don't look after themselves. Too focused on matters of the mind. Your woman's an academic, isn't she?'

Murtov's neck tensed as if in a hangman's noose. 'She is a domestic worker raising two Pioneers. And she has sound teeth.'

'Oh, right,' AAA said, holding his grin. 'Anyway. Poor old Bedya. Turns out he's been part of a ring of intellectuals planning an insurgency. Very bad guys.'

'What kind of insurgency—a sternly worded letter?'

'I don't think you should joke about it.'

Murtov hadn't thought he was.

'Bedya has lodged some kind of plagiarism claim against the author of *On the History of Bolshevik Organisations in Transcaucasia*,' AAA said.

'He can't be that stupid and still be called an intellectual.'

'Ah! So you do know him?'

Murtov stared at the two-storey dental building.

'We've been doing more of these softer operations since you went away,' AAA said. 'Friend Meskhi's influence—working towards friend Beria, of course.'

'Softer?'

'Not so much snatching people and beating the shit out of them until they sign a confession,' AAA said. 'With the General Secretary's coming visit, it's been deemed unhelpful to have vehicles from the organs picking up suspects. So we use ambulances and post office vans, or we just visit them when they're at a medical appointment.'

What had happened to the shocked young man who had come trembling out of that waterfront apartment? AAA had hardened so quickly that he was now showing off his inside involvement like coloured ribbons on his tunic. He had no fear of the Terror. He was a child of October.

'We treat them with the respect to which their ranking entitles them. Friend Bedya'—AAA nodded to the dental building—'will be given a nice bed to sleep in and plenty of books and all he needs to go on with his work. That's usually what these academics complain about: they're so busy and we're taking them away from useful activity.'

'Good for you.'

'Which must be hard for Babilina, no? Going from useful to non-productive activity?'

'I'm not going to talk to you about that.'

AAA gave him a complacent smile. 'Shame, I was so hoping to hear one of your rambling anecdotes. Anyway, I'm looking forward to seeing Bedya's new teeth.'

'Did he confess to the plagiarism?'

'The what?'

'You said he was accused of writing the boss's book.'

'I never said that. I said he accused the boss of writing *his* book.'

Murtov thought: my book, really.

'And this insanity is the intellectuals' plot against the Vozhd?'

'It wouldn't do to have such scuttlebutt circulating at the time of the gala, would it? I believe friend Bedya has said he is prepared to make a verbal confession. But he will ask what's in it for him. Good question! The boss thinks Bedya needs some bridgework.'

They checked the lit windows on the second floor. Murtov had found Bedya an irritating, up-himself writing partner, a raving pedant who threw tantrums over punctuation while allowing the wildest untruths to pass unchecked. Had Bedya merely opposed the fantasies and fabrications, such as airbrushing even Lenin out of the 1912 Prague Conference and making Stalin the founder of Bolshevism, Murtov might have respected him more. But Bedya was the type of academic who kept their place in the Writers' Union while asserting their independence through commas and semicolons.

He didn't need bridgework.

Like liquid . . .

'We might be a while,' AAA said. 'You know how hard it is to find a good dentist.'

✿

Three hours later, the boss and Natia Meskhi emerged from the dental hospital with smiles as broad as if they had received a good flossing themselves. Murtov tried not to picture friend Bedya's teeth.

More pressing was figuring out the changing dynamic between Beria and his number two. As far as Murtov could guess, Natia Meskhi and AAA were spying for Yezhov and the Moscow NKVD. But Beria had been sure of Natia's loyalty. Murtov was scared enough to keep his information about her to himself, but now that Beria was to be working under Yezhov, was it safer to reveal what he knew? Like any reasonable question, it was dangerous even to think about. Did Meskhi know that Beria himself had, since Moscow, become that most dangerous person—the man who has been put on notice to prove his efficiency? As Murtov looked across the front seat at AAA, whose hands rested calmly in his lap, he was confused about whether the young man's confidence had grown to the point of arrogance because he was getting closer to Beria, or because Beria would soon be cancelled.

Having secured a signed confession from Professor Bedya—'We found the enemy within his mouth'—the boss was in a buoyant mood, steering Natia through the plans for the gala down to minute-by-minute transport arrangements.

'Exactly what time would you like the General Secretary's mother delivered to the temple?' said Natia over her notepad.

'Fucksake, I'd forgotten her. Some time next year? He won't want to see Keke for a minute longer than necessary. Let her go to the ballet on Friday; he won't be there for that. On Saturday, have her picked up at five, put her in a holding pen at Ureki, and don't bring her before seven. Then out again by nine. Strict personal supervision. Can't trust her not to get up on stage and grab the mike.'

'Done,' Natia said.

'You do know why she's been under guard all these years?' Beria said to AAA in the front seat.

AAA shook his head.

'To make sure she doesn't give birth to another Stalin!'

Beria always found this uproarious, and Natia joined his laughter despite having heard it more than enough. The really funny thing, Murtov thought, was that Beria was stealing the joke from Nikita Khrushchev, and funnier still, saving the joke to pass on to Stalin himself when he wanted Khrushchev put out of business.

'So what's on now?' Beria asked Natia.

'I hate to say this,' she said, 'but your charity commitment.'

'I have a charity commitment?'

'You undertook to sit for two hours for Charkviani. The prize at the art gallery auction.'

'Christ almighty. Now?'

'We had to compress your appointments,' Natia said. 'We've little room to move.'

'And the venue?'

'As you requested, it has been moved from the Batumi Children's Hospital to the home of . . .' Natia flipped over her page and read out the name of the trustee Beria had taken home with AAA.

When they arrived at the trustee's waterfront apartment, to Murtov's surprise Beria asked him, not the young Post, to escort him upstairs. Natia and AAA were to wait in the car.

The man was always capable of surprising, was Murtov's thought. With broad views up the Black Sea coast to the Green Cape, the main room was beautifully furnished in the unadorned modern style that tiptoed a careful line between self-respect and gloating. All the Soviet eye would allow, Murtov surmised, thinking of rooms he had seen in Moscow: in the Bolshevik elite's complex relationship with the wealth it had expropriated, it was permitted to *use* such material objects but not to *possess* them; that is, one could benefit from luxury only while repudiating its ownership.

Beria's host, Franja, was absent from the living room. Set up with his easel and pencils was Charkviani, convenor of the Georgian People's Painters' Union, in his uniform of white beard, dark blue smock and a paint-spattered beret he laid ceremoniously in his lap to reveal his pristine head, which looked like it had received a French polish.

'What's that?' Beria snapped, seeing a suspicious outline in Charkviani's painting kit. Before the artist could answer, Beria nodded to Murtov, who reached in and took out a miniature lady's handgun.

'The fuck, Charkviani?' Beria said, more amused than annoyed. 'You're here to immortalise me, right, not make me immortal!'

'I do apologise.' Charkviani ducked his bald dome. 'It's just . . . this Yezhov business. You can't imagine what it's been like. We had twenty or thirty decent painters in this country and I'm the only one left. I know you tried to protect us, but . . .'

'You're wrong, friend,' Beria said with a martyrish expression. 'I do know what it's like. Murtov and I, we've lost family members, good friends, members of our staff, haven't we, friend Murtov? I can stand in Yezhov's way, but if I'm too protective of my fellow Georgians I will be accused of nationalist deviation. Understand, I am just as much in the gun as everyone. But you should at least carry something that could put a dent in a samovar. Throw it away, Murtov, or save it for some child who wants a toy.'

The sitting was delayed as Charkviani made a telephone call to his art supplier. Beria could not distract him. 'If there's a way of getting between a painter and a cheap deal on brushes,' he said to Murtov, 'tell me what it is.'

Finally Beria picked up a brush from the artist's easel, dipped it in black paint, and, while the old man was still on the phone, painted a dotted horizontal line around Charkviani's forehead and wrote the words: 'CUT HERE.'

As the sitting was a Georgian *blat* transaction, Charkviani had brought a bottle of vodka which they were obligated to finish. A plate of *khachapuri* was on a side table. Painter and subject nattered like old friends as Beria, rubbing his hands, took his position on a stool with his back to the Green Cape. Charkviani said he was only going to make a sketch of the First Secretary today to save Beria's precious time; he would fill in the colours later.

Charkviani asked Beria questions about his early life. 'My father died for the Revolution,' Beria said, 'and I frequently visit his grave. I have such fond memories of my childhood with him. He taught me how to tend the crops. At night he would wrap me in his fur coat with him, and we would lie awake and gaze at the sky while he taught me the names of all the stars and their constellations.' This was a fresh bulletin to Murtov, who remembered only Lavrushya's bitterness towards his neglectful criminal father and his later carelessness with the ashes. 'My mother's happiest day was when I graduated from school, the first in my family to learn to read.' He proceeded with an appealing cascade of fantasies, the painter nodding empathetically as he lamented the injustices of imperialism and praised the great reforms of the Revolution. Warming to his task, Beria listed his achievements as ruler of the Transcaucasus. Murtov's eyes were glazing until the boss's peroration was interrupted by the entry of the apartment's owner.

'Madame.' Charkviani bowed.

The chairwoman of the hospital trustees was wearing an Oriental-style gown in turquoise silk with gold embroidery. Her grey hair was piled on top of her head and fixed with a tiara. Crimson lipstick glistened on her lips; her eyes were haloed with mascara and her eyelashes were as long and black as whips. On her feet were high-heeled gold sandals. Drawing deeply on a cigarette in a gilt holder, she cradled her elbow in her other hand and appraised the portraitist and his model through a pennant of smoke.

'You will raise a million for my charity,' she said.

Beria's mood underwent a startling change. Charkviani was rambling genially, sketching away, and Beria snapped at him, 'Aren't you done?'

'Oh, you have to pay extra for a rush job!' the painter joked.

'We've no need of you for anything else. If we wanted a proper painter we'd have looked in the prisons.'

Charkviani was still smiling, enjoying the banter.

'Shut the fuck up and fuck the fuck off,' Beria said. 'I've given you enough of my time. Disappear.'

Charkviani packed up his tools without reacting to Beria's instant switch. More Soviet human liquid. Murtov guided him to the door, where Charkviani bowed to him.

'May I . . . may I have my gun?'

Murtov saw, on the groin of Charkviani's twill trousers, a damp stain.

'No!' Beria shouted from the salon. 'Fuck off. Go.'

When Murtov returned, Beria was still on his stool, quivering with anger at the trustee.

'Why have you dressed like a whore? Is this how you want my best friend to see you?'

Franja, drawing on her cigarette and maintaining her sceptical pose, regarded Murtov haughtily. 'I didn't realise it meant so much that your best friend see me in a certain way. Of course, he's seen me masquerading as an important person.'

'You did not have my permission—' the boss said.

'To dress as a madam? Of course I have permission . . . It is what is *demanded* of me . . .'

'All I demanded was your granddaughters. Come, bring them out.'

'Oh, Lavrentiy Pavlovich, I must have forgotten.' The woman slapped her forehead. 'I am so sorry.'

Franja minced across the parquet on her high heels. She lost her balance and jammed her cigarette hand against a sofa. The cigarette fell onto the leather. Murtov realised how drunk she was.

'Disgusting habit . . . you've burnt it!' Beria jumped off his stool and removed the burning cigarette. He gave it to Murtov, who threw it off the balcony. Murtov saw the Emka below. He wondered what Natia and AAA were discussing.

When Murtov came back into the apartment, the chairwoman was on the floor holding her face. Beria wrenched her by the arm and sat her on the sofa. Her hands dropped. Murtov saw that her right eye had swelled shut. She showed no emotion.

'She tripped,' Beria said to Murtov, then began laughing hysterically. 'Oh, fuck it.' He stepped forward, rubbing his hands, and launched a football-style kick into her hip. Franja still didn't cry, though she let out a yelp. She clutched her right eye; her left gazed dully at Beria.

'Your best friend shares your tastes?' she said.

'So where are they?'

The woman still had the energy, or the drunken recklessness, to mock him. 'Poor little Lavrentiy Pavlovich didn't get what he wanted so he's throwing a tanty.'

Colder now, Beria repeated: 'Where are they?'

To Murtov the chairwoman of the trustees said, 'Do you have daughters, friend?'

Murtov turned to Beria. 'Lavrushya . . . I'm sorry, I don't want to be brought into this . . .'

'*Lavrushya!*' the woman exclaimed. 'I do love the pet names!'

She had unstoppered Beria. He began kicking her, again and again, in all parts of her body. As he paused for breath she said, 'Take me, won't you? My granddaughters were indisposed, such a shame, but you don't mind your meat well-seasoned, it's all the same to you, isn't it . . . *Lavrushya?*'

Beria now applied himself scientifically. Franja fell off the divan onto the parquet floor. He kicked her back and he kicked her head. He kicked her genitals. When she arched away from him, he kicked her in the throat. His assault, while energetic, did not lack control. It was gymnasium-educated, schooled in anatomy. He was not kicking her especially hard, but his aim was as chillingly precise as a statement for the prosecution. He was bruising her internal organs. He was barely tapping her, really, and yet his method was turning her body inside out as if she were a rubber glove.

Murtov fell back against the wall, his eyes closed and his hands clamped over his ears, and slid down to the floor.

Beria was redirecting his attention to him. 'Poor little innocent V wants to live in his little bourgeois bubble,' he was hissing with a horrifying steadiness. 'Open your eyes, cunt. Open your *eyes*.'

Murtov opened his eyes but closed them again. Was this the kind of thing AAA had seen here? Or was Beria crossing some new line, entering territory that he would show nobody but Murtov?

'You want to see how I treat disloyalty, Franja?' Beria inquired of the woman as if she were able to reply. 'You want to see what happens to those who betray the people? Ask my friend here.' He pointed at Murtov. 'All that horseshit about my early life I was telling that dill. You know what it really was? Living under the stairs reading *Crime and Punishment*. It was fascinating. Here's this guy, Raskolnikov, who kills his landlady for the thrill of it. He just wants to know how it feels. A thrill kill! But it isn't just a thrill, is it, because they're living in the dark ages of imperialist religion, and Raskolnikov's Christian conscience catches up with him. He can't live with what he's done, the guilt is too great, so he undoes himself. But what if we create a world without religion?

No consequences? What if we liberate mankind? Huh? What would happen if we gave Raskolnikov his freedom?'

Beria waited for an answer. The woman was silent.

Murtov sobbed, 'I don't know, Lavrushya.'

'That's where the better future comes into it,' Beria answered himself. 'Freedom of action is limited only by whether it leads towards an ideal world.'

If Beria began kicking him, Murtov decided he would not react. His hand went into his pocket and felt Charkviani's little toy. Then he let go. What a fool he would be to defend himself when he had not raised a finger to defend this woman.

Franja, curled in a ball, made no sound. Murtov found his voice. 'Stop, Lavrushya.'

'I am interrogating an enemy of the people,' Beria said as coolly as if discussing a chess puzzle. 'She has been betraying the General Secretary himself, leaking details of his plans. You will not interrupt my interrogation.'

'Stop.'

'She has been whispering to the dwarf. I caught you. I *caught* you,' he kept saying as his toe performed its surgical strikes upon her. Her eyes and mouth were bleeding. She was unresponsive to the continued blows.

'Stop.'

'This *wrecker* sold herself.'

'*Stop.*'

'See?' Beria stopped now. He knelt down to Murtov, grasped his neck, and growled: 'See what I am? See what Stalin loves me for? I am an interrogator and a spy. That is my special gift. I have been kidding myself that I am a governor of a republic and can improve people's lives. I thought I was humane, raising the peasants' basic wage, removing factory inefficiencies, listening to their concerns about the collective farms—God, I've even improved conditions in the prison camps!—but ha ha, what am I crapping on about? The joke's on me. Turns out I have been living a pathetic lie. My true role for the Party is what it always was. Duty only restricts my liberty as a man. Given total freedom to be myself, freedom from all constraint, what am I? I am a dirty little Chekist, I'm one of the invisible men, I'm only good for—what do we call it?—*social research*.' He turned to Franja and kicked her again. She had lost control of her bowels and her bladder. 'That's right, isn't it? I've been kidding myself!'

'Stop, Lavrushya,' said Murtov.

'Fuck off. What does it take to show you? *This*'—he gave the woman another, weaker, kick—'is what your comfortable little family life, Vasil, your security and your income and your function when you should be a dead capitalist, *this* is what it's all based on. You can manufacture your pathetic internal migration, but what about the facts? Eh? What about the animal truths that guarantee your comfort and happiness, your "family love"? You have your nice little superstructure, but when are you going to admit to the *base*? Come on, have a go! Have a kick! You're part of this, V, this is what protects you! This is what makes you free to love your girls!'

He put his hands under Murtov's armpits and tried to lift him.

'*Have a go!*' Beria was screaming now, but he was too intoxicated to lift Murtov, who was making himself an inert sack. Finally Beria gave up and let him slide back to the floor.

'That's you, isn't it? Murtov the lump. The big baby, content to be a child, leaving all the responsibility to the parent. You make me want to throw up. You think you have a secret life, but they are a child's fantasies, they are nothing.'

'She has no secrets for you,' Murtov said.

'The fuck would you know?'

Beria's foot was raised, ready to relaunch, but he was tiring. He paused and settled, his knees spaced wide apart like a boxer's. The uppers of his expensive Italian shoes were coated with blood and hair.

'What are you doing, V?'

'Stop.' Murtov had taken his hand out of his pocket. He held Charkviani's pistol. He could not lift his arm to point it at Lavrushya, who took in this sign of weakness, but the sight of the gun in Murtov's hand had altered his mood.

'Why would I stop,' Beria said in a soft voice, 'now that I'm finally enjoying myself?'

'Stop,' Murtov croaked.

'Why? Are you going to throw that stupid little thing at me? That's the only way it's going to hurt me.'

'Just stop. She's dead, Lavrushya. She's been dead for ages.'

XXII

BERIA MADE MURTOV WATCH AS HE TIDIED THE APARTMENT and folded the trustee of the children's hospital into a suitcase. After the years of vainglory, Beria worked with the energy of a man relieved, or condemned, by earthing himself in his truth. A murderer, a Chekist. No great governor, no reformer of production, no guardian of Georgia, no father of the Soviet Florida. What did it matter that he had reintroduced the Georgian language and alphabet into schools, preserved their folk music, saved their traditions? The people had other tasks for him. In the end, Stalin was right: no matter what you *said*, you could never crawl out from under the crushing weight of what you *did*.

Natia and AAA were in a talkative mood as Murtov climbed into the driver's seat.

'He was just entertaining me with a wonderful story,' Natia said. 'I can repeat it, but it will take a while.'

Murtov shook his head.

'No? Oh well, we can't gossip in front of the First Secretary. Any idea when he's coming down, Murtov? Friend Beria is a very good man, wouldn't you agree?' Natia gazed up at the apartment Murtov had just left. 'For ninety percent of the time.' She leant forward and put one hand on Murtov's shoulder and the other on AAA's. 'My boys,' she said, 'the time is coming. Remember your boss.'

Murtov felt five thousand years old. Who was his boss today? Meskhi? Beria, Yezhov? Stalin? The first man? God?

Murtov looked down. His right hand was resting on the car seat. On top of it was AAA's left hand, giving him a comforting squeeze. The kid was no longer a fidgeter.

Murtov started the car. It would need warming up by the time Beria came down.

'Why are you smiling?' Meskhi asked him.

She must possess a clever imagination, he thought, if she was seeing a smile.

✿

Murtov went home on his trolley car to find the apartment stripped. Babilina and the girls were picnicking on the kitchen floor. Melor wore her Pioneer's scarf, Ana a Ukrainian shirt. Nothing remained on the bench and table except the telephone, which belonged to the co-op. Babilina wept silently as Murtov embraced her and the girls. Ana and Melor cried too, without knowing the reasons why.

After Babilina took the girls to their room, Murtov said, 'You are right. I don't want to know your plan.'

'I'm telling you anyway.' Babilina stroked his forehead.

'Why?'

'If you are interrogated and you know nothing, you can never be a good husband and father. Only by concealing information can you be proud of yourself.'

'This is madness,' he said.

Babilina cleared her throat and drank cold water directly from the tap. 'We are going to my sister's house in Sokhumi, and then, on the day of The Steel One's arrival, when the police and security will be distracted by other duties, we will board a freighter, the *Kormuz*.'

Murtov blinked at her. He loved her more than life. Her competency. She was getting the girls out of Georgia, away from him. And from *him*. Of course this was historical necessity. It always was. It only required Murtov to know what was to happen—not because his permission was needed, but because it was better for him to know.

'Where to?' he asked.

'Istanbul. My sister is holding forged passports for us.'

He left the kitchen and went to his secret place. He took out the tens of thousands of roubles, years' worth of packets, that Beria had carelessly tossed his way without the slightest idea of their value. In addition to the cash that Ana and Melor had saved from busking, there was enough to get them to the very ends of the earth, somewhere like Timbuktu or Australia.

Babilina accepted the mountain of money, her tears soaking the notes. She followed Murtov to the girls' bedroom.

'Let Papa tell you a story,' Murtov said in a flat voice, his eyes drawing the girls towards him. He put his arms around them. 'The border guards in Turkey see something coming from our side of the Black Sea. It is a boat being steered by a rabbit.'

'A rabbit? Papa, you're being silly!' exclaimed Melor. Ana stared red-eyed at Babilina, saying nothing.

'The rabbit,' Murtov said, 'sails to the shore and asks the Turkish if she can enter. The Turkish ask her why? The rabbit says, "Our police have ordered that all camels be put in jail." The Turkish guards look at each other. Then they look back at the rabbit and say, "But you are not a camel!" The rabbit replies, "Try telling our police that."'

Melor giggled at the joke, though she did not know what it meant.

Ana said gravely, 'You aren't coming with us today?'

'Not today.'

'When then?'

'I can't say.'

'Why not?'

'Why not?' echoed Melor.

Only Babilina was looking at him with understanding. She had contemplated and absorbed the scale of the sacrifice, the number of lies she had told the girls and would have to keep telling them. And she also knew that Murtov was going to make every lie count.

The enemy within is the enemy within yourself.

'Your special gift,' Babilina said.

Ana put her arms as far as she could around Murtov's middle and rested her head against his ribs. Melor put her arms around Ana.

'Maybe tomorrow,' he said. 'Today there is work to be done.'

Babilina asked the girls to take their bags and wait on the landing. Then she came back, enfolded Murtov in her arms, kissed him deeply, and began whispering into his ear.

SIX, FIVE, FOUR DAYS TO LIVE

XXIII

IN THE FEVER OF PREPARATIONS FOR THE GENERAL SECRETARY'S visit, there was much to do. Lavrentiy Pavlovich Beria conducted the final building inspections, personally supervising every detail down to the ashtrays in the villas. He organised the most personal protection ever seen in Georgia. He provided minute-by-minute itineraries and guardrails against the slightest deviation. He issued a proclamation that the Georgian people refer to Stalin as 'The Shining Sun Of The Soviet Country, And More Than The Sun, For The Sun Lacks Wisdom', a title beyond the Georgian language's powers to abbreviate.

Beria's operations ran like one of his Swiss wristwatches. He had the replacement chief architect of the Ureki compound shortened by a head when it was found that the Vozhd's personal bathroom did not connect through a doorway to his bedroom. Such mistakes were unforgivable. Beria had members of the planning committee cancelled for errors he picked up during late-night re-readings of their blueprints. Every worker, from the chief engineer to the streetsweeper, was on notice that the slightest misstep—even one Beria imagined in his increasingly febrile state—was punishable by sentencing without right of correspondence.

It was AAA who filled Murtov in on these developments. Murtov's life consisted of driving and waiting, ferrying Party apparatchiki along pothole-free roads between newly concreted kerbs painted with white and red stripes. Hessian barriers hid all unplanned vegetation. From the roads, you could no longer see the goats who had got stuck in the trees they climbed in search of green leaves.

Speaking like a son worrying about his father, AAA said Beria was frantic, he was stressed, he was not sleeping, he was subsisting on stimulants and eating hot chillis like they were going out of fashion. Beria muttered about 'the jaws closing on my neck', AAA reported.

Stalin had proclaimed the law of the Fellowship of the Peoples, a cultural policy recognising the republics' freedoms while tying them closer to Moscow. Georgia's years of sham independence were finished. Stalin's closest mates dribbled in: Politburo members Mikoyan, Kaganovich and Voroshilov entered the Ureki compound with retinues swollen beyond Beria's plans. A welter of new problems demanded his attention. Without warning, Yezhov arrived to double-check the security arrangements. He was conducted around Ureki by Natia Meskhi.

Murtov continued in his numb daze. He refused to allow himself to question Babilina's plan for herself and the girls. Babilina was saving Ana and Melor. Of course her plan was for the best! The organs of the entire country would be concentrated on Ureki.

Babilina had found the one crack in the wall, the briefest opportunity to get out.

He felt that he had been wrong all along. He was a ninety-five-kilogram human error. He urged himself to have the courage to obey his instincts instead of that other master.

✿

He did not see Beria until the Wednesday before the gala. The Shining Sun Of The Soviet Country, And More Than The Sun, For The Sun Lacks Wisdom was to arrive on the Friday, in a sealed train to Tbilisi followed by an armoured motorcade to the Black Sea coast. When Murtov got into his Emka, after dropping off two of Voroshilov's assistants at the parking turnabout in Ureki, he found Lavrushya on the back seat with his Tommy gun. Not since the afternoon at Franja's apartment had they been together. Beria made no mention of that event, nor of how he had frozen Murtov out of his subsequent arrangements. He delivered Murtov a set of orders and a handgun. They held a brief, impersonal discussion. Murtov felt like he was nothing to Beria. He was less than one of the cogs inside Beria's wristwatch.

With the gun in his trouser pocket and his mind flipping like a fish in a frying pan, Murtov took the Emka back to the garage in Batumi and caught his tram. He changed to his trolley car and then another trolley car. Public transport was disrupted by the closure of roads for Stalin's visit. The majority of the banners and icons depicting The Steel One would never be seen by the populace, as they were kept for the pristine roads with their painted kerbs that only Stalin would take.

Nicholas II was waiting at the door and Murtov fed him before taking him for a short walk. The closed stores would be shuttered until Georgia had endured its week-long public holiday-cum-lockdown. On each street corner loitered pairs of men in long dark coats and forage caps. The only other activity was that of the squirrels in the plane trees and the rats darting down rails into basements. Murtov was lost in his own world. Only when a guard hissed at him did he realise he had to pick up a turd Nicholas II had deposited and take it back home.

In the apartment, Murtov heated soup from a tin. With his hand he felt the top of the stove; like a peasant, he would sleep on its warmth tonight. He had become one of the people who could not risk having lights on. No longer *Who* but *Whom*. For his purposes, enough moonlight came through the window. The apartment was a desolate place without his family. Many of their possessions still sat in packing cases, like props in a stage play, waiting for transportation back to an empty apartment in Tbilisi.

Having forgotten that he had already eaten his dinner, Nicholas II begged Murtov for his.

'You are suffering from memory loss,' Murtov said to the dog, who was shifting from foot to foot as if in the last throes of starvation. 'You are a good Bolshevik.'

Nicholas II got up and went to the kitchen door and pushed it shut. He had learnt to close doors when he heard Murtov or Babilina speak in a certain cautious, secretive tone. Now he even did it when Murtov was alone. He came back and looked to Murtov for his reward.

It was as he was feeding most of his soup to the dog that Murtov heard the front door close, followed by soft footsteps. Was it someone come to take him away? He had his overnight bag packed at the front door. All things considered, it would simplify his life if one of Beria's men came and put a bullet in his neck.

'My darling.'

He accepted Babilina's embrace in silence. A pulse transferred from her heart into his. She brushed her fingertips across his forehead and kissed his nose.

'You're not looking after yourself,' she whispered. She looked into the shadows where Nicholas II was lapping spilt soup from the floor. 'At least someone's eating well.'

She sat with him at the kitchen table. Murtov asked how the girls were. Babilina said they were enjoying visiting their aunt in Sokhumi. 'The passage aboard the *Kormuz* has been secured.'

'So all is going to plan,' Murtov said. 'Except that you are here, not there.'

Babilina took his hands. 'I came back to ask you to join us.'

'You know that I am watched. I would be followed to Sokhumi and it would mean the end for all of us.'

Babilina's eyes glistened in the light of the moon. 'You can't find an opening?'

'From tomorrow, the whole place will be locked down. You must get back to Sokhumi. You can't spend the night. If they had any brains, they would follow you. We're fortunate in that regard.'

Babilina wiped her nose. Another allergy, perhaps.

'My plan is on track,' Murtov said. 'It is all going to work out.'

'Is your Five-Year Plan as good as old shitbreath's?' Babilina said through her sniffles. Stalin's economic miracle had resulted in millions of deaths by famine, mass deportations to Siberia and engineering triumphs like the White Sea Canal that would never take a ship.

'Hard to believe, but mine is better.'

'And what does your plan consist of? Waiting for some opportunity to present itself? Is that really a plan, or just more internal migration? God, Vasil, sometimes I just wish you'd go chop down a tree or take a shit in the park so that they'd throw you into jail for six months like the rest of the petty criminals. They're the smart ones. It'd be safer there.'

'You wait and see. I will join you in Turkey.'

'Don't toy with me. If we are to say goodbye, then I want to say goodbye to you now with honesty and dignity. I don't want false hope.'

Murtov said, 'No, things changed today. Everything has changed. Look!'

He reached into his trouser pocket and drew out the handgun like a magic trick. Babilina's eyes widened, first at the pistol and then at her madly grinning husband. He plonked it loudly on the kitchen table, making his empty soup can jump.

Nicholas II got up, pushed shut the kitchen door that Babilina had come through, and lay beside it.

'Who gave you this?' Babilina said.

'This gun? I got it from Beria in my car at Ureki today. About three forty-five in the afternoon, we met in the car park. He was cold and charmless. I was one item on a list of tasks he had to check off on a busy day.'

'What state was he in?'

'He's a mess,' Murtov said. 'He's not sleeping, he's jittery, he's speaking a mile a minute, he's had a breakout of pimples, he's amped on uppers. I have never seen him like this. Some demonic force has overtaken him.'

'He has such a capacity for work . . .'

'He's finally found his limits. Work is driving him off the deep end.'

'So what does he want you to do with this gun?'

'When he gave it to me, he began going off his head at "the senile coot".'

'Old shitbreath.'

'He was saying Stalin is a paranoiac, an ineffective ruler, a mediocrity surrounded by idiots. All stuff I'd heard before, but he was putting it with such intensity I could scarcely credit it.'

'I suppose he can only vent his true feelings about Stalin to you. He has nobody else.'

'He said Stalin will undo his seven years of good work as governor of the Caucasus.'

'I thought he was undoing it himself.'

'Beria has convinced himself that Stalin wants to destroy his legacy because he fears him as a rival. Stalin will make sure he wrecks any chance Beria has to build a name for himself. Stalin only wants him to do his dirty work, an invisible man to replace Yezhov.'

'I thought he lived for the dirty work.'

'Lavrushya hates Stalin so much there are no words for it.'

'And . . . ?' Babilina looked at the pistol. 'What does your hyena in syrup want you to do with this gun?'

'Lavrushya referred to our fond memories growing up together, but it was mechanical. Being nice to me was fatiguing him. He was buttering me up to do something. But not even in my worst nightmares could I have anticipated what he asked.'

He picked up the handgun and dropped it again, louder, on the table.

'This is his personal Tokarev TT-30. It doesn't have a safety catch. For a safety, you pull the trigger back into the half-cocked position, like so, see? And when you want to release the safety, you pull it back into the full-cock position and lower it slowly to half-cock again, and then squeeze. Like that. And see here—its grip is embossed with the NKVD initials and Beria's likeness.' He showed Babilina. The grip bore a small circle, in the middle of which, like the heads side of a coin, was an engraved profile of Lavrentiy Pavlovich, the bald head, the nondescript nose and jaw, the lack of spectacles bearing almost no resemblance to him and yet, unmistakably, him. 'And look.'

'Holy fuck, Vasil. He wants you to shoot *Stalin*?'

Murtov held a small ammunition box. 'These bullets are what I am meant to use. See what's on them?'

Babilina leant close. 'The bullets are engraved "Yezhov". Not Stalin.'

'Shooting Stalin now would be over-complicating things.'

'So—Yezhov. But won't Stalin undertake reprisals for that?'

'As Beria sees it, he'll be doing Stalin a big favour. Yezhov's Thing has gone far enough. Stalin wants an end to the Terror and Yezhov will be his scapegoat. Beria wants a grand gesture to show Stalin how efficient he is at working towards his wishes. A heroic assassin is to step in at the gala.'

Babilina and Murtov regarded the gun: a short nose, a simple loading mechanism, a neat magazine. Beria's benign not-quite-doppelganger, the Caesar profile, directed his eyes at the trigger.

'Beria put the gun in my hand, looked me in the eye and said, "Friend Murtov, on Saturday night you will stage one of the greatest acts of courage in Georgia's proud history."'

'But how? If you're armed, they won't let you anywhere near the bigwigs.'

'Beria told me I will be positioned behind the head table with specific responsibility for his protection. He's allowed one armed bodyguard, and I'm it. He will be two places to the right of the General Secretary. Yezhov will be three places to his left. At the moment the General Secretary finishes his address after the main meal, a diversion will be created. I will step forward and put a bullet in the back of Yezhov's neck.'

Babilina gasped. 'But they will shoot you on the spot!'

Murtov clipped the magazine into place.

'Beria will be ready. It is all choreographed. Once I have liquidated Yezhov, the Georgian NKVD will take me to a secret location. Beria will report that I have been sent to the other world. In gratitude for getting rid of Yezhov, Stalin will promote Beria to the Politburo. Beria rides into Moscow on a white horse as the new head of the NKVD. Meanwhile, I am vanished.'

'Why you? Why can't Beria get one of his other hoodlums to do it?'

'He said I am the only person in the entire world he can trust. The sad part is, I believe him.'

'But what assurances do you have? He might trust you, but surely you can't trust him?'

'I asked that too. If he is to have the chief of the NKVD assassinated before Stalin's eyes, it would be neatest to do away with the one witness to his machinations.'

'Of course he will double-cross you.'

'So I refused.'

'You refused?'

'I told him that he was taking me for a fool: he must remember the number of fake assassinations I've helped him put on. Theatrical shows, and he's a veteran director. I told him these bullets are blanks, and in any case I will be arrested before I can get to Yezhov. When I am apprehended, Beria will take credit for saving Yezhov's life—maybe even for saving Stalin's life. Why would he wreck his crowning moment, the gala, with a real assassination? A faked one, where he can play the hero, makes more sense. So I called him on it. It's a charade, I said.'

'I remember one or two.'

'In Baku in 1928, in Tbilisi in 1931, in Moscow in 1934, back in Tbilisi in 1935 . . . When Beria runs out of ideas, he comes back to the fake assassination. He even faked that attempt on Stalin, on the lake. The "shooter" is always disposable. I said, "If you want to get to the top in such a hurry, why don't you cut out the middle man? Forget about Yezhov and just get me to take out Stalin? You want to plot in the big leagues, why not just go for the biggest of all?"'

'You really said that? My god, plotting to kill old shitbreath. What did he say?'

'I thought he was going to shoot me right there, to prove that the bullets were real. "Calm down," I said. "I'll take out Yezhov. But I need written assurances."'

'Beria won't give you a signed document saying he's ordered you to assassinate Yezhov.'

'He was offended. He asked why couldn't I trust him, after all these years?'

'An emotional appeal,' Babilina said.

'There was no emotion in it. He asked me, "Why would you want a document? If I give you such a document, Vasil, who will you leak it to? Journalists? Foreign press? An embassy? Who will safeguard you? Is there anywhere a 'letter' will provide you with one scintilla of protection? There is no press. Could you take it to a political foe? Oh dear, no, we've killed them all. A judge? Every judge has Stalin's cock in his mouth. There are no police, no advocates, no points of reference outside the circle of control. A military coup? Nope. Maybe in the twenties, but Yezhov's liquidated them too. There is nothing left except the Party and nobody except Stalin. Or, could you send your 'letter' outside the Soviet Union?" This made Beria laugh. "Oh yes, send them to your good friends in Britain, your diplomatic contacts in France, or Trotsky in Mexico. Trotsky can tell the world that the Stalin regime is peopled with murderers and charlatans! *You fucking, fucking idiot.* You embarrass me, Vasil."'

'Wow. Beria said all this?'

'Yes, and you know what he did then? He said, "If you really want proof that I trust you, here, shoot me." He handed me the gun, he put the grip in my hand, he slid one of these bullets into the magazine. He grabbed my wrist so that the gun was pointing at his head. And he said, "Go on, V, put me out of my fucking misery." And you know what? I think he meant it. It was the first authentic emotion he had shown. He waited there, holding my wrist so the gun was at his temple. "You don't trust the bullets are real?" he said. "Go on!"'

'Knowing you couldn't do it.'

Murtov placed the gun back on the table with a heavy thud. 'Maybe he was bluffing, but I believe the bullets are real now.'

'You still haven't tested them.'

'They have Yezhov's name. How could I use them on Beria?'

'After everything that's happened, you still love him.'

'He said that after I do away with Yezhov, he will look after me. He asked me where I wanted to be disappeared to. I told him I wasn't going to fall for that one.'

'Good!'

'Then he produced this.'

From the same pocket which had housed the gun, Murtov drew an envelope. He handed Babilina its single sheet.

She read it. 'What is this?'

'You can see. It's a letter of passage, signed by Beria, for the bearer to board a freighter at Sokhumi port bound for Turkey.'

'No! He knows we're on the *Kormuz*?'

'*It is impossible to deceive Beria*,' Murtov said, citing an official Georgian slogan.

'Just like *It is impossible to deceive Stalin*,' Babilina said.

'We were crazy to underestimate him. He knew that he had me. He is upset that you are taking the girls out of the country. "How can Babilina do this to me when we were all going to move to Moscow and have a swell old time together?" He asked if you had been planning to defect for long.'

'But surely if he wants you to assassinate Yezhov, we must all leave.'

'This is the thing, Babi: it's the other way round. He already knew you were leaving, and that's why he decided to get me to shoot Yezhov. He's realised that we're lost to him, so he might as well put me to good use.'

'My god. The mind of that man.' Babilina was shaking her head. She reached down to pat Nicholas II, who had picked up the tenor of this conversation and was whining softly. 'Where does this leave us?'

'The *Kormuz* comes back on Sunday, and returns to Istanbul on Tuesday. This letter is his assurance that I can join you. He says he has NKVD people there who will help us reunite and give us new passports. He's actually offering to make our defection easier.'

'But surely we can't trust him.'

'We always have.'

Murtov stared at the gun on the table. He sighed loudly. His heart felt like it was jumping out of his throat.

'I told him that unless I had proof of your safe arrival in Istanbul,' he said, 'I would not shoot Yezhov.'

'It's a terrible risk.'

'It weighs against the terrible risk he has taken in giving me this gun and this letter. But it's a decent deal. You and the girls get out safely before I agree to anything.'

'You know he will trick you. He will never let us go free.'

'So you and I need to agree on a special code.'

Babilina allowed herself a grim smile.

'You will use the words "ANA IS SAFE",' Murtov said. 'If I see that on the telegram, I will know it is legitimate. If you use any other words, I will know Beria is tricking me and I will not carry out his orders.'

'Oh, Vasil. What inordinate power we are placing in his hands. Our life and death.'

'Has it ever been otherwise?'

They sat in the silent darkness. Babilina reached into the pocket of her trousers and produced a small notebook. She gave it to Murtov. He did not need to ask. He opened its pages and saw her handwriting, miniature but clearly legible. She said: 'This is my diary. It contains everything. All of Beria's plots in the last year. I've written a key to the code on the last page. Should this fall into Stalin's hands, Beria is finished. Finished!'

Murtov fondled the diary as if its secrets might be absorbed by his fingers. After some time, he laid it behind him on the kitchen sideboard beside the telephone. For an endless moment Murtov and Babilina regarded the telephone as if they had, at the end of their story, persuaded it that they were its friends. Babilina smiled even, the tip of her tongue pinched by her teeth against her lower lip. Murtov gave the telephone a last, trustful nod.

Between them on the deal table, because there was nothing else, lay the Tokarev. The conversation, the most extraordinary of his years of marriage to this extraordinary woman, was over.

Nicholas II keened.

Babilina shook her head, wiped her face with the back of her sleeve, and looked up at the ceiling. Her eyes were streaming. At first Murtov couldn't understand, and then he could.

Nicholas II was gazing up at them.

'We could leave him outside and hope someone adopts him,' Murtov said.

Babilina shook her head. 'You know how they treat stray children. They are sending them to orphanages and stripping them of their names and wiping their brains so that their parents no longer exist, even in their memories. And worse.'

'So?'

'Children are lucky compared to dogs.'

Murtov took a deep breath and leant down to Nicholas II. Babilina gasped as Murtov put his hands around Nikita's throat. His fingers formed an iron ring which he closed steadily. He thought he could do it. Nicholas II struggled to his feet and began to scrabble on the wooden floor. His paws made a terrible sound. The worst was seeing the realisation in his eyes that his master had turned into his murderer. After everything, just another Soviet killer. It was the dog's disappointment in him that Murtov could not take. He closed his eyes. Nicholas II fought desperately, wheezing and trying to bark, his paws scratching the floorboards, his growls: if Murtov wanted a fight, then a fight he would get.

Murtov slipped as Nicholas II's mortal strength yanked him off his chair. The dog dragged him towards the door. Finally, Murtov's grip loosened.

'I can't do it!' he cried to Babilina. 'Quick—the gun!'

Babilina, aghast, was frozen at the table.

Murtov took hold of Nicholas II's collar with his left hand and reached to the table with his right. He brought the handgun to the dog's head. But now he could not remember how to perform the motion to unlock the safety. His fingers went tingly and numb, useless as a mannequin's. Nicholas II was more nimble and fearless in the dark than Murtov, who dropped the gun to the floor. The impact flicked the safety mechanism. A bullet hit the base of the stove and ricocheted. One of the special bullets, with Yezhov's name on it, embedded itself in the skirting board. A real bullet.

Nicholas II let off a yelp. In horror and fright, Babilina and Murtov stared at each other.

'I can't do it,' he said again. If he were able to cry, he would have now. But Vasil Anastasvili Murtov had shed his last tear. Instead he hugged the dog to his breast. Nicholas II tried to wriggle free of his loving apologies.

Babilina reached into her pocket and came across the room.

'You can contemplate firing a gun at the chief of the NKVD but you can't bring yourself to kill Nicholas II. Somehow I wonder if they've picked the right man for the job.'

Murtov shook his head. He was not a killer, simple as that. He knew he would not be sleeping between now and Saturday.

He buried his nose in Nicholas II's neck and waited for the dog to trust him again.

Babilina held a large white tablet. She closed her fist, held it to her lips, and opened it again, as if giving the pill a blessing. She knelt, wiped the pill in some of the spilt soup and offered it to Nicholas II. At last, the dog was thinking, one of these humans has decided to be nice, like they used to be.

Murtov closed his eyes as he felt the dog turn ramrod stiff, as if electrocuted.

He laid Nicholas II on his side. For many minutes, he and Babilina held hands and prayed into the Soviet night.

'What was the pill?' Murtov said.

'I have one for myself, in case I need it,' Babilina said. 'I was meaning to give that one to you.'

XXIV

AFTER SLEEPING ON THE WARM STOVE, MURTOV BREAKFASTED on an egg that he boiled hard and a heel of black bread Babilina had left in the larder. He peeled the shell off the egg, salted it and ate it in a single bite. He found an orange from the Soviet Florida under Melor's bed and cut it up. He poured some condensed milk over the pieces, which alleviated the rotting sweetness. The milk was slightly off as well. 'Bitter,' he said as he toasted himself.

He was not in a constant state of worry; it was more that the effort to not think about Babilina, Melor and Ana, to not picture everything that might go wrong, spun his internal dynamo with such force that he could not predict what, physically, his body might do.

The smell of Nicholas II pervaded the apartment and this made him more straightforwardly sad. For all the death and cruelty that was being dealt out, it was heartbreaking to put down one's pet. They said that that mad bastard in Berlin had a soft spot for his German shepherds; Murtov thought, you can strip away every scrap of humanity, every vestige of heart and mercy, and the last feeling that will remain is a love of pet animals. If that wasn't fucked up, he didn't know what was.

He made tea in the samovar. He washed his cup and, as he stood at the door, said a silent goodbye to this apartment where his family had spent summers which, he reflected, had been happy.

✻

On the last day of his life, in May 1938, the Moscow NKVD executioner Dmitri Shchekin paid a succession of visits to families of his victims. He drank and reminisced with them about their lost husband, wife, brother, sister, daughter or son. They did not know about his role in sending their family member to the other world, and he did not tell them. He could have visited thousands of such families but only had time, that day, for six. At sunset he went to his home and shot himself.

On what he expected to be the last day of his life, Vasil Anastasvili Murtov laboured as a chauffeur under Natia Meskhi's direction. He kept the Tokarev pistol and the letter from Beria in a large, sturdy envelope, packed also with Babilina's diary and a set of notes he had made, on top of his navigation set in the glove box of the Emka.

While Beria was unravelling, Natia Meskhi glowed. She had rouged her cheeks and wore a new Party tunic. She smiled at Murtov with the contained self-confidence of one who has backed the right horse.

He drove her to Ureki, where they collected Svetlana Stalina to take her to Batumi and meet her grandmother. Stalin's twelve-year-old daughter was silent and sullen during the ride. She had spent the night in her 'Uncle' Lavrushya's villa, where he put on a movie and invited her to share his wolf-lined fur jacket, big enough to tuck over their shoulders and under their legs.

Meskhi and Murtov delivered Svetlana to Keke's little gatehouse where the black-clad ravens stood guard. Keke came outside to complain about the Georgian State Opera she had seen the previous night. 'Too much didactic socialism, blah blah blah. Who ever heard of an opera about citrus fruit growers triumphantly re-educating imperial saboteurs?'

Still ignoring her granddaughter, Keke gave Natia Meskhi a once-over and shot Murtov a lewd wink. 'She's improved, this one. Oh, don't look so offended. If you want to take a mistress, it's the plain ones who are the goers.' She tapped the side of her nose. 'Take it from one with experience. When I was young and cleaning houses, I didn't waste the opportunity.'

Before she could torment Murtov further, she noticed Svetlana. 'Ah! Who have we here? She's not much to look at either!'

Murtov and Natia waited an hour for Svetlana to complete what must have been a strange meeting. One of Keke's ravens acted as Russian–Georgian interpreter. When Keke emerged at its end, her granddaughter on her arm, her face was split by a snaggle-toothed grin.

'My father thinks you beat him too much as a boy,' Svetlana told her grandmother by way of farewell.

Keke scoffed. 'Those beatings made him what he is.' After a pause, she asked, 'What is he again? Does he work for Trotsky?'

'Don't be silly,' Svetlana said.

'He should have worked for Trotsky. That was a capable young man.'

There could have been few moments in Svetlana Stalina's life where she feared for her safety, but now she was glancing about in a panic, hoping that nobody could hear her grandmother. The only nobody in sight was Murtov.

'But tell me the truth,' Keke said. 'What is it that he does?'

'I guess you'd say he's like a tsar,' Svetlana replied.

'A tsar!' Keke shook her head regretfully. 'I'd have preferred a priest. I knew I should have beaten him more.'

Murtov drove Svetlana and Meskhi back to the Ureki compound. Svetlana uttered one statement, to herself.

'He is a deeply unhappy man. His character drives him to creativity.'

It was so terrible and profound and dangerous, on the lips of a twelve-year-old girl, that it left a numb silence in the car. Murtov tried to assure himself that she was not referring to her father.

Murtov's next job was to ferry Stalin's son Vasili to a brothel. Later, at the appointed hour, Vasili was not ready to leave. Though he did not speak Georgian himself, Vasili Stalin had local connections, an unbeatable collection of young shitheads.

Murtov picked up a delegation of Georgian Party bigwigs including Dumbadze and Kruglov. He collected an abusive Vasili Stalin from the brothel and brought him back to Ureki where he might, if all went well, sober up for dinner. Then Murtov drove back to the Party headquarters in Batumi to pick up Beria.

THE FIRST FRIEND

✱

It was five in the evening when the boss, disgruntled in his western suit with a silver star on each lapel and a fedora on his head, jumped into the Emka. He was without his Thompson submachine gun. He jitterbugged on the back seat, a sign of having prepared for the night with caffeine and cocaine. The first thing he asked Murtov was whether he had remembered the Togarev TT-33. Meticulous to the last, Beria called it by its full model name.

'Of course.'

'This is why you get the privilege of driving me,' Beria said. 'We are the one car that will not be searched. Oh! Before I forget— good news!' Beria took a slip of paper out of his leather binder and passed it to Murtov. The telegram from the Hotel Crown in Istanbul said: ARRIVED SAFELY LOOK FORWARD TO SEEING YOU ANA IS SAFE BEST WISHES BABILINA.

'I still don't get why they left,' Beria said. 'I could have looked after all of you in Moscow; I had a plan to make things safe. But we have good people in Turkey. All right, get a leg on, the traffic's going to be hell.'

It was one of the truly weird features of the leadership, Murtov thought, that they expended such energy on preventing the free movement of the population, and yet when their cordon was breached, they did not give it a second thought. With the escape of Babilina, Ana and Melor confirmed by the telegram, Beria was on to the next thing. Murtov did not want to tempt fate by asking him any more. To see the code words was all he needed.

✱

The road was as clogged as the boss had forecast. A newly built avenue on the beachfront, passing within distant sight of the Temple of the New, was crowded with specially permitted villagers in folk costumes waving flags and strings of onions. They were close enough to slow the motorcade but not so close as to see the cars' occupants. They cheered as if The Steel One might be in every vehicle. The roads had been cleared by government order, but there were so many security checkpoints that even Beria was reduced to impotent huffing and puffing. He had been steadily losing his shit ever since he knew that Stalin was coming to Georgia and now, in his most reckless and megalomaniacal gamble, he expected his best friend to walk up behind the head of the NKVD and shoot him in the neck. Was this the Beria whom Murtov had known for thirty years, whom he had grown up with and befriended, the fearless intriguer whose protection had given him, Murtov, a pathway to survival? Did Beria still believe he could be a builder and a leader, or was he just a *player*? In his heart, was Beria still commanding his own destiny or had the pressure finally made him like everyone else in this forsaken country, driven by the fear of today's sunrise being his last?

Too late to ask now. Murtov had to clear his head so that only one thing fit inside it.

✿

They came to another barricade. Murtov checked his wristwatch. Still, at this late hour, unbelievably, trucks of middle-aged slave workers flowed out of Ureki; the gardening and construction had continued to the last minute.

'I wish we could turn around and follow them,' Beria said.

'Back to their barracks?'

'Ha. They're being sent to the other world. At least the entertainment would be guaranteed.'

Murtov caressed the steering wheel of his vehicle, Soviet on the outside and German on the inside. Lavrushya too: Soviet on the outside and batshit-crazy homicidal maniac on the inside.

'Lavrentiy Pavlovich,' Murtov said.

The boss did not look up from the document he was annotating with his Mont Blanc. It was his speech for tonight, and at three densely typed pages it was by some measure longer than Stalin would like. Beria wanted his voice to fill Yezhov's last minutes.

'Lavrushya?'

Intense with irritation, Beria breathed deeply and palpated his eyes with his thumb and forefinger.

'What is it?' Beria said.

'Do you like me?'

Beria was about to snap out some nasty one-liner but checked himself, no doubt remembering that he needed to keep Murtov onside until the main course.

'Come again?'

'I am asking myself: do you like me?'

'What's this fun and games? Are we in the school playground? Do I *like* you? You sound like a nervous girl.'

'I'm thinking back over the years we have known each other. My parents adopted you, put you through school and university. My father ensured you had an in with the Mensheviks when they controlled Georgia, and this positioned you for the Revolution and the Civil War and our ultimate triumph . . .'

Beria's mask of politeness slipped. 'Oh god, it's potted biography hour.'

'. . . You relied on him for advice right up until this month. Over the next few hours, you will rely on *me*. But I have never known for sure. I've assumed that you liked me when it could be that you hate me.'

Beria's annoyance was beyond his powers of disguise. It touched Murtov that his oldest friend was still fighting to conceal it rather than launching into a tirade. Murtov remembered a poem that Babilina used to enjoy quoting at him, something about 'the beautiful enemy', the friend you grapple to yourself with 'hoops of steel' until you win him over. Soviet friendship only had this one variety. Like the USSR itself, this friendship had no fixed borders or half-measures, and when it was ruptured there was no way of controlling how much pain you inflicted on the other. You were nowhere commanded to forgive your friends.

'Do I like you? This is the strangest question I believe I have ever been asked. And when I have put my own life, my own future, in your hands. You have a loaded gun, my personal weapon, in your pocket. You could turn around and shoot me right now. I have given you a letter which would have me strung up. But I trust you fully to carry out the mission I have given you. And you have trusted me to fulfil my side of our little deal. We are coming up to the most critical two hours of our years in this world, V. Everything—*everything*—I have placed in your hands. And you ask me if I *like* you?'

In a small voice Murtov said, 'It's important to me.'

'Well. Let me ask you: do *you* like *me*?'

Murtov's heart missed a beat. Maybe this was the real question. Lavrentiy Pavlovich is on his way to the Kremlin, where I do not want to go. I am on my way to . . . somewhere else. What the fuck do I care if he likes me?

'I have been in the habit of liking you for so long, Lavrushya, I had forgotten what it was to not feel that way. When you were the strange sour child who refused our hospitality and our kindness, the way you punished yourself and us by living under the stairs, I still liked you. I loved you. When you took your revenge on me—for what, and why me?—when you messed up my personal relationships and humiliated my father and reduced us to the status of your personal manservants ... were you still that boy who taunted the beggar?'

'All young boys are alike,' Beria said with a showy yawn. 'Who cares to remember?'

Murtov forged ahead. 'I have done what I have done because I believe in our socialist future and I still loved you.'

'You do what you do because you are shit-scared, V. Like we all do.'

'But I have always loved you, Lavrushya. You are my brother. Love has been set in the stone of my personality. And I also believe in the good you have done for Georgia. You have made us the luckiest of the republics.'

'I've never heard you so chatty,' Beria said, with a curt smack of his lips. 'You put it better than I could. I would say precisely the same about you. Engraved in the stone of my personality—yep, all that, me too. Now. I need some quiet, if we ever get there.'

'I hadn't finished,' Murtov said.

Behind the pince-nez, Beria's eyes widened.

'I was going to say that the love I bore for you was automatic and unexamined,' Murtov said. 'But in the past few weeks, I have stood back and switched my vehicle from automatic to manual, as it were. I still love you, Lavrushya, but I am concerned about the way you are going and I no longer have any influence over you. And that got me to thinking, maybe you do not like me and never have.'

Beria's glasses had been reflecting Murtov's face for long enough. Murtov reached out and wrenched them away. Beria tried to grab his hand but missed. Now Murtov took him on, in the eyes, for what seemed like the first time. Stripped of their glass masks, however, Beria's eyes, small and colourless, were just more glass.

Beria took back his pince-nez. Murtov did not resist. As he cleaned them with a rag, Beria snorted. 'You think you ever had *influence* over me? I'm sorry, my dear Vasil, but don't you think you have been suffering naive fantasies?'

'Okay, I get it.'

'You do? Sometimes I wonder if you are one of those types who, when they come under interrogation, make as if they are retarded. Internal migration seldom works. We usually manage to bring you back. I am First Secretary of the Georgian Communist Party and head of government for the Transcaucasus region. You are one of several hundred assistant secretaries on my staff, and among them you alone lack the necessary qualifications and have no actual powers or responsibilities. When the most dangerous thing in this place is to be a witness, I have protected you from *witnessing*. Do you appreciate what I have done for you? How much more than *liking* you? I've kept you safe. I know you've grown jealous of young friend Adam. But I have given you and nobody else the critical mission tonight. And then I'm giving you free passage out of this nuthouse. Is that not enough?'

'I understand.'

'I am going to the very top, Vasil.' Beria's hands had gravitated together in frictional reunion. 'After tonight, without the dwarf to impede me, I have a clear run. We don't know how long the old man will last. I'm sure his misjudgement of that German cunt will cost him. We don't know where events will lead. Once the old boy's gone, who's in our way? The Politburo? That lot are as useful as hip pockets on a singlet. Believe me, my friend. You, of course, will have full freedom, after your mission tonight, to opt out, go and chase obscurity; I am sorry to lose you, Babilina and our daughters.'

'I see that,' Murtov said. The Communist utopia: no more *my* daughters, only *our* daughters.

'Do you? I wonder if you do. You insult me by asking this asinine question about whether I *like* you, whether I ever did *like* you when we were running around Sokhumi and Ureki. Contemplate the safe life I have given you and the unimaginable future I still offer. You ask me if I *like* you, such a bourgeois concept, as if personal affections amount to anything when we stand at a moment of historical necessity. You might still happily belong to the past, but I have pledged myself to the great and glorious future.'

Murtov could see his preoccupation and impatience. What was really on Lavrushya's mind was the speech, the gala, the plot against Yezhov. He was irritated that he still had to manage Murtov. The sweat on his brow, the puffing of his cheeks and the rapidity of his speech were betraying him: he'd had a gutful of playing nice, and the last person who should be expecting him to keep up this masquerade was his first friend.

'Just get on with it,' Beria concluded.

As they remained gridlocked, Murtov didn't know what 'it' was. Maybe Beria was talking to himself, because his attention had returned to his folder.

✤

They were waved through the last of the security checkpoints without a search. Beria read his speech, his lips moving silently, as the car came to the turning circle in front of the ghost dacha.

'One thing,' Beria said. 'Your wristwatch.'

'My wristwatch?' Instinctively, Murtov retracted his arm into his sleeve.

'Better leave it here. You don't want any of these Moscow people seeing it.'

'It's an heirloom from my mother,' Murtov said. Giving it to him had been one of her last acts, when she was dying in those faraway days.

'As if I don't know that,' Beria said. 'That's why you'll leave it in the glove box.'

Beria thrust open his door before the Moscow NKVD guards could come. He leapt up the steps into the temple. Murtov parked the car in a specially marked space in a paved area that had replaced a grove of palm trees from which he and Lavrushya had, as boys, thrown eggs at the carriages of passing noblemen. Post-Revolution eggs were too rare to waste. Murtov left his wristwatch in the glove box with his fancy navigation set, took the Tokarev and the documents in their envelope and slid them into his pocket, handed his car key to a guard and followed the boss inside. There was no last security check.

XXV

BERIA'S CHILDREN HAD ARRIVED IN A WHITE EMKA. THE MORON, darker-complexioned than his father, dawdled past Murtov with his customary air of almost knowing what was going on. When a guard asked for his credentials, he smiled vacantly. He was Beria's son. He turned to his sister for help. The bitch, rotten apple of her father's eye, would have been described as being dressed like a prostitute if prostitutes existed in the Soviet Union.

'Not Daddy's favourite anymore?' she said to Murtov. AAA, in a bone-coloured tunic, was shadowing Beria in the hectares of crowded foyer, enjoying champagne and vodka, caviar and salmon on black bread. The girl wrinkled her nose and gave Murtov an impish wink.

'Your mother is not here,' Murtov said. 'Stayed in Tbilisi?'

'Wait, what?' said Beria's son, coming in late. 'Can you get my identity card from the car, please?'

Murtov fetched the card and conveyed the boss's children into the festivities. A lesser man, he thought, a better assassin, a true socialist Raskolnikov, would have taken Beria's Togarev from his pocket and put a bullet in these two.

A thick-fingered hand clasped his elbow. Natia Meskhi. From what Murtov could see, her entourage—or was she now using Yezhov's detachment?—was larger than foreseen in the planning documents. Natia's three female guards wore high-collared bottle-green uniforms and carried batons and handcuffs. No guns. Three hundred unarmed NKVD guards were stationed along the walls of the foyer. Murtov could make out the telltale cluster of nervous energy around Nikita Khrushchev, Lazar Kaganovich and the Leningrad Party chief Andrei Zhdanov. It had not been a part of Beria's original plan to have so many of the Moscow Politburo here, but Stalin was always reluctant to leave them unsupervised. For all the best-laid Five-Year Plans . . .

'You saw the kulaks in the trucks?' Natia said.

Murtov nodded. 'In service to the generation they used to push around.'

'You think?' Smiling, she shook her head. 'They were actors.'

'Actors?'

'Well, not real actors. They were real kulaks. But their work was finished yesterday. Today, Beria wanted the bigwigs to see these old defeated faces. Clever, really.'

Blue-trousered Moscow NKVD guards glared at Murtov and Natia, who shuffled a few steps back. Murtov wondered whether those kulaks in the trucks lived, like him, in a constant reverberant shock at how far they had fallen, or (also like him) in the fear of falling further still.

'Here. Let me show you the layout for . . . the formalities.' Natia guided him to a banquet hall the size of two football fields. The ceiling was hung with Arabian fabrics and the tables were set low to the ground, surrounded by lavish cushions.

'What's with the kasbah theme?' Murtov said.

'The General Secretary's been on an Arab history bender, got his eye on our southern neighbours,' Natia replied.

'Cultural brotherhood?'

'Oil. And with the imperialists circling, your buffer can never be big enough.'

'It's beautiful, anyway.'

'I wouldn't want there to be an emergency. The guests will be battling to get off the floor.'

Murtov gave a start. Emergency? How much of the plan did Natia know? Had she flipped back to Beria's side? Had she ever left it?

She told him to stay by the wall until he received orders. He expected her to rejoin the great and the good, but instead she remained on the margin, as always more comfortable as an observer. They watched Beria, all smiles, guide his son and daughter into Stalin's inner circle. Voroshilov and The Hammer, the Vozhd's two oldest and most ineffectual cronies, were hovering. Murtov could not locate Yezhov.

At a fanfare of bagpipes and *panduris* from the orchestra, the crowd began to filter into the banquet hall. AAA was like shit on a stick, close to Beria who, conspicuous in his western suit, looked more than ever like a mafioso. Apparatchiki cleared a corridor for the VIPs, gleaming like royalty, to make their way to the one raised table, a twenty-seater on a platform beside the orchestra.

Murtov saw Yezhov now, limping up the steps with Keke Geladze on his arm, tiny as Lilliputians. Beria stood at the centre of the high table, waiting for all to take their places. Keke was waving her finger admonishingly at him, for that dull opera or how her son hadn't been to visit her or how she'd rather have given birth to a priest than a tsar. Yezhov was mugging away. Life was good! Life was more joyous!

'I know, right?' Natia said. 'It hurts me too, but we're playing in the big leagues now.'

'It doesn't hurt me,' Murtov said.

The cavern fell into darkness. An excited titter rippled out, but nothing happened until there was total quiet. Then, crystal chandeliers lit up and light flakes fell, giving an impression of snow rather at odds with the kasbah theme. There was a gasp. With a bashing of cymbals and drums and the opening bars of Miley Balakirev's 'Islamey', a scrummage of security personnel, approved cameras and lights, masses of nameless escorts—a kind of centipede with a nicotine-yellow head—made its way down the central corridor. The invitees stood at attention and bowed towards the centipede. Light flashed off something silvery-auburn. Murtov saw Beria, flanked by AAA, pause in his conversation with The Hammer at the high table. While all stood at attention with arms rigid at their sides, Beria rubbed his hands and surveyed the hall with a smug air.

The Shining Sun Of The Soviet Country, And More Than The Sun, For The Sun Lacks Wisdom, and his children, followed by his personal secretary Poskrebyshev and the ever-adhesive man mountain General Vlasik, made their slow approach. The Steel One, as ever, was more an accumulation of effects than a person. Now that it was 1938 and life had become better and more joyous, his dress had turned celebratory, even imperial if you could use such a word, which you couldn't. He wore a white tunic with gold epaulettes and a gilt dagger at his hip. Vlasik's NKVD outfit was scarcely less flamboyant, a sign of the security police coming out of the shadows. The Steel One's most potent organ.

Stalin paused to greet attendees, who threw back champagne in spontaneous toasts. His presence intoxicated them. When he paused to speak with anyone, he made them feel that they had forged an instant and eternal bond, and they would spend the rest of their lives hooked, hanging out like junkies for another fix, even flattered if they found out he was keeping a file on them. He knows my name!

He came to the end of the high table, held out his hand and beamed in a general way at Keke as if she were someone else's mother. She disrupted the script by leaping into his arms. He embraced her stiffly while her little hands grappled his tunic. The Mother of the Nation quivered with ecstatic sobs. The crowd broke into applause before General Vlasik intervened, somewhat roughly, to peel her away.

Murtov felt something as light as dust land on his shoulder and swept it off; dust it was, a fine grey powder. The fake snow? He looked up and saw an enormous fissure in the ceiling. For an instant he thought of a good old Caucasian earthquake, but then came a more logical explanation: Soviet workmanship. The damn place couldn't have been built solidly in six Pre-Revolutionary weeks, never mind four Post ones. It was no sturdier than a film set. The moment this evening was over, the entire temple would crumble. It was probably a safety hazard already.

As he brushed the dust away, his hand bumped against the muscular biceps of AAA. The young man's eyes were glazed onto the Vozhd. He was undergoing some kind of rapture.

'Isn't he, I don't know the word . . .' AAA tailed off. His throbbing purple nose and his bulging eyes, pupils as pinned as if he had taken a shot of morphine, spoke for him. 'He is so . . . *beautiful*.'

Murtov followed AAA's gaze. Beautiful? Each to his own. He pitied AAA and the other adoring Posts, blind to the fact that while they were giving the Revolution its vitality, the important positions were still occupied by old men whose interest in youth was like that of vampires for young blood.

'If you say so.'

'I do!' AAA's eyes glittered. 'Moscow must be so beautiful too! Where the future is created!' He looked at Murtov. 'Have you heard the news?'

So much news, he couldn't take any more.

'My name,' AAA said, 'has been entered in the *nomenklatura*! I enjoy the confidence of the Party!'

With the clarity of a man who expects he has less than an hour to live, Murtov finally figured out how wrong he had been about AAA. He had seen this ambitious kid as a Political on the make, an opportunistic Post like Meskhi. He'd thought that whatever idealism AAA had brought to the job had been shattered by his exposure to Beria's darker practices, causing the kid to take each step with calculating cynicism. But AAA had never lost his pure belief in Marxist–Leninist socialism. It had leapfrogged the tawdry Georgian mind games and attached itself to its host in Moscow. His idealism had not been eroded, only clarified. His ever-intensifying work ethic no longer needed a purpose; it simply needed fuel for the mechanism of faith. Believing had long lost its transitive sense. AAA's generation did not believe *in* anything; it just *believed*. And now he was going to the Centre. He was, Murtov now understood, a truer fanatic than the rest of them could imagine, and considerably more dangerous than Murtov had calculated.

'The people need a single individual ruling over them,' AAA continued. 'But to give birth to a future, much blood must be spilt.'

'Whatever you say.'

AAA tapped Murtov's arm. He was offering something. Murtov struggled to focus in the low light. It was a pack of Soviet-made chewing gum. Before Murtov could respond, AAA took it away.

'I can see I'm needed,' AAA said before disappearing into the crowd.

✺

As Stalin reached the centre of the high table, while the choir trilled a newly composed song in Georgian about the sun's eternal vigour, the surrounding mass was dispersed by NKVD staff. General Vlasik pushed a photographer away and the First Children assumed their seats, Svetlana looking withdrawn, Vasili three sheets to the wind. The General Secretary was still standing, thronged by Politburo-grade grovelling, but now Murtov sensed the leader's impatience. Whereas 'Stalin' projected benevolence, the actual man was mostly in the state of irritability typical of a sixty-year-old with too much on his plate and too little time remaining. Those paying tribute tilted forward to hear his mumbled responses; thinking they were bowing, the General Secretary bowed lower still. Even humility was a contest and they should never presume to outdo him.

Natia had materialised again. She took Murtov's elbow and led him to the curtained wall behind the high table. She positioned him three metres behind Stalin and Beria, with Yezhov a little further away in a solid line of Politburo members that comprised Zhdanov, Molotov, Voroshilov, Mikoyan, Kaganovich and Khrushchev—the Moscow alphabetical order of the day, Stalin's current favourites starting with Z and finishing at K.

General Vlasik towered at Murtov's side.

I'm going to have to be quick on my feet here, was his thought.

Meskhi stood with Murtov for a considerable time. He was intensely conscious of her, as if they were alone in the room except for the walls and their big ears.

Finally, all Meskhi could say was: 'Yes, friend . . .'

And all Murtov could summon in reply was: 'Yes, friend . . .'

After a heavy pause full of understanding, Meskhi said: 'Yes, friend . . .'

Her index finger tapped his arm, her eyes wet, as if she longed to say everything she felt and knew, but then she slipped behind the curtains. Murtov swallowed.

Against his will, Murtov felt himself bend closer when Beria leant across Svetlana Stalina to speak to her father. Murtov was close enough to hear the Vozhd exclaim, 'And how are you . . . friend?

Stalin is grateful to this part of Russia. The Islamic theme was very . . . thoughtful.'

Murtov saw Beria's shoulders twitch. Was Stalin slyly insulting him with his 'friend', or had he momentarily forgotten Beria's name? Was it 'How are you' or 'Who are you?' Surely this evening merited a 'Lavrentiy Pavlovich'?

The Hammer, who as foreign minister and premier knew the diplomatic niceties, provided the missing information, with which Stalin let out a delighted cry as if being introduced afresh.

'Beria! You look so well in your suit!'

The moment was excruciating, an embarrassment for Beria, until Yezhov stepped into the breach with Keke, who had been raising a stink at her end of the table. She wanted another crack at her Soso. She fell, again, on his shoulder. Unnerved, The Steel One shoved her at Beria, who handed her back off to Yezhov. Keke wrung her hands and babbled incoherently. 'He's a kind of tsar, you know!'

Now General Vlasik moved in and carted the Mother of the Nation back to her seat. At a nod from Stalin, Vlasik stayed on guard behind her.

Murtov did not receive food. He waited against the curtain until the entree (Black Sea oysters) and main (Muscovy duck in a wine sauce with blinis) had been finished. Two welcome speeches were made, first by The Hammer, to extol the General Secretary's achievements and pay homage to his connection with his beloved 'Russo–Georgian' homeland, and then at great length by Beria, who lauded 'the industrious Georgian worker and peasant', by which he meant himself.

The Steel One got up. He cleared his throat and brushed something from his hair. His eyes rose and took in the crack—cracks, now—patterning the ceiling.

In keeping with the Revolution's flattened hierarchy, the dictator took care not to be seen dictating. Leave that for the German psycho. Here, change must happen so subtly as to be invisible. He condemned cults of personality, a remnant of the Tsarist-imperialist class system. Beria twitched once more; had Stalin objected to the festooning of the streets with his image? Stalin shunned the limelight while obviously insisting that all the focus be on 'Stalin'. It was an empire-sized double game.

His speech was not so much sub-audible as sub-textual. It was spoken entirely in in-depth language, so when he spoke of Beria's 'plantations of citrus fruit, which he treats as his own Georgian children', what he meant was that he was sick of Beria's bragging. When Stalin commended Beria's book on Caucasian Communist history, he was warning him severely against pushing the fictions too far. If you comprehended in-depth language, as all at the high table did, you understood that the speech, larded with praise for Beria, was a jagged rebuke.

The words evaporated in Stalin's throat and Murtov was soon looking at thousands of faces hypnotised by a yellow-grey cobra. One blow from The Steel One and they were all down. Murtov's legs were cramping and his stomach somersaulted with nerves and thirst. The great banquet hall smelt of desperate effort. He focused on the General Secretary's jaundiced complexion, his pockmarked cheeks and yellow ears; anything that could stop him thinking about how much he needed water.

And then, a tear in the fabric: from the high table came a shriek. Stalin paused momentarily, and then continued.

The shriek repeated, louder. What was it? Suicidal mocking laughter? Involuntary fright?

Nobody looked. That was the next thing Murtov noticed. So compulsory was it to pay exclusive attention to Stalin, not one face turned towards the shrieker, who was now clutching his mouth: Vasili Stalin, the ruined princeling. Murtov had seen Vasili suppressing laughter during his father's speech, but now his head was whiplashing. Completely off his seventeen-year-old bonce, he was having some kind of alcoholic seizure.

As the General Secretary kept rambling through his report on the current plan for a major reconstitution of the Georgian Party's organisational structure—another in-depth strike against Beria—Vasili began to splutter. Then he filled his lap with richly coloured chunder.

The mayhem was no longer possible to ignore. But even then, it was only when Stalin stopped speaking and said, 'Fucksake, somebody do something, will you?' that General Vlasik lumbered forward, picked Vasili up like a bag of manure, threw him over his shoulder and marched off to the bathrooms. Only with a twitch of their eyes did the spellbound audience acknowledge the dictator's son.

Murtov checked the high table. Yezhov was showing nothing. Beria turned quickly to Murtov and shot him a wink. It was planned—the genius of it, Murtov thought. Vasili Stalin wasn't just drunk. Beria had had him poisoned, which removed Stalin's bodyguard. The way was clear.

For a few seconds the General Secretary remained at the microphone in pause mode. Even he had to concede that the evening had been severed. He folded his papers, ended his speech, and, to thunderous applause, went back to his seat where he ignored whatever his daughter was saying to him.

'Come on. Time to shine.'

Natia Meskhi was at Murtov's side. Beria had turned to look him squarely in the eye. At that precise moment, so did Yezhov.

✿

Motion slowed. Even without the insurmountable impediment of General Vlasik, there were so many loyal Politburo members at the table, and so many NKVD personnel in close range, Murtov knew he only had one shot.

He felt the Togarev and the envelope in his pocket. He switched the TT-33, with its lethal magazine of engraved Parabellum bullets, to its sophisticated unlock position. He honestly did not know what his arms and legs would do. It was his time, but would he shine? He did not know that he wouldn't fall about the place, like Vasili Stalin projectile vomiting.

Beria's spectacles, disc-shaped holes, flashed. He reached into his pocket and pulled out his jar of chillis. He jammed one inside his cheek.

Then Yezhov saw Beria looking. And Beria saw Yezhov looking. A split-second was all it took.

Yezhov understood.

Murtov took a step forward. For all that Yezhov knew death was coming, he was still going to do his best to cheat it. He jumped off his chair and crawled under the table.

Beria let a frown transform his features and began to rub his hands.

Vasil Anastasvili Murtov thought of his favourite Bolshevik maxim, the one he had reshaped in 1917 for his personal use, his private property: *The lowest of underlings can be more important than all the generals and marshals put together. He can play tricks which all the big chiefs will be unable to undo.*

He would work towards the wishes of the people. He took three steps to the General Secretary. His hand emerged from his pocket. Stalin turned. When he saw Murtov offering him a sealed envelope, as thick as a weekly 'packet', his withered left arm came out. If Stalin had one special gift, it was receiving information.

His eyes softened and cast upon Murtov the golden light of revelation. *He is The Steel One Himself and yet He sees my singularity . . . We have our own unique connection: Stalin and me, alone in this world . . .*

A voice came to Murtov . . . AAA's.

Stalin . . . is beautiful.

Yes! This is it. He *knows* me . . .

Murtov finally understood the bleeding fucking obvious. He finally *got* the truth that he had somehow avoided in the twenty years since October. So focused had he been on his next move in the relentless snakes and ladders game of life at Beria's side, he had always had a hunch that he must be missing the main point. Now, as he met the yellow tyrant's yellow eye, Murtov got it. He got the invisible force, the Mother Russia and the Papa Stalin who gave birth to the children of the Revolution, who provided socialism's genetic material, whose hearts beat, whose lungs filled, whose electricity fired the neurons in the Soviet brain. The Steel One wasn't a man living in this room; The Steel One was an animating microbe lying dormant in every Bolshevik until its time came to waken. The microbe was The Steel One was the Party was the state. Murtov saw the flash of shock—and respect?—in those yellow eyes as they reassured him that no Soviet citizen, let alone one as weak and flawed and passive as this . . . *assistant* . . . could for an instant think and act outside that state. They all had The Steel One inside them. Schoolchildren had a schoolchild Steel One inside them. Workers had a production-line Steel One inside them. Murderers had a murderer Steel One inside them. And the bigwigs Beria was joining? The bigger the bigwig, the bigger The Steel One inside them.

'This will be very helpful to you, friend . . .'

Murtov was able to say no more before he was tackled to the floor. Fat bald Khrushchev was on him. The Hammer was on Khrushchev. Both were flabby office workers and Murtov was able to push them away. Only Vlasik, of the Stalin entourage, would have been capable of overpowering him, and Vlasik was holding Vasili Stalin's head over a toilet bowl.

On his feet again, Murtov stood face to face with the dictator, whose features resembled a death mask. Murtov met the yellow eye. It was The Steel One who lowered his in a flicker of the most counterfeit obedience.

'Please believe me, friend,' Murtov said. 'This will save your life.'

He saw Stalin's left hand clutching the thickly stuffed envelope.

Just then, a pair of smooth young paws seized Murtov's neck. He spun around and saw AAA, the new model, the pet bodyguard, the golden boy, the little shit who had lied to Beria and gone across to the dwarf's side, the young and true representative of the Post-Revolutionary generation with whom Stalin would form his next alliance to preserve his rule before devouring them as well, because for all he had eaten he could never fill his stomach.

Murtov's hands were free. He reached into his pocket, took out the Togarev and fired. He got off just the one round before the entire banquet hall was either running for the exit or jumping on top of whoever was already on him.

NO DAYS TO LIVE

END

MATSESTA MICRODISTRICT, RUSSIAN SOVIET SOCIALIST REPUBLIC
1 JULY 1938

YES INDEED, THINKS VASIL ANASTASVILI MURTOV, HE WOULD like to put up a fight. But where will that get him? Where will it get the last person to see him alive?

When she draws open that curtain of hair, he sees her face. It was a lie, as Murtov suspected, just not the exact lie he took it for.

'You,' he says.

'Me,' she agrees.

'Where are they?'

'Far away and out of reach.'

'Why did you come back?'

She lowers her face again. He hears her soft weeping but he cannot move his hands, his feet, his head. Nothing but his heart.

'Are we going to die?' he asks.

'From the moment we are born.'

✻

The chaos that ensued in the Temple of the New was uniquely Soviet. No sooner was the General Secretary's safety assured than the facts were being retrofit.

Give me a man and I will make the case.

The man, Murtov, was apprehended by the Georgian state organs in the person of First Secretary Lavrentiy Pavlovich Beria. It was far from usual that the first law enforcement officer on the scene also happened to be the head of the government, but this was 1938: every citizen in the flattened hierarchy of the workers' and peasants' paradise was required to chip in, and Beria was a chipping-in kind of guy. He pinned the assassin to the floor, knees on his shoulders, and cuffed him with a heavy chrome pair handed over by the *nomenklatura* Adam Adamashvili Adamadze, who had leapt onto the stage with heroic disregard for his personal welfare. First Secretary Beria and AAA bundled the assailant to the rear of the banquet hall from which Beria would reportedly escort Murtov down a secret passageway to the underground cells, a thoughtful architectural addition of which he was the author. He told the young hero to go and get his facial wounds seen to.

The chief of the NKVD of the USSR, Nikolai Ivanovich Yezhov, also on the scene, assisted his Politburo friends (in ranking order) Zhdanov, The Hammer, Kaganovich, Mikoyan, Voroshilov, Malenkov and Khrushchev in forming an eight-man scrummage to spirit the General Secretary to his villa. Each would receive an Order of the Red Banner for their bravery under fire—the single gunshot which had caused part of the ceiling to cave in.

The Vozhd was in greater danger, in the end, of being crushed by the guests making for the same exit, a failure of design that would be examined by the subsequent commission of inquiry, leaving questions for the Georgian administration. The ceiling, falling apart with the mass exodus, showered the survivors with a white powder that transformed them into terror-stricken ghosts. No serious injuries were suffered, thanks to the great common sense of the Soviet worker and peasant, although members of the Vozhd's family were bruised and the Mother of the Nation was most unhappy at not being able to finish her meal.

For Murtov, it was more than a little strange to be hustled, by his oldest friend, out of the temple into what he recognised as the overgrown backyard of his childhood holiday dacha. The yard was strewn with discarded building materials. There was no moon but he knew the pathways.

'No secret passageway to the cells?' Murtov said.

'Still in the concept stage, pal.'

Beria sat him at the base of a palm tree and beckoned for his Tokarev TT-33. Murtov held up his cuffed hands by way of excuse. Beria took the gun from Murtov's pocket and slid out the magazine.

'Yezhov's name, on all of them,' he said, pocketing the remaining four bullets. 'They'll have to wait for another day.'

'There's one buried in your temple,' Murtov said, 'and another in my flat.'

'They'll keep.' Beria screwed the lid off his little jar and chewed a calming chilli. 'You remember when you used to follow me up these trees and we'd fire stones from our catapults at aristocrats?'

'*You* climbed the trees, Lavrushya, with *my* catapult. And then you fired the stones at me while I was talking to girls.'

'I don't think so,' Beria said. 'We were side by side in everything we did. You looked up to me, you allowed me to be the leader—which surprised me, given that I was a peasant and you the bourgeois, but your Revolutionary heart was true.'

'You don't even believe that yourself.'

'Well, sometimes I think my memory is a big omelette, everything thrown in and scrambled together. It's work that does that to you. Work and more work. Did you know that the human brain loses seventy percent of information within the first hour of learning it? Even between tonight and tomorrow, I'll have been worked so hard my memory will turn out to be something else again.'

Murtov couldn't help a savage grimace. 'You have the sharpest memory in the Soviet Union.'

'Except for The Shining Sun Of The Soviet Country.'

'And More Than The Sun.'

'For The Sun Lacks Wisdom.'

'And you are its supreme survivor,' Murkov said. 'I'm sorry I won't be around to see you . . . *do* it.'

'Yes, we're both sorry about that. I suppose it is my capacity to survive every threat that has tied you to me for all these years.'

'Actually, Lavrushya, that's true.' And it was. Babilina had always said it. Beria could survive any and every danger. Why would you not attach yourself to, and hide behind, such a creature?

Beria was gazing fondly, nostalgically even, at the lush palms. 'Well, whatever our versions of childhood, I guess I'm the one who wins in the end. You're right: firing stones at you from the tree does sound like a me kind of thing. Anyway, I get to say which memory is true, don't I?'

'Sure.' Murtov gestured with his chin at his cuffed hands. 'I concede. You're the boss. *You win.*'

'And I'm sorry about tonight. I really did think I'd be able to get you out of there. I had a plan but I guess it all got fucked up.'

'Bad luck for me.'

'I suppose it might have turned out better if they'd shown up. But you know, no sign of them at Sokhumi port, not on the *Kormuz,* and we've searched every square inch of Istanbul.' Beria knelt down to him. His breath stank almost as badly as Stalin's. 'You're a lying cunt, V.'

'But you got the telegram, Lavrushya—I saw it myself. The secret code: ANA IS SAFE!'

Beria gave him a narrow-eyed smile that contained, if Murtov's perception was not thrown off by the sheer novelty of it, respect.

'The telegram was sent by your agents in Turkey, Lavrushya. They obtained the secret code. Are you saying they are lying to you? Your own people?'

As he saw Beria's right hand close into a fist, Murtov didn't need to say anything: he saw the pieces falling into place in Beria's head. The NKVD had been listening to Murtov's apartment, and had heard him and Babilina establishing the code: ANA IS SAFE.

Then, when she and the girls didn't show on the ship or in Istanbul, those piss-weak dogs had sent the telegram with the code anyway because they wanted to buy themselves time, to deceive Beria for a few hours while they tried to cover up. The critical hours, according to Babi's plan.

And if the spies had heard the secret code, what else had they heard?

'Fuck, eh?' Murtov said. 'Suppose you can't win everything.'

'You know I'll find them.'

Murtov shrugged. 'Good luck.'

Beria gave him a hard tap across the cheek.

'You should have gone for Yezhov. Instead you just wanted to touch the great one. I always knew in my gut you were a useless prick, Vasil. I should never have given you a man's job.'

'Yep, you should have gone with your gut.'

Beria left him. Murtov sat waiting through the night. What struck him most poignantly was that behind the facade of the Temple of the New, the palms and pines and the carpet of fragrant brown needles were untouched. Their childhood playground was intact.

✿

Near dawn, Beria came back. He looked spruce.

'Come on, let me disappear you.'

Beria took Murtov into a storeroom. Presently, Yezhov arrived alone.

'Busy?' Beria said.

'Busier than a one-armed bricklayer,' Yezhov replied. 'Today alone, before I came to your pissant dinner, I had to sign orders to send three thousand, one hundred and sixty-seven individuals to the other world.' He wrung his fingers. 'It's giving me a fucking cramp. And that was before your shitshow.'

'You'd better be careful,' Beria said. 'Once you've run out of Old Bolsheviks, how will you fill your quotas?'

'We're getting there,' Yezhov agreed. 'You know that since the beginning of this madness, the old boy has personally signed thirty-eight thousand six hundred and seventy-nine execution orders? All up we've done away with six hundred and eighty-one thousand six hundred and ninety-two and sent another one million three hundred and seventy-two thousand three hundred and ninety-two to the camps. Hard to believe.'

'You've got quite a head for numbers. I feel sorry for the fucker who'll have to verify them one day,' Beria said. 'I hope your record-keeping is in order.'

'You'll find my records as pristine as a baby's bottom,' Yezhov replied. 'It's a good thing we've had quotas to keep our commissars moving forward. Some of them annoy me when they decide that the best way to suck up to him is to go above and beyond. I send Khrushchev or Malenkov a quota to put away a hundred, and they'll come back and boast to the old boy they've done a thousand.'

'Better safe than sorry,' Beria said.

'They're all running ahead of the locomotive. Their view is that the more they do, the faster they get to the end, the sooner it's over. The worse it is now, the better it will be.'

'I kind of thought that was your thinking too.'

'Doesn't matter, yeah? When he wants it to end he'll blame it on me. And once I've taken the fall, he'll shift it to you.'

'Hasn't he already told you to wind it up?'

'We've begun disposing of our executioners from '37. Witnesses, yeah? It's like a giant conveyor belt: you step up to kill, you do it, and then you're on the list. You're Who, but once you've done the job you become Whom. It's relentless, it's exhausting—six hundred and eighty thousand, fucksake! I'm done, I can feel it. The day you arrive in Moscow, he'll drop me like a stone. And then it's . . .' He held a gun-shaped hand to his head and pulled the trigger. 'Have you got a bullet with my name on it? To add to the collection?'

Beria offered Yezhov his jar. They both took chillis.

'We all need a holiday,' Beria said. 'Nobody appreciates how much this business takes out of you.'

'I've never understood '37, if you really want to know,' Yezhov said about the year that bore his name. 'All these Old Bolsheviks he wanted to get rid of because they remembered bad things about him? If we'd just provided them with the socialist reward, given them their retirement pensions and their heated toilets, they'd be pushing each other aside to sing his praises.'

'Well, you know the saying: There's no such thing as socialism . . .'

'. . . and the Soviet Union invented it.' Yezhov completed the joke with a grimace.

'Now: business?'

Beria and Yezhov had to negotiate what crimes had been committed last night, by whom, why, and how such information would be passed up the line. By the time Stalin's sealed rail carriage arrived in the Centre two nights from now, he would expect a satisfactory report. Beria and Yezhov agreed that they had to get this right, and to do so to their shared advantage. Yezhov did not trust Beria any more than Beria trusted Yezhov, but their mutual distrust was in perfect equilibrium.

'Let's do the NKVD proud,' Yezhov said. He cast an eye over Murtov, showing no sign of recognising this ruffian chained to a filing cabinet. To Beria he said, 'You know the old boy disapproves of you having so many Georgian friends. You've turned the republic into a personal fiefdom. It's a bad look. I suppose you'll say that personal friendships and national feeling might have helped you here, but when you come to Moscow it'll be frowned upon. Socialist principles must always override those . . . *backward* sentiments, yeah?'

'If you say so.'

'So let me relieve you of one Tsarist cunt.'

Beria nodded, rubbing his hands. 'Mind if I stay?'

Yezhov went to work with some of his favourite methods. He placed a metal rubbish bin on Murtov's head and struck it repeatedly with a truncheon, the vibrations and noise ringing for an excruciating hour.

It didn't work.

Yezhov then had Murtov stand in a corner with his arms raised and legs bent in a crouch. Whenever Murtov's body trembled, Yezhov asked him gently if he had anything to say.

Murtov, eyes on Beria, was resolutely silent.

'Sorry, I'll have to get more serious,' Yezhov said in a sympathetic tone.

He proceeded to slam the storeroom door several times on Murtov's fingers.

Coming close to Murtov's ear, he said, 'True or false?'

Remembering Yezhov's game from Kutaisi, Murtov said, 'False.'

Yezhov sat Murtov in front of the five-hundred-candlepower photographic lamp and ordered him to lay his penis on the desk. When Yezhov smashed his fist on the prisoner's organ, over and over, Murtov winced but had nothing to say. Beria shook his head in admiration.

Then Yezhov put Murtov's testicles in the open drawer of the desk and slammed it shut repeatedly with increasing force. Tears poured from Murtov's eyes but he said nothing.

All Yezhov claimed he wanted was confirmation of his working hypothesis, which was that friend Murtov had armed himself with the intention of taking Yezhov's, life, but had changed his mind and then tried to assassinate Stalin. Yezhov wanted to know whose orders Murtov was acting on.

But Murtov remained staunch. He could have told Yezhov about Beria. He could have told Beria about Yezhov. But Murtov had found his superpower: the talent for withstanding. The words in his head were Babilina's: *Only by concealing information can you be proud of yourself.*

Finally, Yezhov slumped to the floor and had a guard bring him a bottle of vodka. Enjoying the sweet exhaustion that followed a good strenuous interrogation even when it failed to induce a confession, he shook his head in bafflement.

'If we don't get an answer, it's going to reflect poorly on us,' he told Beria. 'I'm thinking we should just shoot him, yeah? Unless I've been using too much stick, not enough carrot . . .' He redirected his gaze to Murtov, who was still, just, conscious. 'You! We're letting criminals serve their sentence by going into the army as frontline fodder when this war starts. That hold any interest?'

Beria's attention remained on the prisoner, who was now incapable of responding. Beria had needed to plan his next move in case Murtov dumped him in it. But Murtov had resisted. Beria was containing his surprise and relief, not wanting to show anything to Yezhov—but he also twitched with a powerful curiosity. What could he learn, for research purposes, from this resilience? Why would Murtov save him now?

Beria assembled a usable set of facts. Friend Adamadze, the young *nomenklatura*, had stepped into the fray when he believed, in good faith, that the General Secretary's life might be imperilled. Friend Adamadze's orders were to defend the General Secretary's life with his own. But an assassination attempt on Stalin would be extremely embarrassing for Beria, and Murtov had not actually drawn his weapon when he approached the Vozhd. The 'assassination attempt', then, was a simple misapprehension by AAA. Murtov was not an assassin but a random simpleton, an idiot fanboy who just wanted to meet Stalin.

Therefore there was no security lapse by either Yezhov's NKVD detachment or Beria's Georgian organs. The whole incident need not reflect poorly on Yezhov or Beria. In fact, it seemed that everybody involved had done their duty to the Party, the Soviet state and the General Secretary.

Beria shared this version with Yezhov. As the last thing they needed was for the General Secretary to find fault with the outcome, Beria proposed that friend Yezhov award friend Adamadze the Order of Hero of the Soviet Union (NKVD Division) before the sealed train arrived in Moscow. Adamadze had shown himself ready to protect the Vozhd at risk to his own life. It wasn't his fault that he had overstated the threat.

'So what we need now,' Yezhov said, 'is to convict old mate here of some crime.'

Beria replied, 'Or he can just be disappeared. Who's to know?'

After friend Adam Adamashvili Adamadze received the award of Hero of the Soviet Union (NKVD Division) from a beaming Yezhov, Beria took Vasıl Anastasvili Murtov into his personal custody in a Black Maria van bound for a seaside resort over the Russian border, where he had been planning for some weeks to host his inner circle on a three-day waterfront retreat. They needed to decompress and debrief after the strain of the past weeks and plan their move to the Centre.

On arrival in the Matsesta Microdistrict, an enclave that the Georgian people had gifted to their Russian friends, Beria supplied Murtov with water and a nurse to bandage his severely damaged head, arms and penis. As the nurse worked, Beria sat in the back of the van, watching.

'You stayed silent for me,' Beria said. 'You want to live.'

'That's the only reason you think I would save you?' Murtov asked. 'To save myself?'

Beria gave an indifferent shrug. 'I must have a limited imagination. But I'm not sure I can help you—*they* won't let me.' Before he shut the van door on Murtov he said, 'Maybe there's something I can do. One last offer. But how can I get you to Babilina and the girls if I don't know where they are?'

Murtov spent two days locked in a room at the Black Sea resort. He could hear the others celebrating. Beria did not visit him, but on the third day his door swung open and he received an invitation to lunch.

Merkulov, Dumbadze, Kruglov, Goglidze and the brothers Kobulov, six middle-aged officials who were paid to laugh, were at the table, plus the newly decorated AAA. They enjoyed a healthy feast of grilled fish and vegetables. They played with their pistols. Beria's Thompson submachine gun rested by the leg of his chair, loyal as a pet dog. They drank only light Georgian wines and coffee to commence their post-gala cleansing program. Natia Meskhi was cleaning up the mess in Ureki, but she would be coming to Moscow with them. Ketevan? Alas, no Ketevan. The longest-serving member of the retinue, she who had survived the Tsarist nobility, the 1917 Revolution, the Civil War, the Five-Year

Plans, the famine, the purges and the Great Terror, would not be coming to Moscow. The prodigious Ketevan, who remembered everything, had been given early retirement.

Murtov was permitted to watch but not partake in the lunch. Beria judged that he was too badly injured to speak, so he bound his mouth.

'Take him back to my room and cuff him to my bed,' Beria finally said to AAA, upon whose pocket was pinned the purple ribbon of his Order of Hero of the Soviet Union (NKVD Division), a perfect tonal match for his nose. 'I'm tired of trying to cheer him up. He's mad, you know? Only a madman would have tried that stunt.'

'Mentally ill,' one of the Kobulovs dared to correct him.

'But I did think of a sweetener,' Beria said. 'Afternoon delight! Something to silence the voices in his head.' He turned to Murtov. 'You'll find company.'

Murtov scrunched his eyes and shook his head.

'Oh, you'll want this.' Beria laughed. 'My treat.'

The cronies, distracted from their guns, also laughed.

When she came in, Murtov could not look at her. Had Beria paid her, or was gunpoint enough? It hardly mattered. Once AAA had stripped him naked, cuffed him to his bedposts, tied his head in a noose hooked to an iron ring in the wall and left him, Murtov wished only to die. A prostitute in the land where prostitution was banned, an assassination in the nation where such things were false flags in the service of politics, a prisoner in a country where he no longer existed.

We are all shadows in life.

✿

She lowers her face again. He hears her sniffling.

'My allergies never go away,' she says.

She takes a tissue from a fold of her kimono and blows her nose.

'Am I dreaming you?'

'You might be,' she says, but she smiles in a way that is no dream.

'Why?' he says. 'How?'

'I couldn't,' she says. 'I thought I could come back and save you. Silly me. I contacted Lavrushya.'

'He would never have let you through unless . . .'

'I promised him I would bring the girls and leave them in a place where he could find them. So he let me come back.'

'You told him where they are?'

'Turns out I was lying. He's furious. He doesn't like being double-crossed.'

'They are safe?'

'Safely on their way to the other end of the earth. Somewhere nobody has heard of, where my sister has gone. Timbuktu or Australia. The plan came off, Vasil. The snoops heard the plan, they heard the secret code. While his men were waiting at the sea port, we got them out through the Ukraine. Hundreds of versts away. He never saw it coming, never saw them leaving. Beria's inner Caucasian got the better of him: he thinks only men are capable of vengeance.'

Babilina's plan—and she always had one, she just couldn't let Murtov in on it. Who the girls went with, where they went, how they were to get out. So many unexplained details, but Babilina had a genius for deception. All he had to do was trust her.

And she is right about the inner Caucasian.

'I have this pain, Babi . . . this noise . . . I think I am about to die.'

'Perhaps you are to die of happiness.'

Murtov's breath shortens. Here it is. It is coming. He will die Lavrushya's prisoner. The last face he will see is this reflection of his failure. But, then, that is Lavrushya's fate, too, isn't it? The state decrees final defeat for all persons except one. Lavrushya is at that table with men who have been forced to be with him. He only has his retainers, allies, servants, agents. He has no friends. Your only permitted friend is old shitbreath who lives inside you, knows everything about you, everything down to the last murderous plot.

'You won,' she says. 'You worked towards Stalin.'

'As we agreed.'

'You've put it all in his hands: the time, the location of the NKVD listening device, a summary of the conversation. He will see the transcript describing all of Beria's intrigue. And my diary?'

'Stalin has your diary.'

'After everything, you did what you wanted to do.'

'I didn't win. We're fucked.'

'If we didn't win, we made sure Lavrushya lost.'

'He lost.' Murtov lets this settle. He could never have outwrestled his beautiful enemy. The hoops of steel that tie them are too strong. Murtov is not permitted to win. Stalin was never going to thank him, free him, reward him for saving his life. This is not the way. On the other hand, yes, Babilina is right. They can ensure that Beria will lose.

'And there is your answer to why I came back, my love. I wanted to celebrate with you.'

'But . . . we have orphaned our girls.'

Babilina reaches down to a place Murtov cannot see. Her hand comes back with a pill the same as she gave Nicholas II. And another.

'I don't think we can trust the hyena in syrup to disappear us the way we would like,' she says.

'The girls.'

'There is no reward for plans, Vasil. Whether they work out or not.'

Why is she ignoring his question? Is she really Babilina? The only reward is love. Love shits all over gangster debts and socialist principles. Only love.

'I came back,' she says, 'because I wanted him to know, from my lips, that I could not leave you. He didn't understand. He asked me the same question: Why have I orphaned our girls? I told him I love you. He still doesn't get it.'

'Babi . . . You are giving up your life for me.'

'The only message that can blow the machine up.'

She cups the pills in her palm. She closes and kisses her fist and then opens it again, the way she did when she gave that one to Nicholas II.

'Are you real?' Murtov asks.

'Can you still love, Vasil?'

'I love.'

'Then I am real.'

'What is love?'

'Historical necessity.'

She slips the pills into her mouth. She leans over him and kisses his lips, opening her mouth. She straightens and whispers, 'I wish I had the key to your handcuffs so you could do this yourself.'

'I think I am dying.'

'It's not a heart attack. It is our hearts breaking. Sweet dreams, my love. See you on the other side.'

Murtov does not wish to speak, for fear of waking from this dream he is having, for fear that the tingle she has left on his lips, the warmth and the softness, might go away if he opens his mouth.

HISTORICAL NOTE

THERE ARE MANY UNKNOWNS ABOUT THE LIFE OF LAVRENTIY Beria, and material of varying historical quality has been recirculated until it assumes the solidity of fact. Archives, a treasury of Soviet history, were made accessible after the fall of the Communist regime but were closed once again by Vladimir Putin. Only when they are reopened can more truth about Beria be sought. Even then, it is likely that too much was destroyed during and after Beria's lifetime.

In 1938, Nikolai Yezhov was demoted and Beria became chief of the NKVD. He merged the secret police with the regular police and during the war commanded a vast force of military security services who were so brutal in their 'discipline' of Red Army soldiers that it was said that those who repelled the German military were those who were too scared to retreat. In the war, the NKVD killed more Russians than anyone other than the

Wehrmacht. Beria was also assigned responsibility for the murder, in 1940, of several thousand captured Polish army officers at Katyn forest in Belarus, a wartime atrocity so shameful that the Soviet Union kept denying its involvement until the 1990s. In his hagiography of his father, Sergo Beria blames Stalin for the Katyn massacre, but most historians find Beria principally culpable. Beria's offsider Sergei Kruglov maintained that the massacre resulted from a misunderstanding of orders.

After moments of self-doubt when Hitler broke the Nazi–Soviet non-aggression pact and launched Operation Barbarossa against the Soviet Union in 1941, Stalin remained supreme leader until his death from natural causes in 1953. After the war, Stalin erected the 'Iron Curtain' around the Warsaw Pact countries, consolidated the USSR's absorption of republics such as Belarus, Ukraine, the Baltic states and the Transcaucasus of Georgia, Armenia and Azerbaijan, and launched new repressive sprees, quashing the Soviet people's hopes that their reward for defeating the Third Reich would be greater freedoms.

Almost to the end of this dismal post-war period, Beria remained at Stalin's side. Beria's home in Moscow was as lavish as those of the Caucasian aristocrats he had helped to dispossess as a young Revolutionary. He collected valuables, had his son Sergo tutored in foreign languages, and installed his own cinema as well as a private shooting gallery, so that on Sundays he could practise with his guns and then watch German and American movies which he had Sergo interpret for him. His other hobbies included collecting pornography and expensive liquor. In Georgia, his dacha had a pool, a tennis court, a volleyball court and a Steinway piano. He loved recitals of Chopin, Berlioz and Rachmaninoff. When Beria arranged a volleyball match among

Stalin's magnates, Politburo member Lazar Kaganovich insisted on playing alongside him, saying, 'Beria always wins and I want to be on the winning side.' Stalin also gave Beria responsibility for appointing and supervising his personal household staff, a sign that Stalin continued to trust him while rebuffing his desire to become the dictator's appointed heir.

At the end of the war, Beria gave up many of his posts to run the Soviet nuclear weapons program. He took credit for the USSR's first successful atomic bomb test in 1949. The nuclear scientist Andrei Sakharov found Beria a reasonable manager until he shook his 'slightly moist and deathly cold hand' and looked into his eyes to find himself 'face to face with a terrifying human being'.

Beria's manoeuvres to position himself as Stalin's successor were undermined by his rivals in the Politburo as well as by Stalin himself. Andrei Zhdanov was Stalin's chosen heir until his death, officially from natural causes, in 1949. Stalin then named the bureaucrat Georgi Malenkov as his successor, another insult to Beria, who adapted by forming an alliance with Malenkov. Positioning himself for life after Stalin, Beria managed to isolate and imprison Stalin's bodyguard, General Vlasik, and befriended Vasili Stalin. He grew comfortable pulling Malenkov's strings. However, in late 1952 a paranoid Stalin turned on Beria, suspecting he was plotting an assassination.

Just as Beria's career appeared over, in March 1953 Stalin died from a stroke. Malenkov became General Secretary of the Communist Party and nominal ruler. At the funerary commemorations of the late leader, Beria broke ranks with his colleagues' emotional eulogies and instead spoke forcefully of plans for a post-Stalin future.

After Stalin's fortuitous death, Beria and Malenkov initiated a program of 'de-Stalinisation', releasing tens of thousands of gulag prisoners, liberalising some of the more repressive aspects of the regime and outlining plans to modernise the economy.

The Beria–Malenkov junta lasted only a few weeks. The opposition faction in the Politburo, now led by Khrushchev, teamed up with General Zhukov, the hero of the war, to have Beria arrested in April 1953, a month after Stalin's death. It is not known whether Beria was kept in prison for a few nights or a few months prior to his execution. The details and date of his death, and the whereabouts of his remains, are unlikely ever to be ascertained. He was tried by a court in absentia in December 1953, but was probably already dead. Beria, that most effective and ambitious of Stalin's operatives, failed to realise his ambitions. In 1953, it could be said that Stalin and Beria cancelled each other out.

After Beria's execution, copies of his book *On the History of Bolshevik Organisations in Transcaucasia* were destroyed. The editors of the *Great Soviet Encyclopedia* ordered subscribers to cut out 'with a small knife or razor blade' the entry on Lavrentiy Pavlovich Beria. As a replacement text box to paste into the space, the subscribers were sent an entry on the Bering Sea.

In Georgia, there were now empty rectangles where Beria's portrait had been. Beria Streets became Malenkov Streets, though Beria's name could still be made out where it had been painted over. In 1956, the year Khrushchev made his 'Secret Speech' to the Communist Party Congress denouncing Stalin and Stalinism, Georgians rioted against Khrushchev's regime and paraded portraits of Beria and Stalin, who remained popular in their home republic.

Beria's widow Nina and their son Sergo lived quietly in the Soviet Union until the 1970s and 1990s respectively. Neither would publish a word against him. Nina obtained a degree in agricultural chemistry. In his biography of his father, Sergo blamed Stalin for the excesses of the years before 1953 and claimed that Beria was eliminated because he planned to modernise and westernise the Soviet Union faster than his Politburo rivals would allow. Sergo became a mathematician, married the granddaughter of the novelist Maxim Gorky, and had two children, ensuring the survival of both family lines.

ACKNOWLEDGEMENTS

IN THE BUSINESS OF PRODUCING FICTION, THE NOVELIST CAN never keep up with authoritarian political leaders. Such leaders offer an invitation to artists, most of all bullshit artists. You want to lie? Thank you, don't mind if I do.

Vasil Murtov, Babilina and their children are inventions, as are Anastas Murtov, Natia Meskhi and AAA. The other principal characters in this book—Lavrentiy Beria, Nikolai Yezhov, Josef Stalin, Sergo Ordzhonikidze, Keke Geladze, Stalin's children and the members of Beria's and Stalin's Politburos—are based to some degree on documented histories. Most useful in researching those lives have been the few English-language biographies of Beria: *Kommissar: The Life and Death of Lavrentiy Pavlovich Beria* by Tadeusz Wittlin; *Beria: Stalin's First Lieutenant* by Amy W. Knight;

and *Beria: My Father* by Sergo Beria. Other essential sources have been *Khrushchev Remembers* by Nikita Khrushchev; Isaac Deutscher's *Stalin: A Political Biography*; Simon Sebag Montefiore's magisterial *Stalin: The Court of the Red Tsar* and *Young Stalin*; *On Stalin's Team* by Sheila Fitzpatrick; *Stalin* by Robert Service; *Stalin* by Edvard Radzinski; *Stalin: Breaker of Nations* and *The Great Terror* by Robert Conquest; *Stalin: Waiting for Hitler 1929–1941* by Stephen Kotkin; *Molotov's Magic Lantern: Travels in Russian History* by Rachel Polonsky; *Conversations with Stalin* by Milovan Djilas; *Stalin's Daughter* by Rosemary Sullivan; *The Last Days of Stalin* by Joshua Rubenstein; *The Unknown Stalin* by Zhores and Roy Medvedev; and *The Dictators* by Richard Overy. For learning about life in the Soviet Union in this period, nothing matches Nadezhda Mandelstam's memoirs *Hope Against Hope* and *Hope Abandoned*, and Alexander Solzhenitsyn's *The Gulag Archipelago* and *One Day in the Life of Ivan Denisovich*. The poet quoted occasionally in this book is Osip Mandelstam, particularly his *Stalin Epigram* and *Canzone*. The phrase 'young men who smell of dog and wolf' originates with Osip Mandelstam, as remembered by his wife Nadezhda in *Hope Abandoned*. Sheila Fitzpatrick's *Everyday Stalinism* was a treasure, as was the truly epic project *The Whisperers* by Orlando Figes. Lydia Chukovskaya's novella *The Deserted House* gave a heart-rending insight into living in the Soviet Union in the 1930s and *Free: Coming of Age at the End of History* by Lea Ypi was revealing about more recent times. From *Secondhand Time* through *The Unwomanly Face of War*, the work of Svetlana Alexievich has a Nobel Prize to attest to its importance and moral beauty. Armando Iannucci's film *The Death of Stalin* had a liberating effect.

Stalin's celebratory visit to Georgia in the late 1930s was a real event overseen by Beria, though I have taken liberties with the reconstruction of scenes and the rearrangement of some historical events, such as the deaths of Sergo Ordzhonikidze and Keke Geladze, which both occurred in 1937. Between that trip and the end of the Great Patriotic War (World War II) in 1945, Stalin would not take a single holiday.

I have also taken liberties with who said what, when events occurred and the accuracy of translations and facts, both alternative and the alternatives to those alternatives. In a novel, even when it uses history, the writer is an absolute and capricious ruler. Tyrannies begin with fiction and their reward is more fiction.

The contributions of individuals who read drafts of this book and helped in many ways are as real as the author's. Sincere thanks to Jane Palfreyman, Ali Lavau, Christa Munns, Greer Gamble, Josh Durham, Jane Novak, Geordie Williamson, Jon Casimir, Lyn Tranter, Michael Robotham, John Edwards, Rob Carlton, Michael Brissenden, Tim Winton and, last and foremost, Wenona Byrne.